PENGUIN BOOKS
The Christmas Swap

T0322114

The Christmas Swap

TALIA SAMUELS

PENGUIN BOOKS

PENGUIN BOOKS

UK | USA | Canada | Ireland | Australia
India | New Zealand | South Africa

Penguin Books is part of the Penguin Random House group of companies
whose addresses can be found at global.penguinrandomhouse.com.

First published 2023
004

Copyright © Talia Samuels, 2023

The moral right of the author has been asserted

Set in 12.5/14.75pt Garamond MT
Typeset by Falcon Oast Graphic Art Ltd
Printed and bound in Great Britain by Clays Ltd, Elcograf S.p.A.

A CIP catalogue record for this book is available from the British Library

ISBN: 978–1–405–95213–2

www.greenpenguin.co.uk

MIX
Paper | Supporting
responsible forestry
FSC® C018179

Penguin Random House is committed to a
sustainable future for our business, our readers
and our planet. This book is made from Forest
Stewardship Council® certified paper.

Dedicated to Grani Frani and Grandpa Derek,
unwavering supporters.

Monday, 18 December

I

Margot

'So, you and I have been together for five months,' I say to the man I met four days ago.

'No,' Ben says lightly, his hazel eyes fixed on the winding icy road ahead. 'Six months.'

'I don't think so.' I glance up at the grey snow pelting down on to the ironically named sunroof of Ben's car. 'Six months is too round. Too uniform. When concocting a lie, you want to avoid box-fresh perfection.'

'Hmm. It's good to see that my girlfriend is such a well-practised liar.'

'*Fake* girlfriend,' I correct him.

'Yes, yes,' Ben mutters, lifting a hand from the steering wheel and waving me away as if this is nothing more than a minor technicality. 'We'll circle back to our anniversary later then. Remind me of your name?'

I whip around to face him. Is he stupid?

'Obviously I know that it's Margot Murray,' he says with a little laugh, both hands back on the wheel. 'But is there anything else? Nicknames? Middle names? Isn't "Margot" French? Are *you* French?'

Ah. Of course Ben remembers my name. He first came across me through my online marketing business, Margot Murray Digital. He'd have to be more than a bit slow to forget the name I've plastered all over my website and socials.

'*Non*, I'm not French,' I say. 'I was named after a random great-aunt who I never met. I don't have any nicknames. And my middle name is May.'

'M, M, M.'

'Mmm, indeed. And is there more to Ben than . . . Ben?'

'Not at all,' he says with an easy smile. 'Just Ben Gibson. It's not even short for Benjamin.'

'Fantastic,' I say. I could do with everything about Just Ben Gibson being as straightforward as his name if I have any hope of putting on a convincing performance as his life partner over the next week or so.

God, it does sound insane when put so plainly. *Yeah, I'll be spending my Christmas with this near perfect stranger, swindling his doting parents into believing that I'm his lovely new girlfriend, how about you?*

I can't help it – I sigh. This Christmas was supposed to be the most magical in all my thirty-two years of life. Taylor and I were going to be spending it in the Bahamas, completely ignoring the significance of the season as we sipped on rum punch by the pool. Obviously that plan fell apart. Everything fell apart. Our tiny Islington flat was stripped of Taylor's stuff, the trip was called off, and my share of the (very) partial refund was sent to my account without a word. In the span of one drizzly November afternoon Christmas was cancelled.

And then there was Ben. Ben who I'd been talking to for weeks already as I worked on a major project his jewellery company had hired me for. Ben who could never grasp what I meant by SEO or PPC but always made sure to tell me I was doing a great job and that the website I was designing looked fantastic. Ben who invited me to his company Christmas party because I was basically part of the team now, and it would be great to finally meet in person, and he didn't think I should miss out on all the fun on account of being self-employed.

To be completely honest, my idea of fun isn't spending a Thursday evening with someone else's inebriated colleagues, but I didn't want to be rude to one of my top clients, so I turned up to the party alone and ordered a large glass of red at the open bar. Ben raced over to me with a huge grin on his face and a paper crown from a Christmas cracker on his head. He introduced me to his employees and their spouses as the Computer Whizz and stuck by my side all evening as we mingled with the obnoxiously happy couples. He skipped past work talk to chat to me about our shared love of wine and dogs, and he ensured that I had a constant supply of canapés and Merlot. He laughed at all my jokes with shaking shoulders and occasional adorable snorts.

His face fell when I said I'd be spending Christmas alone this year.

I hadn't seen what the big deal was. Why would I want to hang out with my mum and her latest toy boy for the day, especially now that Nana is no longer here to act as a buffer and I have no siblings to share the pain with? Why would I accept a pity invite from some friend who'd just seat me between their snotty three-year-old and perverted uncle?

Ben had all but choked on his wine when I'd said that.

I'd made a mental note to be more professional.

He'd made an insane offer to have me round for Christmas.

'It isn't a pity invite,' he'd hastened to add. 'I'd really love it if you'd spend the holidays with me – and my family – for a week – at our manor house – out in the country!' He raised his voice louder and louder over the blaring music. 'All you'd have to do is pretend to be my girlfriend!'

It felt like it was my turn to choke on the wine then. Or, better yet, to back away slowly from the maniac I'd only just met in person for the first time that night.

Instead, Ben was the one to take several steps backwards.

'I'm sorry,' he said. 'I'm coming on too strong. As soon as the words left my mouth, I heard how crazy they sounded. The idea just came to me suddenly and I got all excited because I don't want you to be left on your own for Christmas. And *I* don't want to be alone either. I'm thinking of myself really. I'm asking you for a favour. Because I . . . well, I'm kind of the only singleton in my family. Everyone else is coupled up. Even our Rottweiler Mitsi has bagged herself a mystery man. Year after year, I'm the only Gibson who turns up for the holidays alone. So I thought that if you were going to be alone too, maybe we could be together instead? That way, my family could stop bombarding me with questions about why I'm still single, and you'd have a clear reason for being there. It's a really nice place, Margot. A big country estate in Cheshire, with a manor house that my parents run as a hotel for most of the year. We'd sleep in separate beds, so there wouldn't be any funny business. It would just be a nice holiday, and we could drink loads of wine and hang out with the dog and have a good time. That's all I want, because everyone

6

deserves a lovely Christmas, because it's the most wonderful time of the year, because people come together from far and wide, because we all – we all –'

'Ben,' I interrupted. 'Breathe.'

He stopped suddenly and we stared at each other.

We both fell about laughing.

'I promise I'm not as mad as I sound right now,' he said, composing himself. 'I'm not an axe murderer or anything. I just think this could work out nicely for both of us.'

I searched his face, which was as innocent as a little boy's, and I glanced down at his arms, which were very skinny and could not have wielded an axe even if he wanted them to. An image shot through my mind then: a birds-eye view of myself sitting all alone in my empty flat on Christmas Day, with only the ghost of Taylor's things to keep me company.

'Our house has a wine cellar and a spa . . .' Ben added.

I packed my bags the next day.

And now here I am, on Monday afternoon, four days after the office Christmas party, being driven down the M40 by a strange man to a strangers' mansion.

I do know what's supposed to happen here. If the cheesy films they ram down your throat at this time of year are to be believed, Ben and I are meant to fall in love for real, finally snogging on Christmas morning under the mistletoe or something equally gag-inducing. But there is zero chance of any of that happening. As attractive as Ben is, with his floppy dark curls and clear complexion, and that strong jaw that I can see contracting as he focuses on driving, he is not my type. I'm more a fan of blondes for one. And I prefer longer hair. Freckles really do it for me – as do softer, rounder features.

Then again, Taylor ticked none of those boxes and I was totally lovesick for her.

The real issue with Ben is that he is a *he*.

So, no. There is no threat of real romance blossoming this Christmas. Ben knows that I'm a lesbian, and I know that he's a harmless kook. The whole thing is very simple. I will just be having a nice little holiday and then I'll be on my merry way. Nothing complicated whatsoever.

With that comforting thought, I relax back against the soft leather seat and snuggle up deeper inside the huge woollen scarf that I am basically wearing as a blanket. The sky outside has already darkened to an inky blue, and within minutes I am drifting off to sleep, soothed by the idea of swapping the smoggy grey city for the idyllic English countryside.

2

Margot

When I stir awake, my neck is stiff and my mouth tastes stale. There's a little string of drool hanging from my lips. I will almost definitely have been snoring. It's a good job I don't want Just Ben Gibson to fancy me for real, I think as I pull my scarf over my mouth to contain the worst of my post-nap breath and start circling my head to stretch out my neck.

'Hey, how long was I –'

I stop. I've just seen where we are. We're driving between two long rows of pine trees, which are all dusted lightly with snow although no more is falling; the sky is now cloudless and fully darkened to black. We're moving slowly, gravel crunching under the tyres as we make our way up a long driveway that cuts through a vast estate of manicured lawns. Up ahead: a tremendous mansion.

'We're . . . here?'

I thought I'd nodded off for thirty minutes – forty at a push. But if we've already arrived at the manor, then I've been asleep for well over three hours. I pull my scarf off, suddenly too warm. How could I have slept for so long? Ben and I were supposed to spend this drive getting properly acquainted. We were going to quiz and query and question one another the whole way, until we were both officially filled in on every personal detail we could think of. Now we're here, and we've barely moved past our names.

It's impossible. There's no way I can stroll into this looming estate and convince Ben's entire family that we're in a committed relationship. It was enough of a stretch telling my mum that we're *friends*.

'Ben who?' she had demanded three days ago, when I'd called to tell her about my new Christmas plans. I had of course left out the more unique features of the arrangement, but Mum was still managing to make the whole thing sound ridiculous. 'I don't know any "*Ben*". I've never met him, have I?'

'No,' I said snippily. 'Why should you have met him? I don't bring my friends round for juice and fairy cakes any more, do I? I'm a grown woman.' I wasn't acting like it, and I knew it. Talking to my mum often causes me to inhabit my teenage personality again, and the backslide through time seemed to be happening even quicker than usual during this phone call.

She tutted. 'All right, tetchy. But surely I should have at least *heard* of this guy?'

'Why? I don't have to report who my friends are to you.'

'No, you don't. I just thought that I might have been aware of a friend who you're close enough with to spend Christmas with his family instead of with me, that's all.'

I felt bad then. Mum's voice was still loud and nagging, but now I recognized the thread of hurt in her words. I quickly revisited the idea of eating Christmas lunch with her as usual. We would have burnt potatoes and Bisto gravy, and the radio would blast all my favourite indie bands instead of crappy Christmas tunes. We would fight, definitely, but it would be resolved by the time pudding was brought out, and we would chase the sugar with Quality Streets and mince pies, and watch all the best over-the-top telly and laugh harder than the shows deserved.

Mum continued. 'It was bad enough that you were going to be going away with Taylor. I thought now that your swanky show-off holiday was cancelled, you'd be content to spend the day at home like normal.' She paused. 'Is *she* why you're running off to the countryside? Is this all about Taylor?'

I bristled. It was so typical of Mum to find a way to blame everything on Taylor – to try to stick her nose into my business and cast her petty judgements. She would be even worse at Christmas, given all the excitement and stress and free-flowing alcohol of the day. Suddenly the festive memories that I had been conjuring up shifted, and I saw that Mum wasn't at the centre of them at all. It was Nana. Nana brought the joy and the laughter and the sugar. Mum and I just orbited around her light. Now that Nana was gone, Christmas at home would never be the same again, and it would be best for both of us if we accepted that and let the old traditions go. That was why I had planned to go abroad with Taylor, and it was why I had to stick to my guns and escape to the country with Ben. Mum would be OK. She would spend the day with a boyfriend, who was either already around or would be found some time in the next week.

'It's nothing to do with Taylor,' I said. 'Ben just needed a friend around this Christmas, so I'm stepping in. I'm sorry I hadn't mentioned him before, but we've got a lot closer recently. He's been around for years. He's . . . he's my best friend.'

Here in the real world, he's still a stranger. I look at him now, staring straight ahead at the tree-lined drive with his hands clamped on to the steering wheel. He must be so furious with me for wasting so much time sleeping. *I'm* furious with me.

'Home sweet home!' he says in a sing-song voice, surprising me. His face breaks into a smile, a dimple showing on his left cheek. 'Did you sleep well?'

'Yeah . . . yes,' I say slowly, completely stumped by the calmness and the sing-songing. 'I'm sorry I was out for so long. I know we were meant to –'

'Oh, it's fine. You needed to sleep, so you slept. I kept the music quiet so it wouldn't wake you.'

He nods to the radio. It's turned right down but I can just make out the grating strains of a sickly sweet Christmas song. The one where a squealing popstar tells you that all she wants for Christmas is you. Yes, *you*, sitting on the sofa in your stained sweatpants gobbling down stale gingerbread. You-ooh-ooh.

I reach forward and turn it off. Then I remember my manners and mumble my thanks.

'It's really fine.' Ben shrugs. 'Besides, we've still got loads of time to get to know each other. My family aren't here yet, remember?'

Oh yeah. I do remember. The Gibsons are all away right now. I don't know exactly who is where because I haven't even learned anyone's names yet, but I recall that Ben's parents are off enjoying a few days away after closing their hotel for the remainder of the year so that the family can have the manor all to themselves for Christmas. I guess that's just the sort of thing you do when you're a) family-orientated and b) filthy rich. Mr and Mrs Gibson won't be back here until tomorrow evening.

'We'll do all our homework later tonight,' Ben says. 'Plenty of time for it. And there's no need to stress about the tiny details anyway. It's not like you'll be getting grilled about my favourite colour.' He's silent for a moment. 'Which is blue.'

I laugh. 'Mine's green.'

'Perfect. My *precise* favourite colour is cobalt blue. It's a little bit dark, but also a little bit bright. A lovely deep colour. Very calming. It makes me think of the ocean, and glass beads, and the country of Greece, and –'

I raise a hand to stop him. 'My favourite colour is still green.'

'Cool. Yeah.' He nods. 'Let's stick to the basics for now. I'm a dog person, which you already know, and I like coffee over tea, and apple juice over orange. Oh, and we've been dating for five months – you're right. And we didn't meet through work, I don't think, because the power dynamics could look a bit icky. Instead, we met at a coffee shop *near* my work. You had your head stuck in a book and accidentally spilled your latte all over my best suit. I took your number in place of an apology, and the rest is history. Et cetera, et cetera. It's all sorted, OK? You can relax.'

He's right. I can relax. We have all night to iron out the details of our relationship. And I did need that sleep. I've been working flat out the last few days, spending the entire weekend cramming in all my meetings, completing SEO reports, and pre-scheduling social media posts and marketing emails for my clients, all so that I can actually clock off for Christmas. Taylor always hated me bringing my laptop on holiday with us. We would have such a fantastic time, splashing in the pool and feeding each other new delicacies and making full use of the hotel's king-size bed, but then I'd have to sneak away to get a few hours of work done and Taylor would be furious that I was bursting our perfect bubble of bliss for the sake of reading some emails. I finally realized, too late, that she was right. I need a proper break. So this year, I've left all the stress of my life behind in London, and I am going to relax.

I've clearly picked a fantastic venue for it. Ben is pulling up to the house now, parking next to a pale stone water feature, and I'm getting my first proper look at the place. It's bloody ginormous: three stories high and at least twice as wide, with several pointed triangular roofs and a small army of chimneys on top. Frosted ivy climbs all over the red-brick walls. Through the nearest leaded window, I spot a real Christmas tree, flawlessly decorated with glinting golden lights and ornate baubles. There's none of the cheap tinsel you'd find at my mum's house, and it's a world away from the tiny plastic tree Taylor picked out for us because clutter infuriates her. It's a bona fide winter wonderland. I'd be willing to bet there's even a real fire roaring inside. I might even be able to smell the smoky warmth of it in the air; I'm definitely getting cinnamon and cloves.

'So,' Ben says, 'shall I show you around?'

Yes. Yes, I shall be shown around, and I shall make myself at home sweet home. I might even keep an eye out for interior design inspiration. My flat is due a bit of an update now that half its contents have been removed, and it can't hurt for me to ask Ben where his parents got some of their things from so that I can look online for discounted, second-hand, knock-off versions later.

Other than thinking about redecorating, I have nothing much to worry about during my stay at this perfect palatial place. Ben and I will sort out our story later as we lounge in our beds beneath thousand-thread-count sheets. I will calmly explain that we *didn't* meet by bumping into one another in a coffee shop, because ridiculous things like that do not happen in real life. People are simply not that clumsy and they are not brought together by whimsical slapstick acts of fate. They meet on Tinder. So we'll agree on that, then I will lay my head on a plump goose-feather pillow – which I will pretend is synthetic to fit in with my vegetarianism – and I will slumber. Over the coming week I will unwind in the sauna and dine in the great hall and sip on mulled wine by the fire, letting all the pampering heal me. I will occasionally hold Ben's hand and kiss his cheek and tell some tiny little lies to a bunch of strangers, letting the fake relationship distract me if I'm not healing as fast I'd like.

All of this will be good for me. I'm going to have a splendid time. Behind those grand double doors lies the ultimate luxury holiday – my perfect uncomplicated Christmas. I'm ready to step on in.

I nod to Ben, take in a big hearty breath, and fling open the car door.

It hits something, hard.

There's a horrible thud as the door bangs, and then a surprised little yelp from whatever it banged against. An animal? Oh, please say I haven't hit an animal. I scramble out of my seat, practically throwing myself out of the car – directly into another collision. Before I can work out what's happened, my face has come smack-bang against . . . something. Something unyielding yet soft.

I pull back, dazed. And then I jerk back sharply, all the way. The something is a someone, and I've gone and buried my face in her cleavage. I take a step back. Then another. I try to apologize, but my words are tripping over themselves. As it happens, so am I: as I take another clumsy step back, my foot catches on a stone and I go tumbling backwards. The someone comes lunging forward and catches me, one hand gripping my flailing arm and the other swooping behind my back.

We stay suspended here, like any slight movement could send us toppling out of our ballroom-esque dip. I look up into her face. Half of it is covered by her hair, a bleach-blonde waterfall tumbling down over her face and towards mine. What I can see is a pair of greenish-brown eyes, wide with the same adrenaline that's coursing through me. And full bee-stung lips. Tons of freckles. Round cheeks. She is one of the most beautiful women I've seen in my life. *Who is she?*

'Ellie!'

As Ben's voice rings out from the other side of the car, I remember where I am. Who I'm here with. I pull myself quickly into an upright position then draw back, untangling myself from this someone, this woman. This Ellie.

Ben comes up behind me and places a hand on the small of my back. For a brief moment I'm surprised by the casual intimacy, by the foreign feeling of a man's large warm hand on my body. I push the discomfort away and lean into the embrace.

'This is a lovely surprise,' he continues, beaming at the woman in front of us. 'I didn't realize you'd be here yet. I guess it's introduction time already!' His smile gets even wider somehow, and he stands taller. 'Ellie – this is Margot, my girlfriend.'

I cringe slightly at the lie – then pretend to shiver in the cold. I flash a quick smile at Ellie, allowing my eyes to linger on her face for only a second before returning my gaze to Ben.

'And, Margot – this is Ellie. My sister.'

I blink at him, confused. Because there wasn't supposed to be any family here yet. Because Ben doesn't seem at all worried about how unprepared we are.

Because Ellie looks nothing like her dark, lanky brother.

It's this last bit that sticks in my mind and takes over everything else. I just can't wrap my head around it. I can't make sense of them as siblings. Ellie is blonde. And freckly. And curvy. She's exactly my type.

She's completely off-limits.

I cringe again, this time at myself. I should not be thinking for a second about whether she is *on*-limits. I am here to be Ben's girlfriend. That's it. I can't get all carried away over the very first woman I see on arrival. It's like teenage Margot is back again – and this time she's taken over without my mum being around to annoy her out of me. That has been happening more and more regularly over the last month or so, ever since the break-up with Taylor. *She* would find my awkward hormonal behaviour beyond ridiculous. I especially dread to think what she'd make of me getting up so close and personal with Ellie like that. She'd never believe that our epic collision was an accident. I'm not even sure *I* believe it. Have I seriously just lived out my own clumsy romcom-style meet-cute?

'Oh,' Ben calls out suddenly. 'And this is Mitsi.'

Grateful for the distraction, I look down to where he's pointing and see a Rottweiler standing nearby. She's panting heavily, tail wagging away. She is very fat, with a bloated pregnant tummy and many neck rolls. She looks up at me with innocent puppy-dog eyes then proceeds to ram her head into Ben's car door as if she'd like to be hit with it again.

Again! Crap. I hit a pregnant dog with the door.

'I'm *so* sorry,' I cry. 'I hit your dog.'

'I noticed,' Ellie says wryly. Then she sighs. 'It's not really your fault. She's a nightmarish creature. I was trying to give her some medicine, but she kept running away from me, and then she got out somehow, and she made a beeline for the garden, and . . .'

My goodness. Even her voice is beautiful. It's as smooth as honey, but with the slightest husky edge to it. I could just get lost in it.

Nope. No getting lost in honey-ish voices for me. I've got to focus my attention on something else. Like . . . Oh, like those cars parked opposite Ben's. There are three of them. A tiny sporty one, a huge SUV, and a classic Cadillac.

'Those cars are amazing,' I gush. 'How old is the Cadillac? It's stunning. It must be a rare model? I bet it cost a fortune!'

Ben dives straight into talking about the car. Ellie catches my eye and searches my face. I look away quickly. I try to get lost in *Ben's* voice, but I'm too distracted. I can still feel Ellie's eyes on me, making every inch of my skin feel warm. I don't like it. Her attention is making me want to tuck myself out of sight, to draw in and hide all my long limbs, which currently feel even more gangly and awkward than they did when I was a five-foot-nine sixteen-year-old girl. I am too conspicuous. It's like the smart exterior that I've carefully constructed for myself over the years has fallen away. If only I hadn't arrived at the manor via double prat-fall. And if I only I wasn't continuing to make an idiot of myself by thinking again and again about how gorgeous my fake boyfriend's sister is.

I sigh. My simple, relaxing Christmas is starting to look pretty bloody complicated.

3

Ellie

A strange thing just happened involving a stranger and my tits. Now I'm standing alone in the middle of the driveway, watching said stranger stroll into my house with her little stripy suitcase rolling along behind her. I'm feeling very strange about the strange thing with the strange stranger.

It's odd that I'm so bothered by my intimate introduction to this Margot character. Normally I'd be happy to have a woman motor-boating me within a few seconds of us meeting. Forwardness is a good quality in my book. I've spent years touring party islands, thanks to my summer-job-turned-long-term-career as a holiday rep, and somewhere between Mykonos and Ibiza I mastered the delicate art of cutting to the chase. Saved me from wasting time on straight girls. I like a woman who's as forward as I am, especially when she happens to look like Margot, with her shiny dark hair and olive skin and long legs. A lady like that literally throwing herself at me would usually seem like a lovely early Christmas present.

But there's something very weird about Margot.

She's dating my older brother.

I mean no offence to Ben, obviously. I'm sure he's attractive to a certain kind of woman. It's just that nobody has ever been able to find said woman – not Ben nor our meddling parents nor exclusive, expensive dating apps. I've even tried setting him up before, with a sweet, slightly geeky girl I flat-shared with back in the day. No dice. Apparently she didn't mind when he tucked his napkin into his shirt to eat his spaghetti and she found his cheesy pick-up lines charming, but she was turned off by his interview-style questioning, including whether she wanted children and, if so, how many. That about sums Ben up: overeager and overly awkward. And I'm meant to believe that his life-long losing streak has been broken by a woman like Margot?

Nah. Margot is an alpha. Sure, she stuttered and stumbled a bit when she first tripped and made her acquaintance with my cleavage, but once she was standing straight again, she had perfect posture and a confident stance. Her make-up was subtle but flawless, eyelids brushed with warm browns and lips stained a purplish nude. Her glossy hair was parted neatly down the middle and styled into a sleek long bob. She was even wearing a suit. Seriously! This woman genuinely sat through a car ride all the way from London in a pressed chequered trouser suit. Granted, it looked relatively comfy for such a smart outfit, but it is still oh-so-obvious that Margot is one of those perfectly preened, highly polished, dominant types. I can't work out for the life of me how she's ended up with my brother.

The front door closes behind the two of them now, and the sound of Ben babbling on endlessly about the history of the manor fades away. Oddly enough I turned down the invitation to join a grand tour of 'his' childhood home, seeing that it's, you know, *my* childhood home as well. I've been getting to know my way around here for a good thirty years now, and I have been shown all Dad's rare antiques and Mum's carefully matched furnishings more than enough times to last me another sixty. Besides, I've got to stay behind and give Mitsi her medicine. I swoop down while she's distracted by her own tail and capture her at last. I feed her the chunk of cheese containing her worming tablet, then clip her lead to her collar and march her back to the house.

The ridiculous dog has been rowdier than ever since getting pregnant. I only arrived home from my five-month stint in Thailand yesterday, and she's already staged three break-out attempts. Mum and Dad say they have no idea how she possibly got herself knocked up since she's always kept on the leash at the park and we're in too remote an area for there to be dog-walkers near the house, but they also say she's a perfect angel and never gets outside without them opening the door for her, so Mitsi clearly has a few secrets under this roof.

I tug at her lead to get her through the double doors and into the foyer. The reception desk is deserted. It's always weird to see a reception desk in your own home. Even weirder to find it strange that no one is manning it, thanks to the hotel portion of your family home being closed for the holidays. I walk Mitsi past it, dinging the little bell on the counter as I go, then down the left hallway and into the small family living room at the back of the house. Not for guest use, this wing. Gibsons only.

I swing the wooden door shut behind me and let Mitsi go. She jumps straight on to the old Chesterfield and stretches out her body, generously leaving one tiny corner of the sofa for me to squeeze into. I sit myself down and she plonks her big drooling head in my lap and starts snoring.

I give her a little rub behind the ears. I do love this dollop of a dog – how she has somehow convinced my parents she's a good girl while consistently running amok on the grounds to terrorize the squirrels and piss in the roses. Me and her, we're the loose cannons of the family. Honestly, for all the fuss my parents have made over the years about my 'reckless lifestyle', the dog might actually be worse than I am. At least as a lesbian I've never gone and got myself pregnant on my adventures abroad. That's Ellie 1 – Mitsi 0. *And* I come back home without being dragged in on a leash. So 2–0.

I shift her head carefully so I can cross one leg over the other. Even though she'd fall asleep again in seconds, I can't bring myself to wake her up, so I'm stuck here for a while. Naturally the TV control is on the other side of the room, teasing me from its perch on top of the fireplace. My phone is in my bedroom, attached to the speakers upstairs and pumping music into the wrong room. There's not much to do in here besides look around at the beige walls, heavy curtains and garish chandelier.

It feels a bit weird being back here. Always does. After spending most of the year showing tourists around sandy beaches with sparkling azure oceans and clear blue skies, the snow-topped trees and crackling fires round here don't really feel like home. Two days ago, I was concluding a good night's work with a rowdy group of American holidaymakers by polishing off the last in a long line of cocktails as we all spent a rare quiet moment watching the sun rise at a private beach party in Phuket. Being tucked up on the sofa with the dog at 9:00 p.m. doesn't feel very *me*.

Still, I've got to get used to it if I want to move back

here. A key part of settling down is accepting the whole 'settling' thing. It does feel like it's about time for me to stay put for a while, after spending nearly a decade travelling around the world and earning just enough money as a rep to buy my next flight. The plan is to get myself a nice little place somewhere near here as soon as I've convinced my folks to let me help run the family biz. Maybe a flat in Manchester – that's within commuting distance. I'll be able to get to the hotel easily whenever I want to, so I can see my Grandpa Mo all the time. I'll hear his life stories while he's still around to tell them, and I'll laugh at his ridiculous jokes until my belly aches, and I'll share his extensive supply of fancy whiskies and cheap sweets, and basically just spend hours and hours lounging around with him shooting the shit. And I'll do my job and stuff, too.

I really believe I'll be great at working here. I've organized loads of group holidays on the islands, and I know tons about tourism, and I have loads of fresh ideas for levelling up the hotel's reputation. I'm especially keen to introduce some fun new events in the evenings so that we can start appealing to the younger generations as well as the geriatric gang that my parents currently cater to. Obviously there will always be a new generation of old fogies interested in this place, but we're just not filling up rooms like we used to as so many of our regular long-term visitors . . . well, stop being able to visit. Plus, Mum and Dad may well retire soon themselves, and I'll be damned if I let someone from outside this family take over the business. It belongs to us, and it needs to be protected. That's what I'm going to do here: future-proof the hotel and use it to build myself a future.

I do feel like a bit of a cliché, turning thirty and suddenly wanting to lay down some roots. But celebrating the big three-oh six months ago in Ibiza with a group of people whose names I barely knew, then winding up completely blitzed at an after-party that turned out to be full of teenagers on their first-ever holiday without parents . . . yeah, that did give me a bit of a wake-up call. Not to mention a vicious hangover. And intense fatigue. Obviously I'll still go travelling whenever I can, but I'm finally ready to have a permanent address and a steady job and a wardrobe that isn't my backpack.

All I've got to do is show my family that I can be trusted with the job. The idea is to spend the entirety of this Christmas break demonstrating my maturity and dependability. For starters, I've turned up this year without a girl-of-the-month on my arm. My parents have never minded me dating women, thank heavens, but dating *around* is a different matter. Showing up here single and not looking to mingle will go some way towards making me look more settled and sensible. I've also earned a few brownie points right off the bat by offering to take care of Mitsi while they're away for a few days. Dog-sitting duty usually falls to my sister Kate, so I'm up in her estimation too. When she arrives at the house, I'll step in to help entertain her two unruly sons. I'll cook and I'll clean and I'll make conversation about politics and history and, like, *Strictly Come Dancing* or something. This Christmas I'm going to be on my very best behaviour, fitting seamlessly in with my parents' very detailed idea of what a perfect daughter should be. I'm gonna dazzle 'em all.

Unfortunately that means I can't yell at Ben to shut

up right now. His guided tour of the house has just led him down this hallway and his voice rings out loud and clear.

'So *this* wooden beam is an original period feature,' he says. 'Just like those ones I showed you in the foyer. And in the great hall. And in the other hall. We have loads of period features in the house, and then everything else is a faithful restoration, or an antique of my dad's. Except for the spa! That's all modern, and the furthest thing from a period feature we've got.'

Ugh. I dare him to say *period feature* one more time. He sounds like a bloody estate agent – not a guy settling his new girlfriend into his family home. It's exactly this kind of awkwardness that I can't see meshing with Alpha Margot. Although she sounds like she's enjoying the tour, commenting excitedly on the features she likes most.

'I *love* this wallpaper,' she says. 'The pattern is so intricate and subtle. So classy!'

'It's nearly fifty years old now. Vintage. It's lasted well, hasn't it?'

'It really has. Do you know who designed it by any chance? Or the name of the pattern? How much does fifty-year-old designer wallpaper sell for these days?'

'No idea,' Ben says regretfully. 'But my mum will know everything you want to know. We'll ask her tomorrow – about the wallpaper, and that rug you liked earlier, and those lamps too. In the meantime, here's another original beam! Shall we see the spa next? It's Ellie's favourite place in the house.'

'Oh, is she . . . ?'

'She's not in there at the moment,' Ben clarifies. 'There's

music coming from her bedroom, so she's up there. The spa is all ours, *my darling*. Follow me.'

Their footsteps retreat down the hallway. I'm not surprised that Ben hasn't bothered showing off the room I'm actually in. Far too small and homely to elicit excitement from Margot. The wallpaper isn't even vintage. Instead, Ben tells her all about the 'state-of-the-art' sauna and she even lets out a wolf-whistle as they reach the end of the hall and turn off into the spa room.

Just as their voices start to fade, I hear something odd. 'No!' Margot cries out in surprise. Then she quickly forces a laugh. 'Sorry. I wasn't expecting you to grab me. Not around the waist. So . . . you can let go now.' Another strained giggle. 'Sorry, I only slipped a little bit. Let's save the handsy stuff for later, *darling*. We can do all that when . . .'

Her voice finally trails off. I frown. An estate agent and a prospective buyer would have more chemistry than those two. Why is she so weird about him touching her? I noticed that she flinched when he put an arm around her out on the driveway as well. And that smile she pinned on when she looked at him seemed so false to me. And what's with the 'darling' thing? I've never heard a term of endearment sound so stilted and forced. Almost like a joke.

In a few minutes, they're back in the hallway.

'Don't bother arguing with me about it,' Ben says. 'Let me treat you. You've done so much for me, Margot. You're incredible. The least I can do is give you a little thank you. Consider it a Christmas bonus if you like. It's really not a lot of money.'

Huh? He's offering her *money*? Surely she won't accept tha–

'Fine!' Margot says. 'Thank you. You've worn me down with your complete and utter insistence on being lovely.' She lets out a little giggle and then pauses, having what I hope is an awkward moment to feel embarrassed about all of this. But she quickly breezes on in a new playful voice: 'Shall I spend it all on Christmas prezzies for you, then? Or on new clothes for me? Or maybe new shoes for me? And what about a nice handbag for . . . guess who . . . ?'

Her jubilant voice dwindles again as they climb the stairs to the first floor. I strain to hear more, but they're gone. I flop back against the padded sofa cushions. That dynamic is too weird for words. Poor Ben. His sparkly new girlfriend seems much more interested in shopping than she does in him. Out on the driveway he looked pleased as punch to be standing by her side, while she stood there as stiff as a solider, hardly speaking to either of us. The most she said was about the Cadillac, when she gushed about how rare it must be and how much it must have cost. It's just like how she wanted to know all about the vintage wallpaper and what sort of money it –

Wait.

Shit.

Oh my God.

She's a *gold-digger.*

Suddenly everything makes sense. Margot doesn't seem all that interested in my brother because *she is not interested in my brother.* She's interested in his wallet. His jewellery business. His family home, with its period features and designer wallpaper and wolf-whistle-worthy spa. She has barely been here for an hour and already she seems to be marching around making mental notes about exactly how much everything is worth, from the classic cars to the lamps.

It's undeniable. She's here for his money. *Our* money. This slick, sexy snake in the grass is only here to slither her way into the family fortune.

I feel sick. Anger and outrage form a tight fist in my belly, making it all tense and knotty. There's a heavy lump of guilt in there too. I watched this woman go swanning into my family home and all I could think about was how wonderfully long her legs were and how completely bizarre it was that she was dating my brother. Well. It doesn't seem so bizarre now, does it? Seems calculated and clever to me. Ice cold.

A deep sadness joins the cocktail of emotions swimming around in my gut. Poor, poor Ben. He's being used, and he's so desperate for love that he can't see it. He thinks he's finally found the one – a real girlfriend at last. And it's all a lie. A scam.

Well, I won't let her get away with it. Ben and I might not be the closest siblings around, but nobody hurts him on my watch. *Nobody* messes with my family.

Obviously I want to jump up right now and fling that woman out of our house by her pressed chequered collar. But I have to be smart about this. If I fly into a rage, I'll be seen as hot-headed and impulsive as usual, and everything I say will be dismissed out of hand. My family loves to accuse me of jumping to conclusions – though I can't see why. Instead I'll play the long game. Keep a close eye on Margot; prove that she's a gold-digger; gently reveal the truth to Ben and allow *him* the honours of chucking her out on her arse. Hopefully I'll make short work of the long game and have everything sorted out before we're singing carols and swapping presents under the tree next Monday.

I let my plan calm me down and I slowly stroke Mitsi in my lap. You'd better watch out, Margot – Ellie Gibson is on to you.

4

Margot

I close my eyes and tilt my head back, letting the shower's steaming-hot water wash over my face. I have already shampooed and conditioned my hair and lathered my entire body in vanilla-scented body wash. I am now using the shower for its true purpose: overthinking. Goodness knows there's plenty of material for me to get through tonight. Although I've only had a tour of the house and eaten pesto pasta so far, I'm already completely overwhelmed by how bonkers the situation at Gibson Manor is.

For one, there's the fact that I'm sharing a room with Ben. I did know that was the deal going in, and he has kept his word and got us a room with separate double beds, but now that I'm actually here I can't shake the feeling that I shouldn't be having a slumber party with a client. To this day, nobody on my books has seen me in my fluffy PJs and orthodontic retainer, and I am feeling a bit strange about that changing.

For two, there's the role that I'm here to play. If it's a bit weird that I'm sharing digs with Ben, then it's downright insane that I'm play-acting as his girlfriend. I don't even know any of my lines or directions. The sum of my Ben Gibson-related knowledge is that he works as a jeweller and his favourite colour is a shade of blue that I *think* begins with the letter C.

For three, there's the small fact of this whopping mansion. I swear it grew larger and more magnificent as the tour went on, and as much as I enjoyed looking at the smaller details, the full scale of the place just intimidated me.

And then there's Ellie.

But no. I am not going to think about her. She's just Ben's sister. That's it. Any thoughts I *did* have about her out on the driveway were the obvious result of a moment of madness. Perhaps I was suffering from a very brief concussion after crashing into her. I mean, really. 'One of the most beautiful women I've ever seen'? Ridiculous.

I reach out to turn the heat up even higher. All it takes is the slightest twist of a large metal tap, which is refreshing considering that most unfamiliar showers seem to come kitted out with a complicated series of taps, handles and valves which all need to be fiddled with in precisely the right way before a single droplet of water can be coaxed out.

Clouds of steam gather around me. Vanilla sweetness floats through the air. I take in a deep breath and when I exhale I let every inch of my body relax. I remind myself that there's no use in holding on to stressful thoughts, and then I imagine every one of them leaving my head and swirling down the plughole along with the last suds of my shower gel.

Before the warm cosy feeling deserts me, I step out of the shower and into a huge towel. The fluffy cotton is incredibly soft against my skin and wraps around my body nearly twice over. I rake some argan oil through my wet hair, slather myself in lotion, and step into my PJs: an oversized Pixies band tee and fleecy grey pyjama bottoms. My wristwatch on the basin tells me that it's nearly 11:00 p.m., and I think that seems as good a time as any for a late-night natter with Ben. I'm ready to introduce myself to my boyfriend.

In the bedroom, Ben has set up a full-on classroom. There are pads of paper on both our beds, and the matching walnut side tables are covered with pens, highlighters and Post-it notes. He's even donning a pair of thick-rimmed reading glasses. As I walk in, he lowers a sheet of lined A4 and smiles at me.

'Hey! You ready to study up?'

I grin back at him. The excessive nerdiness of this set-up paired with Ben's dorky smile has got rid of any last remnants of anxiety. I cross the room to my bed, the one under the big leaded window. The view is gorgeous. That's Ben's excuse for us staying in this room, should anyone ask: we wanted the fabulous view. It's hard to argue with his logic. You can see basically the whole estate from here, from the thicket of pine trees to the small lake and from the rose garden to the sprawling lawns, each area lit up by various warm-coloured outdoor lights. It's snowing again too. Not the grey stuff we were pelted with on the motorway, but fluffy white snow that drifts down from the skies and settles over the trees with grace.

In here it's nice and toasty. The room is everything I'd dreamed it would be, with its plush cream carpet and heavy elegant curtains detailed with little glints of gold. There's even a chaise longue in beige and walnut. The pillows on the bed are *definitely* goose-feather – you can just tell. I sit myself down on the mattress, stretching my legs out over the crisp white sheets. I'm more than ready to settle into this new normal. I just have to focus on Ben – on getting to know him so well that I can transform myself into his ideal girlfriend. I will absorb every single word he utters tonight and become the most perfect, most adoring, most attentive partner of all time.

'Margot?'

'Huh?'

'I said, shall we dive in?' Ben waves his piece of paper at me. 'I've written out a few questions to get us started.'

I nod and reach forward to pick up the lined notepad at the foot of my bed. The first page is covered in neat ultra-small handwriting.

'I thought we'd start off with some quick-fire questions,' he says. 'Just to ease us into it.'

I look closer at the paper. At the very top he's written: QUICK-FIRE QUESTIONS TO EASE US INTO IT. I can't help but grin again. I run my finger down the page and land on 'favourite food?'

'I love Mexican food,' I tell him. 'You?'

'I'm a fan of gastropubs.' He writes something down on a Post-it. 'Favourite TV show?'

'*Fleabag*,' I say. 'Or *Russian Doll*. Or *High Fidelity*! You?'

'*The West Wing*.'

'Oooo–K.' I fall back against the pillows, taking my crib sheet with me. 'Music?'

'Coldplay's my favourite. And I also like Snow Patrol, U2, Maroon 5. That sort of thing.'

I manage not to yawn. 'I'm into slightly more indie stuff. I can never pick any favourites, but I've been listening to Girl in Red all week and I'm wearing a Pixies shirt, so let's go with those two for today. How about . . . your favourite film?'

'*The Godfather.*'

'Ugh.' I can't hold it in any more. 'Your taste is so *male*. And mainstream. And middle-aged.' I peek at him to check he's still smiling. He is. 'If you're not careful, I might have to break up with you.'

'OK, darling. But could we schedule our separation for *after* Christmas?'

'Good idea,' I agree. 'I don't want to miss out on my prezzies.'

'Oh, I'm getting you presents, am I?'

'Of course you are. Many presents. All of them shiny and expensive. You own a jewellery shop, darling, so it shouldn't be too difficult. I'll simply take my pick of your stock.' I drop the increasingly exaggerated voice I've been using. 'Actually, I *have* been given freebies by my clients before. Just saying. Maybe working for a jeweller will mean I finally get something a bit more exciting than a multipack of knickers or a free MOT.'

'Hmm. I wouldn't hold your breath.'

I poke my tongue out at him, then dive back into the questions. It's actually really nice getting to know Ben, predictable tastes and all. It's been a while since I made a new friend, and I've definitely never gone through such a thorough introduction process. Together we whizz through pet peeves (me – loud chewing; Ben – slow texters), favourite places we've travelled (me – Cancún; Ben – Montreal), and best subjects in school (both – English). Given that we're reading questions from a script, the conversation feels remarkably natural.

35

'So what's your family like?' Ben asks.

I stiffen. I wasn't ready for that question yet, but I play it off with a shrug. 'It's a small family. Not that much to say. Let's talk about yours first, since I'll actually be meeting them.'

'Fair point.' He pushes his glasses up his nose. 'Now's the time for you to start making notes, then.'

I suppress a smile and reach forward to grab some green Post-its and a pen. Ready, I nod to Ben.

'OK. We'll start with Ellie because you've already met her.'

I give him a double thumbs-up to confirm, then immediately feel silly about the cartoonish move. He doesn't seem to find it weird, though. He simply returns the gesture.

'So,' he says, 'Ellie is a major travel junkie. She's just got back from Thailand – or maybe it was Taiwan – and before that she was in Ibiza. She works as a holiday rep, which basically means she gets paid to party with big groups of people on their holidays.'

'Cool.' Of course she has a cool job. She'd never give someone a double thumbs-up. 'Very cool.'

'I guess. I couldn't do work like that myself. I like my home comforts too much.'

As if to illustrate his point, Ben reaches for a cinnamon cookie. A huge batch of them were baked from scratch by the hotel chef before she left for Christmas break, which explains the warm spicy smell I was hit with when we arrived. Ben takes a big bite, and I pick one up from my own plate and follow suit. The biscuit has a wonderful crunch, then literally melts in my mouth.

'Anyway,' Ben continues with his mouth full, 'that job

works for Ellie, so more power to her. Of course, she thinks all of us are painfully boring and repressed. I imagine she's thought that since she was about six. She's a real free spirit. Horrifically messy. And very funny.'

'Nice.' I jot it all down to keep Ben happy. 'And her partner? What do I need to memorize there? Is she married? Engaged?'

'Ha!' He laughs and cookie crumbs go flying. 'No.'

Oh?

'Ellie is unattached.'

Oh.

'She has a different girlfriend every year.'

Oh.

'Yeah, she isn't big on commitment, my sister. And yet *she* always has someone to bring home for Christmas, unlike me. That's why I consider her part of the "coupled up" crowd. This is probably the first time I've seen her come back home without a new girlfriend in about ten years. That's good for you, though, isn't it?'

I spin to look at him. 'What?'

'Because it's one less person for you to get to know,' Ben clarifies. 'We've still got plenty more to get through.'

'Of course.' I relax back into my natural seated position, laying a hand across my stomach. I just experienced a very strange whooshing sensation in there, but it is subsiding now, and it only happened in the first place because Ben's question surprised and confused me. I suppose I'm also excited to discover that Ellie is queer. That has very little to do with Ellie herself, though, and a lot to do with the fact that I *always* get excited when I meet other openly queer people. I let the buzzy feeling fade into the usual sense of casual kinship. 'Let's move on, then. Tell me about your other sister.'

'Kate, yes.' Ben finishes the last of his cookie in one big mouthful. 'Kate is the eldest, and she's the polar opposite of Ellie. Very organized and very, very dependable. If you're ever in a crisis, you call Kate. She's a part-time paralegal and her husband, Henry, is a solicitor. They have twin boys – Dylan and Dominic. They're five and they're a bit . . . lively. All four of them will come for Christmas but Henry will probably be called away for work at some point.'

OK. That's kind of exciting too. In a way. I make some more notes on my Post-it.

'Then there's Grandpa Mo,' Ben says. 'He's eighty-eight now, and still has almost as much energy as Kate's twins. He managed the hotel for most of his life, and only retired a decade ago. He got into astronomy after retirement, and now owns several telescopes. He's always been a bit eccentric, but in recent years . . .' He trails off, looking around the room as if the walls might finish his sentence for him. 'It hit him hard when my grandma passed away three years ago. He doesn't always make sense any more. But he's lovely. I think you'll like him.'

'I think I will too,' I say gently.

Ben smiles. 'He's visiting friends at a retirement village at the moment. He always goes just before Christmas. He said he'll be back on Wednesday, Thursday or Saturday.'

I tilt my head. 'Not Friday?'

'Apparently not,' Ben says with a bemused shrug. 'That just leaves Mum and Dad. They both work here, basically sharing the role of manager. They met at school. Together they masterminded a big campaign to have a proper end-of-year prom, which was pretty forward-thinking given that this was many, many years before the tradition had made its way across the pond from America. In return they were voted prom king and queen, and they've been together ever since. Dad started working for Grandpa Mo as soon as he left school, and he got Mum a job at the hotel's front desk too. By the time they were twenty, they were working directly under Grandpa as assistant managers. By twenty-three, they were engaged. Twenty-five, married. Twenty-seven, along came Kate. Then me, then Ellie. We all lived in the family quarter that Grandpa had designed decades before, and Mum baked fresh bread every morning and Dad collected rare antiques, and to this day they still hold hands. They're perfect.'

He is still smiling as he talks, but it doesn't quite reach his eyes. 'Sometimes they're a bit too perfect,' he says quietly, looking down at the papers in his lap. 'They're perfection-*ists*. Like . . . OK, so they picked out my "favourite colour" for me before I was even born. It was supposed to be orange. My clothes were orange, and my room was orange, and my new toys were almost always orange. They picked a different colour for each of us kids. And they called us Kate and Ben and Ellie – not Katherine and Benjamin and Eleanor – because they couldn't stand the thought of us being given the "wrong" nicknames later in life. Grandma was even discouraged from calling me "Ben-Ben" as a child. And *I* was discouraged from finger-painting, because I did it too messily and I was much better at colouring in. It was the same thing with drama club in secondary school; I never got the big parts, so they made me quit once the rehearsals started clashing with football practice.'

He sighs. 'Everything has always had to be just so. The very best.'

I consider this. It's hard to imagine Ben's childhood being *too* perfect, even if he was surrounded by orange and occasionally had to sacrifice one extracurricular activity for another. I for one would have been delighted to grow up in a huge country house with acres of land as my garden, instead of a council flat in Tottenham with one dinky window box and mould growing in the shower. I'd love to have been raised by happily married, doting parents like Ben's. My own dad walked out when I was eight, heading off to start a sunny new life in Australia without me. Mum took his departure as a chance to rewind the clock, parading around town with as many men as she pleased, often ones about ten years her junior. She still hasn't grown out of her taste for younger men; the depressing fact is that if I were straight, the two of us could share a dating pool. The only family member I ever really felt connected to was my nana, who always baked me sweet treats, and danced around the living room to old jazz songs, and printed out pages from the websites I designed to keep in a scrapbook by her bed. But she died in March. So there you go. That's my lot in life.

And yet . . . all struggles are relative. Somehow I don't seem to resent Ben for complaining about his own lot. Looking over at his bed, I see him sitting cross-legged with his big glasses slightly askew and his pages of notes fanned out around him. He's wearing a matching pyjama set made from pale blue cotton, with little buttons and a collar and everything. He looks so harmless and sweet, and although his problems might seem a tad trivial to me, I find myself fighting the urge to get up and hug him.

'All parents are a little bit rubbish,' I tell him softly. 'Mine are a lot-a bit rubbish. My dad's not in the picture and my mum's a cougar.'

'Yikes.'

'Yeah, yikes.' I try a small smile, and Ben mirrors it. I know instinctively that I could tell him more and he would listen with kindness, but I think I'll put a cap on my sob story for now. There's plenty more gossip for us to get through at this sleepover. I get myself under the covers, pulling the duvet up to my chin. 'So, tell me. Your parents. The unattainable standard of perfection. Is that why you've brought an undercover lesbian round to masquerade as your girlfriend for Christmas?'

Midnight is long past by the time Ben finishes explaining why he's still single. Fittingly, the main issue seems to be that he talks too much. He has self-diagnosed verbal diarrhoea at the best of times, and the symptoms get worse when he tries to talk to eligible women. Apparently he once spent a romantic evening at the cinema telling his date about all the other films he'd seen each of the starring actors in, along with a short biography of their lives thus far. He did this because he was worried that he wouldn't get a second date unless he proved himself to be interesting, knowledgeable and engaged. He did not get a second date.

'That's crappy,' I say. 'But the right person is out there. The future Mrs Just Ben Gibson will be even chattier than you are, and she'll be delighted that you can keep up with her. You just need to meet someone who's on your wavelength, that's all.'

He sighs. 'I'm sure you're right. But I've only ever met

one person who's on this particular wavelength of mine, and that was years ago.'

'Ooh! Tell me more.'

'Oh, we were just kids.' He shrugs, while simultaneously sitting up taller in his bed to prepare for storytelling. 'I mean that literally: we spent our childhoods together. Her name was Bobbi. She was the groundskeeper's daughter. She lived with her mum for most of the year, but every summer she would stay at her dad's bungalow right here on the estate. We got on like a house on fire. We would spend hours on end running around the grounds together, getting very out of breath because we'd both be talking non-stop the whole time. My sisters found us irritating when we were together, so they left us alone. It was just me and Bobbi. I loved talking to her, and I loved her curly ginger hair, and when I was old enough to work out that I loved *her*, I told her so. We were both seventeen. My hands were sweating like mad, but she held them anyway. She said I was her best friend, and my heart sank, because that was exactly what I had been afraid of – that I had mistaken her friendship for something more – but then she kissed me. It was my first kiss, and she said it was her first good one. We were under the tallest tree in the rose garden when it happened, out of sight of both our families, and we kept meeting up in that exact same spot every single day for the next five weeks.'

He pauses for a while, seemingly lost in his memories. I find that I'm eager to hear more, despite the fact that a story like this would normally trigger my gag reflex.

'But that was the last summer I spent with Bobbi,' he says at last. 'On the last day of August, she went back home to her mum's house without saying goodbye, and she never came back to the estate again. I still don't know why. I don't know what I did wrong. I couldn't call her to ask because she didn't leave me her number, and also I was a teenage boy, so I was terrified of seeming desperate or pathetic or in possession of functioning tear ducts. I just had to get over it and move on. By now I've mostly made my peace with the idea that it was only a summer fling and we were too young and inexperienced for it to ever last. But sometimes I still wonder about her. It would be nice to know how she's doing at least. I've looked for her online a few times, but I can't find her anywhere on Facebook or Twitter or even LinkedIn. She must have got married and changed her last name.'

'OK,' I venture, 'but couldn't you ask her dad? Does he still work here?'

'He does actually. Stan's still in his bungalow at the bottom of the garden. But he never mentions Bobbi and he doesn't visit her as far as I know, so I'm not sure how much he'd really have to say, and I wouldn't want to upset him by bringing her up in case it's a bit of sore spot. I also wouldn't want to be creepy. I probably shouldn't still be thinking about her after all these years. I *definitely* shouldn't still get a bit excited when I see someone with curly ginger hair. Actually, that's another reason not to approach Stan; he has the exact same hair as Bobbi, and I wouldn't want to get confused and start projecting my old teenage-fling feelings on to him.'

I laugh. Ben barely musters up a smile for his own joke. I stop laughing.

'It will all work out, you know,' I tell him. 'I can't promise you that you're going to track Bobbi down on LinkedIn and get all the answers you deserve to be given, but you *will* find someone who's perfect for you. You'll have a proper happily ever after – and I don't usually believe in those for anyone other than animated princesses. Animated princesses and you. OK? You are so clearly a lovely, gentle, thoughtful guy – and there is an ultra-chatty woman out there somewhere just waiting to ride off into the sunset with you. I know it.'

'Thank you.' Ben sniffs, but he has brightened considerably. 'And thanks for not thinking I'm a loser.'

'Well, I never said that . . .'

'Ha! Whatever.' He shifts in his bed, kicking one leg out of the duvet. 'Come on, it's your turn now. Tell me about your ex-girlfriend.'

Oh. Yeah. Taylor. I realize suddenly that I *haven't* been thinking about her. Not since arriving at the manor. That has to be the longest stretch of time without having her on my mind since she left our flat a month ago. I feel a bit weird about that, both sad and happy. And far less defensive than usual.

'Taylor was also my first girlfriend,' I say. 'But our relationship wasn't as sweet as yours and Bobbi's. We met at university, shortly after I came out of the closet in my second year, and the whole thing was defined by typical teenage angst. There was jealousy, lust, anger, obsession – the works. We broke up soon after we graduated. Then two years ago, just before I turned thirty, I met her again at a music festival in Croatia. We got back together quickly, and things were perfect the second time around.' I pause. 'Well, they were nearly perfect.' Another pause. 'No, they were actually perfect. Or very, very close to perfect, quite a lot of the time.

'She tried to be the perfect partner this time, is what I'm saying, and I tried my very best to be worth the effort. We went on these splashy date nights and gifted each other bouquets bigger than our torsos. After a few months she bought me a huge crystal vase, labelled "for our new place". We moved into a flat in Islington, and we painted all the walls in rainbow pastels, and we spent as much time as we possibly could curled up together in bed. We were all set to grow old together. Then she dumped me. It was a horrible shock. I mean, Taylor and I argued sometimes, but who doesn't? Every happy couple has the odd disagreement from time to time. I didn't think we were on the rocks or anything. But there you go. She accused me of being emotionless and closed off, then of having too many mood swings and being oversensitive. She screamed the house down when I suggested that she was contradicting herself.

'In the end, she left quietly. She sent me a long text a few days later, explaining that she'd simply got bored. She didn't want to sit around at home any more, watching me give all my attention to my job instead of to her. It turns out that I'm "all work and no play". Taylor wanted to play – to be "out there" enjoying her thirties. She signed off by saying that she'll always love me, and that was that. I haven't heard from her since. She won't answer my calls.'

Floorboards creak in the middle of the room. A moment later, Ben stands beside my bed with a cookie in one hand and my glass of water in the other. The gesture almost makes me want to cry. Instead, I take the offerings gratefully. I have a big bite of the cookie and a sip of water, and then for some reason I keep talking.

'The worst thing about the break-up is that I haven't just lost Taylor. Our lives were so intertwined that all our friends were mutual. They all knew Taylor before they knew me, so they've obviously stood by her side. And the other friends I had before, in my twenties, are long gone. I neglected them all when I got back together with Taylor. I only wanted to spend time with her – and with her friends, if that's what she wanted to do. Now that that's all gone, I'm alone.'

I pause for another bite of cookie, then say in a very small voice, 'The truth is, I didn't even actually receive any pity invites for Christmas this year. Nobody really asked me to come over and sit between their snotty three-year-old and their perverted uncle for the big day. The only option I had was going over to my mum's and staring at the empty chair that my nana used to sit in at the head of the table. I couldn't do it. I had nowhere to go.'

Ben is silent for a moment. I'm silent too.

'I'm very glad you're here,' he says quietly. 'And you really should feel at home.'

I can only nod, all my words apparently used up. He waits for a little while, then nods back and returns to his own bed, switching off the lamp as he goes. We lie in the dark, together and apart. I know that we have said everything we need to say to each other and that nothing more is expected of me. It is a comforting thought. Fairly soon, my eyes start to feel heavy, and I drop off to sleep surrounded by the warm smell of cinnamon, feeling like I might have made myself a friend.

Tuesday, 19 December

5

Margot

I walk into the dining room with a big yawn. Ben is in the kitchen next door, making us breakfast. I offered to help him, of course, but he wouldn't hear of it. My only job is to choose us a table. There are several dotted around the room, each covered with a pristine white tablecloth. I pick one right in the middle and slip into a padded chair.

The room is gorgeous. I saw it last night on Ben's tour, but it looks different today, the morning's soft winter sunlight making everything look warmer and more inviting. There are exposed ceiling beams, sandy-coloured walls, and a huge patterned rug laid over the wooden floors. A large fireplace is decorated with an intricate festive garland, and through a tall archway I can see into the great hall, where the picture-perfect Christmas tree I spotted yesterday stands proud. It is the perfect blend of cosy homeliness and luxury excess, and I am slightly in love with it all.

Now I'm just looking forward to Ben joining me. He'll bring with him tea, toast, and easy conversation – everything I want this morning. We definitely deserve a hearty breakfast after our bumper study session last night. My brain is now so full of Ben-related facts that I could choose him as a specialist subject on *Mastermind*. I even know what it's like to wake up with him. It turns out that my roomie is a very heavy sleeper who will remain conked out well into the afternoon unless he has three different alarms blaring simultaneously at full volume each morning. I won't hold that against him, though. If it hadn't been for Ben's symphony of alarms, I think I would have slept right through to the afternoon as well. I may well have stayed in that warm cosy bed upstairs for the entire day. It gave me one of the best sleeps I've ever had. I have come to the conclusion that the manor has restorative powers, and I cannot wait for the rest of the house to work its magic on me over the next week.

Suddenly something catches my eye from over by the archway. A big round blob barrelling this way, red tongue lolloping out of its mouth. Mitsi! She's through the archway and running towards my table, and I can't help but smile. I learned a lot about Mitsi last night. Or, rather, I learned that I cannot learn a lot about Mitsi. She is considered to be one of nature's greatest mysteries. She came from a litter of black Rottweiler puppies, yet she has an all-brown coat. She knows how to roll over and give a high-five, but cannot be trained to sit or stay. She got pregnant somehow, even though Mr and Mrs Gibson never let her out of their sight at the park and she lives in the middle of nowhere with no neighbours and no other dogs nearby.

Mitsi abruptly stops running and switches into a casual waddle. Mysterious indeed. She saunters up to my table, gives my leg a cursory sniff, then plops her head right down in my lap. She's drooling on to my favourite corduroy trousers, but I don't care. I give her a scratch behind the ears, and she rewards me with a big wag of her tail, before curling up on top of my feet for a nap. She definitely doesn't seem to be holding a grudge over Car Door Gate. I am immensely relieved.

Someone else is walking into the room now. I look towards the archway eagerly, excited for my breakfast, but it's not Ben that I see.

It's Ellie.

She stops under the arch, eyes closed, and stretches her arms out overhead. She looks like she's still half asleep. It suits her. Her blonde hair is mussed up in parts, but the tangles fit into the beachy waves she's somehow managing to rock in the middle of December. Her face is free of make-up, making her scattering of freckles even more pronounced. She's wearing an oversized knitted jumper that falls halfway down her bare thighs, riding up even further as she stretches. I can't seem to take my eyes off her. All ruffled with sleep, she looks even more beautiful than she did last night.

She blinks open her eyes and suddenly she's looking right this way. I smile. She flinches. My presence in the room has clearly caught her by surprise. As she recovers herself, she lets out a sharp exhale. She squares her shoulders. She narrows her eyes.

She's glacial.

I can't say I blame her. Finally coming back to my own senses, I realize that I have just been caught full-on gawking at Ellie's naked legs. And then *smiling* about it. I look away. Should I apologize for staring at her like that? She clearly didn't like it, and the last thing I want to do is make her feel uncomfortable in her own home.

'I'm sossy.'

I'm . . . sossy? Did I really just say that? 'Sossy' is how Nana and I always used to apologize to one another, because that was how I pronounced the word 'sorry' as a baby. Which is exactly what I sound like right now. A big baby.

'Sorry,' I say. 'I meant to say "sorry". For . . . um . . .'

For what? Do I come right out and apologize for being a creep? Or will I seem even creepier if I acknowledge my own creepiness? Ellie hasn't said a single word yet, and I don't want to overwhelm her.

Before I can work it out she's striding towards me. In what looks like one fluid motion, she uses her leg to pull out the chair opposite mine and sits down with her arms stretched across the table.

'It's all right,' she says without any traces of coldness. She is smiling at me now, apparently making an effort to push past my weirdness. 'You just scared me for a second cos I didn't realize anyone was in here. No harm done. Actually, I'm glad I've caught you. I'm dying to have a proper chat so we can get to know each other. Shall we have brekkie?'

I don't see how I can say no. It's such a reasonable request, and one that would be horribly rude of me to turn down. I'm just not convinced that I can make it through breakfast without making a tit of myself. I don't seem to have anywhere near enough control over my hormones, words or eyeballs. It is so important that I make a good impression on Ben's family, and I really haven't been doing my best work with Ellie so far.

Then again, I made the worst possible first impression on Mitsi last night, and now she's cuddled up on my feet like we're the best of friends. I could turn things round with Ellie too. Maybe it's not even as bad as I feared. She seemed to glare at me from the archway, but maybe she was just tired. I bet she didn't even notice me looking at her legs. And I'm sure she won't judge me too harshly for stumbling over my words a bit.

I don't need to overthink this. Ellie wants to make the effort to get to know me, and I want to be friendly in return. Appropriately friendly. I can do that. I am not, in fact, a horny teenager and I am perfectly capable of making polite conversation over breakfast. If I find myself getting awkward again, I can just shake it off. Literally. I can shake my head until I've got rid of any nagging thoughts about how I am not acting naturally around Ellie, or, if things take a different turn, about how I am acting *too* naturally around her due to getting lost in her eyes or voice or something. I can shake my head at any thoughts that are not strictly about being Ben's 'girlfriend'. He'll be joining us soon, which will help. I won't have to chat to Ellie one-on-one for very long at all. And I'll probably be able to avoid alone time with her completely once the rest of the Gibsons arrive at the manor this evening. Until then I can always excuse myself if I absolutely have to. It's all chilled out and casual.

So I confirm that Ellie and I will 'have brekkie' together by giving her an enthusiastic double thumbs-up. I even manage not to fall into a spiral of cringing over making that ridiculous gesture again.

I've got this.

Ellie

I've got her. Margot has fallen right into my trap of friendly conversation. She has no idea that as we chatter away over breakfast I will be carefully weighing up all the information she gives me about herself to see whether any details don't quite add up or unwittingly point to her true intentions with my brother. I know there's no chance of her coming out and saying, 'I love money and I want loads of it from Ben,' but she might give away little snippets here and there that indicate an unsavoury character or outlandishly lavish tastes. I'm bound to find something if I keep her talking long enough.

And I *know* there's something. No doubt in my mind. There was a moment there last night when I considered attempting to hold off on my judgements because the voices of my family were ringing in my ears, telling me that I was being rash and looking for the worst in others 'as per usual'. I was gonna be sensible and sleep on my gold-digger theory. But then I didn't sleep. Not enough anyway. It was way too cold. I always find it hard to readjust to the freezing English weather when I come back home, and last night it felt like I woke up every five minutes to pull my extra blankets back on. They just wouldn't stop sliding off the narrow single bed I've had since I was a child.

Meanwhile, Margot and Ben slept in one of the swanky guest rooms. I shouldn't be surprised that they swerved Ben's childhood bedroom in favour of a top-floor suite with not one but *two* double beds and a sweeping view of the estate. I'm sure Margot would accept nothing less. I was pissed off about sleeping arrangements from the moment I woke up this morning, and I have been pissed off every second since.

Still, I have to play nice so that Margot doesn't work out I'm on to her. I think she picked up on my distaste when I first came into the room, and it made her all stuttery and skittish. Very suspicious. She wouldn't be so nervous if she had nothing to hide, would she? I've just got to soften my approach a little to keep her from closing off completely. It's gonna be a tricky balance to strike, but I know I'm up to the task.

'So,' I begin, stretching my arms out further across the table, 'I hear –'

'Breakfast!' Ben calls out.

Margot's face lights up as she turns towards the archway. It's the first time this morning that she's seemed genuinely happy. Is it because of hearing Ben's voice? I must admit that would be pretty sweet and unexpectedly . . . Ah. No. Following Margot's eyeline, I see that she's looking only at Ben's *tray*. It's a round silver tray loaded up with a pot of tea, a jug of milk, a bowl of sugar cubes, two mugs, two plates of toast, a few pats of butter, and a broad selection of mini jam jars – and it makes Ben look like a bloody butler. It breaks my heart seeing him so eager to please Margot. Even worse to see it working.

'*Yum*,' she says. 'It looks delish.'

'It is delish.' Ben puts the tray down on the table. 'Are you joining us, Ellie?'

'She is,' Margot says. She's still smiling, but it looks a little forced now. Something in the eyes. 'Shall I get another plate?'

'I'll grab it,' Ben says, making for the door.

Margot had already started to get up, and now sits back down. Mitsi huffs over the disturbance and moves off Margot's feet and on to mine. That's my girl. Dogs are excellent judges of character. Now that there is someone else for her to nap on, she has moved away from the shady character in the room. I'll ignore the fact that it took her several minutes to do so. Sometimes laziness overrides good judgement.

'So –'

'I love breakfast,' Margot says suddenly. Her voice overlaps with mine, cutting me off just as I was about to start asking questions. None of them were going to be about her opinions on breakfast. Although it might be good to get her talking about her favourite places to splurge on an extravagant brunch. How often is Ben footing the bill for eggs benedict and bottomless mimosas? Margot starts shaking her head before I can think of a way to ask subtly. 'I don't love breakfast,' she says. 'That was weird, sorry. I just like it. A lot. A normal amount of a lot.'

Ben comes back in with an extra plate and mug, and Margot looks relieved. Maybe she is a similar sort of awkward to my brother after all. I need to get a closer look at their dynamic, so I reckon I'll let the conversation move naturally for a while. I'm not having much luck getting my questioning started anyway.

I butter my toast and Ben pours us all some tea, and we

work our way through all the usual small talk. No, I didn't sleep that well. Yes, the snow was beautiful last night. No, it's not forecast for today. Yes, it will be great to see everyone later. No, I don't have any plans before dinner.

Margot doesn't join in. She hasn't uttered a single word since she came out as a breakfast fanatic. She just nods along to the conversation, her glossy dark hair bouncing on her shoulders with the movement. After a few minutes, I get fed up of waiting for something more 'dynamic' to happen.

'So I assume you're a London girl, Margot?'

'Me?' she asks. Then she shakes her head. 'Obviously me. Yes, I am.' She switches back to nodding. 'London born and raised.'

'Cool,' I say. 'Whereabouts in the city?'

'Um, I grew up in Tottenham, but I live in Islington now.'

'It's near your old warehouse,' Ben says to me. Then he turns to Margot. 'Before Ellie went travelling, she rented this amazing converted warehouse in Angel. I bet you two know all the same local haunts.'

Margot seems to perk up at this. 'Camden Head?'

'The one in Angel or the one in Camden?' I ask steadily.

'Angel for comedy, Camden for drinking.'

I'm surprised. She's completely right.

'I love them both,' she continues, 'but the Camden in Angel is my favourite. You just can't beat free live comedy. I've seen some *hilarious* acts there.'

'And loads of shit ones?'

She laughs. 'Yep. But I always go back for more. You know where else is good . . .'

'Inside Out!' I call, surprising myself.

'Yes! And The Bill Murray!'

'And Top Secret Comedy Club!'

'Yes!' she cries. 'You know, some of those are –'

'Run by the same people!' I join in.

Margot beams at me. Another one of those real smiles that lights up her eyes.

'We go to see comedy all the time,' Ben says, placing a hand over Margot's. 'It's one of our favourite date nights.'

Margot's smile falters slightly. She looks awkward again, and maybe a bit . . . guilty? She starts shaking her head back and forth again, more dramatically this time.

'Yeah, comedy is the best date night,' she agrees, still shaking. 'For us.'

I narrow my eyes, finding the sudden change in her mood and behaviour very confusing. My suspicions are reignited. 'That's so sweet that you two get to go out a lot. I bet you don't only go to the pub clubs, though, right? I'm sure my brother here splashes out on plenty of big-name comedy tours?'

She opens her mouth as if to reply, but then she stops herself. She just nods. It's no less awkward than the head shaking. She scratches her neck. Returns to her overly milky cup of tea.

A few moments later, she scrapes her chair back. 'Sorry. Um. I have to go.' She pulls her hand away from Ben's, picks up the toast she's slathered with apricot jam, and takes a quick bite. 'I'm not super hungry this morning. And I really need a shower. I have to wash my hair. So . . . yeah. Thanks for breakfast, Ben. Ellie, nice to see you again. Bye, guys.'

As she rushes past me, I smell her perfume. A lovely

delicate scent. Sweet like vanilla but with a hint of something warm and spicy. It smells expensive. So why would Margot have put it on this morning if she knew she was going to have a shower so soon? She's also all dressed for the day ahead already in a pair of wide-leg black corduroys and a tight rib-knit jumper in jade green, and her hair has obviously been freshly washed. It's even shinier today than it was last night. She definitely doesn't 'need' a shower or hair wash. Something else has made her want to abruptly end our conversation – something pressing enough to make her leave her beloved breakfast behind. Something like me mentioning Ben 'splashing out' on their date nights? She seemed uneasy and strange before that, but it was my comment that pushed her over the edge and sent her running.

'Is she all right?' I ask once she's left the room.

'Oh, yeah,' Ben says, although his furrowed brow tells another story. He looks totally perplexed by Margot's sudden departure.

Why is he wasting his time with someone so strange and shifty?

'Yeah,' he says again with more confidence. 'She's fine. I think she's just tired. We didn't get much sleep last night.'

Ew. That will be why.

'I don't need to hear about that,' I say.

'Oh! No. I mean –' He stops. A blush has spread across his face and neck. 'Er. Yeah. Fair point. Um. Maybe she'll have a nap or something after her shower, and then I'm going to take her on a tour of the gardens. We're going to go swimming later too. And then in the afternoon I have a few bits and bobs I have to get finished for work.

I just have to check how they're doing at the shop and finalize some orders. I had signed off for the week, but duty calls! After that, I'll hopefully be free for the rest of Christmas. Unless Ramesh really needs me, of course. You remember Ramesh, don't you? My business partner? He and his family don't celebrate the holiday, so he's covering for me . . .'

I nod as he babbles on and on. He always does this when he's anxious or embarrassed. No point in trying to interrupt. I sit back in my chair and take a long sip of my black tea, feeling sorry for my brother but also secretly pleased that Margot already seems to be feeling the pressure from me. Maybe she'll become so ashamed of herself for taking advantage of poor, sweet Ben that she'll crack and fess up to what she's been doing. It might only take a few more questions from me at this rate. I'll have to find a way to ask her some more after her 'shower'.

Twenty minutes later, I just so happen to be walking down the top-floor corridor. And up it. And down it again. Maybe I lost something up here, or maybe I'm stretching my legs. Dunno. I'm just here. Just pacing up and down the narrow corridor that happens to have Margot and Ben's room on it.

Ben is safely out of the way downstairs, doing the washing-up. While I won't stand for Margot taking advantage of his generosity, it's my birthright as his little sister to have him do all the stuff I can't be bothered to do. I'm busy enough up here, strolling up and down the hallway.

One of the doors creaks open.

Oh. How strange. There's Margot. What an absolutely

crazy coincidence to bump into her here. I raise my brows in 'surprise' and walk over to meet her.

Oh. How doubly strange. She doesn't seem to have showered. Her hair isn't wet and her clothes haven't changed. As I get closer, I can smell that she's still doused in that sweet and spicy perfume of hers. All that's changed is that she's now got a bit of mascara and nude lipstick on.

When she sees me, her eyes widen slightly. 'Oh, hi.'

'Hey!' I step closer. 'Funny seeing you here. I was just looking for . . .' I cast a quick look around. 'I heard this lamp wasn't working.' I reach over to a tall floor lamp next to Margot. Pull its cord twice – on and off. 'Oh. It does work? Good.'

She smiles tightly, leaning out of the way of my outstretched arm. 'Good, good. Um . . .' She takes a small step backwards and starts patting her trouser pockets. Then she pulls out her phone, angling the screen away from me. 'Ah. Sorry, I've got to take this call.'

In one swift movement, she disappears back inside her room.

I fight the urge to kick over the floor lamp. I can't keep loitering around now that I've used up that stupid improvised excuse. I wanted to ask Margot more questions as soon as possible to really pile on the pressure, and to get as much info as I could before the rest of my family came rushing in to pull her attention in all directions. But I guess I still have the rest of the day to play with. I file her probably fake phone call away in my mind as minor evidence of her major caginess, and make my way back down the stairs to the ground floor.

In the dining room, Mitsi is still lounging on the rug,

and I bend down to give her a quick pat before rolling up my sleeves and getting to work.

The only solid plan I have today is rearranging all the tables in this room. Every year, once all the hotel guests have cleared out, we push all the tables together to make one long dining table in the middle of the room. The smaller square tables were custom-built for this so they all fit together seamlessly, and any tell-tale cracks get covered up by a mega-sized tablecloth. It's pretty smart, and also pretty silly. I've never seen the point in reconfiguring this whole room just for Christmas, when we already have a perfectly nice dining room in the family wing. It's pointless and showy, and I have never helped move the tables before. I try not to engage too much with my parents' ideas about how to make every single little thing perfect – which is probably why I became a professional beach bum halfway across the world instead of sticking around here and spending my time arranging tables into the ideal position for the month of December. But this year I'm trying to fit in. I'm turning over a new leaf. When everyone gets home tonight, they'll see that I've already put myself to work. Team player of the year. MVP.

I pull all the tablecloths off and pile them up in a corner. Mitsi crawls on top of the pile and falls asleep, and I'm free to drag the tables around the room, their sturdy legs occasionally catching on the rug.

I guess it's kind of nice to reclaim this room from the hotel guests. Make it Gibson territory again. And I suppose there is a lot more space in here than in our compact private dining room. Maybe it's not just a collective flamboyance that makes my family want to spend time in here over Christmas. We *have* always needed plenty of space to lay out all the food we get through at this time of year. Pretty much from the moment the table is set up to the moment it is dismantled again, there will be something edible on it. A freshly baked loaf of bread. A giant soup kettle. A tray of mince pies. All just sitting out throughout the day so that anyone can help themselves at any time.

We're lucky we have such a big kitchen. That is one upside to my own home being run as a business: we have a professional kitchen at our disposal. The chef only ever uses it to make breakfast and the occasional sweet treat, but it's still properly kitted out with a huge double fridge and a commercial range cooker and stainless-steel work surfaces. This gives us a fantastic advantage when it comes to cooking Christmas dinner. Of course, once it actually comes down to it, the huge fridge still gets filled to bursting point, and there's a last-minute panic about oven space, and all the surfaces disappear under dishes and saucepans and chopping boards. But that's just Christmas: no matter what, there's gonna be a calamity on the big day.

I stand back and admire my handiwork. The dining table is all set up now, stretching out dramatically through the centre of the room. I washed the big tablecloth myself yesterday, and I've topped it with a patterned burgundy runner and a few taper candles, plus the garland that was arranged on the fireplace before.

It looks properly Christmassy, and I'm filled with a sort of fizzy excitement. I've never really been that arsed about Christmas – never felt very joyful or triumphant – but seeing the dining room set up in all its glory might just be getting me into the spirit. I suppose over the last year or so, the islands I escaped to have been getting a bit samey. Blue sea, blue sky, hot sand. Bloody beautiful, but it's the same story everywhere I go. Now, for the first time, I'm enjoying being back home and experiencing a proper English winter, complete with chilly weather, warm jumpers, and perfectly decked dining halls.

I suddenly can't wait for the rest of the family to get here and get excited too. They're gonna be thrilled when they see this room. They'll all marvel at how I've set it up so beautifully – and ahead of schedule too. I grin. I've nabbed myself a lovely festive feeling *and* loads of brownie points with the parentals.

The smile is wiped off my face when I hear the front door clattering shut.

I rush to the nearest window in time to see Margot and Ben walking away from the house, both huddled up in big coats and heading for the gardens. *No.* I missed them. I was meant to be keeping an ear out for them coming down the stairs. Then I was gonna 'run into' them in the foyer, casually ask where they're off to, then accept Ben's kind offer to join them on a tour of the grounds. Ben would somehow drag the tour out to over an hour, and Margot would have no choice but to stick around for the duration, answering all my carefully selected questions along the way.

That would've been the perfect plan, if I hadn't forgotten all about it while I faffed around with these tables. I can't chase after Margot and Ben and ask to tag along for the tour now. So that's it. She's dodged me again.

For a while I resign myself to watching the two of them as they trek across the lawn leaving boot prints in last night's snow. Margot keeps a careful distance from Ben the whole way. She has her arms pinned down at her sides, not letting them so much as brush her boyfriend's body. The only time she does touch him is to give him a playful little shove on the shoulder. Just enough flirting to keep him sweet, then right back to her rigid straight-backed posture. She cranes her neck as they walk, taking everything in greedily. The huge lake holds her attention for the longest, as she stops to gawp at the evergreen foliage surrounding the water's edge and the small stone waterfall that feeds down to a lower, wider level of the lake. I'm not surprised that she likes it so much, given that it's the most expensive feature of our garden by far. Manmade natural wonders don't come cheap, as I'm sure Margot can sense by some kind of avaricious instinct.

I turn away suddenly. I can't stand watching her any more. I leave the window and march out of the dining hall, leaving Mitsi and her towering pile of tablecloths behind.

When the front door swings open again fifty minutes later, I'm ready. I wander out of the kitchen and into the foyer to meet Margot and Ben, armed with a simple plan.

'Oh, hey, you two,' I say. 'I was just about to make some soup for lunch. Will you join me? Help warm yourselves up?'

'Ooh, soup would be lovely,' Ben says, rubbing his gloved hands together. 'What do we have?'

'Carrot and coriander. Minestrone. Probably some French onion in the pantry.'

'Yum. Minestrone, please. What would you like, Margot?'

'Oh.' She pauses in the act of shrugging off her boxy black overcoat and glances around the hall. 'No. None for me, thanks. I . . . I don't want to eat right before we go swimming. But, Ben, you can . . .'

'Oh, no, it's fine,' Ben rushes to say. 'Yeah, no. You're right. We should swim *then* eat. Otherwise we'd get cramps!' He pushes out an awkward little chuckle, then flashes me a rueful grin. 'Let's take a rain check on lunch? Sorry, Ellie.'

Before I can even tell him it's fine, Margot is walking away. Her heeled boots click on the wooden floors with each confident stride. She finally pulls her coat all the way off in one sharp pull as she reaches the stairs.

'I'll just grab my swimming costume,' she throws over her shoulder.

No. I can't let her slip away again. I'm running out of time before my family gets here to make everything ten times more complicated. I have to up the ante. Stop pussy-footing around and finally get to the action. Luckily I came armed with a back-up plan in case soup failed me.

'Margot!' I call after her. 'Would you like to go to a Christmas market with me?'

She pauses halfway up the stairs. Turns round to look down at me. I meet her gaze with my very sweetest smile.

'Today is the last day it's in town, and I *really* want to go. It's in Chester – only about twenty minutes away. I thought you could come with and get any last-minute Christmas shopping sorted out? You and Ben.' I gesture sideways to him, but I keep my eyes fixed on Margot. I need *her* to agree to this. And surely she has to, to avoid appearing too rude. I keep smiling sweetly up at her. 'We could head out after you've been swimming.'

The poor thing looks like a deer caught in headlights. Eyes round and wide, hand gripping the banister.

'Yes,' she says at last. 'Yes, of course. That sounds lovely.'

'Fantastic.' I finally break eye contact. 'Ben?'

He shakes his head sadly. 'I'd love to, but I have to work this afternoon.'

'Oh no! During your holidays? I totally forgot.' (I totally did not.) 'I guess we'll just make it a girls' trip then, Margot. Give you something to do while Ben's locked away working!' Another innocent smile. 'I'll meet you back down here in an hour.'

7

Margot

So, my plan to avoid alone time with Ellie isn't going very well. I am currently buckling myself into the passenger seat of her car so that we can head off to a Christmas market together. Spending the afternoon just the two of us, strolling beneath string lights and sipping on hot chocolates, definitely wasn't what I had in mind.

I did try to think of a way to get out of this. Immediately after agreeing to go, I headed back to my room and thought of reasons to cancel. Maybe I had some work to do, just like Ben did. Or maybe I had to stay behind to take a phone call. Maybe I was too shaken up after nearly sinking to the bottom of the pool during my swim.

It was no use. None of those would wash. I couldn't go around saying I'd done a bit of light drowning every time Ellie wanted to talk to me over the next week. It just wasn't sustainable. And I no longer felt like going swimming, anyway.

After only one morning of avoiding her, I was already out of excuses.

Besides, I knew I would annoy her too much by saying no. Ellie was being very friendly, trying so hard to connect with me and help me feel welcome in her home, but I was also noticing some frustration from her. It was probably because I was still being so awkward around her despite all the effort she was putting in with me. I could tell from the start that Ellie was way too cool to have much patience for bumbling idiots. The trouble was, the more frustration I sensed from her, the more awkward I felt, and that awkwardness was only bound to frustrate her even more. It was a vicious cycle. I was starting to think that I was only a few wrong moves away from Ellie not liking me much – and a Gibson not liking me much would defeat the whole purpose of me being here for Ben. I had to meet Ellie halfway and spend some proper time with her.

With a heavy groan, I resigned myself to an afternoon of festive fun.

A few moments later, Ben came into the room. He knocked on the door first, then padded across the carpet and sat down on the chaise longue.

'Hey,' he said softly. 'Just checking that you're OK going out with Ellie? It's only your first day here, and I don't want you to feel thrown in at the deep end. Are you sure you're comfortable going?'

No! No, I wasn't sure at all. Something inside me took desperate hold of the lifeline Ben was throwing me, and I started going through my excuses again. Work to do. Phone call to make. Drowning to . . .

Enough. Ben's brow was furrowed with concern as he looked at me, the only blemish on his kind, open face. He was waiting so patiently for my answer. So sweetly.

'I'm fine,' I fibbed. 'I'm looking forward to getting out and about. It'll be fun to hang out with Ellie, and even more fun to get my mitts on some mulled wine.' I plastered on a bright smile. 'Plus, this is a great chance to practise being your girlfriend and getting to know your family. I can show off all my Just Ben Gibson trivia.' I performed jazz hands in the general direction of our notebooks. 'Seriously. Thanks for checking in, but I'm going.'

Before I could even think about changing my mind again, I skipped off to the bathroom to get ready: to touch up my make-up and spritz on some extra perfume.

And now here I am. Less than twenty-four hours after driving up to the house with Ben, I am about to drive away from it again with his friendly but frustrated but fucking gorgeous sister.

Ellie hasn't actually got into the car with me yet. She's crouched a few metres away near the water feature, begging Mitsi to eat a cube of cheese containing a supplement. Mitsi, of course, is having none of it. I listen to Ellie's desperate pleas and Mitsi's defiant growls, and mentally thank the stubborn dog for buying me a few extra moments alone.

I turn away from them both to look out of the driver-side window, out across the stretching lawns of the estate. Glittering frost clings to the grass, as well as a few lingering patches of melting snow. I know the layout of the gardens now, thanks to Ben's detailed tour this morning. I have a quick look at the almost hidden rose garden to the north, and the little bungalow behind it in the far distance. I catch sight of a person heading inside, so far away that they look like a toy figure. Their only discernible feature is a puff of bright ginger hair. The groundskeeper. I keep looking around, tracking my gaze back to the rose garden and then to the insanely beautiful lake just left of that. I wonder idly about stepping out of the car, walking across the lawns, and somehow falling into the lake. It might be cold enough to give me a lovely case of frostbite. Maybe even hypothermia? I could always splash around wildly like I was being pulled under.

I shake my head sharply. I have got to stop with this drowning gambit.

In fact, all the melodrama has to end. If I feel awkward, I can push through. If I feel drawn to Ellie, I can deal with it. There is really nothing weird or wrong about me finding an objectively attractive woman attractive. It's not like I'm going to do anything about it. I am committed to being Ben's fake girlfriend – and over in the real world I have only been single for a month. Taylor deserves better than me throwing myself at someone else already. 'What about loyalty?' she'd say, and she'd have a very good point. I would never want to upset Taylor, or Ben, so I definitely wouldn't make a move on Ellie. All that is going to happen this afternoon is friendly conversation.

'I'm so excited to have a proper chat with you at last,' Ellie had said when we left the foyer together a few minutes ago. 'We'll have *plenty* of time to talk because my radio's broken. A lot of my car is broken, to be honest. Nothing dangerous, it's just a bit old and banged up, but hardly worth upgrading since I only drive it a few times a year. My parents hide it in the garage the rest of the time. Anyway. The point is, there's no music, so we'll just have to chat!'

Her chirpiness set the tone for our afternoon together. All I have to do is follow suit. From the moment she gets into the car with me, I will start up some casual chatter, and then we will have a casual afternoon together, and then I will become casual around her. I will get my confidence back. That is how I deal with problems at work: with confidence and poise, facing any issues head-on. I can do the same thing here. Spending this much time with Ellie will normalize her for me and banish my nervousness. Like exposure therapy. By the end of the day, I will be back to my usual self and I will be able to get on with doing what I came here to do in the first place: enjoying a luxury holiday in a gorgeous manor house without any complications.

I hear gravel crunching and I turn to see Ellie walking away from Mitsi. The cube of cheese is still in her hand, uneaten. Within nanoseconds, the dog leaps up to grab the cheese, snatching it right out of Ellie's fist, then runs back to the house at top speed with her stolen treat stashed safely in her mouth. Ellie rolls her eyes at Mitsi's bounding behind, then wipes her cheesy, slobbery hand on her jeans and keeps walking.

This is it. I sit up straighter in my seat. Pull my beanie down over my ears. Tell myself I can do this. All I have to do is be myself – and pretend to be Ben's girlfriend.

Ellie pulls open the car door and slips into her seat. The tiny space fills up at once with a fresh citrussy smell that seems like it belongs to summer, not winter. She flicks her hair over her shoulder, so that the blonde waves tumble down her back. She flashes a smile my way. 'Sorry about that. Ridiculous dog.'

'Oh, it's fine.' I wave away the apology and smile back. 'She's very cute.'

'She is. Adorable little nightmare. I've only been back home a few days and I reckon I've already run half a marathon chasing her around out here. But now Ben can deal with her for the afternoon.' Her smile widens at this, eyes twinkling. 'So, do you like animals? You a dog person?' She starts the engine. 'Ready to go?'

'Er . . . yes. Triple yes.'

Ellie nods and puts the car into drive. I wonder whether I should apologize again for hitting Mitsi, but before I can say anything Ellie is spinning the car quickly around the water fountain and asking about my favourite dog breeds. I leave the past in the past and tell her about my love of cavaliers, corgis, and any and all mixed-breed mutts.

'I love mongrels,' she says, looking half delighted and half confused. 'Are you into those designer cross-breeds?'

'No, no. The scruffier the better.'

'Really? But your taste in purebreds is so . . . posh. Cavalier *King* Charles spaniels. And didn't the *Queen* have corgis?'

I shrug, a half-smile on my face. 'That's just what I like. My nana had a cavalier and two corgis when I was growing up and they were really lovely dogs. They'll always be my favourites. But I do have an extra-special soft spot for mutts. When I get my own dog, it will definitely be some kind of mix.'

'Cool.' Ellie spins her steering wheel with one hand to turn us on to the long gravelled driveway out of the estate, which she zips down at speed. 'Is Ben on the same page?'

Crap. I forgot about him. Already.

I keep my face relaxed and resist the urge to tug at the collar of my coat. Ellie has switched the heating on, and the car is filling up with artificial hot air. I roll back my shoulders. I'm fine. This is a good sign actually. Forgetting about Ben proves that I am doing exactly what I set out to do: being myself.

Still, I must remember to stay in character as The Girlfriend.

'Yeah, Ben and I definitely want to adopt one day. A dog. Obviously. We want to adopt a dog. It will work out nicely because I'll always be at home to look after it.'

'Oh? Do you not work?'

'I do. I just work from home.'

'I see.' Ellie stops at the end of the driveway, glances left and right, then pulls us out on to a narrow country road. 'What do you do?'

'Digital marketing. I was at an agency in Soho for a long time, but a few years ago I finally took the plunge and set up on my own.'

'You own your own business?' She sounds surprised and impressed, and I feel a little glow of pride. 'Is it . . . going well?'

'Yeah, it is.' I think about stopping there, because I don't want to brag, but I'm meant to be chatting, so I may as well . . . chat. 'It was a steep learning curve, but business is really good now. I poached a few clients from the Soho agency, and I've attracted some new ones too. A couple of them are pretty big brands, like that lingerie company that all the politicians buy undies from for their mistresses. Their reputation is a little iffy, but they always give me free samples, so that's cool. I also work with an *incredible* artisan ice-cream company. And then there's Ben, of course.'

'Ben? He's one of your clients?'

Shit. That isn't part of our story. He was worried about how the power dynamics would look if I worked for him.

'No,' I answer quickly. 'He's not a client. He's just . . . very supportive. That's all I meant. He, uh, introduced me to a new client recently. A business friend of his. Networking is so important, you know? I actually met my first investor at a coffee morning for north London business owners. His backing made all the difference for me at the start.'

'Huh,' Ellie says. 'Who is this generous guy?'

'Oh, I can't really tell you. Sorry. He likes to invest "silently".'

'Huh,' Ellie says again. 'Very mysterious. They only do that when it's a lot of money, right?'

'I guess so.' I give a small self-deprecating laugh. I find talking about finances a little uncomfortable, but at least I've moved us away from the idea of Ben paying me. 'It was definitely a bigger investment than I was expecting so early on. I owe him a lot.'

Ellie smiles faintly. 'Clearly.'

I shift, and the seat belt tightens against my body. Was that a bit curt or . . . ?

'Sorry,' she says, her voice immediately brighter. 'I was focusing on the road. Tell me more. Please.'

'Uh . . .' I loosen the seat belt, relaxing again. 'There aren't many more interesting things to say about marketing,' I joke.

She half laughs. 'There must be.' She waits a moment for me to prove myself wrong, but before I can think of a riveting anecdote about customer acquisition cost metrics, she shrugs. 'Is it nice working from home?'

'Oh yeah.' I'm relieved to be off the proper businessy talk. 'I love it. At first it was a bit difficult to focus, but I don't have that problem any more. The trick is still getting dressed up for work every day, even though nobody's around to see it.'

'You're telling me you wear trouser suits in your own home?'

I laugh. 'Yes. They're actually very comfortable. Especially the Harvey Nichols ones.'

'Harvey Nichols! Those must cost hundreds?'

'Nope. I get most of my stuff second-hand. There are so many great charity shops in London. You can find amazing deals if you're patient.'

'Oh.' Ellie arches a thick brow as she peeks into her rear-view mirror. 'I wouldn't have pegged you as the thrifting type. I am too actually. But then I can spend *loads* on nice jewellery. Rings especially. What do you splurge on, if not designer suits right off the rack?'

'Hmm. Food, I guess. Holidays. Theatre trips. More food.' I tilt my head. 'Mostly food.'

'So you and Ben eat out a lot, then?'

'Oh yeah. We go out all the time. He's taken me to so many great restaurants that I'd never even heard of before.'

'Aw. He really is generous, isn't he?'

'Very.' I sigh dreamily, like I'm in love with him. 'He's always treating me.'

Ellie just nods at that. The quiet doesn't bother me, as I know that more conversation will follow soon enough. Even with the odd hiccup, I've really started relaxing into the casual chit-chat. I've barely even noticed how the soft sunlight catches the golden streaks in Ellie's hair, or how her lemony scent mingles with my sweet perfume. Mostly I've just been treating her like a potential sister-in-law. I gaze out of my window, at the endless frosty fields that fly by as we zoom down the country road, and I know that I can get through this afternoon. I might even be looking forward to it.

8

Ellie

I really thought I had her. She gave *so* much away early on. Ben being 'very supportive' of her business and almost definitely being the anonymous investor she bragged about. Ben taking her out to fancy restaurants that wouldn't even be on her radar without him. Ben financing every single aspect of her life by the sounds of it.

But she shut up after that. My fault for stopping with the questions. I didn't want to push so hard that she'd realize I was prying – which I think I nearly did with that investor thing. Plus, I kind of figured that she might keep bragging of her own accord, incriminating herself without even being prompted. I guess I took some pleasure in that idea. Stupid. She didn't say another word for ages. Just kept gazing out of the window. I couldn't even fill the dead silence by putting the radio on, since I'd lied about it being broken so she'd have to talk to me.

I cracked first and got the conversation going again.

'So,' I said, 'you mentioned that you and Ben watch a lot of live comedy together?'

'Yes! We can't get enough.'

'Sweet. So what's the best show he's taken you to? The biggest name? Go on – make me jealous.'

'Oh, I don't know,' Margot said. 'I've always preferred

the smaller venues, to be honest. I like watching new acts finding their voices, and big comedians testing out works in progress. That's why I love all the small clubs dotted around London. I saw a new Scottish guy recently. Brilliant. And I – *we* went to see Rose Matafeo last month. Extra brilliant.'

'Ooh, did you watch her sitcom?' I asked automatically.

'Yes. I loved it. Ten out of ten.'

'*Eleven* out of ten!' I stopped the car at a junction. Refocused on the task at hand. 'And you said you like the theatre? Like big, splashy musicals?'

'No, no. *Not* musicals. Well, only if they're really good ones. I much prefer plays. I'm not the biggest fan of dance numbers or spontaneously bursting into song about the weather and love and . . . cats.'

I couldn't help but smile. 'So no cheesiness for you?'

'None. Not unless it's on a cracker. Or a toastie. Or a pizza.'

'A quesadilla?' I offered.

'Yum. Exactly. Any edible cheese is fine by me. I've even tried a Colombian hot chocolate with mozzarella in it before. It was surprisingly all right.'

'Would you have it again?' I asked.

'Oh, never.'

I laughed. I wondered aloud about other weird food combos, then I asked a little more about Margot's life in London, and her business, and her family. There were no more indications of villainy. In fact, she almost came across . . . well, *well*. It is kind of cool that she's an entrepreneur. And it's even cooler that she's a lover of cheese and cross-bred mutts. She shared her thrifting tips and tricks with me, and she recommended a bunch of underrated sitcoms, and she remained chatty and friendly and sweet for the rest of the drive to Chester. Somewhere along the way, I realized I was enjoying talking to her.

Still. I haven't let my guard down completely. I have to remember that Margot is good at turning on the charm. She must be to have ensnared Ben. For every funny thing she says or impressive titbit she shares, I must remind myself that she has been taking my brother's money. For her business; for her swanky nights out; for her 'Christmas bonus', whatever that was all about yesterday. I force myself to list these things again and again in my mind as we walk away from the car, down cobbled streets, towards the market in the city centre. I am still on the ball, asking plenty of questions, keeping my eyes peeled for Margot's true colours.

'I only volunteer for a couple of hours each week,' she says now. 'Every Sunday afternoon at the local library. Anyone over sixty can come and sit down with me, and I teach them how to use a computer. I try to get them interested in email and Zoom and online banking, but they mostly want to play solitaire.'

Huh. When I asked how she spends her weekends, I'd been angling for more stories about those fancy dinners and posh plays financed by Ben. At the very least, I'd expected her to talk about going out for posh cocktails with her 'girls' – a group of women I imagine to be just as sleek and stylish as Margot. Instead, she tells me all about her favourite library drop-in, a retired headmistress who always has 'the best stories' and is a master of FreeCell solitaire.

Margot stands tall and swings her arms by her sides as

she walks, flashing bright smiles at everyone we pass. It's a total transformation from her awkwardness this morning. The only thing about her that isn't in perfect alignment is her knitted black beanie, which keeps creeping up so that it's no longer covering her ears. Every now and again, she reaches up to pull it back down. The gesture stops her from looking too cocksure and instead makes her seem sweet and harmless and –

I stop myself. I am *not* getting swept away.

I know that some people would call my cynicism 'trust issues'. I call it common sense. I've met plenty of people in my life who seem lovely at first but are really anything but. Worst offender was the girlfriend who stole money from under my pillow as I slept with my head on her chest. Or the best friend who bad-mouthed me to our boss at a crappy Ibiza resort until he fired me and promoted her. Both those women came bounding into my life all smiles and giggles. I trusted them. I don't fall for that sort of crap any more.

I still attract a lot of that kind, though. I think they assume I'm ditzy and naive – just because I like to party and don't take life too seriously. But these days I can see a chancer coming a mile off. Alarm bells start ringing at the smallest sign of trouble, and I always trust my gut. So there is no way I will let Margot fool me. I will *not* be fallin–

I trip.

It's like the pavement just disappears. My foot plunges down into nothingness and the rest of my body is following at speed.

Then someone grabs me.

I am still.

I smell vanilla.

'You're OK,' Margot says softly, right into my ear.

She's above me, I think. Still on the pavement. Her arms are around me. Breath tickling my neck. I feel her pulling me closer, and then I'm standing fully upright again. One foot on the pavement and one foot in the road. She lets me go.

'You're OK,' she says again.

I'm still facing away from her, out into the road. It's empty. No cars. It's lucky that I opted for free parking on a quiet side street outside the city walls, or else I could have been playing in traffic.

I step back up on to the pavement and turn towards Margot. 'Thank you. I . . . thank you.'

'It's fine.' Margot's arms are hovering in front of her body as if reassuring me they can catch me again at a moment's notice. 'I guess we're even now.'

I blink at her.

'I fell over yesterday, out on the driveway, and you caught me. Now I've caught you. So we're even. No more falling necessary. We can both remain vertical for the rest of the year.'

I'm so dazed that I giggle. 'I never fall over like that.'

'Me neither,' she says. 'I always thought that kind of thing only happened in cheesy romcoms. And maybe Charlie Chaplin films. To be honest, I've always found women who are clumsy in real life really, really irritating.'

'Same! I was so annoyed when you tripped yesterday!'

I stand there smiling dumbly for a second before I realize what I've said. Then my hands fly up to cover my mouth. Another slapsticky move. Dunno what's come over me. I slide my hands back down my face and get ready to apologize. But Margot is laughing. A proper throaty chuckle.

'I must have looked so ridiculous,' she howls. 'I mean, seriously, spatial awareness is not that hard. Never have I *ever* been that clumsy in my life before.' Her laughter peters out. 'I really am sorry for crashing into you like that, and for hitting your poor dog with the door.' She winces at me. 'Are you sure Mitsi's OK?'

'Oh, she's fine. That animal could fall off Mount Everest and live to tell the tale. She'd probably climb right back up to the top to do the whole thing over again.'

Margot almost sags with relief. Then, of course, she recovers her perfect posture.

'Thank goodness. But I don't think I'll make a habit of bungling around like that. My days of being a clumsy, klutzy clown are officially over.'

'Mine too.'

'Perfect.' She starts striding down the pavement, her surprisingly strong arms swinging again. 'Come on, then. Let's get a couple of cheeseless hot chocolates.'

The market looks exactly how it looks every year. A long parade of wooden chalet stalls. Fairy lights on their pointed roofs. Huge Christmas tree. Fairy lights all over that too. Even more fairy lights strung between the black-and-white mock-Tudor buildings. It's still daytime, so the effect of the twinkling lights is a bit lost. Margot doesn't seem to mind – she's gazing around at it all as if she's just entered her own personal heaven.

I lead her towards the drinks stall, weaving us through the milling crowd. Everyone seems to be carrying something edible, and the warm smells of cinnamon and ginger fill the air. It mingles nicely with Margot's sweet perfume, I think. Strange. That thought came out of nowhere. I put my head down and keep pushing through the throng.

We reach the stall selling hot chocolates, mulled wine, and cask ales, and we join the queue. We're stationed right under the cathedral, which is strung with – guess what? – fairy lights. I suppose they do look kind of cute. The day has got darker as it's gone on, and the golden lights add a welcome glow.

Soon enough, we're being handed a couple of hot chocolates, each topped with a mountain of whipped cream and a dusting of cinnamon. Margot reaches for her wallet.

'Put that away,' she says, glancing at the purse in my hand and extracting her debit card. 'I'm getting these.'

I'm slightly surprised but do as I'm told. I say my thanks and we touch our brown paper cups together in a silent toast. Neither of us takes a sip yet, knowing we'd burn our tongues.

As Margot lowers her cup, she grimaces.

'What's up?'

She looks at me in surprise, as if she hadn't realized I could see her face. She rearranges her features into a look of sheepish apology. Waves her hand up towards a nearby speaker. Tinny music is being pumped out of it. Your standard festive fare: heavily auto-tuned pop with added jingle bells and vocal runs.

'It's not really my kind of music,' she says. 'Actually, it makes my ears bleed.' She uses her free hand to tug her beanie down. 'There's just no escape from it. It's relentless.'

I smirk. We're in agreement on that point. 'What is your kind of music then?'

'Indie-type stuff mostly.'

Interesting. We're in agreement on that too.

'You know,' she continues, 'Phoebe Bridgers, Lizzie McAlpine, Girl in Red.'

Ah. Never mind. Those artists are not who I think of when I think of indie music. Sure, they might technically fall under the indie umbrella, but they're a bit soft for my tastes. Especially Girl in Red. I know I'm meant to like her because she's a lesbian and she writes lesbian love songs for lesbians to sing along to – but she's not really up my street. It's always straight girls like Margot who tell gay girls like me to listen to her. The kind of music I like is grittier than that. Clashing layers of guitars and drums. Gravelly voices. Proper *bands*.

'And bands too,' Margot says. 'Like The Strokes, Pixies, the Stone Roses.'

Oh. Yeah. That's more like it.

'How about you?' she asks, moving out of the way of a woman with a pram by stepping closer to me and the drinks' stall.

'Same as you really. Not so much the solo artists, but I love a good indie rock band.'

'Nice. Who have you seen live? I went to the Pixies' reunion tour in 2004 and it was *in*-credible. I was only thirteen. My first proper gig! My mind. Was. Blown.'

My mind is blown too. 'I saw them as well. In 2004. London. My grandpa took me.'

'Wait. That's crazy. They only did a few dates in London, right? It was so hard to get tickets. So we were both there? As out-of-place pre-teens? Possibly on the same night? That's *so* crazy!'

84

It is. Almost unbelievable, actually. Margot's eyes are as wide as saucers as she stares at me, and I'm pretty sure I have a similar dumbstruck expression on my face.

'It really is crazy,' I say. 'Maybe you were right next to me. Boogying with Grandpa Mo.'

She laughs. That deep husky chuckle. 'It's so cool that he took you to that gig. From what Ben's told me, he sounds like a wonderful man.'

'He is.' I finally break goggled eye contact with Margot. Scoop a bit of whipped cream up with my finger and pop it in my mouth. 'My grandma was amazing too. They're still the coolest people I've ever met. I always told them everything. They were actually the first people I ever came out to.'

'Same for me!' Margot is all wide-eyed with wonder again, but then a shadow passes over her face and she shakes her head sharply. 'I mean, I was always very close with my nana. Not that I came out to her. Obviously. That's . . . Not that. I mean that I always told her everything, too, like you did, too. As well.'

Weird. Margot is being weird. She lifts her drink and takes a big gulp. Winces at the heat. Tries to hide her wince. Ends up looking a bit constipated.

She stops. She rolls her shoulders back, like she's resetting herself, then steps away from the stall and back into the crowd. Back to normal. I follow her lead.

'So you said you like to travel?' I prompt.

'I do, yes.' She looks into a stall selling handcrafted ornaments as we pass it, presumably to avoid making eye contact. 'Not the sort of travelling you're used to, I'm sure. I mostly stay in hotels. See the sights, swim in the pool, go for dinner.'

'Where's the best place you've ever been?'

'Oh, *definitely* Mexico. I went to Cancún with some friends years ago and I still have dreams about the food. We obviously did a lot of partying, but the days were even better than the nights. Like, I went for a day trip to Tulum to see the Mayan ruins and the hidden beach, and another day we went snorkelling to see the underwater museum. Those sunken statues are seriously awe-inspiring. And did I mention the food?'

I smile slightly. 'You did.'

'Well, the food is phenomenal,' she says. 'Those flavours. So zingy and spicy and . . . just wow. I was beyond obsessed with all the street food downtown. Still. I'm sure my experience of the country was very westernized, in my big fancy hotel.'

'Oh yeah?' I stop smiling. 'How big and fancy is big and fancy?'

'To be honest, not very.' She gazes into a chalet filled with funny little wooden toys. 'I went when I was twenty-one so it's not like I was splashing out on a five-star resort or anything. But it did have this big beautiful swimming pool and it was right on the beach, and at that age that felt like the height of luxury. I'd love to go back one day and stay somewhere a bit more authentic.' She appraises a display of gingerbread. 'I bet you've stayed in loads of cool, *real* places.'

'Kind of. When I'm working, I've got to be in the big tourist hotspots, but when I travel by myself between jobs, I try to stay among locals. Then *I* become the tourist. I'm sure all those places are tourist traps too – just for more seasoned, pretentious travellers like myself.'

Margot grins. We keep walking. Slowly, so that she can

have a nosy at all the bits and bobs. She stops a few times to make purchases: some candles, a bottle of red for mulling, a *nice* bottle of red for drinking. She pays her own way at every stall, even as she checks with me that my family will enjoy the wine she's picked out. As we pass a food stall, she offers to buy me a late lunch.

'Oh,' I say. 'I had one of those soups earlier. And I don't think they have any veggie options here anyway.'

'You're a vegetarian?!' she asks, immediately rubbing me the wrong way. I don't think she has to sound so astonished. I'm sure she can think of nothing better to eat than an overpriced, undercooked lump of steak, but she must understand that's not for everyone. 'Me too!'

Wait, what?

'Let's just get some mince pies then,' she says. 'If you've already had soup, we can have fun foods. I'm sure there will be somewhere selling chips. Or we could get some fancy artisan cheese.'

We get all the above. She pays for everything. We leave the market with our arms full of goodies and find a low wall to sit down on.

'I'm glad there's another vegetarian around this Christmas,' I say as I pop a chip into my mouth. It is crispy, salty, and delicious. I pick up five more. 'It's normally just me, and my parents have no clue what to make for me. I've tried buying in something from the veggie range at M&S, but they insist that everything has to be homemade at Christmas. I get saddled with such rubbish. They've tried cooking me chicken a bunch of times, because it's "*not like a real animal*". Then last year they expanded their horizons and made me this vile oven-baked tofu thing.'

'Oh, yuck.'

'They cooked it in goose fat.'

'Oh, double yuck.'

I nod grimly. 'I almost always end up with a plate full of vegetables.' I dunk a few more chips into a pool of ketchup. 'But not this year. If they have to make something veggie for you, they'll make sure it's actually good. Never anything but the best for our guests.' I cram my ketchup-covered chips into my mouth. 'So thank you for being here. Having another plant-muncher around bodes well for my Christmas dinner.'

'I'll come up with something,' Margot says. 'A good centrepiece for us. Maybe a pie? I could make it myself. I mean, my cookery skills aren't the best, but I can promise I won't use any goose fat.'

'We can cook together!'

That slipped out all on its own. But I find that I don't regret it. It could be kind of fun. We might both be crappy cooks, and I might still have to watch Margot in the kitchen to see if she gets excited about our silverware, but I know that if we work together on this we'll make something much nicer than whatever bonkers dish my parents would cook for us.

'We can go shopping for ingredients later this week,' I say. 'Maybe do a test run before the big day. See if we can't make something edible.'

'That sounds *great*.'

She sits there beaming at me, nibbling on a chunk of Brie, and I finally have to admit to myself that she's been good company this afternoon. She's nowhere near as awkward *or* as serious as I first expected. She's pretty cool. I feel like my suspicions about her are slightly less urgent — like I can hold off on asking her more questions until we get together in the kitchen later this week.

For now I'll just ask one more.

'So. Other than a delicious pie baked by yours truly, what is your ideal Christmas present? Like, if you could be given anything in the whole world, what would it be?'

She lowers her Brie and looks at me. Properly looks. Like she's searching for something in my face.

I look right back at her. See the guarded look in her eyes. It's not cagey or withholding. More insecure. Uncertain. It makes me feel suddenly desperate for her to share her answer with me — but this time it's not because I think she might say something incriminating. I know instinctively that she won't.

'It's silly,' she says.

I hold her gaze. 'Tell me anyway.'

'I'd want cake.' Her eyes slide away from mine. She shifts her weight on the wall. Tugs at her hat. 'My nana used to make us this special cake at Christmastime. Only once a year. It was a French recipe that had been passed down to her, and it took hours and hours to make. She'd bake all these tiny pastry balls and fill them with vanilla cream and cover them with spun sugar. I think it's called croquembouche. You're meant to stack all the pastry into a tall triangular shape, like a golden Christmas tree. Nana used to bake a cake to go in the middle too. Salted caramel flavour. A huge column of it to hold up the pastry balls. Definitely not French tradition, but tradition for us.'

She pauses to take a bite of cheese. For strength, I suppose.

'Nana died in March this year. Breast cancer. This will be my first Christmas without her. So . . . well, I guess that if Santa can't put her under the tree for me, then the next best thing would be having that cake. I know I could make it myself, or I could buy a regular croquembouche somewhere. But there's something about the fact that *she* made it for me. Someone who loved me. It's . . . yeah.' She looks down into her lap. 'It's cake. If I could have anything for Christmas, it would be that cake.'

We're both silent. It doesn't seem right to say anything; to chime in with my own experiences or offer up empty words of solace. I think there's a small lump in my throat anyway. So instead of talking, I shift a little on the wall, sliding closer to Margot so that my arm presses gently against hers.

I believe her. It's as simple as that. Whatever else might be true or false, I believe that all she wants for Christmas is an obscure French dessert. I believe that she is completely genuine in this moment with me.

I glance across at her. Her back is still held perfectly straight, and her shoulders are rolled down and back. She takes a deep breath in through her nose. Brings her hands together, clasping them in her lap.

Her hat is askew again. Both hands now covered in cheese. I reach up slowly and carefully, and pull the beanie down over her ears for her.

9

Margot

I never thought a woman putting clothes *on* to me could feel so intimate. Ellie's touch is gentle as she pulls my hat down into place. I'm surprised by the gesture, but it doesn't startle me. It isn't unwelcome. In fact, it is very comforting. I have to resist the urge to lean in to it, to rest my head against her hand. I'm sure she lingers for just a moment before pulling her arm away again.

'Thank you.'

She doesn't reply. I appreciate it. I like that she hasn't rushed in with pointless platitudes about Nana being in a better place now or her suffering being over. I'm grateful that she hasn't claimed to know exactly how I feel. It's nice just having her beside me.

After a while, my stomach starts rumbling. I'm ready for more comfort food. The Brie has got a bit squashed in my hands, but that doesn't put me off. I take a big bite. Nana would be so relieved to know that I kept my appetite after her death, even at the height of my grief. She was a feeder through and through, forever offering me second and third helpings of dinner, always giving me an extra-large portion of dessert. She was obsessed with getting *some more meat on my bones.* She would be delighted to see me now, tucking into my doorstop wedge of cheese with such gusto.

'Here,' Ellie says, reaching over to break off a bit of the Brie and smear it over some chips. 'Try this.'

I do. It is outrageously delicious. The salty, oily chips and the rich, fruity Brie clash in the best way, creating an explosion of flavour in my mouth. It certainly takes my mind off the pastry balls and spun sugar and salted caramel cake that I won't be having this year. I go in for some more. And more. And more. In a few short minutes, Ellie and I have polished off all the chips and all the Brie, and we turn our attention to the mince pies.

'I think you and I dispel the stereotype that vegetarians only eat salad,' I say as I pull off the foil case.

Ellie nods, her mouth already too full of buttery pastry to answer with words. We both laugh. It doesn't take us long to eat a pie each, and then we're hauling ourselves up off the low wall we've been squatting on.

I feel fit to burst, and Ellie is cradling her stomach like she's heavily pregnant. We make our way back to the car slowly, chattering idly about nothing in particular. I'm drowsy after my feast. If not for the cold wind hitting my cheeks and keeping me awake, I reckon I'd curl right up on the pavement for a quick nap. It's like I'm in a pleasantly hazy dream: comfortable, a bit out of it, and wholly unbothered by anything outside my current reality. My entire world is just Ellie and the after-effects of our lovely afternoon together. I am so very glad that I didn't use any of my excuses to get out of this.

We reach the car and swing our tote bags off our shoulders, placing our stash of wine and unopened cheese in the boot. As I slip into the front seat, I pull my hat off my head and my phone out of my coat pocket. I haven't checked my phone since leaving the manor, so I've got a fair few notifications waiting for me. I kick back and click on the top one.

My heart stops.

With a slightly shaking hand, I click away from the text then back on to it, just to check I'm really seeing what I think I'm seeing.

I am.

Taylor has texted me.

I stare at the screen, unblinking. There at the top is her name, still littered with the heart emojis I never got round to deleting. Then two simple words:

Hey you.

So casual. Like we just spoke yesterday. So plain and so simple, and yet the two words have bought a sharp pin to the dreamlike bubble of my day. My air of carefree bliss evaporates and my mind fills up with frantic messy thoughts. Why is Taylor texting me now? Is she OK? Is she safe? I can't help wondering: does she miss me? Does she still love me? Does she know that my feelings didn't simply vanish when she did?

My head is spinning. I don't look up as Ellie gets into the car. I have enough sense left to angle my phone screen away from her.

I keep staring at the text. I think I feel relieved. I've been wanting to hear from Taylor for ages. I spent the first two weeks after our break-up calling and texting her constantly, and then I decided to get some self-respect, and so spent the next two weeks sitting around all day waiting for her to contact me. And now she has. Of course I feel relieved.

But I'm annoyed as well. The feeling is too hot and prickly to ignore. I had just been getting used to the idea that I may never hear from Taylor again. I had stopped pining for a few hours and got on with enjoying my day, disappearing into the joys of good food and great conversation. And now she decides to reappear. I resent that. Taylor's text is an invasion; it has bolted out of the blue to ruin my perfect day.

But that's an awful thing to think. Guilt floods in and overwhelms me. I have technically known Taylor for my entire adult life. How can I begrudge her sending me a quick text? All because I'd rather carry on chatting to Ellie. Taylor would despise that. Now that she's texted me and returned to the forefront of my mind, it's like I'm seeing things from her perspective. Me laughing with Ellie becomes an outrageous display of flirting. Letting her pull my hat down becomes a major crossed line. And the fact that I've noticed her looks . . . well, that isn't an understandable casual attraction any more. It is evidence of the 'wandering eye' that Taylor always accused me of having, even though I never so much as considered straying from her in all the time we were together. Somewhere deep down I know that my ex-girlfriend's opinion about me getting to know Ellie as a friend shouldn't matter, especially since Taylor is the one who left me, but I can't help but care about her feelings. That instinct hasn't gone away yet.

'What shall we listen to?' Ellie asks brightly.

I don't look up. I'm too focused on this two-word text and the myriad of feelings it has bought up in me. It's always like this with Taylor. She gets me all tangled up in a web of messy contradictory emotions. They are all-consuming. A bit too all-consuming for me to think about music right now.

'My radio works sometimes,' Ellie explains. 'You just have to give it a proper thump, and even then it's touch-and-go. That's why I said it was broken earlier. But I have a good feeling that it's going to treat us well on the drive home. So choose any music you like.' She turns her keys in the ignition. 'As long as I like it too.'

I force a small laugh, then shrug. Out of the corner of my eye, I see her shrug back – a big pantomime-y movement that she does with a silly smile on her face. Earlier I'd hoped for this kind of casual and fun atmosphere between us, but now I can't enjoy it. My head is swimming and I need time to think.

'I'm really tired,' I say. 'I'm going to rest my eyes until we get back to the house. You listen to whatever you want.'

My words come out clipped. Now silence fills the car, broken up only by the faint hum of the engine. Despite the awkwardness, I just keep staring down into my lap. I double-check that my phone screen is still angled away from Ellie, then I reread Taylor's text several more times, needing to ensure I am adequately analysing all two words she's written. Eventually I lock the phone and put it back in my pocket. I will reply to her later – when I'm alone.

Finally I glance up. My eyes meet Ellie's. Her smile isn't as bright now, and her forehead is starting to crease slightly. Suddenly I want to forget it all and flick through all the radio stations with her until we find something good; to take us back to the hazy contentment we'd been basking in just a few minutes ago. Then I imagine Taylor's perspective again, seeing me seek happiness with this beautiful blonde woman, and the guilt comes back with a vengeance. It is not a logical thought process, but that is exactly why I can't interact with Ellie right now. I'm all over the place. I'm not myself – or I'm too much myself to handle.

I turn away from her and close my eyes.

There is a long beat of silence. Then the radio comes on and I hear the gear stick clicking, and we're moving.

I do my best to look relaxed, letting my head loll to the side like I'm about to enjoy a post-food nap. I'm definitely stuffed enough to warrant one, but I know I won't really be able to sleep.

My brain feels like it's tied in a knot. I wish I had someone to help me untangle it. Frustratingly I think that Ellie would be good at that. I know that she'd listen to me without judgement, just like she did when I spoke about Nana, and she'd probably stop the car to grab me some more cheese to eat once I was done. It's just that telling Ellie what's on my mind would require telling her that I am not really dating her brother and that I like women, and then she might recognize my initial awkwardness around her for what it was, and I'd become all awkward all over again, and . . . Yeah, it's a no. Discussing all this with Ellie would only lead to further complications.

What I need is a friend. Someone who isn't tied up in my messiness, who I can tell the whole story to without having to edit out any details. Someone who will insist I treat myself to an entire tub of ice cream to soothe my sorrows.

There is no one.

I guess I lost my old friends so gradually that I hardly

noticed it happening. I answered the phone less because I was busy with work, and I skipped a few brunch dates to stay home with Taylor. It didn't help that she didn't like my friends much. They just didn't gel, and she noticed all these little things about them that I must have been missing – like bitchy looks she'd spot between them about me, and ways they would subtly judge me. Over time I withdrew, and now if I wanted to talk to any of them I would have to reintroduce myself first. I couldn't just dive in with a complete rundown of my feelings and insist on being offered dairy products to help me numb the pain.

I miss them. I miss my friends. I miss having someone to talk about my problems with who isn't just the ramble-y voice in my head. More than that, I miss having someone to laugh with and muck about with and generally chat absolute unfettered nonsense with.

I especially miss lovely Nikita from my old office in Soho. I never thought I'd lose touch with her. We were immediate friends when we met at work, and quickly became part of each other's lives outside the office. She was a firm fixture through my twenties, and we even remained close after she got married and moved out of London. But Taylor wasn't sure about her. She said Nikita was distant, and seemed jealous of my business, and should really have made the effort to visit us in London rather than having us trek out to Reading for her. It all made sense. Taylor loved me and had my best interests at heart, and as an outsider she could see things I'd become blind to. So I took her word as gospel and slowly stopped making an effort with Nikita.

But now I think about it, I'm not so sure Taylor was

right. Nikita wasn't distant, just prone to shyness. If she was jealous of my career, she never let it stop her congratulating me. And of course I visited her in Reading that one time – she'd come to see me in London the time before, and the time before that. Nikita was a wonderful friend, until I stopped answering fifty per cent of her texts and seventy per cent of her calls. Until I let Taylor pull me away from her.

Sadness seeps its way into my tangle of feelings. I am starting to feel very, very full – of too many emotions and too many thoughts and far too much food. It is quite sick-inducing. The car jerking along the uneven country roads is not helping matters.

The only silver lining is that we must be getting close to the house now. I take a quick peek and, sure enough, there's the manor up ahead.

This means I can lie down soon. Goodness knows I need it. This 'nap' I've taken in the car, in which I've squeezed my eyes shut and pretended to be dozing so that I can overindulge in overthinking, has not done much to relax me. I need a proper rest, with the curtains drawn and the blankets bundled on top of me. That will sort me out. My game plan for the next hour is clear: say a quick thank you to Ellie for a nice day out; say a quick hello to Ben; go straight to bed. I will sleep all this confusion off and then I will wake up with a clear head, no longer feeling sick or emotionally knotted. All I need is some alone time.

'Margot! Ellie!'

As the car comes to a jolting halt, I see Ben running across the driveway. He reaches the car and stops just short of launching himself through the window.

'Fun news,' he says breathlessly. 'Everyone got home early. I texted you both about it, but maybe you didn't see. They're all inside. Mum and Dad; Kate; Henry and Dylan and Dominic. They're all waiting in the hall with tea and cake. Margot, they can't wait to meet you!'

10

Margot

Ben opens the car door for me and pulls me into a hug as soon as I get out. He plants a kiss on both my cheeks, then throws an arm round my shoulders. I manage not to flinch away from any of the sudden intimacy, partly because I am stiff with shock. Ben must notice this, because he pushes me into action, using the arm he has round my shoulders to shepherd me towards the house.

As we walk, he tilts his head towards mine and whispers, 'I'm so sorry for springing this on you. I wasn't expecting everyone to get back home until much later tonight. I tried to let you know but you didn't read my WhatsApps. Neither did Ellie. I really didn't want to catch you by surprise.'

Suddenly he's talking much louder, which ironically catches me by surprise. He calls out, 'They're he-eeere!' as we approach the window with the huge Christmas tree in it. I see a flurry of movement through the glass, and then we're approaching the front door and I'm being ushered into the foyer and the flurry of movement has transformed into a crowd of people rushing in to meet us. They all know my name and they keep saying it, and there is a series of introductions I can't quite catch. Too many new faces smile at me, and Ben keeps his arm clamped round my shoulders, and Ellie appears beside Ben with our tote bags, and two small boys run rings around us all. Out of the chaos steps a short wavy-haired woman. She strides towards me, arms open wide.

'Margot!' She pulls me into an embrace the second she reaches me, squeezing both me and Ben. 'It is so wonderful to meet you.'

She pulls back slightly to link an arm through mine and starts walking me through the foyer and away from Ben, completing a seamless hand-off I hadn't realized was happening.

'I'm Ben's mum, by the way, in case that wasn't obvious. Oh, I'm just delighted that you're here. I've heard so much about you.'

I manage a weak 'All good things, I hope.'

She laughs like she's never heard that cheesy line before, the sound tinkling. 'Of course. Only good things. *Endless* good things, since he finally told us about you last week.'

She keeps up her light laughter as she leads me onwards: down the long hallway lit on both sides by warm lamps, through the dining room now home to a large table with all its places set, and into the great hall with its roaring, crackling fire. I am whisked through the archway and pulled over to a two-seater sofa opposite the ginormous Christmas tree. Mrs Gibson sits down, crosses her legs daintily, and gestures for me to make myself comfortable beside her.

'It truly is a joy to meet you,' she says as I sit down.

I finally remember my manners. 'It's so lovely to meet you too.'

She beams. I smile back, a little wonkily. The two boys come darting into the room, skidding across a patterned rug, and everyone else pours in after them. A neat-looking couple settle into another two-seater; a man in a tweed jacket takes an armchair by the fire; the boys dive on to the biggest sofa, settling down on their stomachs; and Ben and Ellie perch either side of them. Everyone is chattering away happily, and I hear Mrs Gibson sigh a contented sigh.

Then she jumps right back up to her feet. 'Tea!' she trills. 'How is everyone taking it? And you'll all have cake, of course. You will allow the boys to have cake, won't you, Kate? It is Christmas, after all. I got three flavours from a splendid bakery near the hotel we were staying in. We've got carrot cake, chocolate cake, and lemon drizzle.'

'Cost me a small fortune,' laughs the man in the tweed jacket.

'And it will be worth every penny!' Mrs Gibson bounces over to a long side table laden with tea paraphernalia. 'Guests first – Margot, what can I get you? A bit of all three? Go on, just a sliver of each.'

Before I know it, I'm holding a plate loaded up with three huge slabs of cake.

It's all a bit Wonderland-esque, my stumbling into the middle of a tea party I hadn't realized I was going to attend. I feel disorientated and quite sick. I ate too much at the market to manage this mound of sugar. But it would be horribly rude of me to leave it untouched. Mrs Gibson smiles at me expectantly from over by the table, and I force myself to eat a forkful of lemon drizzle.

'Ben? Just carrot cake? Are you sure you won't try one of the others, too?' Mrs Gibson hovers her knife over the chocolate cake. 'Just a tiny bit.'

Ben shrugs his acceptance, then turns to flash me a rueful smile. I shake my head to let him know it's all right.

He looks relieved. Mrs Gibson leans over to pass him a plate identical to mine, with all three flavours of cake piled high.

A quick glance around the room confirms that everybody has been given the same treatment, regardless of what they asked for. As my gaze slides past Ellie's triple-loaded plate, our eyes meet. She puffs out her cheeks at me and widens her eyes, her mind clearly boggling at all the food we have to get through. I purse my lips to keep from laughing. I think about Ellie's laugh, and how it lights up her entire face like she's made of sunshine, and –

I look away.

Mrs Gibson squeezes herself back on to the sofa next to me and I rush to put another forkful of sickly sweet lemon cake into my mouth, making a loud mmm-ing noise as I do so. She responds with another happy sigh, then turns her attention to her own plate. The room is mostly quiet now, aside from the gentle clattering of cutlery on china. I remind myself that I have studied hard for this moment, that Ben and I are fully prepared for our debut performance as a couple.

I look around at everyone again, this time paying attention to their faces rather than their plates. It isn't hard to work out who's who. Mr Tweed Jacket has to be Ben's dad; the neat-looking couple will be Kate and her husband Henry; the two little boys are the twins, Dylan and Dominic. As I look at each face, I can almost see the flashcards Ben and I drew up last night. Mrs Gibson is a former prom queen who loves to bake. Mr Gibson is her prom king and a keen collector of rare antiques. Kate and Henry are strait-laced members of the legal profession, and their sons are unruly agents of chaos. Grandpa Mo is not here right now because he's busy living it up at the local nursing home with his oldest friends and a big bottle of whisky.

Mitsi arrives late to the party. I watch as she waddles into the room and curls up by the fire. Aside from the dog, there is a very strong Gibson family resemblance. They all have button noses, almond eyes and thick wavy hair. All of them are brunettes, besides Ellie who has dyed her locks blonde. She also has the greenest eyes in the room, the rest being more hazel-coloured. And she got the lion's share of the freckles. Anyway. I am not looking at her in particular. I am looking at everyone. I am noticing how Ben and Kate have their father's strong jawline, while Ellie has the rounder features of her mother. Even non-Gibson Henry looks like an uncanny male clone of his wife. Obviously I won't comment on that. I have to charm these people.

'This cake is delicious,' I say, making a show of loading some more lemon drizzle on to my fork. 'You must tell me the name of the bakery, in case I ever find myself that way. Where was it you stayed for your long weekend?'

'Oh, I'm so glad you're enjoying it.' Mrs Gibson practically vibrates with pleasure beside me. 'The bakery was Millie's Sweetie Pies. Only a five-minute drive from the hotel, a lovely country lodge with gorgeous grounds.'

I ignore the fact she hasn't told me where in the UK any of this is. 'I bet it was lovely, but it couldn't have been as nice as this place.' I gesture around the room. 'It's such an incredible building and you have it kept so beautifully. Mr Gibson, the estate has been in your family for a long time, is that right?'

Mr 'Tweed' Gibson sits up straighter in his armchair.

'That's right. It was passed down to my father from his father, and it was his father's before him. Et cetera, et cetera.'

'Well, I'm honoured to be staying here. Thank you all so much for having me.'

'Of course!' Mrs Gibson says. 'The pleasure is all ours. I've been waiting a very long time for Ben to bring home a lovely young lady. And here you are – every bit as beautiful and charming as I knew you would be.'

Well, that was easy.

Mrs Gibson leans closer to me conspiratorially. 'You know, Henry visited us for the very first time over Christmas. That's a good sign, don't you think? All we need now is for Ellie to find a nice woman to settle down with. Maybe next Christmas, darling?'

Ellie pauses with a fork halfway up to her mouth. She lowers it back down. 'Maybe. Will she still be welcome if I bring her round on Ash Wednesday instead?'

I try not to laugh. Mrs Gibson tries to laugh.

'Of course she would. I'm only teasing. Although there is something especially romantic about Christmastime. Don't you think, Margot?'

I keep watching Ellie. Her long hair looks golden thanks to the twinkling lights on the tree beside her. She lifts her fork back up and pops it into her mouth. Like me, she has made a beeline for the lemon cake and only picked at the rest. I look into her green eyes from across the room, and she looks right back. For a moment it's like we're back in Chester on a crumbling brick wall in the freezing cold, eating chips smothered in Brie.

She suddenly looks away.

I remember where I am, and what I'm here to do.

'Yes,' I say to Mrs Gibson brightly. I shift my gaze to Ben. I try to look at him the way I just looked at his sister. 'That's why I'm so happy to be spending this magical season with your wonderful son.'

II

Ellie

Tea was delicious but it went on forever. I've now got about an hour to myself before we reassemble and do it all over again for dinner. My belly is stuffed full of hot chocolate and chips and Brie and mince pies and tea and chocolate cake and carrot cake and lemon drizzle cake, and I have no idea where Mum's homemade pumpkin soup is going to fit into the mix. Ditto the crusty bread rolls from Silly Milly's Sweetie Treaties, or whatever the name of that bakery was.

I'll find space, though. Have to. Nothing offends Mum quite like someone turning down food. I'm not gonna rock the boat like that this evening. Especially not after today has turned out to be so much nicer than expected. I head up to my room and change into a pair of soft stretchy flares with an elastic waist, leaving my worn jeans in front of the overflowing wardrobe. I want to try on the chunky silver rings I bought from a craft stall at the market. As I rummage through my tote bags, I remember that I've still got hold of all Margot's shopping too. I retrieve my rings, chuck them on to my bed, and gather up the bags to take up to her room.

She was a bit strange on our drive back home again. All quiet and stiff, and kind of frosty with me. I wondered whether our nice afternoon together had been a fluke – whether Margot could only sustain being warm and friendly for a few hours at a time. But she *did* look exhausted, slumped there in the passenger seat, and I thought that maybe she was just emotionally drained after sharing that story about her nana. I decided to give her the benefit of the doubt. At least for twenty minutes. I was surprisingly relieved when she brightened up again once we got home. The mood swings are a little odd, but I can't see how fluctuating emotions might tie in with being a gold-digger, so I'm not too worried right now. I don't even mind hand-delivering Margot's shopping. Not that much, anyway. I climb the narrow staircase to the top floor, holding the tote bags close to my body to keep the wine bottles from knocking about.

I can hear Margot and Ben chatting before I reach their room – just the general shape of two voices and lots of laughter. It's nice to hear. I get to their door and raise my hand to knock, but my curiosity takes over once I realize I can make out their conversation now, and I leave my hand hovering.

'No, no, really,' Margot is saying, 'I want to hear more about your afternoon at work.' She pauses. Laughs. 'Don't look at me like that – I'm really interested. Didn't you finally get your end-of-year figures back?'

'We did.' Ben's voice is level. 'Nothing too interesting.'

Another pause. Another laugh from Margot. 'You're lying, aren't you? They were great, weren't they? Tell me they were great!'

'They were great!' Ben says, finally laughing along. 'Really, really great. We've had a fantastic year, with loads of click-through from the new website. Business is booming!'

'That's the best news *ever*,' Margot cries. 'I'm so pleased for you. And for me, of course, since I'm the wonderful woman behind all your success. How shall we celebrate? I could buy us some nice wine – and you could give me a new necklace from your range?'

Ben keeps chuckling. On the other side of the door, I can't see the funny side. Margot might be passing this off as a playful joke, but it troubles me that she could even consider asking to be rewarded for Ben's business doing well. It isn't *her* hard work that they're celebrating. She clearly takes a keen interest in his finances, though. The light, casual way she's discussing all of this suggests that it's a common occurrence for her to ask about his profits and how they might benefit her. How often does she 'jokingly' ask for expensive gifts? How often does he give them?

'Oh, by the way,' Margot says, serious now. 'I noticed the standing lamp in the corridor earlier, and I was meaning to ask you where it's from. It's gorgeous.'

'I'm not too sure to be honest – I'd have to ask my parents,' Ben says.

'Would you? Something like that would look just perfect in my flat.'

I feel my body tensing up. Not only is she angling for jewellery, but now the family antiques as well, so that she can decorate her flat in the chic country style that she's obviously set her sights on. It's an outrage. She can't just survey all our things to see what might fit into the lifestyle she's aspiring to. I do not like her aspiring. I do not like the role that Ben might be expected to play in facilitating her goals.

Suddenly I can't bear to hear another word. I drop the

bags in a heap and stalk back down the corridor. Past the lamp that *I* brought Margot's attention to this morning. Down the stairs that I climbed laden with the spoils of her shopping spree. Into my room that is half the size of her suite.

I am now completely convinced. Margot Murray is a gold-digger. She has fooled my brother good and proper, and this afternoon she nearly fooled me too. I never should have given her the benefit of the doubt. Not even for twenty minutes.

I launch myself at the bed. My new silver rings dig into my belly. I squirm around, my right leg slipping off the narrow single bed and my left leg brushing against the overlapping tapestries on my wall. I huff and flop on to my back.

I was actually starting to like her.

What an idiot.

By the time I'm making my way downstairs for dinner, I'm calm. Or, rather, I'm able to do a decent enough impression of a person who is calm. I had a cuddle with Mitsi, I took a nice hot shower, and now I'm ready to get on with my evening. I'm just going to ignore Margot for the night and focus on myself. On getting what I want. A job at the hotel.

To kick things off, I'm gonna impress everyone with the fantastic job I did setting up the dining room earlier. I can't wait to see their reactions to the place being all done up ahead of schedule.

I take a seat at the table and await compliments.

'My apologies for the mess in here,' Mum says as she breezes into the room. 'Hopefully I've got it cleaned up nicely enough for you all. The room was in such a state when we got back! There were old tablecloths in a heap on the floor, and the new cloth was all wrinkled. The garland from the fireplace was cluttering the *table*. I have no idea what could have possibly happened in here, but I think I managed to tidy it all up for us.'

I stare at her as she straightens out the already straight tablecloth.

I don't think I'll bother saying it was me who did all that.

Don't think I'll bother saying anything at all.

'Oh, please,' Margot pipes up. 'It looks incredible in here. If you truly think this is messy, Mrs Gibson, you would be horrified to visit *my* mother's house. Or my flat, for that matter. I could never keep my place as pristine as you keep this house.'

Mum practically swoons. Ben looks on with pure adoration as he and Margot take their seats opposite me. I turn away from them.

'You know,' I say, 'if there are any other scruffy spots around the house, I'm happy to help you do some cleaning tomorrow, Mum.' I take a napkin and lay it carefully in my lap. 'Or I'll just do it myself, if you fancy a bit of a rest.'

'*Boys!*' Kate yells, scraping her chair back and jumping to her feet. 'Sit down, please. You are being very rude. Everyone here is sitting down nicely. We're all waiting for *you* so we can start eating. Henry, tell them.'

'Listen to your mum,' Henry chips in, sounding bored.

Dylan and Dominic had been chasing each other around the dining table in a frenzied game of tag. Games like that were not allowed inside the house when I was a kid, but Mum and Dad don't seem to mind it when their grandsons play. The twins hunch their shoulders and trudge over to their chairs. I see Dad wink at them from his seat at the head of the table. Mum starts collecting bowls to ladle soup into.

'Here, let me help,' I offer at the exact same time as Kate.

'Ah,' Mum passes Kate the ladle. 'Thank you, darling.'

No one so much as glances my way. I was already halfway out of my chair, and I'm left hovering in a squat. I sit back down. I let conversation move on to talk of how hyper the twins have been lately, and I manage to refrain from pointing out that they've been exactly this energetic since the day they were born. I slurp down a few spoonfuls of rich, creamy soup.

'This is so delicious,' I say over the chatter.

Mum finally smiles at me. 'Thank you! I got the stock going as soon as we got back home this afternoon. It is so handy having full use of the bigger kitchen when we're closed to guests.'

I lean forward. 'You know, you could probably make more use of the kitchen even when you're open. Have you ever considered offering meals for the guests? Other than breakfast and cake, I mean.'

'Cake?!' Dylan yelps.

'Is there cake?' Dominic demands.

'Brilliant.' Kate glares at me. 'There isn't any cake, boys. You've already eaten it.'

'Oh, there's plenty left over,' Mum says. 'They can have some more after their soup.'

'No they can't,' Kate snaps. 'They've had more than enough sugar for one day. See, *this* is why they've become so hyperactive. The other day, they bounced off . . .'

I tune out as the conversation returns to exactly where

it was before I tried to get involved. Shame. I *was* going to introduce my idea about hosting supper clubs at the hotel. It's kind of brilliant. We would set aside one evening every month to serve up a special tasting menu. A one-night-only kind of thing. Our breakfast chef could try her hand at some fine dining recipes if she fancies, but I think the best option would be showcasing a different local chef every month. They could each come up with a unique one-off menu of their own design and style. It would be the perfect way to get some proper use out of the kitchen, and it could attract loads of foodies to the hotel. It *will* attract loads of foodies. They'll get a good look at the hotel each time they visit, and it won't be long before they start booking rooms to stay in after the big feast. It will be a huge success.

After several minutes, I find an opening and try again. 'So I was having a chat with an old friend from school recently. Ashwin. He's a really great chef. Has his own catering company, doing authentic Indian dishes with a modern twis–'

'I fancy a curry now!' Dad calls.

'Right.' I force myself to smile. 'Yeah. His curries are really fab –'

'That's always the way, isn't it?' he chuckles. 'As soon as someone mentions curry, you fancy curry.'

'Absolutely,' Mum agrees.

'Hands down the best takeaway,' Ben reckons.

'No, that'd be a Chinese.'

'What about sushi?'

'Or kebabs?'

'No votes for pizza?'

'Italian style or American style?'

'Whichever one is thin-crust.'

'I'm partial to a good burrito.'

'I like Thai!'

'Has anyone mentioned pizza yet?'

I feel my cheeks burning and the back of my neck prickling. I leave them to it. There's no point interrupting their casual, impromptu chat about takeaway foods to deliver my 'casual' and 'impromptu' business presentation. Nobody would bloody listen anyway. I have a feeling my forced grin is starting to look like gritted teeth, so I let my face relax. Reach for a bread roll that I don't really want and set about buttering it.

Once I've finished that roll and half of another, I'm ready to have another go. I'm just gonna come right out with my idea. I wait until there's a proper pause in conversation, and then I launch into it.

I get about five words in. Those words are: 'I have this great idea . . .'

'Sorry,' Henry interrupts, grabbing his loudly ringing mobile. 'Don't mind me. It's just a work call. I have to take it. Sorry. Ignore me.'

Yet he lets it keep ringing at top volume as he saunters out of the room. Asshole.

'Where were we?' Mum asks once he's gone. 'Oh yes. Margot. Weren't you telling us about your trip to the theatre, dear?'

Seriously? Irritation keeps rising. Neck gets hotter. Belly tightens.

Margot looks right at me.

Her gaze surprises me. Freezes me almost. Her eyes are full of sympathy.

'Actually,' she says gently, 'I think someone else was talking.'

Does she mean . . . ? Am I supposed to . . . ? Hang on. Is *Margot* really trying to guide everyone's attention away from herself and towards *me*? It seems impossible. But she is still looking at me, almost expectantly now. Like she's waiting for me to talk. Urging me to –

'I guess not.' She looks away. Shakes off her own interruption. Dives right into telling everyone about her theatre trip for the second time tonight. Holding court happily.

Of course she didn't want me to talk. Her little pause was probably all for show. Like when you offer someone the last biscuit, even though you're already mentally dunking it into your tea. She just wanted to appear humble.

'I became a bit obsessed with the director, and immediately booked tickets to the next play he had in the works,' she bangs on. 'It was even better if you'll believe it. The acting, the stage design, the *plot twist*. Phenomenal. I had to go and see it again before it closed. And then once more for good luck.' She laughs. 'In the end, I visited the West End four times in as many weeks.'

Ugh. She's not that arsed about appearing humble, then. How braggy.

Mum's lapping it up, of course. Lauding Margot for being so cultured. Wishing she herself could go to the theatre more often. Waxing lyrical about the sheer joy of all-singing, all-dancing musicals.

'Oh yes, I love those too,' Margot says. 'They're just . . . magical.'

I thought they were too cheesy for her? Huh. Either

she lied to me earlier, for no discernible reason other than taking pleasure in petty deceptions, or she's now lying to Mum in an attempt to charm her even more.

The two of them quickly enter into a back-and-forth about their favourite musicals. Margot picks out *Les Mis* and *Miss Saigon*, which in fairness include less jazz-handing and high-kicking than most other corny classics. But she is still able to name a hell of a lot of show tunes as she and Mum run through the greatest hits.

'You have really good taste,' Mum compliments her. 'What are your favourite songs outside of musical theatre? Ooh, what is your favourite *Christmas* song?'

'Ah.' Margot pauses. '"Frosty the Snowman".'

Annnnd I'm zoning out. That is officially one cheesy song too many. This whole chat has been beyond ridiculous and irritating, and clearly the only way for me to remain sane is to block Margot out as I'd intended to do. I tear a chunk off my bread roll and wait for another opportunity to talk. I can make room for *myself* in this conversation, thank you very much. I'll give it one more go. Take it back to basics. Simply offer to do a bit of cooking.

'So, Mum,' I finally say, several long minutes later, 'I was thinking that I could help you make Christmas dinner this year. I could do some of the roast vegetables for you, and I could take the vegetarian option off your hands too. Thought I'd make a nice pie. Maybe with some –'

'Sorry about that, everyone.' Henry comes striding back over to the table, phone in hand. 'One of my clients needed a bit of reassurance from me. I did tell him he could call me night or day. You know what they say: there's no rest for the wicked!'

There's a little ripple of laughter, and jokey reassurances that Henry isn't wicked.

Margot is looking at me again, unsmiling.

'Ellie was just saying that she's going to make a pie for Christmas Day,' she says quite loudly.

I stare back at her. So she *was* trying to help me speak before? And she is again. Could it be that while I've been trying to ignore Margot, she's been the only person paying attention to me?

'We were talking earlier about making the pie together,' she continues after a long beat of silence. 'We thought since we're the only two veggies at the table, it would be nice for us to sort out our own centrepiece for the big day. Not that you wouldn't have made us something delicious, Mrs G – I'm sure you would. But this way, you'll have one less thing to worry about.'

Mum brings a hand to her heart. 'Oh, *Margot*. You are such a sweet girl. What a lovely offer. How thoughtful of you!'

My pleasant surprise is immediately replaced by anger as I watch Margot get all the credit for *my* idea. Or maybe it was *our* idea, but now she's totally taken it over. That must be why she jumped in just now. It was nothing to do with helping me out, and everything to do with further impressing my mum. It's always a bloody act with this woman, and I nearly fell for it. Again.

I toss my spoon into my bowl, letting it clatter against the sides.

I've had enough of this.

I've had enough of everyone.

Unfortunately Mum keeps prattling on. 'I would love to

have you in the kitchen with me, Margot! And you, Ellie. Thank you, girls – that's a lovely offer. I must admit that vegetarian cooking is not my forte, although I have tried my best over the years. I made a very nice tofu bake last year actually. You should have tasted it, Margot – it was really quite meaty. But, yes, if you two want to take the lead on the veggie option this year, I won't stand in your way. Just as long as it's all homemade. I take great pride in cooking every single element of our Christmas dinner from scratch. Even the Christmas pudding! There is really no greater joy as a woman than cooking for your family.'

'Yeah, if you live in the 1950s.'

Everyone at the table turns to look at me. Even Dylan and Dominic stop splashing soup at one another for long enough to glance my way. Mum narrows her eyes, glaring right at me.

'If wanting to spoil my family at Christmas with home-cooked food is old-fashioned, then I am a proud traditionalist. Thank you, Ellie.' She sniffs, then turns her head away. 'Can I get anyone some more soup? There are more bread rolls in the kitchen if we're running low. Ben, darling, let me refill your bowl. Come on, just a little drop. Pass me the bowl.'

Just like that, everybody moves on. Ben hands his bowl over to Mum for seconds. Mum demands more bowls to dole out more seconds. Dylan and Dominic get back to decorating each other's jumpers with bright orange soup; Kate gets back to hissing at them to stop at once; Henry gets back to leaving her to it. Dad ignores everyone and instructs Margot to tell him some more about her marketing business.

Naturally I have no role to play here. Everyone has moved on without me. I only managed to get their attention for two measly seconds, and of course those were the two seconds I spent being snarky. Hot-headed, tempestuous Ellie strikes again. Immature Ellie with nothing of value to contribute. Wayward Ellie who can't play nice and fit in.

I push my napkin off my lap and lean back in my chair, crossing my arms over my chest. I know one way to get my family to notice me, and that's by exposing the snake in their midst. The one they've all been fawning over all evening. Treating like a member of the family. *Better* than their actual family. But not for long. I am done with sitting around and waiting. This is going to be the last dinner that woman eats in our house.

My new, old goal is simple.

Get. Margot. Out.

12

Margot

I think tonight went really well. I like the Gibsons, and I'm pretty sure they like me too. There was a bit of a weird vibe coming from Ellie, but I can hardly blame her for that. I'd also be irritated if I was interrupted and talked over all night long. I did what little I could to help, and I let myself move on when it didn't seem to work. I had a truly lovely evening.

Now Ben and I are climbing the stairs towards bed. My arm is linked through his – a final show of affection before the curtain falls.

I remember walking down this staircase this morning in a sleepy haze. I can't believe I've only been at the manor for a little over twenty-four hours. This one day has felt more like a week. The strange warping of time has allowed me to settle in very quickly. The manor already feels almost like a home away from home.

We make it to the top floor and Ben opens the door to our room. As soon as we step inside, we unlink our arms and both laugh.

'And . . . scene,' I say.

'Ha! Who knew we had such good acting chops?' Ben shakes his head. 'Seriously, you were amazing. Thank you so much. And I'm sorry again that everyone got here earlier than expected.'

I wave his apology away. 'It's fine. It was a good thing. Not knowing I was about to meet everyone saved me from overthinking and freaking myself out in advance.'

'Well, if you were nervous at all, it didn't show. You hid it very well. Yet another example of your extraordinary acting abilities.'

'I'll be expecting my Oscar any day now.'

I cross the room to my bed and scoop my PJs up off the pillow. I'm going to have a quick shower before diving into bed. As I head for the bathroom, I start taking my first layer off, pulling my jumper up over my head. I don't feel self-conscious about Ben being nearby. Sharing this room with him doesn't feel strange any more. I got over that silly worry last night.

I'm getting over all my worries actually. I have made my first impression on the Gibsons, and it seems to have been a good one. I behaved naturally and appropriately around Ellie all evening. I haven't checked my phone obsessively for more texts from Taylor, instead leaving it switched off and buried in my pocket. I still don't feel tempted to turn the phone back on and see if she's contacted me again; I leave it on the side of the bathroom sink as I pull the rest of my clothes off and get ready to step into a shower with the most phenomenal water pressure I have ever felt.

I am no longer worried about anything.

I am still worried about everything.

I lie flat on my back in the darkness, staring up at a ceiling that I can't see. My phone is planted screen-down on my chest. I don't want to sting my eyes with the artificial light spilling out of it any more.

I don't want to reread Taylor's most recent texts.

Ben is still talking to me from his bed, continuing the casual conversation we were having before I turned my phone back on. I try to listen to him. He has just finished explaining why Mitsi wasn't around at dinnertime. It had something to do with her only being allowed in certain rooms of the house, and the dining hall not being one of them.

'Of course, she only follows that rule when my parents are around,' he chuckles.

I can't make myself laugh with him about something so mundane.

He just keeps talking. 'I suppose I also behave differently when I'm with Mum and Dad. I go quiet. So it makes sense to me that Mitsi lives a double life. Still, it's a bit extreme for her to sneak out of the house and get herself pregnant by some mystery dog. I really can't work the whole thing out. Mitsi couldn't have . . . erm, *met* this dog at the park in front of my parents. And there are no other houses anywhere near ours, so no neighbours and no dog-walkers this many miles from the beaten track. There's only the grounds-keeper nearby, and he doesn't have any pets. He never has. Maybe he's not allowed them? Or he just hates animals? I don't know. He never even had a goldfish, or the hamster that Bobbi used to beg him for night and day. She was *obsessed*. She even wrote a song once to argue her case, and of course there was a dance break and glowsticks and . . .'

I'm glad that Ben is babbling on, really. It's soothing to hear his voice in the darkness, even if he is waffling on about unimportant matters that I can't make myself join in with. He keeps talking and talking, seemingly about anything that comes to mind, almost as if he is getting out all the words he held in around his parents all evening. His endless stream of chatter is quite comforting.

Comforting, yes, but not distracting. I pick up my phone again.

There's Taylor's first text: Hey you.

Then, forty minutes later: Hello?

Margot?

Are you there, baby?

Another hour later: What's going on?

Is everything OK?

Another hour: What the fuck?

Where are you???

Why won't you reply to me?!

SERIOUSLY, WHERE THE HELL ARE YOU?

Two minutes later: Whatever.

Be like that.

Even if you won't, someone else will tell me where you're staying.

One minute later: I'm sorry, baby.

I just want to know that you're OK.

Let's talk tomorrow. Goodnight xxx

I flip the phone over and lay it back down on my chest. I return to staring up into the pitch-black nothingness. I feel dread wash over my body.

What Taylor has written doesn't surprise me. It doesn't scare me either. In fact, I'm not so sure that I am worried at all. I don't think that the prickly feeling running up and down my body *is* dread.

It's anger.

I clench and unclench my hands into fists. I feel heat surge through me from head to toe. Normally I would have a sense of relief right now – I'd be shaken but relieved that things had ended on a good note, with a nice good-night message and a string of kisses. But now the thought of being so easily won over just makes me angrier. Taylor has no right to manipulate my emotions like this. My *ex*-girlfriend has no right to know where I am, or to demand to hear from me, or to send me digital kisses immediately after oh-so-subtly threatening to track down my location after a full month of radio silence. I am overwhelmed with resentment. I do not want Taylor to come crashing back into my life right now, making her presumptuous demands on my time and attention.

'Margot?'

I start, snapping my head to the side.

'Margot?' Ben repeats softly. 'Are you asleep?'

I let out a big exhale. Some of the tension in my body releases, and I drop my head back on to my pillow. What exactly was I thinking? That it was Taylor calling to me in the darkness? Ridiculous. I am always so irrational when she's involved.

'No. Sorry. I'm awake. I was just . . .'

'Resting?' Ben supplies.

I could say yes. Ben might keep talking then, and I could try to find some more comfort in the sound of his chatter. Or he might decide it's finally time for sleep and leave me alone with my thoughts. I could lie here in the dark for hours, alone with my anger, obsessing about Taylor, letting her take over my brain yet again.

I don't want to do that.

I don't want to be alone in this.

'I was reading my texts actually. My ex has got back in

touch with me.' I clench my fists again. 'She sent me some threatening messages.'

Ben is quiet for just a moment. Then: 'Would you like to talk about it?'

I squeeze my fists tighter. This is new for me. Taylor and I never used to speak to anyone about our relationship, except for one another. I guess I'm a naturally private person, and Taylor didn't like our personal affairs being broadcast to anyone else. She hated the thought of every Tom, Dick and Harry knowing our business. So we kept everything just between us, from big blowout fights to tiny disputes about which takeaway to order for dinner. It was the norm for us, and now it feels unnatural and treacherous to talk about her to someone else. It was strange enough for me to tell Ben about our break-up last night, and what I said then barely scratched the surface. Now I can literally hear Taylor's voice in my head warning me not to go blabbing to people who don't understand our relationship. I hear her asking when exactly she fucking *threatened* me?!

I don't want to hear her voice any more. If she absolutely must take up residence inside my head, then I don't want to listen to what she has to say. She has no right to have that much power over me.

So would I like to talk about it?

I unclench my fists.

'Yes, I would.'

I talk quickly, with no particular order in mind and more than a few repetitions and contradictions.

I explain that Taylor has anger issues, and that it isn't her fault because she had a tough childhood, and that it is her fault because she wouldn't go to therapy. It was worse back in our university days. The first time we ever met, at a seedy club far away from campus, she broke a bottle on a stranger's head. But she did it for a good reason. The guy had shouted the D-slur at us when he saw us dancing close together. So Taylor was my hero. She kissed me right there in the middle of the dance floor before security could take her away. I think I kind of liked the thrill of it all. She pressed her lips so hard against mine that it took my breath away, and she tasted like vodka and smoke, and I couldn't help but follow her out of the club and back to her house.

In a quieter voice I admit that when we started officially dating her anger sometimes turned towards me. She would scream at me for hours at a time back then; turn up at my house drunk in the middle of the night; bang on the front door until one of my housemates finally let her in, then shoulder her way into my room to stand at the foot of my bed and tell me she knew I'd been cheating, or that I'd been flirting with other girls, or at the very least that I clearly had my eye on someone else.

I stress that she never hurt me. Obviously. She never, ever lay a finger on me. And she could be so romantic too. She would declare her love for me via the sound system at our favourite club on date nights. She'd find a way to sweet-talk the DJ into giving her the mic so she could tell everyone on the packed dance floor that I was the one for her. If I didn't seem happy enough about her gesture, she'd circle back to her infidelity theory, and the screaming would start again. I sometimes shouted back. One time I even poured a drink on her. She laughed at that, breaking the tension, and it became a kind of inside joke that I wasn't allowed to have my own drink on our nights out. I would take sips from Taylor's cup instead, and she'd hold the straw steady for me, and the whole thing would kind of turn us on.

Suddenly I feel ashamed, embarrassed. I don't know how to explain the thread of excitement that was always tangled into the chaos of our relationship. I certainly don't want to admit to Ben that we always ended our big fights with mind-blowing sex, and that I sometimes looked forward to the drama because of how passionate it all was.

I move away from the old memories, and quickly push onwards to describe how much calmer everything was when we met again years later. We were both nearly thirty, and Taylor had mellowed out a lot. She'd got a job as a personal trainer, and she'd stopped drinking (except for special occasions or weekends or days that would generally be made better by drinking). We laughed together about how toxic and melodramatic we'd been as teenagers. She told me she loved me a week later. Our two lives became one, as we moved into our rainbow flat and made our toothbrushes look like they were kissing by the sink and invested in a king-size duvet for us to cocoon ourselves in on long, lazy mornings. Often Taylor would hold me in her arms and whisper into my ear that nobody would ever love me like she did. It was romantic. She prided herself on keeping our home meticulously clean, and she did all the cooking, and I paid all the bills. That was stability. Love. She tried really hard to shout less, instead releasing her frustrations by going into another room and breaking things. My mugs. My vases. My plate with my dinner on it. She always cleaned up the mess quickly, and she apologized for losing control, and she explained that she was hurting in a way that I would never be able to understand.

I accepted it all. I never once thought about leaving. Even with the broken pottery and the occasional row and the spells of punishing silence that could go on for hours at a time, things were good. It was nothing like how it had been we were younger. I was happy.

I pick up my phone now, battling against a pang of almost missing Taylor to look at her erratic texts. I want to remind myself of how she threatened to find out where I'm staying, weaving the menacing idea in between calmer messages. Were our good times like that? Did they all have the threat of escalation hanging over them?

I don't know. I have never considered anything like that before. I can't pull on those threads right now – it's too much – but it does feel somehow important to hold on to my anger over these texts.

So I read them all out loud to Ben.

There is a deep silence in the dark room once I'm done. I feel discomfort and guilt creeping in, and I rush to clarify that Taylor would never actually track down my location. She was just trying to get my attention so that I'd reply to her. Besides, only my mum knows where I am, and she would never divulge that information to Taylor because the two of them hated one another from the moment they met. Taylor used to say it was normal for two strong women to butt heads like that. She was always really good at making light of difficult things. She could change my perspective so easily when I was the one getting angry or upset. Which I did sometimes. I feel the need to clarify that. I could get angry and annoyed and aggressive too, just like I had when we were younger. I wasn't perfect in that relationship. I really wasn't perfect, and I am not trying to pretend otherwise. I tell Ben as much three times over. Four. Five. I wasn't perfect, and Taylor isn't the only one to blame.

I stop there. My anger has faded away, and I am suddenly completely spent after spilling out so many words and so many secrets, so I let the silence open back up again.

'You are not to blame.'

I hear the quiet rustling of Ben's duvet cover, and I imagine he is turning to face me.

'Even if you weren't perfect, Margot. Even if you got angry sometimes too. You are *not* to blame for how Taylor treated you. She . . . well, it sounds like she treated you very badly. That's all I will say about it unless you want me to say more. Taylor treated you really, really badly. And that is not your fault.'

I sit with this. Or, rather, I lie on my back spread out like a starfish with this. I imagine a bird's-eye view of myself, captured through night-vision goggles, and I almost want to laugh. Then I pull myself together and try to absorb what Ben has just said.

'Thank you,' I say at last. 'And I'm sorry that none of that was very . . . festive.'

'You have nothing to apologize for. I'm really glad you spoke to me, and I want you to know that I am here to talk any time you need. Or I can just listen. Any time.'

I consider this. I like the thought of talking to Ben, but I'm not sure I can manage any more vulnerability tonight.

'I think I'm done for now.'

'That's OK,' Ben says gently.

'I want to talk about something silly.'

'All right. Like wha—'

I cut him off with a huge yawn. 'Sorry,' I say, putting a hand over my mouth. 'Maybe the silliness will have to wait until tomorrow. Then we'll only talk about candy canes and gingerbread houses and our favourite ever Christmas films.'

'Are you sure?' Ben asks, but he's lightened his tone to match mine. 'My favourite Christmas film is *Die Hard*, which you said doesn't count, and your favourite Christmas film is, and I quote, "none of them".'

'Well remembered!' I finally release the little laugh that has been bubbling up inside me, which also morphs into a yawn. 'OK, so maybe we could talk about *good* films. And you'll take me to the spa, since we never got round to it today. And you'll tell me more about Bobbi and where in the world you think she is these days.'

'That's silly,' Ben says. 'I can't bang on about Bobbi after —'

'I want silly,' I remind him. 'I want to hear about how you're still pretty much in love with the girl you snogged a few times when you were seventeen. Remind me that you're an adorable, lovesick loser, so that I'm not the only one with girl problems.'

He chuckles softly. 'You're on. If it's really what you want, I will spend all day tomorrow telling you how I still miss my childhood sweetheart and you can call me a loser up to five times.'

'Perfect. And you'll take me to the spa, remember.'

'I will also take you to the spa,' Ben promises. 'We can sit in the sauna and have a swim and do some gossiping. And if you want to talk about anything else, you will be welcome to do so. If not, you can just put on a nice clay face mask and call me a loser.'

I nod my agreement, even though Ben can't see me, and then I pull my duvet up around me. Ben does what he does best and follows my lead; I hear his mattress springing slightly as he shifts into a more comfortable position for sleep.

'Goodnight,' he says a moment later. 'Sleep well, Margot. I promise that tomorrow will be a more relaxing day.'

Wednesday, 20 December

13

Ellie

Right. It's Wednesday morning, five sleeps until Christmas, and I have no intention of Margot getting another wink of sleep in this house. I'm gonna have my eyes on her all day long, and I *will* find concrete evidence against her.

Before I have to think about that, though, I get to hang out with my lovely grandpa. He has a big hug waiting for me downstairs, according to the text he sent a few minutes ago, and I can't wait to claim it. I quickly pull on a pair of faded jeans and throw yesterday's jumper over the T-shirt I slept in, then race downstairs.

Gramps is waiting for me on the old Chesterfield in the family living room. As soon as I walk in, he casts aside the paper he's reading and throws his arms open wide. I clamber on to the sofa and snuggle up. He cups a hand on the back of my head, just like he's done since I was a little girl, and I burrow my face into the gap between his shoulder and neck.

'I said I had a hug waiting for you, Ellie, not a *cuddle*.'

'You're welcome to let go any time you want.'

He doesn't move an inch. 'I missed you, kid.'

'I missed you too. How were the Jailbirds?' This is what Grandpa calls his friends at the retirement home. 'Did you behave yourselves?'

'Of course. We just played board games and watched television.'

I lift my head off his shoulder. 'And the whisky you took with you?'

'Oh yes, we polished that off in two days flat. But don't worry – it was all very above board. The home has a small room in which the Jailbirds are allowed to have a drink. We set up a game of Scrabble in there and fixed it so that you had to take a sip of whisky each time you played a four-letter word. Sandra got completely sloshed!'

We finally break apart. I rearrange myself into a cross-legged seat next to Gramps and ask after Sandra and the rest. He talks briefly about hip replacements and new medications, then moves back on to the fun and games portion of his visit, the highlight of which was a 'joyride' on Ann's mobility scooter with Gerald.

'And what about you, kid? How has it been around here?'

'S'OK. Same as always. Mum came home with a bunch of cakes yesterday and made everyone eat three massive slices right before dinner.'

'Any leftovers?'

'Loads.' I picture the huge hunks of cakes waiting on the kitchen counter and my belly rumbles. Looks like the feeling I had yesterday of being uncomfortably full is already a distant memory. 'Shall we have some for breakfast?'

Grandpa nods, a naughty twinkle in his eye. We sneak through the halls towards the kitchen, even though nobody else will be awake yet to catch us out. Grandpa and I are both early risers. Even when I stay out all night on the islands, I get out of bed before 7 a.m. I don't necessarily wake up fresh – I usually feel like a zombie – but something inside me wants to be up and at 'em nice and early. There's always time for a nap later in the day. Grandpa has been known to wake up at 6 a.m. and settle down for his first nap by 8. Right now it is still dark out, the sun only just starting to think about rising. I turn on every lamp that we creep past.

In the kitchen, I grab two bowls. Gramps chooses carrot cake and I go for lemon drizzle. We take our bowls through to the nearest room: the hotel dining hall.

'I set up the table in here yesterday,' I say as we sit down near the window. 'And Mum changed it all around while I was out. Even swapped the white tablecloth I put down for a much-improved white tablecloth.'

'I would have preferred your white tablecloth,' Grandpa confirms. 'But I do think it looks wonderful in here. Between you and your mum, you've made the room look splendid. I especially love these candles.'

'I picked those out!'

He nods knowingly. We each take a few mouthfuls of breakfast cake – a thing that only happens around Christmastime or birthdays but should really be a part of everyday life. Outside, a blustery wind blows. A couple of robins start up their morning song. The tiniest sliver of orange sunlight starts to creep into the sky.

Grandpa leans closer to me. 'So. Have you caught the pony yet?'

I look into his face. His light brown eyes are expectant. Brow furrowed. Forehead creased with the wrinkles that seem to be getting deeper every time I see him. He's being serious. And I don't know how to answer him because there is no pony. There have never been any horses at the manor.

This is how it's been going lately. Grandpa seems totally fine – just like his old self, talking and cracking jokes. Then he comes out with something that doesn't make any sense. Something that highlights his age and his tendency for confusion. It's been happening for a few years now, pretty much since Grandma died. He tells us that he's going to find a new star in the sky, or he says he's getting ready for a dinner date with his wife. He claims there is an unidentified pony running around in our gardens early in the mornings. My parents have had him tested for dementia, but the doctors say his memory is good. He still has all his faculties. He can function completely independently. He seems so normal so much of the time. But his mind is clearly deteriorating.

My heart sinks as I look at him. His milky eyes hold on to mine, waiting for answers. This is why I have to move back home. I need to be near Gramps. The rest of my family might prove a bit difficult to work with, but I'll put up with anything so long as I get to spend as much time with Grandpa as possible while I still have the chance.

'I haven't caught the pony,' I say gently. 'I haven't even seen it yet. What does it look like?'

Grandpa tells me about the pony's black coat and swishy tail. I nod along. I read online that 'indulging the delusion' can help avoid additional confusion and upset, and I obviously don't want Grandpa to feel alone in his new reality. Plus, the two of us have been making up silly stories together my whole life, so it's kind of like old times. I ask if we know anything else about the mystery pony, and Grandpa says she is a friend of Mitsi's.

'Oh? Does she have loads of friends around here?'

He looks at me like I'm crazy. 'There are no other animals on the estate, Ellie. It's just her and Mitsi.'

'I see.' I hold up my hands in surrender. 'My bad.'

He tuts, the twinkle reappearing in his eye. 'What an imagination you have.' He waggles his spoon at me, then digs back into his breakfast of nutty carrot cake and cream cheese frosting. He scoops up some of the icing to eat on its own. 'I suppose Mitsi and the pony could be friends with some of the birds and squirrels.'

'Mitsi would never be friends with a squirrel.'

'You're right,' he concedes. 'What an imagination *I* have. Mitsi, making nice with a common squirrel.' He chuckles to himself. 'She'd sooner be friends with the vet.'

We finish off our breakfasts. Grandpa makes a pot of strong black tea. Conversation moves on to more ordinary topics: my latest flings, Grandpa's recent bout of constipation, my big nights out abroad. There's so much for us to catch up on. Although Grandpa and I speak almost every day when I'm away, we have to rely on text messages or crackly phone calls, and so much gets missed out. Now I get to talk in way more detail, with no dodgy signal getting in my way and with nobody interrupting me. We talk and talk and talk until we've finished the pot of tea. Grandpa has returned fully to his usual self. The sky outside has lightened and become entirely orange and pink, the robin's song is in full swing, and the wind has calmed down. The whole world feels peaceful and serene.

Then Margot walks into the room.

It feels like aeons have passed since she came striding across to us, a big fake smile plastered on her face. In reality it has been seconds. But I am reeling, in sheer disbelief that she has turned up at the exact moment I was letting myself relax. I suppose I should have known the peace couldn't last long. What's that rhyme about red skies? Those dark orange streaks across the clouds were obviously a warning sign. Even the sky knows Margot is bad news.

I don't stand up to greet her, even as Grandpa does. Ben has rushed in behind her and is making enthusiastic introductions. Margot gives Grandpa a quick one-armed hug. Calls him 'sir'. Says how nice it is to meet him, and how beautiful the house and its grounds are, and how incredible it is to spend Christmas here. After all that, she gives me a small cursory smile. I return the favour from my seat. Everyone else remains standing as they get on with their small talk.

'So,' Grandpa asks after a few minutes, 'how did you two lovebirds meet?'

'In a coffee shop,' Ben says. 'I wasn't looking where I was going, and neither was Margot, and then boom!'

'I spilled my latte all over his freshly pressed suit!' Margot shakes her head and covers her face. 'I was so embarrassed, but Ben was really sweet about it. We got to talking, and when I offered to have his suit dry-cleaned, he asked if I'd consider going for dinner with him instead. And that was that. I've never been happier to spill my coffee.'

Ugh. *I've never been happier to spill my coffee.* That's a rehearsed line if I've ever heard one. She used it word-for-word when she told this story towards the end of dinner last night. Oh, everyone thought it was so cute. Sweet little Margot with her butterfingers, serendipitously meeting the love of her life by pouring boiling-hot coffee all over him. She is clearly so proud of the adorable anecdote. Strange, because she told *me* that clumsiness irritates her. It's just another little thing that doesn't add up about her, like the love/hate, bull/shit thing she has going on with cheesy musicals and Christmas songs. I mean, she already proved herself a liar by claiming to have a favourite festive tune after telling me Christmas music makes her ears bleed – but to then go with 'Frosty the Snowman'? Any self-respecting eight-year-old would consider themselves too mature for that crap.

'Yes, thank goodness you spilled that coffee,' Ben says.

'What an introduction,' Grandpa laughs. 'I'm sure it set the tone for a lot of fun to come. How long have you been together now?'

'Six months,' Ben says.

'Five months,' Margot says at the same time.

There's a brief silence, and then Margot laughs. 'Six months apparently! Goodness, time flies. I guess I'm just having too much fun.'

Hmm. Could be that, yeah. Or could be that she doesn't even care about Ben enough to remember their anniversary.

Ben doesn't seem fazed. 'Talking of fun,' he says cheerfully, 'let's go and have that morning swim I promised you.'

He pats a couple of white towels he has rolled up under one arm. There are also two robes slung over his shoulder. He and Margot are clearly all set for a morning in the spa. The perfect luxury activity for your friendly local gold-digger, I'd say. Sure enough, Margot's face has completely lit up. A real smile at last, with her eyes all crinkled at the corners.

It's infuriating that she has such a gorgeous smile when it's genuine.

I won't have to be infuriated for long, I remind myself. I will be finding a way to get the truth out very soon and that will wipe the smile right off her face.

14

Ellie

I have not managed to wipe the smile off Margot's face. She has actually been getting happier and more relaxed as the day has gone on, settling herself in and joining in with the festive fun and getting along swimmingly with everyone – all because I've failed to find any real proof that she's a horrible human being. I've also made zero progress with my family, because they've all been far too busy being enamoured with *her* to give me a second glance. And, to top it all off, dinner was disgusting. The whole day has been a bust.

I was off to a bad start from the jump. I obviously couldn't lurk around outside the sauna, creepily spying on Margot in her bikini, so I was forced to take my eye off her for ages. Hours had passed by the time she and Ben left the spa. At the exact moment that they emerged, Kate appeared out of nowhere and grabbed me by the elbow. Asked if I'd help her look after the twins for a bit. Just while Henry was on a work call. She looked completely knackered and desperate – and she usually only looks knackered. I cast a longing look over my shoulder at Margot, and then followed Kate in the opposite direction.

Henry's work call went on for two hours. I wound up spending most of that time running in circles around the garden with Dylan and Dominic while Kate sat down on a bench and watched. I guess we kind of had fun. The twins are good for a laugh if you're in the mood for high-energy hijinks. And I thought I'd get some props for babysitting my nephews. Eventually Kate got off the bench and did some star jumps with the boys. A moment later, Mum leaned out of the kitchen window.

'Oh, aren't you just adorable,' she cooed. 'Kate, my darling, you're so hands-on! I don't know where you get the energy. Boys, isn't your mummy the best? And aren't *you* the best jumpers! Dylan, you can get up so high. And, Dominic, look how wide your arms go. You are all so *wonderful*!' Mum turned her head towards the bench, where I was taking a quick breather. 'Oh, hello, love.'

She ducked back inside. The warm smells of her baking drifted out of the still open window, and Kate and the twins squealed with glee as they bounced around, and I dug my fingernails into my palms until it felt like my skin was splitting. My mistake was ever thinking I could fit in around here in the same way that Kate and Ben always have. That, and not trimming my nails for a month.

Lunch wasn't any better. Grandpa was off having his second nap, so it was the exact same crowd as last night. We ate leftover pumpkin soup with cheese on toast on the side, and everyone made a big fuss over Margot between mouthfuls. They lavished praise on her business, and her smart clothes, and her taste in lovely Gibson men. She brushed all the attention off like it was nothing and she complimented Mum's granary bread approximately one hundred and fifty-eight times. Other than that obvious bit of suckuppery, she didn't give me anything to work with. I did catch her looking at her phone under the table a few times, but that's just bad manners, not grounds to accuse her of plotting to steal the family fortune. Still, if *I* checked my texts at lunch, I'd . . . Well, I would say I'd be given a good ticking-off, but that would require somebody actually noticing me in the first place. Fat chance of that. No one seemed to look my way for the entire meal, except for when Dad asked me to pass the salt, and even then Ben got to it first.

I didn't bother trying to talk for the duration. I distracted myself instead with thoughts of what I'd get up to if I were invisible.

After lunch, Margot helped Mum clean up. I wanted to keep an eye on her and have a crack at impressing Mum, but not enough to wash dishes. I took Mitsi out for a walk instead. The little weirdo tugged at the leash all the way to the end of our furthest field, then spent ages sniffing around near the groundskeeper's bungalow. She ended her adventure with five laps round the lake – a display of athleticism that exhausted her so much I had to carry her back to the house. By the time I got back inside, sweating buckets, Margot and Ben had disappeared upstairs.

I didn't do much for the rest of the afternoon. I helped Dad get the fire going. Shared another pot of tea with Gramps. Watched the first half of *Elf* with the twins. Watched the second half of *Elf* on my own.

Margot and Ben came downstairs about half an hour before dinner and cuddled up together in front of the fire. They actually looked quite sweet. Relaxed and natural, sipping on hot chocolates and leafing through well-thumbed paperbacks. There was none of the stiff awkwardness I'd spotted from Margot on the night she arrived here. Just an aura of comfort and intimacy.

It really pissed me off.

Dinner was more of the same and I hardly paid attention to any of it. A lot of chatter – none of it directed at me. Another work call for Henry – some world-class frowning from Kate. A mushroom casserole that tasted like sweaty old boot – and Margot's compliments to the chef. She was perfect, as per. She seemed a tiny bit distracted at first, but she still didn't put a single foot wrong and did an excellent job of pretending to be delightful all throughout dinner and dessert and drinks in the hall.

And that's it. The day is over. Now I'm stuck in the kitchen with Mum (who asked me for help before I could offer it), furiously drying the dishes she passes to me from the sink and cursing this day for ending before I could gather a single shred of new evidence against Margot Murray.

From where I'm standing, even my *old* evidence is starting to look flimsy. It's just a few overheard conversations (that Ben himself was a part of and so will not be too scandalized to hear about), and a general sense of bad vibes. I don't have anything solid against Margot, and without that I will never be able to convince Ben to chuck her out. I will also never get through to my parents, and never be given a job at the hotel, and never, ever get the taste of this rank casserole out of my mouth. I am undeniably the loser of the day, while Margot comes out on top, getting away with her nasty scheme yet again.

'Careful!'

I look up. Mum is frowning at the china plate in my hand.

I follow her gaze. I am holding on to the dish so tightly my knuckles are turning white. My other hand is working on autopilot, rubbing a chequered tea towel against the patterned china with extreme force. The plate is already bone dry. I put it down on the counter.

'That was your grandmother's.' Mum takes her hands out of the soapy sink and pulls off her rubber gloves. 'It is very special and very delicate.'

The truth is that Grandma got the plate in a set of twelve at a car-boot sale. It's highly unlikely that it is really made out of china, although it may well have been made *in* China. I am the only person that Grandma and Grandpa told this secret to. The three of us used to giggle together about how everyone thought the plates were priceless, when really they did have a price and it was roughly two quid for the lot.

I don't say anything about all that to Mum. I just mumble an apology under my breath. Take another plate out of the sink. Start drying it. *Carefully*. Mum comes over to take the first plate off the counter and inspect it. She turns it over to look at the blue-and-white pattern on both sides, then wipes it with her own tea towel, inspects it again, and puts it away. She also picks up a couple of the glasses I've dried up and has a go at them too, wiping away smears that are visible only to her eyes. I don't say anything about this little performance either. I hold my tongue until she finally goes back to the sink and pulls her rubber gloves back on.

'Thanks for finishing those off,' I say, because I know that's what she wants to hear.

She nods. Picks up a sponge and gets to work on

cleaning her red Le Creuset. It still smells like the non-veggie option: like beef and gravy and again, somehow, boot. Everything seems so unappetizing while I have this bitter taste in my mouth. Murky water sloshes in the big double sink. I go over all the glasses twice with my tea towel to get rid of any invisible smears.

'We have a food delivery coming in from the local market tomorrow,' Mum says. 'It might be quite early in the morning. You'll be awake, won't you? Do you think you could be around to answer the door and bring in the bags?'

'Oh, yeah, no problem.'

'Marvellous. Then we'll have everything we need for the next few days, until your dad and I go out for the big Christmas Eve shop. I got you those peppermint creams you like, and I ordered the ingredients for your veggie pie, so you can practise your recipe for the big day. Margot told me what you'd need.'

My hand tightens round the damp tea towel. The thought of Margot still being here tomorrow, making herself at home, making a pie – it makes me bloody furious. Who gave her permission to waltz in here and start tinkering with a recipe in our kitchen? I mean, I guess the *technical* answer to that question is: me. But I made that suggestion when I was slipping under Margot's spell. Now that I've come back to my senses that permission should have been revoked. She should have been on a train home already. Instead, she is making herself all comfortable in our house, reeling off a long list of demands to my mother in the form of a pricey shopping list.

I so wish today had been the day I'd got her kicked out of here.

I leave the kitchen with dirty water all down my front. My fault for trying to move Mum's Le Creuset while it was still soaking in the sink. Now my jumper is wet through and I stink of garlic and beef fat.

I try to breathe in through my mouth instead of my nose as I stomp down the hallway. Don't particularly want to be sniffing at the remnants of dinner right now. It might just tip me over the edge.

I walk under the archway. Hanging above me is the sprig of mistletoe that my parents put up every year. At least once a day for the entirety of December, the two of them will stop right here and share a quick kiss for everyone to see. The thought makes my day even worse.

Even higher above me, Margot will be getting ready for bed. I can picture her fluffing up her goose-feather pillows, even though she claims to be a vegetarian. Lounging around on the chaise longue, just for the sake of saying she has lounged on a longue. Stepping into a steaming-hot shower, reaching for her selection of spendy smellies.

I turn out of the dining hall and back into the hallway. I just want to go to bed. Get back into my cosy childhood bedroom with the tapestries on the walls and the soft, squidgy pillows made without harming any geese. I want to dive under my collection of blankets and for this frustrating day to be over.

Something stops me in the middle of the corridor.

A phone. Lying there, screen-down, on the hard wooden floor. I bend to pick it up and check the background image to see whose it is.

There's a text on the screen.

It's from some bloke called Taylor.

His name is surrounded by emoji hearts.

It says: Baby! When can you call me? I miss you so much, Margot.

As I climb the stairs, my heart shatters into a thousand pieces for my poor brother. But it also lifts. Because now Margot can't mess with us any more. I finally have the proof I need to bring her down and keep her far, far away from the people I love. My broken heart swells more and more with every step I take.

There's no way she can talk her way out of this one. She has a bloody *boyfriend*. Maybe this is the guy she's truly in love with. Taylor fulfils her emotional needs and Ben her financial needs. It's not a bad system. Shame it won't be working out for her any more.

I have the incriminating message right here in black and white. I used my phone to take a picture of it, then I put Margot's phone back where I found it. I hope someone treads on it and breaks it. Ben certainly won't be stepping in to buy her a new one now.

At the top of the stairs I stop. I feel suddenly sick.

This is going to ruin Ben. Even though it is for the best – even though he needs to know the truth – it is going to completely destroy him. The idea of his pain hurts me even more than I thought it would. I normally love being proven right, but this time around the triumph feels hollow. I am aching with the weight of what I have to do, the awful news I have to deliver. I feel guilty somehow that I am the one holding all the cards. That I have taken even an ounce of pleasure in unravelling this whole facade.

Still. The truth has to come out. I roll up the sleeves of

my sodden, stinking, greasy jumper, and put my game face on. It's time for me to do what I've been waiting to do since that awful woman arrived here.

I'm about to blow this case wide open.

15

Margot

Today has been a lovely day.

I woke up this morning feeling rejuvenated, having had a wonderful deep sleep despite all the heaviness last night. It was as if, having unburdened myself to Ben, a weight I hadn't realized I'd been carrying had lifted just a touch and a new sort of serenity had entered in its place. I wasn't even bothered by the trio of top-volume alarms waking me at 8:00 a.m. I was determined to get up and enjoy my day. The spa was calling me.

We stopped to chat to Ben's grandfather first, who seemed delightful although not half as crazy as advertised. Ellie was there too, and I managed to be casual around her again. The two of them didn't keep us long so we were off to the spa in no time. It was just what I needed after yesterday. The water in the pool was gently warm; the sauna was ferociously hot. Ben and I slathered on fancy clay face masks, and used the foot spa, and spoke for hours about nothing in particular. He didn't push me to talk about Taylor again, and I was grateful because the morning of pampering was really helping me put her and those nasty texts to the back of my mind.

But then she started sending more of them. The first one came almost as soon as I left the spa. Ben was right next to me, and I showed him the message without thinking too much about whether I should. It only said 'Hey'. Ben asked gently if I was all right, and I found to my surprise that I was. I had walked out of the sauna feeling relaxed and refreshed, and those feelings hadn't simply vanished when I read Taylor's text. Admittedly there was a slight sense of unease creeping in, but I was realizing that I could hold on to my happiness at the same time.

I vowed then to focus on the lovely parts of my day as much as possible, and I did it all with Ben by my side. I ate loads of good food, including some truly exceptional granary bread baked fresh by Mrs Gibson this morning. I went for a long walk around the gorgeous grounds and got to know Kate and Henry a little better. I had a nap in the middle of the afternoon. I relaxed in front of the fire, and chatted easily with the Gibsons, and ate plenty of cake. Basically I found every little bit of joy the day had to offer.

It didn't stop the texts from coming, of course. I received so many in the early afternoon, each with contradictory implications of love or hatred or concern or indifference, that I ended up locking my phone in a drawer upstairs. Unfortunately keeping Taylor's messages out of sight didn't keep them out of mind, and after a few hours it started to feel like I was waiting around to open an unwanted present. I retrieved the phone just before dinner. Ben came up with me. He didn't judge. I have continued to show him each text as it arrives, and doing so has helped a lot. It feels easier to let go of Taylor's words when I'm not the only one holding on to them.

Now I am alone for pretty much the first time today. I fancied an after-dinner mooch around the garden to further clear my head, and I told Ben I would follow him upstairs soon. I have my coat and scarf ready, and I have a torch on my . . .

Wait. Where's my phone?

I turn back down the hallway, away from the door to the garden that I had just been about to open. I retrace my footsteps. Before I can look for my phone in the loo, I see it lying on the floor. It must have fallen out of my pocket.

Naturally there is yet another text waiting for me. Another romantic one this time. **Baby! When can you call me? I miss you so much, Margot.**

I take the phone and head straight outside, now craving the fresh air even more. I've always loved the outdoors, no matter the weather or time of day. I get that from my mum. It's one of the few things we have in common, and I am still grateful to this day that she always found time to take me to the local park as a child any time I wanted to go. With a slight pang I think of how she would happily sit on the swings with me in the middle of a blizzard.

Now I see a bench not too far from the house and I cut across the dark, quiet garden to sit down. A nearby tree has been strung with solar-powered fairy lights, so there is some gentle golden light filtering down to me. It is a mostly cloudless night, and the stars are out. I am wrapped up inside my black jacket and huge woolly scarf. I have found some more peace.

But I don't *feel* peaceful.

Not quite.

Maybe I've been fooling myself all day. It can't have been that lovely and joyful if I have had to tell myself time and time again how lovely and joyful it is. Taylor's texts *have* been bothering me. Of course they have. And I still feel a bit guilty for sharing them with Ben. Especially after reading that article he showed me earlier.

It was when we went upstairs to retrieve my phone from the drawer. He had been nothing but supportive, saying that it was totally my choice how I dealt with everything, and that he was right here with me if and when I wanted to read the latest messages. It turned out there was only one.

You do realize you're not good enough to play hard to get?

I felt it like a spear through the heart.

'Why is she so horrible to me?' I asked myself aloud.

Ben crossed our room in three long strides and wrapped his arms round me. I sank into the embrace, exhausted. He held tight. Only once I pulled away, several long moments later, did he reach for his own phone. He guided me gently to sit down with him on the chaise longue.

'There's something I want to show you,' he said softly. 'It's an article I found earlier. You don't have to look at it if you're not ready.'

I was confused until I saw the title. *Fifteen Signs of Emotional* . . .

I stopped reading there. The next word was horrible. It was not a word I would ever use. Not to describe my relationship with Taylor. Not at all.

And yet I felt numb when I saw it. Ice cold.

'Would it be OK if I read some of it to you?' Ben asked.

I turned my back to him.

'There's no pressure,' he said, inching away to give me more space instead of closing in. 'But I do think it could be good for you to hear some of this. Even if some of the specifics don't resonate . . . even if some of the language isn't quite right for you . . . it could still be worth a look? Maybe I could just read the first point? See how you feel?'

I wanted to say no. I knew I *should* say no. But I felt a strange pull towards the article. It was a similar sensation to wanting to put your hand on a hot stove. I found myself nodding.

Ben spoke slowly and clearly, but it was still difficult to follow what he was saying. I only picked out a few key words and phrases. 'Belittling'. 'Putting down'. 'Undermining self-esteem'. Those all sounded very loud, even though Ben's voice was not. They made my skin burn – that same ice-cold feeling again. Freezer burn. Was it shame? Or anger?

Recognition?

I nodded again when he finished the first point, so he kept going. I felt colder and colder, and the words felt louder and louder, and I was starting to understand too many of them, full sentences and paragraphs, and the shame and the anger and the recognition made me feel sick, because they were not feelings I was supposed to feel, not right now, not about *this*, because even if some of this stuff resonated with me it was just a fluke, just the odd detail, and the rest was too much, too dramatic, too –

I stopped him suddenly at number eight.

He put the phone away without a moment's hesitation. He held my hand. I'm not sure how long for, but it was at least long enough for me to stop shaking. I only realized that was happening once it started to wear off. I stopped feeling quite so cold as well.

Eventually Ben squeezed my hand and said, 'Would you

like to have dinner up here tonight? We can say I'm not feeling well.'

I thought about it. I was comfortable where I was, settled on the firm cushions of the chaise longue, but I was also removed from the festivities downstairs.

I stood up. 'No,' I said as firmly as I could. 'I want to be downstairs. I want to keep having a nice evening.'

'OK,' Ben agreed. 'Let's go down and sit by the fire, then. We'll warm you up a bit.'

Now I sit outside in the cold, alone, staring at my phone. The screen is black. A blank rectangle. Yet I can still feel the presence of Taylor's messages, as if they are three-dimensional, all those declarations of love and hate and love again.

I can also feel Ben's article *with* me somehow. I think that's why I feel so guilty: because I keep thinking about it. Because I feel it settling into my mind. It is getting all muddled up with Taylor's messages. One of the sections that sank in the most was all about mixed signals and emotional extremes. Apparently those patterns are deliberate, designed to confuse and destabilize. The only solution is to remove yourself from it all. Otherwise you'll keep being drawn back in. Almost everyone is drawn back in – again and again, like it never ended. They keep going back. They can't help it.

Suddenly I unlock my phone. I open the messages. I click on her contact name – Taylor, with all those emoji hearts. I hover my finger over the button for a moment. And then I do it.

I block her.

*

Twenty minutes later, I am still trying not to think too much about what I just did. If I do, I'll undo it. I'll feel bad. I'll think that I've betrayed Taylor, when really all I've done is put a stop to betraying myself. I just want to be free to enjoy my Christmas. There is too much happiness and comfort for me here at the manor to let Taylor keep dragging me into the messy past.

I look up at the sky above me. The moon is quite round tonight – maybe a week or so away from being full. The stars are twinkling, just as they always are, whether we can see them or not. They have their fixed point in the sky, always. They are completely unchanged by my actions, which is a thought I find far more comforting than any silly poetic ideas I could have about their beauty. To me, the stars are just balls of gas. Pretty, twinkly balls of gas.

A fresh wind blows all around me, rustling the evergreen trees. Behind me the house is solid and reassuring. In front of me there are signs of life from the bungalow on the other side of the estate, as a golden light glows out and a figure walks back and forth past the window. The world is still turning, and I am still a part of it, even as I sit here alone. I feel connected, yet tethered to nothing. I feel light and free, and once again aware of all the loveliness life has to offer.

I want to do more than just sit here and watch, though. I want to go a step further than simply allowing myself to be carried along by the lovely things happening around me. It is time for me to *make* good things happen for myself. By myself. I think blocking Taylor has been a good start, even if an undercurrent of guilt is attempting to rise up within me. I think that instead of backing down now,

I need to continue to take control and do good things for myself.

So I'm going to make a phone call.

It isn't the boldest move in the history of the world, I know that. But it's what I want to do in this moment. There are some aspects of my past that I don't want to leave behind, and I have to take action to bring them forward with me. I have to go back and at least try to repair the friendships that I let fall by the wayside when I was with Taylor. In particular, I need to talk to Nikita. I feel empowered right now in a way that I haven't in a long time; bold enough to put myself out there and try to make things right with her; energized and brave and impulsive. Most of all, I miss her. I want to talk to her. So I'll try to make that happen.

I tap on her number and press the little green call button. No overthinking. No talking myself out of this. No worrying that she won't answer, or that she will answer and she'll lay into me for being so distant, or that she won't lay into me because she won't speak to me at all, because she doesn't want to hear from me, because I –

'Hello?'

'Nikita? Hi. You answered quickly. Wow. It's Margot. Um, Margot Murray.'

'I know. I have your number saved.'

'Oh! Good. Yeah. I have yours saved too. Obviously. I just didn't know whether . . . I thought maybe . . .' I stop and take a deep breath. 'Listen. I'm just going to jump right into this because it's so long overdue. I'm really sorry. For going quiet on you. I – I don't really know how to explain what happened. If you're willing to hear me out, I'd love to try, at any time that suits you. But if not, I need you to know that I'm so sorry. I've been a horrible friend. And I miss you. And maybe it's been too long, and we can't be close again. And maybe I'm not supposed to ask you outright if we can be friends. That's probably a bit weird. But I have to try. I miss you, Nikita, and I'm sorry, and I want to be friends again.'

There's a static-y silence.

And then: 'So where have you *been*? Jupiter? Scunthorpe? I missed you too.'

'You did?' There is so much hope in my voice. I don't try to conceal it.

'I did,' Nikita says. 'I'll cut to the chase as well, to save us wasting any more time. I've been angry with you, and sad, and confused. I wondered at first whether you might have changed your number and forgotten to give me the new one, but I didn't reach out on Instagram to ask because I was worried the answer would be yes. Or no. I wasn't sure which would be worse. If it was a no, then there had to be some other reason you weren't replying. Maybe you were just busy with work, or maybe you'd outgrown me, or your girlfriend didn't like . . .' She stops, just as her voice starts to crack a little. 'Well. I didn't know, was the point. And I was resentful about not knowing. But when I saw your name come up on my phone just now, the only thing I felt was happy. And maybe relieved. And puzzled.'

'So happiness wasn't the only feeling?' I ask, hoping my slightly cheeky tone is OK.

'I guess not,' she says, a hint of laughter in her voice. 'But since when have either of us stuck to one emotion at a time?'

'Never.' I smile to myself, even as I feel the bittersweet sting of having missed out on so much time with Nikita, who I had always considered a kindred spirit. 'I'm sorry for giving you all those extra emotions to work with, both back then and right now. I know it's a bit presumptuous to call after all this time.'

'I didn't have to answer,' she says, and I can picture her shrugging. 'I even stopped doing my laundry to get the phone. Which . . . I do need to finish hanging this all up. Can I call you back? I want those answers I've been waiting for. And I want to tell you about . . . well, everything. I'll ring back in five minutes, OK? Do you promise to answer?'

I swear that I will. I won't move from this bench until Nikita calls me back. I will wait here beneath the pretty, twinkly balls of gas lighting up the night sky, and then I will catch up with my old friend, who might just become a new friend again, and it will make me incredibly happy.

There could be no better end to a day I have fought so hard to make lovely.

16

Ellie

I step into the bedroom as soon as Ben opens the door. It's the only way to keep myself from chickening out and dodging this horrible responsibility. I have to tell him the truth *now*. Even if it is getting late. Even if today has already felt like the longest day ever.

'Is Margot here?' I ask, looking around.

'Er . . . no?' Ben says, following me into his own room. 'She's out for a walk.'

OK. That calms me down a bit. At least I don't have to find a way to pull Ben aside without Margot getting in the way. Her little evening stroll will be her last chance to enjoy the grounds, so I hope she makes the most of it. Or that she trips and twists her ankle. Whichever.

'Listen,' I say gently, 'there's something I need to tell you.'

'OK . . . ?'

'I think you should sit down for this.'

With a confused frown he obliges, perching on the end of one of the double beds. He smooths out the slightly wrinkled sheets beneath him. I notice that the duvet on the other bed is also rumpled up and that some of Margot's clothes are folded on top of the pillow. Is she not even sharing a bed with him? Fucking hell. How hasn't he spotted the signs?

I try to suppress my anger towards Margot. Now is a time for calmness. I remain standing in the middle of the room, shifting from foot to foot. Wringing my hands. I'm not exactly nailing the strong and confident yet open and approachable body language I'd been going for, but at least I'm not storming off in search of a murder weapon.

'What's this about?' Ben asks.

Oh, this is so sad. Maybe being angry would be easier than letting my heart break for the fiftieth time tonight. My poor brother really has no idea what's been going on. I have to be extremely careful about how I approach this. Sensitive and tactful. Ease into it slowly.

'Margot's a gold-digger!' I blurt out.

Silence. Ben's mouth falls slightly ajar, and his eyebrows draw together in confusion, and he . . . Oh. He stays just like that. Completely still. Like a computer buffering.

It's not a great start. I think I lost control because of how badly I've been trying to keep everything together. It's frustrating. If I was going to slip up and come out with the most shocking information right off the bat, I should have at least told him about the two-timing texts first. But I guess the gold-digging thing has been on my mind for longer, so that's what slipped out when I didn't know where to start. Now I'll have to wait for at least a little while to tell him about the cheating, because I can't deliver info like that as a one-two punch. He's already got enough to process. His facial expressions are only just coming unstuck again, his eyes starting to rove around the room as if he might find an explanation for all this madness somewhere in the air.

'I –'

'Don't say anything yet!' I hold my hands up to stop him.

'Please. I'm sorry – that came out too bluntly and I know it's overwhelming. But you deserve to know the truth. Will you hear me out? Please. There's more. There's . . . a lot. Just let me say everything I need to say, and then you can talk. OK?'

He looks unsure. Unable or unwilling to trust me. He keeps searching around for his invisible answers, looking anywhere but at my face. Eventually he seems to realize he can't work this out on his own. He nods.

I launch right into it, talking as quickly but gently as I can. 'Some of this will sound silly or irrelevant, but it all adds up to something, so bear with me. So on Monday when you two got here and took a tour of the house, I overheard you offering her money, and her accepting it right away. Now, obviously you already know that happened, but you didn't seem to know that it was weird. Maybe you're too close to it, too tied up in this dynamic that you guys have. And I'm not trying to judge you or anything. I think it's lovely that you're so generous and giving. But it's not lovely that she's so . . . taking. I don't think it's at all normal how eager she was to accept the cash and how she started listing off everything she could buy with it. I was concerned, so I started keeping an eye on her. I think she knew I was on to her, because she was really awkward and jumpy around me, and she even tried to avoid me on Tuesday. That didn't work out for long, so she started trying to charm me instead. She's been trying to charm *everyone*.'

'Right . . . ?' he says, sounding dazed.

'It's not just the charm offensive,' I say quickly, wanting to get all this out sharpish so that the horrible talking bit can come to an end and I can get on with comforting my brother. 'Listen. Margot is *very* interested in our house. Excessively so. I've seen her face light up when she sees original features and Dad's vintage pieces and "designer wallpaper". She keeps asking where everything is from and how much it cost. And she asked all about our cars on Monday. And on Tuesday she asked you for jewellery! I overheard that too. She made herself sound all flirty and playful, and she asked you to give her a new necklace since you're doing so well at work. That isn't normal. I'm sorry, but she shouldn't be using you like that, and she shouldn't be so intensely interested in your profits at work. It's . . . these are all red flags, Ben. And I understand why you haven't seen them for what they are. I totally get it. You're not looking out for them. You're in love.'

'I'm . . .'

'Shh. Please. There's just one more thing. An even worse thing. You need to hear it. You . . . she . . . Margot . . .' I feel myself running out of steam, slowing down as I approach the final horrible hurdle. Ideally I would keep this last piece of information held back for even longer, as I'm still not keen on hitting him with a double whammy, but I've realized now that it's probably best to lay it all out for him to process in one go, as awful as it will be.

'Ellie?'

Deep breath. 'I think she's cheating on you, Ben. I saw a text on her phone that was too romantic to be from a friend. I'm sorry. I'm so, so sorry.'

I look closely at his face. He's so confused. I can literally see him trying to digest all this information and work out what to do with it. I think I even spot the exact moment that he accepts his relationship is over. His face slackens, and his shoulders loosen.

And he laughs.

A proper laugh. A guffaw. Head thrown back and everything.

I stare at him. Is he deranged? Is this a trauma response? Should I be calling a doctor?

'Oh, Ellie. Oh no.' He shakes his head, trying to compose himself. 'No. Margot is not cheating on me. She's not a gold-digger.' He snorts at this, but then his smile fades. He stares at his feet. Fidgets on his bed. 'Look, I really wanted to keep this a secret – I really didn't want to embarrass myself – but, no, none of what you said is possible, because she's . . . She's . . . Oh, damn it.' He looks up. 'Margot's not really my girlfriend.'

The poor boy's denial is even worse than I expected. He's so blinded by –

Wait.

'What?!'

He nods. 'We're not actually together. She can't be dating me for my money, because she's not really dating me. We're just friends. Well, we're becoming friends. We met through work.' He cringes. 'Our whole relationship is fake.'

'I –'

I think I'd better sit down for this. I sink down on to the chaise longue and ask the only thing I can think to ask.

'*What?*'

I am still trying to process everything Ben just told me.

'So . . . Margot seemed fake . . . because she was faking a relationship with you.'

166

'Yes,' Ben confirms.

'That's why it seemed like she wasn't really in love.'

'Yes.'

'And why it felt like she was lying.'

'Yes.'

'And hiding something.'

'Yes.'

I flop backwards, rubbing my forehead.

'Yes,' Ben agrees, placing his own head in his hands.

I understand why he's so exhausted. I have been asking for a *lot* of clarification. Why did Margot joke about Ben giving her a necklace? (She was joking.) Why did Ben give Margot a 'Christmas bonus'? (It was a Christmas bonus.) I can definitely see how answering my questions has become wearing.

'Why did she . . . ?' I start, and Ben peeks at me through his fingers. He is covering up as much of his face as possible. Hiding a pink complexion and a sheepish look and . . .

Oh. I realize suddenly that he isn't tired from answering all my questions. He's embarrassed. I suppose you would be if you'd just admitted to pretending to have a girlfriend.

'You're really telling the truth, aren't you?'

'I am,' he says. 'Yes.'

I rub my forehead some more.

Ben drops his hands and stands up. 'I have proof actually.' He starts crossing the room before I can tell him I'm already convinced. He opens the top drawer of the nightstand and pulls out a jumbled pile of paper and notebooks and Post-its. 'Margot and I made notes about one another the night we got here. We wanted to make sure we had all our facts straight, so our relationship would seem believable.'

He spreads them out for me across the chaise longue. There is an A4 page dedicated to how they met. Five months ago; at a coffee shop; Margot spilling a latte all over Ben's favourite suit. This last detail has been crossed out then written in again. They must have disagreed over it. One of them didn't think the clumsy-girl meet-cute thing was realistic. I think I know which one of them it was.

'Ben.' I brush the notes to one side and look at my brother in a way that I hope conveys kindness and encouragement with minimal judgement. 'Why did you do this?'

'Ah. Yes. That's a very good question.' He sits back down at the end of his bed. Eyes trained on his feet again. Cheeks still blazing. 'Other than wanting to give Margot somewhere nice to go for Christmas . . . I suppose I was fed up of being asked when I was going to find myself a girlfriend. Every time I talk to Mum and Dad, they want to know whether I have finally found myself a nice woman to settle down with. It's always made me feel like I was lagging behind, or like I was disappointing them. I didn't want to be a let-down any more. I didn't want to field their questions for another year and give them the wrong answers yet again. It was stupid, I know. And pathetic. I just wanted to impress Mum and Dad. I wanted to live up to their idea of what I should be.'

For once in my life I am stunned into silence.

'You think I sound stupid. Stupid and pathetic and so, so stupid. I know. The whole thing was a stupid mist–'

'No!' I interrupt him. 'No. I mean, this was a pretty weird thing to do. But I get why you did it. I guess . . .' My voice fades away. Words are escaping me again. I fiddle with a green Post-it. 'I don't know. I guess I didn't realize you felt that way too.'

Ben looks up at me.

'Our parents are horribly perfect,' I say. 'I always thought I was the only one who was bothered by that. You and Kate fit so perfectly into their idea of perfection. You with your successful business in London; Kate with her beautiful sons and lawyer husband. I've always been the odd one out.'

'You've always been the cool one! You've always been above it all. Too cool to fit in, too cool to care. Mum would grill you about finding a wife, and you'd just shrug and make some clever joke about it, and she'd leave you alone. I never got how you could do that. You're just like, *this is me, deal with it.* And then I'm over here, obsessing over how I can make myself good enough for our parents.'

That hurts my heart. I tell Ben as much. I tell him that I never felt good enough either, and that I truly thought I was the only one. We say words to that same effect back and forth and back again. We lean close together, hunching over like kids telling scary stories over a campfire. We talk about some of the times in our lives that we've felt less than. Like let-downs. We end up getting a bit competitive.

'When Dad watched me in my school play, he said my performance was *adequate.*'

'Oh yeah? When I was in the Nativity, Mum said I made a *semi-believable* shepherd.'

'When I was six, they took my drawing off the fridge to make room for Kate's.'

'When *I* was six, they put my drawing straight into a locked drawer.'

'I got a B in Geography.'

'I got a *C* in *Maths*.'

'I got picked last for PE.'

'Oh, that happened to you too?'

It feels strange to talk to Ben about all this. Confusing and cathartic at the same time. Kind of funny too. It is bizarre to discover that Ben has felt just how I've felt all these years. My Golden Boy brother – as insecure and eager to prove himself as I am.

It is genuinely bending my brain. I thought I was coming up to Ben's room tonight to blow his mind with a truth he was foolishly blind to. It turns out *I* was the blind fool. I was wrong about being the only one to feel the pressure of Mum and Dad's exacting standards. I was wrong about everyone in the family fitting in except for me.

I was wrong about Margot.

I apologize to Ben now – for misreading the situation he was in with his 'girlfriend' and for thinking he was a gullible idiot.

'That's OK,' he says. 'Although you never said the idiot bit out loud.'

Oh. I grimace at him. He glares at me. We both burst out laughing. There's no confusion or apparent derangement this time. Just a shared silly giggle. Two people enjoying a joke they are both in on. Two siblings finally starting to understand one another.

I'm looking at the jumbled pile of notes again, dropping the pages on to the floor when I'm done with them. The info about Margot is especially interesting, because it confirms so much of what I already knew about her. Like, it turns out that she really is a vegetarian and has been since she was a pre-teen, and her first gig was the Pixies reunion in 2004. Her favourite holiday was Cancún; she loves indie music; she shops second-hand. Basically, everything she told me about herself at the market is true. I wasn't taken for a fool. I was right to be charmed.

I was right to like her.

I push the notes away, marking the official end of my spying. I now know that Ben's fake girlfriend is as genuine and interesting and quirky as she seemed in Chester. No further evidence required. Anything else I want to learn about Margot Murray, I want to learn by chatting to the woman herself.

There's just one last thing I don't understand.

'Ben, why is she here for Christmas instead of at home in London? Surely she would want to be with her real boyfriend for the holidays? And he can't be too pleased about her shacking up with you for the week?'

He purses his lips, hiding a smile. 'Margot doesn't have a boyfriend.'

'She . . . ? Er, yeah, she does. Taylor. I saw that text from him, remember?'

'I remember. But I promise you, Margot doesn't have a boyfriend. She's single. She had nowhere to be this Christmas, so I invited her here to pose as my girlfriend. Win-win. End of story.'

'But the text? *Taylor?*'

Ben sighs. 'Taylor is Margot's ex. They're not together any more. It isn't for me to talk about the specifics, but I can guarantee you that they are over. Taylor has been sending some texts, but Margot has been ignoring them all. She's done with her.'

She's . . .

Her?

Taylor is a . . . her?

I don't think Ben meant to say that. His eyes have opened wide and his mouth has clamped shut.

Which means it's true.

Margot likes women.

I sit calmly with this news, letting it sink in. It's strange that my gaydar failed to pick up on her, but being queer is no big revelation any more. Especially not after all tonight's surprises. I shrug.

Then I leap out of my seat and land in the pile of Post-its.

I have to see Margot right away. We have so much in common! So much to talk about. People have often joked that I get overexcited about making friends with other queer people, and I've never denied it. I need to connect. I have a million and one questions for Margot, and I clearly cannot be trusted to work any of the answers out for myself because I am the newly crowned queen of jumping to the wrong conclusions and staying there. I need help with understanding the truth. I need to hear it all from her.

I need to apologize! That's the main thing. Margot never deserved my harsh judgements and conclusion-jumping. Even if I only made my misgivings known by asking a few prying questions and dishing out some dirty looks, I need her to know how sorry I am for getting it so wrong. I spring on my toes, feeling like I've downed ten shots of espresso. Or eaten a car battery.

'I need to see her,' I tell Ben. 'I owe her a massive apology. And maybe a high-five.'

I run out of the room.

Out in the hallway I grind to a halt. I need to slow down. I need to take a moment before I go racing off into the night to find the woman I loathed up until a few minutes ago.

I need to take off my jumper, that's what I need to do. It's still damp and smelly, and I can't have that. I also need to check my hair looks OK. Maybe spritz on a little body spray. And *then* I need to race into the night to find Margot.

17

Margot

I officially have a date. Me and Nikita; early January; all-you-can-eat sushi. It's a friendship date, just like the ones we used to go on every single month before she left London.

It was amazing talking to Nik again. We've only just got off the phone now, after over an hour spent chatting non-stop. I'd expected a few awkward silences at first, but there was nothing of the sort. We just had too much to say to each other. I told Nikita about my bonkers Christmas set-up, and my new clients at work, and my break-up with Taylor. Nikita told me about her never-ending home renovations, and her recent promotion, and her brother's stint in rehab.

She also told me the best news ever: she's trying for a baby! I am so glad I'll be around for this new chapter in her life. I am so, so glad I pinned my heart to my sleeve and told her outright that I want us to be friends. She appreciated my vulnerability, she said near the end of our call. It made her feel close to me again. It made me feel strong. I knew what I wanted, and I put myself out there to ask for it. Now my little world feels a little bit lovelier – restored to how it should be, with me and Nik going off on a fancy friendship date to eat too much food and drink too many cocktails.

My phone lights up again. It vibrates insistently in my lap. I pick it up.

'Nikita?'

'Hi, hi,' she says. 'Sorry, I almost forgot to tell you something really important.'

'Oh?' I sit up taller. 'What is it?'

'I had a burrito last week.'

I gasp. '*No way*. Did you really? Did you like it?'

'I didn't dislike it!' she says proudly. 'I would even consider having another one. Or at the very least, I'd happily have some nachos and several margaritas while *you* have a burrito. You can finally take me to that Mexican place you always used to rave about. That can be the next thing after sushi?'

I grin. 'I'll hold you to that.'

'I'll count on it. OK, talk soon. Remember to send me that article you were telling me about. Do it now, before you talk yourself out of it.'

'I'm not going to –'

'Yes, you are. You were arguing against yourself even while you described it to me. *Oh, it's just a silly thing Ben showed me. It's hardly even relevant. I shouldn't blab.*' She rolls her eyes. I can't see her, but I know she's doing it. 'Seriously, Margot. Don't double back on yourself now. I was so pleased when you asked me to read through the article. I promise I'll be gentle when I tell you which details resonate with the things you've told me about Taylor over the years. OK? Send the link. Right now. While we're on the phone.'

I only consider protesting for a millisecond. Maybe a full second. Then I pull the phone away from my ear and send the article.

'Perfect. That's my bedtime reading sorted. I'm so proud of you, babe. Sushi is on me when we go out. You can buy the burritos.'

I smile again. 'I can't believe you like them now.'

'Believe it, baby. Things change.'

We say our goodnights, and then she's gone. I shake my head in disbelief. I could never get that girl to eat Mexican food with me – not after a rogue taco at Glastonbury '13 gave her food poisoning for two whole weeks. Also, she despises coriander. And she can't handle spice. Basically, Nikita eating a burrito is almost as big a lifestyle change as her trying for a baby. It's very easy for me to focus on that instead of on anything else.

I pocket my phone and finally get up off the bench. My bum has started to go a bit numb, as have my fingers. I bury my hands deep inside my coat pockets and start making my way across the garden, back towards the house. The cold hasn't bothered me over the last hour. I've felt all cosy, wrapped up inside my big jacket while the sharp wind blows around me. Now I enjoy the feeling of it lifting my hair. I like the sound of my boots crunching on the frosty grass. I am the only thing out here that is daring to move against the wind.

Suddenly the door to the house flings open – long before I'm anywhere near it. Someone comes rushing out, looking around wildly. They turn their head this way and that, their wavy hair flying.

It's Ellie.

She spots me and immediately comes hurrying across the grass. Her long coat flaps in the wind. Her hair keeps streaming all around her.

She comes to a stop. Right in front of me.

For a moment she looks as bewildered as I feel. And then her eyes meet mine, and her face softens. Her features transform into an easy smile. Her chest rises and falls, but her breathing isn't too heavy. She has calmed down. I calm down with her. To be honest, I hadn't really had enough time to work up a panic.

'Are you O–'

'I know about you and Ben.'

–K. Maybe I do have enough time to panic. She *knows*? How could she have worked it out? Did I give the game away somehow?

'Ben told me,' she explains. 'Sorry! I must seem like a madwoman right now – sprinting across the garden in the dead of night then coming out with that dramatic line. I didn't mean for it to sound like *I know what you did this winter*. I just wanted to say: I know. Ben told me all about the fake relationship, and the revision notes, and the . . . Well, I know everything. Obviously I'll keep it quiet for you both. I just thought you'd want to know that someone else knows, you know? So there's another person you can talk to properly around here. Less pressure. Because, oh *boy*, is this a big secret to keep. A real juicy one. I need to know how you're doing it. *Why* you're doing it. Not in a judgemental way, though! Sorry. Just . . . it's all a bit "wow".' She finally takes a big breath. 'Wow.'

I blink at her. She seems so excited to be in on the secret that my initial worries dissipate. This is good news. I now have one less person to lie to while I'm here – one more person I can be fully myself with.

'Surprise,' I say. 'Also, I'm a raging lesbian.'

Ellie nods. 'Nice. Me too.'

'Nice.'

We stand opposite one another in the middle of the vast moonlit garden, both of us staring openly. With the truth out, Ellie is finally seeing me for exactly who I am. It's almost like we're meeting again for the first time.

'This is brilliant,' Ellie says. 'You're like a whole new person, and I'm being introduced to you for the first time all over again.' She holds out her hand. 'I'm Ellie.'

I'm stunned. It's like she plucked the thoughts right out of my brain. I don't dwell on what that means. I don't give myself time to overthink. Instead, I reach right out and take Ellie's hand. Her skin is super soft against mine, but her handshake is pleasingly firm.

'I'm Margot.'

'It's a pleasure to meet you, Margot. Funny coincidence: I met another woman called Margot recently. Turns out she wasn't who she said she was, though.'

'Oh, is that right?' I give her hand a final squeeze, then pull away. 'I'll have you know that that other Margot has a lot in common with this Margot. The two women are practically identical. The same person even.'

Ellie arches a brow playfully. 'So you really do love the song "Frosty the Snowman"?'

I have to cast my mind back for a moment, then I remember the little white lie I told at dinner last night. 'OK, that bit was made up. But I had to pick out a favourite Christmas song to answer your mum. I need her to like me. You know, I take my duties as Ben's pretend girlfriend very seriously. It is of utmost importance that the in-laws warm to me.'

'Ah, everyone adores you already. *Despite* your taste in Christmas tunes. I mean, *"Frosty the Snowman"*? What possessed you?'

'It seemed like a neutral choice!' I protest. 'But I am very sorry for telling such a diabolical lie. I'm also sorry for telling the teeny-tiny fib about me dating your brother. Genuinely – I'm sorry for lying to you and your family.'

'Nah, you're all good. It's a great scam. I totally admire your powers of deception. Never once did I suspect the truth.' Ellie pauses. 'Well, I did think that something might be going on, but I didn't guess *this*. I thought – Ah, it's a long story. Maybe a bit intense to get into right now.'

'Intense? Wha–'

'I'll explain another time. I promise. First, I wondered if we could get to know each other a little better?' She tugs at the bottom of her coat. 'If it's not too late at night for you, d'you fancy going for a quick walk together?'

We head north towards the sunken rose garden. Ellie is walking close enough to me that our arms brush every now and then, coat fabric grazing coat fabric.

'So,' she says, 'pretending to date a man. Is it like being back in the closet?'

'Ha! No, I wouldn't say so. I can see why you'd think that, because I'm having to hide my sexuality, but no. It doesn't feel the same. Back when I was actually in the closet, I was constantly scared that someone would find out that I was gay and then my whole life would change. I guarded that secret with my life. This time the lie is for Ben's benefit. I don't have the same intense fear of being found out. I'm pretending to date him because he asked me to and because I got a nice free holiday out of the deal. The stakes are a lot lower. It feels very different.'

'Makes sense. When did you come out, then?'

'When I was nineteen.'

'Nice.' Ellie's arm brushes past mine again. 'I came out in my teens too. I was more like fourteen, fifteen. I knew I liked girls from a young age. Was always obsessed with the pretty girls in my class; got very jealous when said girls became interested in gross boys; thought all of us ladies should just skip out on the male species altogether and marry each other instead. All the classic signs really.'

'It took me a bit longer,' I say as we walk down the steps into the rose garden. I pull out my phone to use its torch, as it's pitch-dark this far away from the house. 'My friends used to go on and on about the boys they fancied, and I could see how they were attractive, so I thought I must be attracted to them too. I even kissed a few of them, and I didn't find it completely repulsive, so I took that as a sure sign of heterosexuality. When I got to uni, I joined the gay–straight alliance. I wanted to be a good ally to the LGBTQ+ community. I went to all the meetings and all the nights out. I kissed the treasurer. She was incredible. I realized I wasn't just an ally.'

Ellie snorts.

'Things with the treasurer fizzled out quickly. I wasn't ready to come out, and she wasn't willing to put up with that. I spent a good year and a half hiding who I was. I wouldn't even come out to the other people in the alliance. Looking back the closet may as well have been made of glass, because I kissed as many girls as were interested. I swore them all to secrecy and maintained that I was straight and experimenting. On my own, I spent a lot of time trying to get used to word "lesbian". Finally, in my second year at uni, I started coming out to people officially. The first person I told was my nana.'

'No way!' Ellie swats at my arm in amazement, so forcefully that she nearly knocks my phone-turned-torch right out of my hands. 'Oops, sorry. But this is crazy. The first people *I* ever came out to were *my* grandparents. Remember? I told you yesterday!'

'Of course I remember. I thought it was a crazy coincidence as well. I nearly even shouted out "same". I managed to style it out, though.'

'Oh!' Ellie grins. 'No, you did not style that out. This all makes sense now. I remember thinking you were being super weird – I just didn't know why. You immediately started talking like a malfunctioning robot after that.'

I can't help but laugh. 'I also burned my tongue on my hot chocolate.'

'Mmm. Hot liquids do tend to make robots malfunction.'

'Ha! Why can't I be a regular person around you?!' I groan. 'Seriously, I am never going to prove to you that I am *not* an awkward, clumsy idiot. I fear it's only a matter of time before I trip over and bring that huge Christmas tree in your hall crashing down with me.'

Ellie laughs – a proper full-on belly laugh. I noticed how lovely and infectious her laugh is at the market yesterday but hadn't heard it again until now. I feel like it perfectly matches my deep, almost masculine chuckle, which is something I've always been insecure about. I want to keep making Ellie laugh, so instead of trying to prove that I am not an idiot by brushing my awkwardness under the rug, I come up with yet more examples of my buffoonery over the years.

'Oh, I've done that one too,' she says when I tell her about the time I saw a friend of mine at the shops and pulled her into a bear hug before realizing that the woman in my arms was a total stranger. 'Mine was even worse. I asked the lady I was cuddling up to whether her haemorrhoids had cleared up yet.'

'*No.* I bet you think about that every time you're struggling to sleep.'

'Yep,' Ellie says. 'And every time I wipe.'

I throw my head back. 'That reminds me . . . I was once having a nosebleed and rushed into the toilets for some tissue. The first stall was unlocked and also, unfortunately, home to a middle-aged couple going at it. This was at about nine a.m. on a weekday, by the way. I was so shocked by what I was seeing that I asked whether I could reach round them and grab a bit of paper.'

'That's perverted!'

'I know right. Who does that in a grotty public toilet?'

'I meant you, you little perv! Why did you want to get into that stall with them?'

My mouth gapes open. Another deep loud laugh comes out of it. Ellie and I go on and on like this, strolling through the dainty rose garden full of elegant blooms, chuckling away like dirty old men.

'It's getting pretty late,' Ellie says.

We have settled on a bench by the lake. I've switched my phone's torch off again because it is a bit brighter here, thanks to the silver moonlight bouncing off the water and the countless stars up above. Ellie and I are sitting close together for warmth, looking out at the lake. It must be at least midnight by now. But Ellie's acknowledgement of the time doesn't prompt either of us to make a move.

We have been doing this dance for a while now. When we left the rose garden, I commented that it was late. When we walked in circles round the lake, Ellie mentioned that it was late. When we sat down on this bench with our legs touching, we both agreed that it was late. The lateness has been very well established, but at no point has there been a suggestion that we should head back inside and go to bed. We have just kept on talking about music and food and comedy and travel and life.

Now, here, there is no chatter. The quiet is comfortable. Peaceful.

Ellie turns to me. 'It's *very* late,' she says.

I face her. I wonder whether she's trying to say that she's finally had enough of hanging around in the cold with me. But I decide quickly that that's not it because she's still settled comfortably beside me, looking as if she could spend the entire night right where she is. I don't know what she *is* saying.

I look into her eyes.

I look down at her lips.

I see how round they are. How pink. How they are parted ever so slightly. I think about this perfect slice of night coming to an end. About time running out. I wonder what her lips feel like. As soft as her hands? Softer? I imagine finding out. I –

Stop. I look away quickly. Back to the water. I think about going in for a kiss and Ellie pulling away, both of us muttering apologies and then avoiding eye contact for the rest of Christmas. I think about there being no more lovely evenings like this, where we talk and talk and talk because we have so much to say to one other about nothing in particular. I think about misreading signals and being a fool and destroying a friendship before it has even really begun. I think about Ben finding out that I tried it on with his sister. I think about how one moment of impulsive unthinking stupidity could ruin everything.

Ellie presses her leg closer to mine. 'You OK?' she asks gently.

Her voice brings me back to myself. The warmth of her body soothes me. I tell myself that I did the right thing. I held back and avoided doing anything foolish. So everything is OK. Nothing is ruined.

I nod. 'I'm fine. Thank you. You're right, though. It really is getting late. Shall we call it a night?'

She is quiet for a moment. Still. I can feel her gazing at me.

Eventually she nods back.

'OK,' she says. 'It was a real pleasure to meet you tonight, Margot Murray.'

Thursday, 21 December

18

Ellie

I wake up at 6:30 in total darkness, feeling light. I hop right out of bed and turn on my salt lamp. A pinkish glow fills the room. I sort my duvet and blankets into a semi-made arrangement (in that they are all actually on the mattress where they belong), then I rummage around for a big jumper, pull it over my PJs, and head down the hall to the bathroom.

At the large round sink I splash water on to my face, brush my teeth, and beam at my reflection. I slept so soundly last night and now my head feels clearer than it has in ages. It's just so good to finally know the truth about Margot and Ben. To have spoken openly with my brother, to understand what's been going on around here, to be able to let go of the hot ball of anger inside of me. To *know the truth about Margot*.

She is *so* lovely. Now that she doesn't have to put up walls around me to protect her and Ben's secret, she is so relaxed and funny and sweet. She's smart too. I clocked that right from the start, except that I expected her to be stuffy and boring as a result. She's anything but. Margot is like a proper settled adult, but a fun one. Full of energy but not fleeting – not restless and impatient to move on to the next new thing like so many of the people I meet abroad. At least I hope she's not fleeting. I'd really like us to be friends. I think we're getting there.

From the bathroom I go straight to the living room downstairs. The smaller family one. I have to look out for this delivery from the local market for Mum, which is supposed to get here 'early', probably meaning anywhere between now and midday. Gramps should be down to join me within the hour and Mitsi will waddle in soon enough, so I don't mind hanging around here waiting. I settle down on the Chesterfield and pull my legs in towards my body, curling up all cosy.

It took a long time to warm myself up last night once I got back to my room. I had to layer up every single one of my blankets, and I strongly considered nabbing a rug or two from the floor for good measure. It was all worth it, though. I had such a blast chatting to Margot. It was as if we'd known each other for ages. We talked and talked and talked, covering an infinite range of topics from the potential origins of the universe to bagels. We had more to say about bagels. We laughed ourselves silly, and we finished each other's sentences, and we had more in common than I could ever have expected. We sat very close together. Our legs touched.

At one point I thought she was going to kiss me.

I thought I wanted her to.

It didn't happen, of course. She withdrew very suddenly, looking away from me and then promptly saying it was time for bed. Which was good. For the best. We're only just becoming friends, and I don't want to complicate that. I just got caught up in the moment. It's normal. When a gorgeous woman looks at you like she might want to kiss you, it's totally natural to feel a bit pleased about the prospect. But the feeling was fleeting. It passed. I'm not gonna get hung up on it. I have plenty of smoking-hot friends and I manage not to make out with them. Mostly. This isn't any different. Margot and I chatted a bit more about bagels on our way back to the house, and that suited me perfectly. The universe was aligned.

'Morning, kid.'

I look up to see Gramps standing in the doorway. He's wearing the chequered dressing gown and brown loafer slippers of an old man, and the mismatched fluffy socks of a teenage girl. Mitsi is right behind him, wagging her tail like crazy. I scooch over on the sofa to make room for them both.

'How did you sleep?' Gramps asks, taking his seat next to me.

'Really well, thanks. Bloody freezing, but that meant I could –'

'*Get all snuggly!*' he finishes for me. 'Absolutely. That's the best thing about winter. You know, it's still rather nippy this morning . . .'

I take the hint happily, cuddling up close. Mitsi climbs on to the sofa to stretch herself across both our laps. I sigh, contented. This is exactly where I want to be.

'Oh, the shopping is coming tomorrow, darling. I changed our delivery time to the Friday-afternoon slot. Did I not tell you?'

I stare at my mother as she busies herself making coffee in the kitchen. The answer is: no, she did not tell me. I waited for the doorbell to ring for hours before she got

189

around to mentioning it. I was a whole day early for our slot, plus change.

I tell myself that it doesn't matter. I would have been up early either way, and I loved spending the morning cuddled up on the sofa. I'm sure Mum has her reasons for changing the delivery slot, like ensuring that the food doesn't go bad before Christmas or holding out for a superior variety of Brussels sprout. Maybe she was even doing the green-grocer a favour, who has become a friend of the family over the years and who understandably gets a bit over-whelmed leading up to the holidays. Mum didn't do this just to piss me off. Probably.

'Never mind,' I say. 'Can I have two sugars in my coffee?'

She nods and reaches for the sugar jar. She also gathers up whole milk for Dad, semi-skimmed for herself, and oat milk for Kate and Henry, who both decided last year that they might occasionally be lactose intolerant. Mum does work pretty hard to keep everyone happy around here. That goes double at Christmastime. I suppose it makes sense that a few minor things would slip her mind.

I'm trying to be more patient with her than usual today. A bit more generous. After all, I was wrong about Margot. Maybe I've also judged my family a touch too harshly. I'm going to keep more of an open mind from now on. See the good in everyone, especially Mum.

'Ellie, you are breathing far too loudly. Try to breathe through your nose, darling. It's much more ladylike.'

Right. I exhale loudly. Through my mouth. I think that maybe I'll start with baby steps. Open my mind, but only a crack. I take another gulping breath in through my mouth. I exhale through my nose, as a concession.

On the counter in front of me, there's a pile of cards waiting to be posted. My mum would never leave it late with the Christmas mail, so these must be her thank you cards. She sends them out to everyone she's received a Christmas card from so far, and everyone she *expects* to receive one from before the big day. It's her signature hyper-organised way of going above and beyond with the season's greetings, and I imagine it occasionally doubles as a passive aggressive nudge to anyone who forgot to send a card. I start flicking through the large stack to distract myself, slowly reading all the names and addresses. One in particular catches my eye. I pick it up and wave it at Mum.

'Why on *earth* are you *posting* a card to *Stan?*'

'Why not?' she asks. 'Help me with these coffees.'

I put down the stamped envelope addressed to the groundskeepers' bungalow in our garden and pick up two mugs instead. But I do not let the matter go.

'He lives here. Right here. Why would you post him his card?'

'I post everyone their card. Why should he be any different?'

'Because he lives here – I just said that.' I pause to take a quick breath in. I remember to take it through my nose. 'Wouldn't it make more sense to hand-deliver it instead?'

Mum ignores me as she walks into the dining room and passes out coffees. I try to work out why I'm even pissed off about this when I'm supposed to be in a good mood today. I think it's just too silly a notion for me to accept, posting a *second* seasonal card into a post-box so that a postman can take it to the post office to be given to another postman who will drive it all around Cheshire before bringing it right back here to this estate.

I crane my neck to look through the archway and into the hall. Nobody's in there. Margot and Ben must not be awake yet. I put down the mugs I'm holding. Go back to the kitchen to get my own coffee. Glare at the stupid card on the counter.

When I get back into the dining room, Mum says the most unexpected thing: 'You're right.'

'I am?'

'We should take that thank you card over to the bunga-low ourselves.'

'*We* should?'

'Yes. Of course. The whole family will go together to deliver it personally, like you said. I'm sure that when Stan's Christmas card finally arrives it will be addressed to all of us, so we should deliver our thank you as a group. Right now.'

Just like that, everyone is roped into an all-family expe-dition to the bottom of our garden. It takes well over an hour to get everyone together: awake and fed and wrapped up in bulky winter coats. At 10:45 we are all finally gathered in the foyer ready to go.

'I need a wee,' says Dylan.

Kate takes him.

'I need a wee,' says Dominic, as soon as they get back.

Kate heads back to the toilet.

Dad goes upstairs to change his tweed jacket.

Ben squats in front of a mirror, fiddling with his hair.

Mum fills her purse with snacks for the twins 'just in case'.

I stand in the open doorway the whole time, exchanging

192

sideways looks with Gramps. Explorers heading off to Antarctica for a year would make fewer preparations for their journey than this lot.

Kate runs off for a quick wee of her own.

Dylan and Dominic swap shoes.

Then finally we're off.

There are only two people not joining us on our voyage today. Henry, who predictably has to work, and Margot, who unfortunately has to do the same.

'One of her top clients has a social media crisis,' Ben told me half an hour ago, when we thought we were about to leave the house any second. 'An MP used taxpayers' money to buy his girlfriend some lingerie – which he probably would have got away with if his wife hadn't found out. Early this morning, she went online and shared her husband's credit card statements to expose him. Margot's client is named five times, right there in black and white. It's not their fault obviously – they were only selling undies, which an underwear company is wont to do – but you know how it goes. Angry public equals angry posts. It has only blown up like this because the company is called "Mistress Lingerie". It's quite unfortunate. Margot has to do damage control on Twitter so that the brand's reputation can survive long enough for this all to happen again in six months' time.'

I'd smirked. I was fairly sure I was hearing Margot's words being parroted by Ben.

Now we trek across the fields as a group. Mum and Dad hold hands; Kate holds on to Dylan and Dominic; Ben holds the premature thank you card; I hold a bottle of red from our wine cellar as an extra gift; Grandpa holds

Mitsi's leash. Mitsi is not attached to it. Dad told her to sit and stay before we left, and she obeyed. If I gave the same command, she'd probably do a backflip and land in the next county, but there you go. Gramps had already picked up the leash in anticipation of Mitsi joining us and didn't put it down again. He walks an invisible dog all the way to the furthest field and up the slight hill that leads to the groundskeeper's bungalow.

Mum knocks on the front door and steps back, all of us arranged behind her. We look like a gang of deranged carollers. The Von Trapp Family presents 'Jingle Bells'.

The door only opens a crack. A puff of wiry ginger hair appears and then half a face. A brown eye widens at us, smoothing out many of the deep wrinkles surrounding it – evidence of a life spent smiling, although the man's mouth is set in a straight line right now.

'It's you,' he says breathlessly. 'All of you. Hello. I'm sorry. Hi. I'm so sorry. I know I should have –'

'Stanley!' Mum interrupts him with cheer. 'Merry Christmas! We're just here to give you a card. I trust you received your Christmas card already? We thought we'd deliver our thank you in person this year, along with some wine. It is Malbec you like, isn't it? I hope it is – otherwise we've been giving you the wrong gift for decades. Now, as usual, don't think for a *second* about giving us anything. Please. There's nothing to apologize for! This is just a small token of our appreciation for you, and for all the wonderful work you do for us. And . . . Merry Christmas!'

The rest of us stand around and add our Christmas greetings. From what we can see of half Stan's face, he still looks bewildered. He doesn't open the door any further.

Part of me wishes we really were here to sing carols, so we could cover up the awkward silence with music.

'Thank you,' Stan says at last. 'Can I . . . help you with anything else?'

I see Mum's face screw up the tiniest bit, before she quickly recovers her saintly half-smile and shakes her head at him. I can understand her reaction. Stan is usually very friendly – he always has a bright smile for everyone, and he whistles to himself while he's working around the grounds. This caginess is highly unusual. He hasn't even said Merry Christmas yet.

'Merry Christmas!' he says suddenly. 'Um, thank you for coming. Sorry for . . . Well, I'd invite you in, but . . .'

'Oh, that's OK,' Mum says. 'We're very busy. Must get on. But enjoy the wine!'

I take my cue and step forward, holding out the bottle. Ben brings forward the card. Stan opens his door another few millimetres and reaches out. As I hand over the gift, I see through the crack and into the bungalow. And suddenly Stan's behaviour makes sense. There is a woman's light purple coat hanging on a peg in the hall. He clearly has company in there. For the first time in . . . forever. That's a big deal. I can see why he wouldn't want his employers and their entire family to disturb him right now.

I take a big step backwards as soon as he's got hold of the wine. I hope he and his mystery guest enjoy it very much. I shepherd everyone away from his home as quickly and efficiently as I can.

'Thank you!' he calls after us. 'Thank you so much. And you're welcome for your Christmas card; it's on its way in the post!'

*

Somewhere on the short walk home, Mum took over shepherding duties from me. Now that we're back inside, she ushers everyone straight into the dining room.

'Since we're all already together, shall we use the time for a family tradition?'

She is making a show of sounding casual, as if she is thinking this up on the spot, but it's obvious that a) she's about to suggest we make gingerbread houses and b) she cooked up this idea a while ago. Literally. The whole ground floor smells warm and spicy, so she has clearly already put the big slabs of biscuit in the oven to bake. Must have done it before we left to deliver the card, since the biggest pieces can take over an hour to bake.

Sure enough, she soon produces a tray loaded up with the freshly baked biscuits, several bowls of icing in different colours, piping bags with assorted nozzles, sprinkles, candy canes, mini pretzels and, of course, gumdrops. Grandpa takes one look and excuses himself for a nap. I accept defeat and flop down into a chair.

You'd think that decorating gingerbread houses would be a fun family activity. It certainly looks that way in Christmas films. In reality, in this family, it is wildly stressful. All the houses have to be structurally sound to please Dad and decorated perfectly to please Mum. Each design has to be distinct to avoid monotony. Yet nothing *too* distinct is welcome, as gingerbread houses have a traditional look that should be adhered to.

All in all, the process takes hours. When it's finally over, the prettiest house is displayed prominently and the ugliest ones are eaten first.

I get to work with a grimace. Margot is so lucky that she's managed to wriggle her way out of this. My grimace turns into a smile as she pops into my head. It's funny to imagine what I would have thought of her disappearing to work if this had happened yesterday instead of today. I'd probably have assumed she was lying about the client emergency so that she didn't have to bother with Ben or the family for a while, instead using the free time to plot clever new ways to extract extra cash from my brother. Now I just wish she'd come down for a minute to say hello. That's one thing that has stayed the same since yesterday: I'm still waiting around hoping to catch a quick glimpse of Margot Murray.

I start plastering red royal icing on to my gingerbread roof. Opposite me, Ben has selected the colour blue. Our eyes meet over the biscuit building blocks, and he puffs out his cheeks in playful irritation. I'm surprised, because I'd always thought that everyone else somehow enjoyed this festive torture session, and then I'm not surprised, because now I understand that Ben also feels the pressure of perfection in every little thing we do. I respond to him by rolling my eyes, and he gives me a knowing smirk. It feels good. Really good. Like being part of a team.

I keep holding eye contact and reach for a gumdrop. I place it, very carefully, in the middle of my roof. Just off-centre.

Ben's eyes widen. Slowly he takes a small handful of sprinkles and pours them on to his roof. Freestyle.

I fashion some more gumdrops into a zigzag.

He puts a pretzel in one of his windows.

I bar my door with candy canes.

He removes his chimney.

I nibble a wall.

We keep making silly mistakes. We laugh silently and egg each other on and make a bigger mess than either of our hyperactive five-year-old nephews. We end up with two miniature houses that look as if they've been through a few natural disasters, and which will definitely be eaten first.

We are delighted with ourselves.

The rest of the day passes uneventfully and with very few sightings of Margot. She ate lunch in her room with Ben, then continued working right through the afternoon. Even Henry came downstairs before she did, showing Kate a bunch of work emails for them to share a pained laugh over and then racing into the garden to play with the twins for a while. He got another 'urgent' phone call about an hour later, and promptly disappeared again with a defeated sigh and a quick kiss on Kate's cheek.

Both the workaholics were present at dinner. We ate mushroom risotto, and I amused myself by watching Margot and Ben put on their performance as lovers. He placed a protective arm round her shoulders; she batted her eyelashes at him; I stifled my laughter. It was fun being in on the lie. I felt like part of something. Margot's eyes met mine a few times with a little twinkle of mischief lighting them up.

Then she was gone again. Off to do some reading with Ben after a long day. I took myself off to bed as well, incredibly early by my standards. I watched some crap TV on my tablet. I played some good music on my headphones. I texted a few friends and ignored their replies. I'm still lying here hours later, spread out like a starfish and fully dressed. Today has been a pretty brilliant day, but it feels unfinished somehow. Like there's more for me to do.

I sit up and swing my legs out of bed, picking up a jacket from the floor. Who cares if it's nearly midnight now, I need some fresh air. A nice walk will get rid of the last of my energy. I zip up my jacket and creep down the stairs. Slip out through the back door. Wander across the garden. I'm not heading anywhere in particular – not until I see the lake. I feel a strong pull towards the water. Where the moonlight is brightest. The scenery is beautiful. The air fresh.

When I arrive, Margot is already sitting on the bench.

19

Margot

I only came out here to see the stars. I was having trouble switching off after a hectic day spent cleaning up social media messes, and I knew I wasn't going to get to sleep any time soon. I figured I may as well go for a walk – get outside for a bit, stretch my legs, see the midnight sky. I still wasn't having soppy poetic thoughts about the stars, but I will admit that I was drawn to their beauty. I wandered outside in pursuit of celestial objects and light exercise.

Instead, I found her.

Well, actually, I suppose she found me: sitting on this bench, already bored of walking around in the cold on my own. Ellie rounded the lake and emerged from the navy darkness just as I was getting ready to head back inside. I immediately shifted along the bench to make room. Now she sits down beside me, and our legs fall together, touching right away. The hush of midnight settles around us. We both gaze out at the water.

It's like we've been transported back to last night. Everything is exactly as it was. Even the stars seem to be shining in all the same places, appearing in all the same gaps between all the same wispy clouds.

'I heard you got your knickers in a twist today,' Ellie says.

I grin. She's all the same too.

'I'll have you know that *my* knickers didn't cause any problems,' I say. 'It was someone else's dirty laundry being aired in public, thank you very much.'

'I'm well aware,' Ellie says. 'I've been retweeting the angry posts all day.'

'Oh, so *you're* the reason I've been staring at a screen for ten hours?'

She holds up her hands. 'I didn't *write* the tweets.'

I glare at her. She winks at me. I don't think anyone has actually winked at me before. For some reason it makes my stomach flip. Just the tiniest bit. Like a roly-poly.

'Ten hours, though,' Ellie says. 'That's a long old slog for a holiday day.'

'Yep.'

'I missed ya.'

My stomach flips again. Like a triple backflip with two full twists and a pike.

'Missed you too.'

'Good.' Her eyes glint. 'You're not working tomorrow?'

'I shouldn't be,' I say. 'Hey, maybe we could make that pie together? Like a practice run to get the recipe right. I think the ingredients should be here by the afternoon – your mum told me she'd changed the delivery day.'

Ellie seems to grind her teeth for a moment, but somehow grins at the same time. The bizarre face she's making still makes my stomach flip. I really hope she'll say –

'Yes! We should definitely make that pie. Yes.'

'Fantastic,' I say. 'It's a . . . Well, that's tomorrow sorted. What did I miss today?'

She fills me in, painting a vivid picture of cross-garden hiking and gingerbread ruining. I tell her a bit more about my work day, and the book I'm reading, and the non-crap TV I've been watching since she's in need of recommendations.

'And I'm sure you've seen it already, but *Feel Good* is a wonderful show. And *Crashing* is definitely worth revisiting too. Ooh, and *Russian Doll* is –'

'I've seen that one!' Ellie says. '*Russian Doll*. Incredible. I love Natasha Lyonne.'

'Me too. She's phenomenal.'

'And gorgeous. And hilarious. And a full-on lesbian icon.'

'Absolutely,' I say. 'I was so shocked when I found out she's straight.'

'Same! I thought she was queer for the longest time.'

I nod vigorously. 'Right? She just plays lesbian characters so well.'

'And so often,' Ellie says. 'You know, when I first saw *But I'm a Cheerleader* on DVD, I decided that Natasha was gonna fall in love with me one day.'

'Don't,' I laugh. 'I watched the film at a gay–straight alliance night, and I was *convinced* we'd be together. She'd see past my hormonal acne and fall for the real me.'

'Oh, I thought she'd like my spots. And my braces. They showed off my youth.'

'Ha! We were both so deluded.'

'Speak for yourself.' Ellie fluffs up her hair. 'I reckon I'm still in with a chance.'

I laugh and nudge her with my elbow. She elbows back harder. I try to knock her hand away from her hair to stop her posturing. She grabs my arm before I get there. I keep pressing forward, and she keeps pushing back, and I breathe: 'I knew it.'

'You knew what?' she giggles.

'I knew we'd be similar. Same celebrity crush, same play-fighting techniques, same stubborn refusal to back down.' I drive forward. 'No wonder I liked you right away.'

She stares at me, giggles subsiding, chest rising and falling in sync with mine.

Then she seems to stop breathing.

She lets go of my arm.

She turns away.

I'm left with my hands held up in a fighting stance, a leftover smile spread across my face. I know that I look like an idiot, but I can't seem to move. I can't understand what's going on.

'Ellie . . . ?'

'I have to come clean,' she says. 'I can't let you be so nice to me. Telling me how you liked me immediately. It isn't fair. It wasn't . . . Well, the feeling is mutual now. That's why I have to tell you this.' She releases her breath. 'I hated you.'

Oh. My hands finally drop into my lap.

'Not hated. Sorry. That's a strong word. A *wrong* word. I didn't like you, that's what it was. When I first met you, I disliked you.'

'Thanks for the clarification,' I say dully.

'Sorry. I know. I'm sorry. It's all coming out wrong. I just want to own up to how stupid and misguided I was before, instead of sweeping it under the rug and pretending I was never at fault. You deserve better than that. You deserve an apology. I like you now, Margot, and I feel so bad about not liking you before yesterday.'

I stare out at the lake. This was still going on *yesterday*?

How was I so oblivious? I knew I sensed some light irritation from Ellie when I first got here, but I never suspected full-blown hatred, or even dislike. I thought we were getting on well once I stopped being so awkward around her. I even thought we had a real connection when we went out to the market. I was an idiot.

At least things can't get any worse from here.

'I thought you were a gold-digger.'

Right. Things can always get worse.

'I'm sorry,' she says. 'Obviously I don't think that any more, and even when I didn't like you, I irritatingly kind of liked you, like at the market on Tuesday. And now that I know you, I really think you're great, and I'm already shocked that I could have ever thought anything bad about you. I don't want to upset you with this. I just have to be honest. We said last night that it was like we'd just met for the first time, right? That means we have to start fresh. Properly. No weird guilty secrets. No hiding. I want everything to be out in the open between us.'

I kind of like that. In the tiny part of me that doesn't feel dark and cold, I like that.

'Do you want to know why?' Ellie asks carefully. 'I did have my reasons for thinking that, but they are obviously all stupid reasons that would boggle the brain of any actually reasonable person. I don't want to boggle you. I'm sure you're already overwhelmed enough as it is. So it's your call. If you want me to explain, I will; if you want me to shut up, I will. I can explain some other time as well – this isn't a one-time offer. Whatever you need right now is what we'll do.'

I like that too. I like that Ellie is putting the ball in my court, that she is offering up the whole truth if I want to hear it. I'm not used to that. I'm used to begging for the truth and still being denied it, to finding clear evidence of some wrongdoing yet still being told I'm imagining things. Ellie is doing the opposite: coming clean even though I had no idea that there was even a truth to uncover in the first place. I like that a lot.

I do not, however, like the idea of being boggled. 'Explanations later. Apologies now.'

'Of course,' Ellie says immediately. 'Yes. I'm sorry. I just got the stupid gold-digger idea into my head, and then it stuck. It got bigger and bigger the more I thought about it, so I thought about it more, and it got bigger still. But that's no excuse. Sorry. I'm not trying to justify myself. I was wrong and harsh and nasty, and I'm sorry. I'm so sorry. And also, for a change of pace, I'm sorry.'

The corners of my mouth start twitching upwards.

'Sorry for making a joke there,' she adds. 'I don't get to joke. I'm sorry.'

I press my lips together to flatten my smile. But the light has already been let in. I don't feel dark and cold any more. There is still some residual shock and upset, of course, and plenty of confusion, but I don't feel the need to squash any of it down. I trust that Ellie would accept and welcome any of my emotions. She would help me work through them all in any way she could.

I shift a little closer to her on the bench. More than anything else, I feel at peace. Everything is officially out in the open, and nothing awful has happened as a result. I am simply sitting on a bench beside a lake in the misty silver moonlight with Ellie very close to me and no secrets left hanging between us and her leg pressed up against mine. For once I don't feel the need to disappear into ruminations. I simply allow myself to exist in this weird, wonderful moment.

'I forgive you,' I say at last. 'Done. Fin.'

'Really?'

'Really. I can understand a fixation. I'm a massive over-thinker too.'

Ellie looks me square in the eyes, considering this. Finally she says, 'No. I'm not an overthinker. I'm not letting myself off the hook that easily. Truth is, I don't think *enough*. I get one thought into my head and that's it – I don't consider any other possibilities. If anything, I'm an underthinker.'

'OK.' I hold her gaze. 'I guess we balance out, then.'

I'm not sure whether that is a romantic line. I'm not even sure whether this is a romantic moment that calls for romantic lines. I don't dwell on it. I have been put in the driver's seat tonight and given licence to feel all my feelings, so it's about time I act on them. Without wasting another second on thinking, I lean even closer to Ellie.

The space between us has all but vanished. Our bodies are connected. Her breath is on my cheek. Slowly I look from her almond eyes to her full lips. As I glance back up, she looks down at my mouth, questioning. I close my eyes. My hand finds hers in the blind darkness. Her skin feels even softer tonight. I stroke her palm, then I tangle our fingers together. I breathe in her citrussy scent. I keep leaning closer.

I kiss her.

Her lips are even softer than her hands, and they are

parting to welcome me. We kiss gently, softly, softer than her hands and her lips and the flutter in my chest. Ellie tastes sweet. Ellie tastes salty. Ellie tastes like I could taste her for the rest of my life and never tire of it. I kiss her deeper. She kisses me harder. We meld together as one, and my whole body fills with electricity, the flutter in my chest spreading out into every inch of me.

When we come up for air again, we barely break apart. Our fingers remain tangled, our breathing is synced. Her leg is still pressing against me, now in between my legs. Neither of us moves a muscle. It's just like the first time we touched – when Ellie caught me as I fell, and we stood suspended in space for what felt like an eternity.

Our faces are so close together that all I can really see is her eyes. Her pupils are dilated in the low light of midnight, the black almost entirely taking over the green. Right in the corner of her eye, there is a reflection of glittering starlight. I suspect that if I pulled away and looked out at the stars, I would finally be able to see what all the poets of the world have been describing all this time. I would see how the stars stud the darkness like brilliant diamonds, or like scattered moondust, or like the twinkling lights of an unexplored city in the sky.

But I don't look.

I don't take my eyes off Ellie.

The thousands of beautiful stars hanging in the velvet sky can get on without me. I'd rather look at this tiny glint of silver in Ellie's eyes. The freckles dotted across the bridge of her nose are almost like constellations anyway. I finally move again, bringing my free hand up to her face to trace my fingers across those scattered markings.

She laughs softly. 'It really has been a pleasure to meet you.'

'The pleasure's all mine,' I say, and then I kiss her again, and again, and again.

20

Margot

I am on cloud nine right now. I'm practically skipping up the stairs towards my room, barely feeling the wooden steps beneath my feet because I am floating on an actual cloud of pure happiness.

Before I levitate all the way to the top floor, I chance a quick look over my shoulder. Ellie is still standing outside her bedroom, half in and half out of the door, looking over her own shoulder at me. My heart flutters yet again as our eyes meet. I don't mind that she has spotted me skipping slash floating slash levitating up the stairs in a state of pure bliss. It's not like I have to worry about her realizing that I'm attracted to her any more, and I don't feel the need to hide my joy from her either. She seems just as happy as I am. Moments ago, when we shared our last lingering kiss goodnight, I felt her lips curling up into a smile while they were still held against mine. Now I beam at her, silently mouth the word 'goodnight', and twirl around to continue my jubilant ascent up the stairs.

Tonight has been perfect. Ellie and I spent well over an hour snuggled up together on our bench, kissing and talking and laughing. Mostly kissing. We have had our first kiss and probably our hundredth. I could have had a hundred more, but eventually it got so cold out that all our fingers and toes had gone numb, and we'd had to call it a night. We hurried across the dark frosty gardens hand in hand, and breathed synchronized sighs of relief once we were back in the warmth of the house.

'We should be careful,' Ellie whispered, 'now that we're in here.'

We untangled ourselves. I walked her up to her room. She immediately discarded her own advice and pressed me up against her bedroom door, kissing me deeply. Her fingertips got lost in my hair and my heart beat against her chest. Then she pulled back, whispered the word 'careful', and guided me over to the staircase. She brought one arm behind her back and extended the other to direct me upstairs in an exaggerated display of good manners.

'Once again,' she said, 'it has been an utter delight to make your acquaintance these past few evenings.' She hesitated, dropping the formalities. 'See ya tomorrow for pie?'

I grinned. 'It's a date.'

Now my fluffy cloud of happiness carries me along the top-floor corridor. I feel like a starry-eyed teenager again, but for once I'm only experiencing the good bits: skipping along home after my first-ever Proper Snog; marvelling at all these brand-new Big Feelings; already daydreaming about the next time I'll see The Girl. All I need to complete the picture is a friend to share my precious gossip with. Luckily I have one, and he's waiting for me in the room that we've already been using for chatty, giggly sleepovers.

Ben is the perfect person to talk to. He is exactly the friend I want to share my joy with *and* he's the one that Ellie and I agreed must know about the kiss pronto. I will fill him in on this wonderful thing that happened, and he will be safe in the knowledge that nothing weird went on behind his back, and we will natter away into the early hours of the morning about how romance really is real. I'll be sensitive, of course. I won't tell Ben how it felt when his little sister nibbled on my lower lip, for instance. And I'll make sure he knows that our fake relationship is still a go. I will still be posing as his girlfriend for the remainder of the holidays, and Ellie and I will be very discreet about anything that might come next. We'll be *careful.* I am not going to let Ben down or embarrass him in front of his family. So long as I make all of that very clear, and am open with him from the start, and edit out some of the racier details of my evening, everything will be golden.

I start humming to myself as I near our room – a sweet little tune to match the lyrics stuck in my head, about stars shining for you and everything you do. As the melody joins with the lyrics, I realize it's an old Coldplay song. Ben's favourite band. Maybe the two of us will play a few of their songs as we chat. I so can't wait. I sweep open the door, already grinning and brimming with lovely news.

I find all the lights switched off.

The room is completely silent.

Except for Ben's snoring.

It looks like my planned sleepover is going to include a lot of actual sleeping, then. Even if I wanted to wake Ben up, I'm not sure I could muster up the volume of three wailing alarms going off simultaneously. I definitely can't make that much noise without disturbing everyone else in the house. It's gone 1:00 a.m. now. I'm going to have to leave it.

Ah, well. I guess it was always a longshot that Ben would

still be awake up here, considering that he was barely conscious when I crept into bed at midnight last night. I'll just chat to him in the morning instead. That's no big deal. I can bask in the glow of my post-kiss euphoria all on my own.

I drift across the room and snuggle up under the covers, not bothering to brush my teeth or put my retainer in first. There's just too much daydreaming to be done before sweet dreams take me. I lie still, remembering the softness of hands and the smell of lemons and the taste of salt and sugar. I smile into the velvet darkness, my mind filled with memories and music.

Sleep arrives swiftly and easily. When I fall, the feeling of Ellie's soft warm lips are still lingering on mine.

Friday, 22 December

21

Ellie

This morning I was smiling as soon as I opened my eyes. Maybe even before that. I had this lovely tingle on my lips. I even thought for a moment that I could still taste Margot's mouth lingering there – until I brushed my teeth and could only taste spearmint.

Now I'm sitting down for breakfast with Gramps. No cake this morning – we're being sensible and having porridge with caramelized apples and cinnamon. The sugar content is probably about the same. I set our two steaming bowlfuls down and sprinkle some extra brown sugar on top. Grandpa pours on lashings of maple syrup.

Right away, I want to spill the beans about what happened last night. I can already feel myself smiling again as I think about it. Me and Margot Murray. Margot Murray and me. That has got to be the surprise of the century. This time two days ago, I was still plotting to have her expelled from the house. Now I'm desperate to see her again. Her shiny dark hair; her smooth flawless skin; her sultry catlike eyes. And, oh God, her legs. Her *lips*.

That first kiss. It was otherworldly. Totally unlike anything I've ever experienced in my life. The very second Margot's lips touched mine, my body came alive. Reacted to her immediately and intensely. It was like being on fire.

Yet, at the same time, I felt safe. Grounded. Almost like I was arriving home. The fire was uncontrollable and controlled. I was shockingly alive and peacefully calm all at once. It was a brand-new sensation, and it stayed with me throughout the rest of our night together, throughout every kiss we shared. It is still with me now. It is making it very hard not to think about Margot non-stop, and that in turn is making it very hard not to tell Grandpa Mo all about her.

But I know I mustn't get too carried away about something so new. It's only been one night. Only some kisses. However electrifying it all felt, I've got to resist the instinct to jump to conclusions. I don't know what will happen next, and I can't go around talking about Margot as if it's a sure thing that there are more kisses in our future.

Really, I can't go around talking about Margot at all. I have to protect Ben's lie. The two of us are closer now. I have connected with him more in these last few days than I ever have before. It has helped a lot knowing that he also struggles under the pressure of Mum and Dad's strict standards of perfection. It's helped even more knowing that he's willing to put a sugar-coated middle finger up to them in the form of gingerbread-related tomfoolery – the silliest and loveliest form of sibling bonding I've experienced since we were toddlers fashioning Santa-style beards out of bubble bath. But the thing that's helped most of all is something I thought I already knew. He's a loser. Truly. It turns out that nothing can humanize your Golden Boy brother quite like finding out that he feels the need to fake a relationship with a near stranger for the duration of Christmas so that nobody discovers he's still single in his mid-thirties. I find the lengths he has gone to strangely endearing. Of course I'll keep his secret safe.

All of that means no gossiping with Gramps. I dig my spoon into my porridge and focus on poking around for chunks of apple. I'm relieved when he starts telling me about the latest drama at the retirement home.

'. . . and Ann is always forgetting to charge her mobility scooter's battery. Gerald tries to remind her about it, but I think he forgets quite how often he is jogging her memory, and the nagging irritates her so much that she "forgets" out of principle. *I* think that the nurses should take over and do it for her, but that's just me. I'm not a Jailbird, so I don't get a say. Anyhow. Yesterday afternoon, Ann's scooter broke down again. Directly outside Gerald's bedroom window. He hit the roof, shouting about the scooter being a safety hazard and a huge danger and an unnecessary risk. Finally he lodged a formal complaint against Ann for obstructing his view of the garden.' Grandpa shakes his head. 'I'm worried that the fallout might finally spell the end of our little group.'

'It won't,' I promise him. 'Ann lodged a formal complaint against Gerald last month for cheating at bridge, and you're all still friends.'

'That's true. Although that complaint turned out to be a false alarm. Gerald wasn't signalling anything to his bridge partner in that game – he just had an itchy nose. Oh, do you know who *has* been cheating, though? Sandra! Not at bridge – at Scrabble. She's been pocketing letters to use at her own convenience. It doesn't make any sense. She only ever plays low-scoring four-letter words.'

'Imagine how bad she'd be if she played by the rules.'

'I dread to think. She's lucky that Ann and Gerald's drama has eclipsed her scandal. Everyone will forget about the whole thing by the time Christmas is over, and Sandra will be free to illegally lose at Scrabble in peace.' He tuts. 'Old people, eh? You know, they attempted to organize a Secret Santa gift exchange this year, but they've all lost their slips of paper and can't recall who they were supposed to buy a present for. It's a disaster. That place falls apart without my youthful influence.'

I purse my lips and make a sarcastic mmm-ing sound. Really, I'm loving every second of this. It's great to see Grandpa chatting and laughing. Being his usual self. He doesn't say a thing about ponies running wild on the estate or Grandma joining us for breakfast any minute now. Of course he doesn't. Everything is perfect today.

In the main kitchen I start unloading a small army of shopping bags. The delivery from the market arrived a few minutes ago – seven hours before it was due. Mum must have changed the timeslot again. Grandpa did his usual vanishing act when the bell rang, so I'm left putting away all the shopping on my own, but I don't mind. Means I get first dibs on any goodies I come across. Like the peppermint creams that I'm currently hiding at the back of a high-up cupboard, out of reach of my nephews' sticky fingers. Or the jar of chocolate spread that I dig into right away with a tablespoon, licking at the hazelnutty goodness like it's a chocolate lollipop.

I pull colourful heritage carrots out of a particularly heavy bag, along with some fat parsnips. I stow them away at the bottom of the fridge. Put a huge packet of vegan soya mince into the freezer. Marmite into the cupboard. Whenever I come across something that I think might be a potential pie ingredient, I leave it out on the counter ready for me and Margot to cook with this afternoon. At least I know we have that 'date' in our future. I'm sure she called it a date last night. I'm sure she was only half joking.

The sound of running footsteps echoes from the hallway. A moment later, Dylan races into the kitchen, closely followed by Dominic, then Mitsi.

'Any chocolate, Auntie Ellie?'

'Yeah! What he said! Any chocolate?'

Mitsi lets out a hearty bark.

Kate sprints into the kitchen. 'No chocolate! It's barely nine. Breakfast first.'

I slip the chocolate spread and accompanying spoon behind my back. Kate notices and mouths a quick 'thank you' at me, before grabbing hold of a box of Weetabix and a stack of bowls then shepherding her boys and the dog out of the kitchen again. A full minute later, Henry strolls along after them all.

After that Dad comes in. He grumbles a single word: 'Weetabix'. I point him towards Kate and the others in the dining room. He shuffles out with a low grunt in place of a thank you. Not really a morning person, my dad.

'Morning, my love!' Mum chirps as she passes him in the hallway. 'And good morning, Ellie, darling. Thank you for getting the shopping in.'

'No problem,' I say, putting a carton of almond milk into the fridge.

Mum opens the fridge door as soon as I close it and

takes the carton back out. She also picks up the cranberry sauce I'd just put in there, and the carrots and parsnips.

'None of this is fridge stuff,' she says brightly. 'Not until it's opened or peeled.' She deposits everything in the walk-in pantry, then gets to work on relocating everything else I just put away.

I leave her to it. This sort of thing from her would usually irritate me to no end, but not any more. Not if I don't let it. I eat another spoonful of chocolate spread and take a deep breath in through my nose.

'OK, Mum. Tell me where to put things, and that's where I'll put them.'

She beams at me, and her shoulders drop down a whole inch. I hadn't even noticed they were tense. Together we move around the kitchen, and within minutes all the shopping is tidied away, the bags balled up and placed in a bigger bag in the pantry. Mum looks around, satisfied. I see her gaze hang momentarily on the pie ingredients standing out on the counter, but she says nothing and makes no move to eliminate the mess.

I'm glad. It makes me so happy seeing everything laid out ready for me and Margot to make our pie. Hanging out with her again will be so much fun. I can't bloody wait.

Luckily I don't have to. Margot is here.

She looks amazing, as per usual. Her hair is even glossier than I remember it, hanging loose down to her shoulders. Her naturally tanned skin is radiant. She's wearing her chequered suit trousers from the night she arrived here, dressed down with a black long-sleeved top and trainers. I feel a burst of heat looking at her.

Then I remember I shouldn't be looking at her. Not like

this, at least. Not right now. Mum is standing here with us. The rest of my family is in the next room. I have to be careful for Ben's sake. And also for mine. If I go feeling bursts of hot passion and shooting openly hungry looks at the woman that everyone believes is my brother's girlfriend, I'm not gonna come off too well. I am still trying to impress my family, after all. I need to make *some* effort to avoid drama.

Besides, I think I kind of like having a secret. I'm pretty sure that's where some of this heat is coming from. The excitement of having something to hide. The warm glow of keeping it close to my chest. Right now, this brilliant budding thing only exists between me and Margot. Whether she's already told Ben yet is irrelevant. This is ours. Only ours. As we stand at opposite ends of the kitchen, in the open and in hiding, I feel it held between us. Special and delicate and safe. Electrifying.

I slide my gaze away, giving Margot a small smile as I do so. I ask casually how she slept and involve Mum in the conversation too. Mum asks where Ben is, saving me the trouble. Turns out he's upstairs doing some work. It's his turn to sort out a crisis today — some dispute between his business partner, Ramesh, and one of their diamond suppliers. He'll be stuck on the phone for a while.

'So . . . we could make that pie, Ellie?' Margot performs a casual shrug. 'I have some time to kill.'

I battle to keep myself from grinning. *It's a date,* right now! And she is such a fabulous actress. I nod and gesture for her to come on in.

'Would you like an extra pair of hands?' Mum asks before Margot even takes a step forward. 'I wouldn't want you girls to spend hours making your own Christmas dinner. I could get the pastry started for you . . . ?'

I battle to keep myself from scowling. Must remember to be patient. Mum is not trying to be annoying and stick her oar in where it doesn't belong.

Margot steps in, approaching the kitchen island. 'We're fine, thanks, Mrs G. You're already doing more than enough this Christmas. Ellie and I wanted to do this one small thing for you so that you can take a well-deserved break. You go and enjoy your breakfast. Please. We'll be just fine on our own.'

'Oh, Margot,' Mum sighs. 'You are so very lovely.'

I couldn't agree more. Margot Murray is so very lovely. And she's all mine for the morning. It's such a wonderful thought that I'm not even pissed off when Mum stops on her way out of the kitchen to double-check that she can't lend us a hand. Margot dispatches her effortlessly yet again, and then finally: we're alone.

I smile at her. The sort of smile I'd wanted to give her when she arrived in the doorway. The sort of smile I woke up with on my face this morning.

She grins back. 'Hi.'

'Hi.'

We just stand there smiling at each other. Flashes of last night play in my mind. My leg pressing close to hers. My fingertips caught in her hair. Her lower lip between my teeth.

'So,' she says at last, 'we should probably . . .'

'Yes! Yes, we should.' I pull myself back into the present moment – the one where Margot and I are doing a spot of cosy Christmas baking. 'I got everything out ready.' I slide across the island to where all the ingredients are laid out. Hold out an arm to gesture at them with a proud flourish. 'It's all here.'

'Umm.' Margot sucks in her cheeks, laughter dancing in her eyes. 'No.'

'No?'

'None of these ingredients are for the pie. Not one.'

'Not . . . one?'

She's already disappeared into the pantry. She comes out holding the carrots and parsnips. 'For sweetness,' she explains. From the freezer she pulls out the soya mince. 'For a meaty texture.' She takes Marmite out of a cupboard. 'For a meaty flavour.'

She also gathers up onions, garlic, veggie stock, butter, and flour. Bog-standard, all-purpose *flour*. How did I miss that out? Now that the correct ingredients are laid out in front of me, it all seems so obvious. What sort of pie did I think we were going to make with tofu, kale, Brussels sprouts, and pre-made filo pastry?

Margot is clearly wondering the same thing. Her eyes are still shining with amusement, and finally she lets her laughter out. I can't help but join in. Together we dissolve into a helpless fit of giggles.

'Oh,' I say, holding my side. 'This is going to be a disaster, isn't it?'

'Yep,' she says gleefully. 'Let's jump in.'

22

Margot

Both our aprons are covered in flour and our scruffy patch-work pastry case is in the oven before I work up the nerve to say what I need to say.

'Ellie,' I whisper, so that the other Gibsons in the room next door don't overhear, 'I haven't told Ben about our kiss yet.'

She puts down the peeler she's been attacking the pars-nips with. I can feel her eyes on me. I pretend I can't and keep looking down at the multicoloured carrots I'm chopping.

'I'm not trying to hide anything or sneak around,' I say. 'I know how important it is that we're as open and honest as possible. It's just that he was asleep when I got back up to our room last night, and then I was in the shower when he woke up this morning, and by the time I came out of the bathroom, he was already on the phone to Ramesh. I'm sorry. I'll tell him as soon as I can.'

I finally glance at Ellie. Her face has lit up.

'What?' I ask.

'Well,' she says in a low voice, 'maybe we don't have to tell him yet?' She sneaks round to my side of the kitchen island. 'I'm not trying to sneak around either, but I kind of like the idea of this thing just being . . . *ours*. Just for a little while. We could stay in our own private bubble together. Only if you're comfortable with that, of course. We can tell Ben everything right away if that's what you'd prefer. I know that's what we agreed on. I just . . . I think the most important openness is between me and you, Margot. That's really what I meant last night. As long as we're honest with each other, I think we're peachy. We could keep this kind of . . . sealed. Just while we're getting to know each another. Like, maybe we give ourselves one more night before we talk to Ben? Have a proper first date first?'

'Oh yeah?' I say levelly, as if my stomach isn't swarming with butterflies right now. 'Are you asking me on a date?'

'Yep,' she answers immediately. She is the picture of confidence, standing tall with her chest puffed out and her chin raised, but I do notice some colour rising to her cheeks. 'I want to take you on an official first date. Midnight tonight? Our bench?'

Our bench. I had also been thinking of the seat next to the lake as somehow belonging to the two of us. The butterflies in my stomach go wild upon hearing that Ellie has been thinking the same. Still, I continue to feign cool composure.

'I could see if I'm available tonight. I might be able to shuffle around my sleep schedule for you.' I pause. 'Yep. I'm free. I'll see you at midnight for our official first date.'

The blind-baked pastry comes out of the oven looking predictably slapdash. There are a few gaps threatening to open up at the bottom, and I'm not convinced they will survive the filling being added to the pie. Ellie and I push on with cooking the soya mince filling regardless.

'Here.' I lean round her to add another spoonful of Marmite to the saucepan on the stove. 'This is the secret ingredient. It'll make the pie salty and rich.'

She nods approvingly and stirs the pot. I remain where I am, despite the fact that my task at the stove is complete. My chest is pressed lightly against Ellie's shoulder blades. She leans back against me, pressing closer. I rest my chin on her shoulder.

Her body suddenly becomes rigid. She peels away from me and spins round to look at the open door.

'I'm sorry,' I say automatically, collecting myself and backing away from the stove. 'Sorry.' I take the jar of Marmite and hurry off to the pantry to put it away.

Ellie follows me in. She swings the door shut behind her, throwing the pantry into darkness. She takes hold of my forearms.

'*I'm* sorry,' she whispers. 'I shouldn't have pulled away like that. It's not because I don't like being close to you. I like that. A lot. It's just –'

'We have to be careful. I know. I was being reckless.'

'Recklessness suits you,' she breathes, taking a micro-step closer to me in the tiny space. My back comes up against a shelf. Ellie runs her hands up and down my arms.

I feel warmth, and I lean close to her. I bring my mouth to her shoulder. My lips graze the soft exposed skin. Slowly, slowly I move across to her neck. My mouth nearly forms a kiss, but I hold back. I trail barely parted lips up along the full length of her neck, and up to her jawline, up to her earlobe.

Then I pause. Dampened lips on her ear. A slow exhale.

'Careful,' I whisper.

And I move round her to get out of the pantry.

On the stove the saucepan is bubbling and spitting, and I race across the kitchen to turn down the heat.

'Oh, it smells *divine* in here,' Mrs Gibson says, bouncing into the kitchen a minute after the pie goes into the oven. She sniffs at the air, breathing in garlic, onion, rosemary and thyme. 'You've done a fantastic job by the smell of things. You must be exhausted now. Go and have a clean-up and a sit-down, both of you. I'll do the washing-up. Now don't try to argue with me, Margot, I insist. I'm just about to wash up the breakfast things anyway. We all had a very long, slow breakfast, so I'm glad of something to do. Off you go, girls. They're about to start watching *Home Alone* in the other room, so you're just in time to join them. I'll stay in here and take your pie out of the oven when it's done. Go!'

We go. We haven't got much choice in the matter. With a quick shared look, Ellie and I agree that we'll join the others for the film.

The great hall has been set up for the screening with all the thick curtains drawn and a huge projector screen pulled down over the opposite wall. The fire is lit and the Christmas tree lights are twinkling. Wordlessly Ellie and I take our seats on two different sofas. Mr Gibson is in his armchair near the fire; Kate is on the middle sofa with Henry, who is engrossed in his phone; Dylan and Dominic are splayed out on their fronts on the patterned rug.

After the boys make a failed bid for some chocolatey movie snacks, Kate presses play on the projector.

I make sure to keep my eyes on the screen the whole

time. If I start flicking little looks at Ellie, I don't think I'll be able to stop. I'll wind up watching her instead of the film. Up until last night, I'd been doing a good job of keeping my attraction to her hidden, but now that we've kissed and that attraction isn't a solely abstract concept, I think I'll struggle to be so subtle.

Around about the time Kevin McAllister starts setting up his booby traps on screen, Ben shuffles into the room and sits down on the sofa with me. I whisper hello and try to work out whether I should be cuddling up to him. It's pretty dark in here, so who's going to see us? Who would I be putting on the act for? I decide against a cuddle and elect instead to hold his hand. He gives me a grateful squeeze as I slip my hand into his. He pulls away again when his phone starts vibrating in his pocket. By the time the *Home Alone* villains are breaking into Kevin's house and falling victim to his booby traps, Ben has left the room again.

As the credits roll and the orchestral score fills the room, Ellie and I both stand up.

'We have to check on our pie,' she tells nobody in particular.

Our pie might have been better left unchecked. Mrs Gibson has removed it from the oven and left it cooling on a wire rack, and somewhere between then and now the soggy bottom has collapsed and leaked filling all over the rack. There is a puddle of mince and gravy spreading across the kitchen counter. I dip a finger into it and discover that it tastes even worse than it looks. The excessive amounts of Marmite and stock I added have made the filling way too salty, and the abundance of mushy carrots and parsnips has made it too sweet. The balance of flavours is non-existent, and to top it all off it tastes burnt.

'Oh no.' I cover my face with my hands. 'I guess now is the time to admit that I've never made a pie before. I knew all the ingredients for this one because I've read the recipe a million times. I've read loads of recipes actually. I kind of have a cookbook addiction, but I never quite get round to the . . . cooking. I'm just too busy with work. I pore over all these recipes, and I memorize all these delicious-sounding ingredients, but I've never really needed to look at the quantities bit. Or the method. Ever.' I peek through my fingers. 'I'm sorry.'

Ellie cackles. 'You seemed so confident before. I was totally intimidated.' She licks some burnt gunk off a spoon. 'It's a good thing we practised ahead of Christmas Day. I'll look up an actual method for us to follow next time. And maybe we'll let Mum make the pastry for us. Attempt number two on Sunday? Christmas Eve?'

I let my hands drop. 'Isn't that cutting it a bit fine?'

Ellie shrugs. 'The practice round is always a flop. We'll be making the real deal on Sunday, so it will work. It has to. And besides –' she looks me up and down in challenge – 'I thought you were being reckless today?'

A sudden, wild impulse flares within me to prove her right by sliding our mess of a pie out of the way and picking her up, putting her on the counter, and kissing her right here in the middle of the kitchen.

I ignore it.

Obviously.

Instead, I make myself busy dumping the failed pie into the bin and cleaning up the mess it has left behind. Once the wire rack and pie dish are washed up and the counter is gleaming, I say loudly, 'I'd better check in on my workaholic boyfriend.'

Ellie nods her understanding.

I leave her with a whispered promise to see her tonight.

Upstairs in our room, Ben is still on a work call. I had half expected to find him flustered and skittish, but he seems totally in control. He is clear, direct and confident as he tells whoever is on the other end of the line that the issue needs to be resolved within twenty-four hours or else another supplier will be found. He then calls somebody else and promises that everything is sorted and the stock is secured. Finally he rings Ramesh and says that everything is very much not sorted, but that they are well on their way to a solution and there's nothing more to be done today.

As soon as he hangs up, he flops down on to his bed, limbs sprawling.

'I'm so sorry,' he tells me, looking up at the ceiling. 'I didn't mean to get so sucked into all that work stuff. It's this big boring mess with one of our suppliers. Don't worry, it's nothing that you as our marketing pro need to worry about. There was just a tiny communication error a week ago, and today a huge amount of communication was required to get everything back on track. Ramesh was too busy with clients to deal with it all on his own, and he and this supplier don't get on too well at the best of times. I had to step in. I'm sorry. I never would have left you to fend for yourself with my family all morning unless it was really urgent.'

'It's totally fine,' I assure him. 'We all have to work sometimes. *I* had to work yesterday, and you wouldn't let me apologize for that. And honestly I had a lovely morning. I made a terrible pie with your sister, and I watched a brilliant film with your family. You have nothing to be sorry for.'

Ben sighs. 'Thanks for saying that. I just hate it when I have to be the glued-to-his-phone, married-to-the-job kind of guy. It's so not my style. You can save that for the Henrys of the world.'

'Ugh,' I scoff, as if I haven't been that guy myself many times. 'You know he was texting the whole way through *Home Alone*.'

'I bet he was.' Ben turns on to his side to face me, where I'm sitting cross-legged on my bed. 'It's only a matter of time before he gets called away for work. I'm amazed it hasn't happened already.'

'Is he really working?' I ask carefully. 'That much?'

'He's really working. I think we've all wondered at one point or another whether he might be . . . doing something else. But he's a good guy. Kate's best friend works at his law firm, and any time she works late, he's there even later. He eats dinner at his desk and only takes breaks to call Kate and the boys. The man is just genuinely obsessed with his job. I guess he has to be, as a top solicitor. You mark my words: he'll be out of this house and back in the office before Christmas Day rolls round.'

When Ben and I head downstairs for lunch, Henry is frantically replying to emails on his phone, a plate of food left untouched in front of him. We're having a 'grazing lunch' today, as Mrs Gibson calls it. The dining table has been laden with crusty loaves of bread, cheeses, red grapes, salad and jars of chutney for everybody to help themselves to whenever they fancy. I don't see Ellie during the drop-in meal, only Ben, Henry and one of the twin boys, though I'm not sure which one.

After lunch, Ben and I volunteer to take Mitsi for her afternoon walk. She takes us around the whole estate, sniffing desperately at the ground the whole way. At the neat little bungalow on the outskirts of the grounds, she sniffs so hard I think her nostrils will grow wide enough to inhale the entire building. She only runs back home again when she sees Dylan and Dominic racing around in the garden near the kitchen.

The rest of the day is very relaxed. Ben and I go for a swim and an extended stay in the sauna; we sit by the fire reading our books; we eat a dinner that is way too big and way too rich and that I enjoy way too much considering both of the above. Ellie and I only interact to tell everyone about how disastrous our pie-making mission was. We bounce off one another to infuse as much comedy into the tragic tale as we can, and I feel so close to her but also a million miles away and the whole thing makes me miss her in a way that almost hurts. Somehow I think she feels the same way. After that the two of us avoid talking or making prolonged eye contact. When dinner is over, she heads off somewhere with her grandfather, and I help Mrs Gibson with the washing-up.

Before I know it, I'm back upstairs with Ben, getting settled down in our separate beds for an evening of chatting nonsense. I've got changed into my fluffy PJs even though I know I'll be getting changed out of them again soon, and Ben has put his blue cotton pyjama set on. We turn off the lights, leaving just one lamp on in the centre of the room for a gentle glow, and pull the duvet covers up to our chins.

Now that we're settling into sleepover mode, part of me feels tempted to tell Ben all the goss about Ellie. But another much bigger part of me wants to keep the secret to myself. It *is* nice being in a private bubble with her, keeping our tentative new connection safe and unsullied for a while. Plus, I've been doing such a good job of not overthinking this whole thing. I mustn't ruin that by over-talking about it.

'Do you want to talk about it now?' Ben asks.

'Huh?!'

'The stuff with Taylor,' he says. 'The other day you said you might want to talk some more about it later. I'm not trying to push you into anything, but if you do want to talk, I'm right here.'

I relax. For a crazy moment there I thought Ben somehow knew about me and Ellie. But of course he doesn't. In fact, he doesn't know about a lot of things. Between both of us having work crises in the last forty-eight hours and our sleep schedules drifting ever further apart, I still haven't told Ben about blocking Taylor's phone number and reconnecting with Nikita. Leaving out the key Ellie-centric detail, I fill Ben in on all my recent good news.

'I genuinely haven't thought about Taylor all day,' I finish proudly. 'A huge weight is starting to lift, and a lot of that is thanks to you. Talking everything through the other night was really good for me. I mean, it was tricky and upsetting obviously, but it also kind of made me see a bigger picture that had somehow passed me by. And thinking about that article of yours has also been . . . helping. Slowly. I might read some more of it some time. Just out of interest, you know.' I shift slightly on the bed. 'Anyway. Maybe the best thing of all has been being here at the manor. Since I stepped away from my life in London, I've stopped obsessing about the past so much. From the moment I got into the car with you on our way here, I've thought about Taylor less and less. So. Yeah. Thank you, Just Ben Gibson.'

'Oh, Margot – that's amazing. You're so welcome. I'm so happy for you, and I'm so, so proud of you. If I've helped you even a little bit, then I'm pleased. Remember you can still talk to me any time you need. You know that?'

'I do. Thank you.' I smile at my friend across the room. My best friend, probably. Then I clap my hands together loudly. 'Right. Enough about me. Enough about my ex. Let's talk about you, my current lover.'

Ben laughs. He says there isn't much to say, and then promptly proceeds to say plenty. He tells me more about his boring businessy stuff (his words, not mine, but also probably mine); and the new song he is considering for one of his morning alarms; and how many litres of water he drank today; and the unusually loud music he heard coming from the groundskeeper's bungalow earlier; and the battered old soft toy in the shape of a horse that he found abandoned in the garden, which neither of the twins will claim as their own. Finally he returns to one of his favourite topics of conversation: the ongoing mystery surrounding Mitsi's pregnancy.

'I just don't get it,' he says through a yawn. 'There are no other dogs anywhere nearby. She must be the next Virgin Mary.'

'If she is, the timing is spot on.'

'Ha, ha,' Ben says, stifling another yawn. He's clearly too tired for actual laughter. 'It's a real puzzle, isn't it? Hmm. I don't think I can work it all out tonight. I have to . . . Hmm. G'night then, Margot.'

'Goodnight,' I say, but he's already snoring. Within minutes he'll be so deep into sleep that nothing could wake him – not even Mitsi climbing up on to his bed, sitting down right on top of him and telling him, in perfect human English, the full truth behind her Immaculate Conception.

Very soon, I will be free to slip out of my PJs and into something a little less comfortable. The clock is about to strike midnight, and at last my day can properly begin.

23

Ellie

Contrary to how I'd normally prepare for a date, tonight I've put on extra underwear. A thermal vest and two pairs of thick socks. Also a huge woolly jumper, a fleece-lined denim jacket, and an extra coat on top of all that. The cold weather can do its worst – it will not be cutting my date with Margot short tonight.

At least it's dry outside. The snow we had at the start of the week is long gone. Whichever omnipotent force it is that controls the weather must have realized it was the festive period and that a seasonally appropriate white Christmas was inching dangerously close. Couldn't have that. No doubt the snow will be back in abundance in early March, just when everyone assumes winter is drawing to a close. Tonight, three sleeps away from Christmas Day, the night sky is completely cloudless.

I've done a bit more than don some extra undies to get ready for this date. I've brought a pile of blankets down from my room for us to snuggle up under, as well as a string of battery-operated fairy lights, which I've hung across the back of our bench. I also brought wireless speakers for us to play some music from and brewed up some mulled wine for the two of us to share via matching Thermoses.

I'm hoping it's enough.

Also hoping it's not too much.

Could really do with Goldilocks dropping by to confirm it's just right.

I fidget on the hard slats of the wooden bench. I suppose it's possible that I'm out of practice at this sort of thing. Over the last few years, my courting technique has largely consisted of buying a lady a round of drinks in the club and asking her flat out whether she likes women. Of course I've gone on to take plenty of those ladies out for a quick bite to eat or another night out on the town. Some of them have even wound up coming home with me, all the way to England for Christmas. But I wouldn't say I've pulled out all the stops for anyone. It's been a very long time since I put any real thought into planning a proper date.

I really hope I don't screw it up.

At quarter past twelve, Margot walks along the edge of the lake towards me. She's bundled up inside her black overcoat and matching beanie, with a huge scarf wound around her neck.

'Sorry I'm a bit late,' she says. 'This is . . . wow.'

She's close enough now that I can make out her face properly, and there is pure joy lighting up her eyes. She's taking in my messy stack of frayed blankets and the dim fairy lights as if they're a work of art at the Louvre. She's holding herself even taller than usual, truly looking pleased as punch with what I've put together for her. It is impossible to me that I ever thought this woman was anything less than lovely, when she exudes such warm enthusiastic energy.

'Seriously, wow.'

I brush off the compliment like it's no biggie and stand up to say hello. Give her a kiss on either cheek. Place my hand on the small of her back to guide her to her seat. Pass her the thickest blanket and a Thermos. Pick up the speakers.

'What would you like to listen to?' I squint at the tiny buttons. 'Any album or any artist you'd like. I've left it totally up to you.'

'What I'd like is for you to sit down.' She pats the space beside her and lifts up the corner of her blanket. 'Relax, Ellie. Please. This is all amazing: beautiful but super low-key. It's perfect for me. You can officially consider me swept off my feet, and now you can get off yours too.'

I sit down next to her and pull half the thick blanket across my lap. I'd hoped that we'd end up sharing. Already our legs are touching under the quilt.

'*Now* will you tell me what you want to listen to?' I ask. 'I've connected my Spotify to the speakers, so you can pick anything you like. I've already downloaded a few albums from artists I know you listen to. Got some indie rock with jangly guitars, loud drums and depressed-sounding singers, and then some softer, sweeter stuff from solo artists. Assuming you'd rather the soft stuff?'

'Nah, bring on the loud drums. We're far enough away from the house that no one will hear the music, right? Put some rock on. This is the perfect evening – there's no need to ruin it by playing sappy love songs.'

I melt into relaxation and press play on the Stone Roses' self-titled album. Then I shoot Margot a sideways look.

'Are you sure you're not a fan of sappy love songs?'

I ask in an innocent voice. 'Cos I'm certain I heard you humming something earlier in the kitchen? It definitely sounded like a love song to me . . . ?'

She slowly lowers the Thermos she'd just brought to her mouth. 'Did you hear me humming a Coldplay song?'

'Yes. Yes, I did hear you humming a Coldplay song. That famously underground independent band. "Yellow", was it? I don't think anyone could argue that that isn't a love song, Margot. If there is a person who could make that case, I'd wager that they also think the sky is pink and honeydew is the best kind of melon.'

'Funny,' she says drily. 'Would this person also think that what you're doing right now is a good way to woo their date?'

'Are you not wooed?! I thought you'd be ready to sere-nade me with another Coldplay song by now?' I get an elbow jabbed into my side for that, but I'm not put off. 'You know, they are my brother's favourite band of all time. Maybe you two *are* meant for one another. Should I be stepping aside?'

'No. Don't step aside.' Margot pauses with her elbow still digging into my waist. 'You need to stick around, because I have nothing better to do at midnight on a random Wednesday in the middle of nowhere than to sit on a bench in the cold with you.'

'Aww. Are *you* wooing *me*?'

'Maybe. We'll have to see how tonight goes.'

'I'll drink to that.' I pick up my Thermos of wine and clink it against hers. 'To our first official date, to expert-level flirting, and to taking it slow and seeing how it goes.'

*

Margot's fingers grip my hair to pull me closer to her, her mouth hot and insistent on mine. I press back against her with equal force, parting her lips and slipping my tongue into her mouth. The fire that started inside me last night is reignited. Blazing hotter than ever. I slide my hand down her back and feel it arch in response. She tangles her fingers deeper into my waves. Our tongues clash and wrestle. We burn together.

Just when I'm about to be consumed fully by the flames, I pull away. It takes an amount of willpower that I didn't know I possessed. It does not please Margot, who lets out a soft moan of disappointment.

'Sorry. If I keep kissing you now, I won't be able to stop. And we're meant to . . . umm . . . we're meant to be . . .'

'Talking?' Margot supplies breathily. 'How's that going for you?'

Not very well clearly. Maybe my willpower is not as strong as it seemed. Talking can always wait. I lean in again, eyes closed, searching blindly for Margot's mouth.

I can't find it. I blink open my eyes to see that she's leaned away from me. She untangles her hands from my hair. Pulls the blanket up over her body. Picks up her Thermos and takes a long, slow sip.

'You're right. We should talk. A first date is for getting to know one another. We might have jumped the gun by getting under the covers already.'

Damn it. Why couldn't I have kept my mouth closed and pressed against hers? Why am I willing to forgo making out with this gorgeous woman so we can chat instead? What has Margot Murray done to me in such a short space of time that has so drastically transformed my approach to dating?

With a little sigh, I grab the speakers and turn down the volume. Guitars, bass and drums fade into the background. Can't say I'd been paying too much attention to the music anyway.

'Where do we start then? I'm Ellie Gibson, I work in the travel and tourism industry, and my favourite colour is green?'

'Ooh, green is my favourite too. But no. We already know each other fairly well, don't we? Sixty seconds ago, I was getting myself acquainted with your tonsils. So I say we jump straight into the meaty stuff.' She pauses. 'Why did you think I was a gold-digger?'

Oh. I blink. I blush. I wonder whether I could change the subject with another kiss.

But Margot deserves an explanation about this. I promised that I'd give her one last night. I made a big fuss about being honest with each other.

I take a long drink of mulled wine before I get started. It is still steaming hot inside the Thermos. I left some slices of orange bobbing around in there, so the fruity flavour is intense, balancing perfectly with the warm spices. Have to say, I nailed the catering for this date. The fairy lights are twinkling away as well, some of their light bouncing off the lake's rippling surface. And we are warm and snug under the soft blanket. All in all, the atmosphere is perfect for telling my date why I loathed her at first sight.

'Do you want the full story?' I ask.

'Yep. I've got all night. Give me the fullest version of the full story.'

'OK. I guess there's a prologue, then, in that I was already in a horrible mood before you got here on Monday. I was jet-lagged and hungover, and I'm always on edge when I first get back home. And then you arrived, and the very first thing you did was hit my pregnant dog with your car door.'

'We weren't exactly set up for a meet-cute, were we?'

'No. But that doesn't excuse my gold-digger delusion. That was like a whole year's worth of crazy from me. Basically, I thought . . . Right. I'm just going to fire off all my pieces of "evidence" and you're not going to laugh at me. OK?'

She laughs at every point I make.

'I accepted a Christmas bonus from my employer,' she says. 'Someone arrest me!'

And: '*Everyone* has lied about "washing their hair" to get out of social plans.'

And: 'The fanciest meal Ben's treated me to was pesto pasta in our room upstairs.'

Then finally: 'What did you think I was spending his money *on* anyway? Five-quid dresses from the charity shop and the odd bit of cheese?'

I shrug helplessly. 'You do like fancy wine.'

She concedes my point with a long drink from her Thermos, her laughter finally subsiding. I go in for another sip of liquid courage myself.

'I know I was ridiculous,' I say in a level voice. 'The truth is, I was trying to find fault in you from the start. I always do that. I see the worst in people as soon as we meet, so that they can't surprise me later. It's not like I have trust issues exactly, just that I have some . . . issues . . . trusting people.' I pause. 'It's all because of a girl, of course. My first proper girlfriend – the one I had in my teens. She was a few years older than me. A few years more than a few years really. She lied about everything. Her job, where she lived, her relationship with her parents. She once told me that her friend had died in a tragic car accident, then a month later we bumped into said friend at the post office. The lies were constant. By the time we broke up, years later, I didn't know what was real any more. I couldn't take anyone's word for anything.'

Margot has slipped her hand on top of mine, and she gives it a gentle squeeze. 'I know a thing or two about crappy ex-girlfriends.'

'Do you want to tell me a thing or two about them?'

She is quiet for a long time. Only the low rock music breaks the silence. And then: 'Yes,' she says. 'My most recent ex was a liar, as well. Taylor. She lied in a more subtle way. Like, she would claim that an argument never happened even though it just did, and she would scream at me that she wasn't raising her voice like I'd suggested. It's called gaslighting. Apparently. I don't know. I've been googling it a bit over the last few days, after I had a long talk with Ben about that whole relationship. I'm starting to realize that Taylor was sort of manipulative. I think she might have treated me kind of poorly.'

I think there's a much stronger word than 'poor' for Taylor's behaviour, but Margot doesn't seem ready for further analysis and I don't want to push her.

'I've blocked her number now,' she says proudly. 'It's finally over. I'm free.'

We both drink to that. I'm glad that I opted for mulled wine over hot chocolate. We keep drinking in comfortable silence. I'm also glad that I filled our Thermoses to the brim.

'Your turn for soul baring again,' Margot says after a while.

'OK. I love my grandpa.'

She tilts her head. I can almost hear her asking whether that's really a soul-baring statement, but she doesn't say a word. She understands the depth of this love. She might even be able to tell there's already a lump in my throat.

'He's my best friend in the entire world,' I say thickly. 'And he's fading. He's getting old, and he's getting confused. I don't know how much longer he'll be himself for. I want to be around for every day he has left – or as many of them as humanly possible. I'm hoping to get a job here at the hotel, and then I'll spend every spare moment with him. Playing music from his childhood. Looking at old photo albums. Trying to laugh. That's the future I want for us, but I can already see all the sadness that's going to taint it all. It's like every bit of heartache to come is laid out right in front of me. Just waiting. I've already started the process of grieving him.'

Margot squeezes my hand again. 'I understand. It all gets so muddled, doesn't it? You want the time you have left together to be full of joy, but it's impossible to avoid the sadness when you're so aware that the happiness is finite.'

I sigh. That's exactly it. 'Was it the same with your nana?'

'In a way,' Margot says softly. 'I definitely had the internal battle of joy and sadness, but the bittersweet feeling wasn't quite so drawn out. Nana's illness was the opposite of your grandpa's. It was sudden. She was happy and healthy, and she'd just celebrated her eighty-fifth birthday. The diagnosis of stage-four breast cancer came out of nowhere. She refused treatment and got on with her life, baking cakes and going for short walks to feed the ducks whenever she had the energy. Within two months she was gone. I hardly had the chance to register what was happening before it was time to say goodbye. Sometimes I wish so hard for a few extra weeks with her that my heart aches. The rest of the time I'm glad that she didn't have to suffer for long. The only constant through it all is my love for her. I still love her, just as fiercely as when she was alive.'

'I feel the same about my grandma,' I say. 'I never stopped loving her for a second – not even when I was furious with her for dying so suddenly of a heart attack and leaving us too soon.'

Margot nods. 'There's no good way to lose someone you care about. I guess the best thing any of us can do is keep holding on to our loved ones after they're gone and hold even tighter to the people who are still with us.'

We sit with our hands interlocked, now tucked under the blanket. Margot rests her head on my shoulder. I rest my head on her head. Several minutes pass, with the only sounds being the whisper of the wind and a quiet guitar playing.

Finally I say: 'I'm sorry, Margot. I'm sorry that I ever thought anything remotely negative about you. I like you so much. And that's the end of the story. Fin.'

'I like you too. I have all along. That's my full story: I fancied you from the start.'

Warmth spreads out in my chest. I like Margot's story. She'll have to retell it often. I also like her knowing mine. It is a bit dark and contains some confusing twists and lapses in logic, but I trust her not to hold any of that against me.

I let the warm sensation flourish in my chest, and I drop

a kiss on to Margot's head. Get a mouthful of wool from her beanie. Do the same again. I smile to myself, and somehow I know that Margot is smiling as well. I reach down and pull the beanie over her ears for her, and she leans into my hand, then shifts slightly to plant a soft slow kiss on my lips. Sure enough, I can feel her smiling. And I know with absolute certainty that I got our first date just right.

Saturday, 23 December

24

Margot

The weak light of a winter sunrise is filtering into the dining hall when Ben and I come downstairs for breakfast. In the window seat at the far end of the room, Ellie is sitting cross-legged with Mitsi on her lap. She is scratching the dog behind her ears with one hand, scrolling through her phone with the other, and just generally looking as laid-back and effortlessly beautiful as she always does.

The other people in the room are behaving less typically. Dylan and Dominic are sitting in silence at the table with their heads bowed, eating their bowls of Weetabix without complaint or demands for chocolate. A few seats away, Kate has her back turned to them. She is talking to Henry in a cold, controlled whisper, and he in turn is ignoring his buzzing mobile to hiss back at her.

Eventually they reach some sort of impasse and lapse into a stony silence. Kate glares at her husband until he stands up and clears his throat.

'OK, everyone. Boys. I'm afraid I have some bad news. I've been called into the office. There's an urgent case that needs my attention and I can't work on it remotely. I'll be leaving in the next hour, and I won't be back until late tomorrow night. That's Christmas Eve, boys. Don't worry, I'll be back before Santa visits. I'm sorry I'm being pulled away, everyone. I'll see you all on Christmas Day.'

Kate puts on a tight smile. 'He has no choice but to go. Even though it's a Saturday. During the holidays. Two days before Christmas.' Her nostrils flare but she fights to keep her smile in place. 'Isn't his boss such a Scrooge?'

Ben manages a polite laugh in response. I echo him, and Ellie echoes me. Dylan and Dominic remain quiet and start sniffling a bit, pushing their soggy Weetabix around in their bowls without eating any. Kate widens her smile for their benefit and narrows her eyes for Henry's. She ends up looking quite demented. The rest of us pretend not to notice.

My gaze slides across the room and back to Ellie. I find her already looking at me. She tilts her head to one side in a barely perceptible movement, and I understand the question she's asking me at once. *Should we still tell Ben about us?*

Late last night, we decided it was time to tell him the truth about us going on a date. We didn't want to wait until after Christmas because that felt like too long to keep it a secret, and we didn't want to tell him on Christmas Eve or Christmas Day just in case he was at all upset and the conversation put a dampener on festivities. Today was our only option. Our plan was to 'feel out' the situation this morning – see how Ben's mood was, try to work out the best time to tell him – and then sit him down together to talk everything out. Now it is clear that the situation at the manor is tense, the mood in the room is awkward, and the timing could not be worse for a big revelation.

I give Ellie a small shake of my head, *no*, and she gives me an even smaller nod of agreement. We will not be telling Ben today.

I'm not too worried about it, really. We'll wind up telling him early tomorrow morning – which hardly counts as Christmas *Eve* given the time of day – and I'm sure he'll be fine about it. I really think he'll be happy for us. I mean, look at me and Ellie: communicating so easily from opposite ends of this huge room without a single word passing between us. We work so well together. Nobody could argue against that. The only issue I have to deal with here is remaining in my private bubble of bliss with Ellie for a little while longer, and that certainly doesn't feel like an issue at all.

Mr and Mrs Gibson enter the dining hall through the archway from the great hall. Mitsi jumps down from the window seat as soon as she spots them. She is lucky that her owners are momentarily distracted by the sprig of mistletoe hanging in the archway; they stop to share a quick kiss on the lips, giving the fugitive dog just enough time to make a daring escape from the room she is supposed to be barred from. She flees through the double doors to the hallway, her wagging tail disappearing from view a split second before Mr and Mrs Gibson break apart.

I watch Mrs Gibson brush some invisible lint off her cardigan, and then she claps her hands together to command everyone else's attention.

'Right!' she calls. 'I overheard something about Henry being called away for work? That's a shame for you, dear. We'll miss you dreadfully. I suppose you'd better go and get on with packing an overnight bag. We'll see you bright and early on Christmas morning. Bye-bye now.' She pauses for half a breath. 'Everyone else, we will have to find a way to have fun without him. I'm thinking that we all go ice skating today. There is a lovely outdoor rink about half an hour away. The man who owns it is an old friend of mine, so I'm sure he can get us some last-minute passes for this afternoon. What do you all think? Dylan? Dominic? Would you like to show Grandma how fast you can ice skate?'

The boys glance at one another, wondering whether to break their silence.

'Grandma can skate faster than you think,' Mr Gibson puts in. 'She's like a cheetah on the ice.'

'I love cheetahs!' gasps one of the twins.

'We *both* love cheetahs,' says the other.

'Oh, really? Maybe you two can be as fast as cheetahs, then. Just like Grandma.'

The boys share another look.

'Are you really fast as cheetahs, Grandma?'

Mrs Gibson taps her nose. 'You'll have to come with me to the ice rink to find out. And do you know what we'll do when we've finished skating? We'll all sit down and have . . . *hot chocolates*!'

That does it. Dylan and Dominic come back to life, pushing away their breakfasts and jumping down from their chairs. They march around the dining hall, wiping their runny noses on the backs of their hands and asking what other kinds of chocolate they can have today.

'Maybe chocolate bars?'

Wipe.

'And maybe chocolate buttons?'

Wipe, sniff, wipe.

'And even chocolate from advent calendars!'

Wipe, blubber, snort, wipe.

'You know,' Ellie says in a stage-whisper, 'I've heard there's some chocolate spread in the kitchen. Top shelf. I'll get it down for you.'

The twins jump up and down around her, overjoyed by this input.

'Are you gonna skate too, Auntie Ellie?'

'Course I am!'

They turn to Ben.

'Count me in,' he says.

Everyone looks at me.

'I'm there.'

The boys erupt into roars of delight and start tugging at Kate's trouser legs with their snotty hands, insisting that they have to hurry up and get ready so they can skate like cheetahs and eat all the chocolate.

'You'll have to put on your Christmas jumpers!' Mrs Gibson calls after them as they race out of the room, dragging Kate by her trousers behind them. 'You too, Kate. I want everyone in Christmas jumpers.' She turns to me and Ben. 'Does everybody here have a jumper? I have plenty of spares if anyone needs. Margot, do you need to borrow one, darling? Ben? Ellie? You all just come to me if you need one. OK? Good. I'll see you all this afternoon. It will be perfect!'

I am unexpectedly excited about donning a tacky Christmas sweater and going to the local ice rink for a day of full-on festive cheesiness. There's just something so infectious about the happiness of five-year-olds. I feel swept up in this whirlwind plan along with Dylan and Dominic, and cannot wait to see how fast we can all skate and what sort of chocolatey goodies we'll get our hands on afterwards.

Also, it will be nice to have another outing with Ellie, somewhere other than a bench in the back garden. It doesn't matter that I'll be there as Ben's date; I'll still be able to gaze across the glittering ice at Ellie all bundled up in a hat and gloves and pretend that I'm there in a winter wonderland with her. Any proximity to her makes me happy. Being with her has made me a permanent resident on cloud nine.

My phone rings in my pocket. It's my mum. I head out into the hallway to answer with a spring in my step. I haven't spoken to Mum since I arrived here in Cheshire. We always get on best when we've had a bit of a breather from one another, and I am actually looking forward to catching up with her and filling her in on my luxury stay at the manor.

'Mum! Hi. Merry almost Christmas! How are you?'

'I'm fine.' She sniffs. 'But what about you? Are you all right? Are you safe? I was just told that you're unreachable at the moment. Very worrying. I didn't even know whether I'd get through on the phone. I need to know that you're OK.'

'I'm fine! I'm better than fine. But . . . I don't understand. What's going on? Who told you I was unreachable?'

'Taylor.'

I come tumbling down from cloud nine immediately, landing back on earth with a thud. The wind is knocked out of me and my energy is drained. The sudden low feels even lower than usual thanks to the fact I was just flying high.

How is it possible that Taylor is still muscling her way into my life? I blocked her number. I made my peace with our break-up. I travelled all the way to a remote manor in rural Cheshire to get away from her. And still she has followed me.

Oh God. She hasn't *followed* me, has she? She might have found a way to hound me by going through my mum, but she hasn't actually tracked down my location.

Has she?

I grip hold of my phone with a clammy hand and take a deep breath. 'Mum, what exactly did you say to Taylor? Did you tell her where I'm spending Christmas? Did you mention that I'm in Cheshire? At this hotel?'

'No! Of course not. I didn't tell her a thing. I said that you were all right and that I've been able to reach you just fine, and now I'm calling you to check if that's true.'

My relief is so intense that it washes everything else away. 'Really, Margot. *Did I tell Taylor where you are?*' She sniffs again. 'When have I ever told that woman anything? I wouldn't tell her where I keep my garden hose if I was on fire.'

I hoot with unexpected laughter. Mum is so funny sometimes, skipping any BS to get straight to the point. And she is fiercely loyal. That can make her come across as a bit prickly and meddling at times, but it also means that she is always on my side. One hundred per cent.

With sudden clarity I realize that this is why Taylor disliked her. It wasn't to do with them both being 'strong women' who 'butted heads'. It was more about Mum having my back.

From the moment she met Taylor back in my uni days, Mum knew she was bad news and she never hesitated to tell me as much. Because I was a teenager and chronically stupid, I immediately relayed this information to Taylor. She was not pleased. She said that Mum was crazy and overprotective; inappropriately involved in my love life. She questioned what right that old crone had to judge us anyway when she couldn't even date someone her own age, constantly shacking up with toy boys. There was even a suggestion of homophobia. Mum might have accepted me when I came out, but maybe she was uncomfortable actually seeing me with a girlfriend. She certainly wasn't being very supportive of my first lesbian relationship, was she?

It was more than enough to stop me listening to Mum's concerns. After that, Taylor eased off a bit. She introduced some subtlety. At random but regular intervals she would tell me all the things she liked about my mum, *despite* all her shortcomings, which would then be listed in minute detail. Bit by bit she put me off my only parent until there was a nice little distance between us.

It's the same thing Taylor did with Nikita and the rest of my friends. I think she wanted me isolated so that I was easier to manipulate. According to the article Ben read to me, this is a very common sign of . . . Well. It's common. When Nikita read the article for herself she confirmed for me that she'd noticed Taylor keeping me shut away. It is getting harder and harder for me to deny the evidence right in front of me. Or, maybe, it is getting a little bit easier to accept the truth. There was just so much of Taylor's behaviour reflected back at me in that article. The gaslighting; the emotional blackmail; the erratic moods. And now the attempts to isolate me so that she could have total control.

Unfortunately for Taylor she has started to lose her hold

on me. She knows it too. That's why she has reached out to Mum, to let me know that she's still around and won't be ignored. It's ironic that she worked so hard to sever my connection to my mum, only to exploit that same connection to get close to me again. Or to get into my head. Or to intimidate me. To be honest, I'm not sure exactly what Taylor's game plan is here. I think I still have a long way to go before I fully understand her and everything that happened between us. Maybe I will never get all the way there.

What I do know is that I'm making progress. Thinking more and more about Ben's article and accepting that it might be relevant to my relationship with Taylor is a huge step forward. So is the way I reacted to hearing her name just now. It was upsetting to feel upset, of course, but I think it's a good sign that my response to the situation was wholly negative. I wasn't happy to hear that Taylor had asked after me or relieved to know that she cared. I didn't feel guilty for being unreachable to her. I was just upset. Taylor affected my emotions, but she didn't send them into a confusing, contradictory frenzy like she normally does.

Most importantly of all, I am not isolated any more. I am laughing with Mum. I am reconnecting with Nikita. I am forming a new friendship with Ben, and a new romantic connection with Ellie. Taylor doesn't dominate my entire personal life any more.

I am not alone.

I think of the advice mentioned in the article about 'support networks', and Ben's endless earnest offers to lend me an ear, and Nikita's claim that her phone number is a 24/7 hotline – and I decide that what I need to do next is reach out. I know that it's the right thing to do, because it is the exact opposite of what Taylor would want. Her voice still lives somewhere in my head and right now it is telling me to keep quiet, so I know I have to speak up. I have to open myself up and trust my loved ones to rally around me in the same way the Gibson clan just rallied around Dylan and Dominic.

First things first, I bring my focus back to this phone call. Which is apparently . . . over.

Mum has hung up.

I try not to feel too rejected or annoyed. I *was* stuck inside my own head for a while there. I wasn't being very chatty. Maybe Mum tried to keep the conversation going and I was too absorbed by my own thoughts to notice or respond. Maybe she got distracted by something at her end. I don't know. I suppose our mother–daughter relationship isn't suddenly perfect. Still, it's worth trying to make things a little better. I do want to talk to her some more now, so I will push through any feelings of abandonment and call her back.

She picks up on the second ring. I can hear her eating before she's said hello. I try not to get irritated by the chomping sounds, and I also decide not to get into any sort of argument about however the previous call ended.

'Hi again, Mum. Listen, I just wanted to say thanks for keeping . . . er, "mum", about where I am.'

'Oh. Not a problem,' she says with her mouth full. 'I mean it when I say I wouldn't tell Taylor anything. She doesn't deserve to know squat about you.' She gives another bitter sniff. 'I'm glad you're not speaking to her any more. She makes you . . . spacy. I don't like it.'

I don't respond. Almost by instinct, that comment has

got my back up a bit, but I still don't want to argue. I definitely don't want to defend Taylor.

'I won't answer any of her calls if she tries me again,' Mum continues. 'But *you* call me any time, all right? I'm free to chat whenever you need.' A pause. 'I'm free during the days, at least. I'll ring you back if I miss the call. Promise me you'll call.'

I smile to myself, loosening up a little. 'I promise.'

'Good. Your secrets are always safe with me. "Mum's" the word!'

'I just made that joke, Mum.'

She sniffs her biggest sniff yet. 'Fine. But I'm still taking credit for it, because you got your sense of humour from me.'

'Mmm. And you got yours from Nana?'

'Yup. It goes right up the family tree. I'm sure there's a Neanderthal woman buried in a cave somewhere that we should visit to thank for our funny bones.'

'Yeah? Is that the great-aunt I'm named after?'

Mum laughs. It's a great sound. One I realize I haven't heard in a while.

'Listen,' I say, 'we should do something for Christmas. A belated something. Maybe a lunch next week when I'm back in London? I'll cook. Or I'll try to, at least.'

'I'll host. I can probably cobble together a dessert. . .'

My smile widens at the thought.

'. . . and Daniel can sort out the drinks. He's a bartender.'

This is the first I'm hearing of Mum's latest man. I had been thinking that this belated Christmas lunch would be for the two of us only, but I suppose it would hardly be traditional if there wasn't a new boyfriend at the table. I tell myself to keep on keeping cool. 'The more the merrier' is an expression for a reason, and maybe Bartender Daniel makes my mum very happy.

'That sounds good,' I say. 'Ask him to bring a bottle of red.'

When we hang up a few minutes later, I feel light in a way that I rarely do after a conversation with Mum. 'Reaching out' felt pretty good. I tap the details of our post-Christmas Christmas lunch straight into my phone's calendar. While I'm at it, I shoot off a text to Nikita.

> Hey, Nik. Had a bit of a shaky morning and could use a laugh. Any help?

Two minutes later, she sends me a video of a tiny tabby kitten 'walking' a German shepherd on a leash. Then another clip of a black cat eating a lemon wedge and leaping a metre into the air with shock. She finishes off with three GIFs (cat-related), two pictures (cat-related), and one menu (not cat-related; from the sushi restaurant we're visiting in January).

> Did any of that work? Xx

> I would have preferred more dog content . . . But I did crack a smile. And that sushi sounds DELISH xx

She follows up with a GIF of a ginger cat turning away from the camera as if in disgust, and the cocktail list for the restaurant.

> Even more delish. And how are you? Xx

> BUSY!!

Not too busy for cat vids?

I'm never too busy for cat vids. And I'm never too busy for you. D'you need some more cheering up? Need to talk?

I pause, tapping the back of my phone with my finger-tips. Actually, I'm OK. Thank you, babe. Now get back to your busy life!! Xx

I slip the phone back into my pocket and head through to the dining hall with my shoulders rolled back and my head held high.

It is brighter in here now that the sun has fully risen. Ellie and Ben are sitting at the table, chatting and laughing. I pull up a chair to join them. I'm not going to talk to either of them about Taylor just yet, because I want my breakfast first. I will have a towering pile of toast and jam, and a huge mug of milky tea, and maybe a spoonful of the chocolate spread Ellie mentioned to the twins. I will talk to Ben later this morning and I know he will be immensely supportive. I will talk to Ellie even later than that, if I can get a moment alone with her, and I will ask her out on a second date tonight.

Finally I will grab myself a Christmas jumper and get ready to go out ice skating. I'm sure I'll still be feeling a bit shaky when we leave the house, and I'll probably find my borrowed sweater a tad itchy, and I'll likely not be able to skate as fast as a cheetah. But I'll be damned if I let any of that prevent me from enjoying my day.

25

Ellie

The ice rink is as bustling as expected two days before Christmas. Big families with small children. Groups of chattering teens. Couples skating hand in hand. Everyone whirls around the ice, long scarfs flying in the wind behind them. Or else they shuffle unsteadily, clinging on to the side for support.

I watch all the icy action from a warm cafe overlooking the rink. Us Gibsons got here early, like we always do when my parents are in charge, so we have half an hour to kill before our session on the ice begins. We've opted to have our hot chocolates now to fill the time, plus a round of mince pies, a few slices of fruitcake, and a whole gang of gingerbread men. Why anyone thought it was a good idea to give my hyperactive nephews that much sugar before letting them loose on a body of ice with blades attached to their feet, I do not know, but it's done now. I suppose the sweet treats are tasty enough to be worth the chaos, and it is good to see Dylan and Dominic perked up again after their brief bout of mopiness this morning. They are currently decapitating gingerbread men and drowning their headless bodies in hot chocolate, so it's safe to say they're back to their usual selves.

Margot is looking happier than she did this morning

as well. She was a bit quiet and withdrawn over breakfast, but she's back out of her shell now, laughing at a joke that Ben's telling her on the other side of the table. Her eyes are all crinkled up. Head tilted right back. Hand over his.

I guess it's a little strange watching her cosy up to my brother like this, but it doesn't really bother me. I'm the one who has a *real* date with Margot tonight. It's at midnight. Obviously. That is fast becoming a tradition of ours. Like something out of a fairy tale: the two fair maidens stealing away into the starry night to meet lakeside at the first stroke of midnight. Or like a couple o' birds sat on a bench for a bit. It doesn't matter how you describe those midnight meetings – they are the best part of my day.

Tonight's adventure is gonna feature a picnic. That was Margot's idea. She asked me out via text message earlier this afternoon, because we couldn't seem to find a moment alone at the house. It's a lucky thing I gave her my number last night. Seemed the proper thing to do at the end of a first date, even though we are currently living under the same roof. Her text arrived when I was up in my bedroom, getting changed into my mandatory uniform of an old Christmas jumper in red and white.

Hey, I had a wonderful time last night. Glad I got your number! ;) I would love to take you out for a second date tonight if you're free? I'll be at my favourite local haunt, The Bench, at 12 tonight with food & drink. I got some lovely cheese & a gorgeous bottle of red at a local Xmas market recently that I'd like to share with you. I hope to see you there x

Who's this? I replied.

Right, the date's off. I'll have my cheese all to myself.

Nooo! I'd love to join you for a 2nd date, MARGOT MURRAY. I'll bring a blanket to put down on the grass for our midnight midwinter picnic!! x

Is the picnic idea too out there? I was going for something quirky & romantic, but romance is defo not my strong suit . . .

The picnic idea is perfect!! V. romantic. I'll be counting down the hours x (PS I knew you were trying to woo me!) (PPS Are you OK? Seemed a bit out of it this morning? Xx)

I'm OK. I just had a bit of a shock before breakfast. I got a weird phone call from my mum, who had got a weird phone call from Taylor. Don't worry, I'm still not talking to her & Mum's gonna block her number too. I was just thrown for a moment. Feeling better now that I've had a good chat with Ben & a strong cup of tea :) I also landed myself a hot date for tonight, which has defo helped raise spirits!

I'm glad. I'm so sorry that happened, though, & I'm not worried about Taylor – I just want you to be OK. Let me know if / when you want to talk more about it. I'm always here xxx

I know :) See you later xxxx

Now I watch Margot giggling with my brother from across the table, and the sight makes my heart burst with joy. The fact is, seeing her happy makes me happy. It's as simple as that.

Gramps leans over from the chair next to mine to elbow me in the ribs. He has that naughty twinkle in his eye that I know so well, and he's gesturing towards the inside pocket of his jacket.

I nod my understanding and agreement. In one swift movement I scooch my chair closer to his, angle my body away from the others, and stretch out across the table with my head propped up on an elbow. Gramps is now obscured from view. He pulls a small leather hip flask out of his jacket, unscrews the top, and splashes a bit of whisky into both our hot chocolates. Within seconds the flask is back inside his jacket and I'm straightening up to give our drinks a stir.

Mission accomplished. That was the best undercover work I've done since I tried out being a detective to spy on Margot. More successful too. No one has so much as looked our way; the little pockets of conversation happening all around the table are continuing as if nothing ever happened. Gramps and I get to enjoy our afternoon tipple in peace without having to share any with the other adults or explain to the kids that, no, that was not a type of syrup, and, no, they cannot have any in their own drinks.

We clink our mugs together and gulp down some new-and-improved hot choc. Grandpa lowers his cup to reveal a frothy moustache. I slide a napkin his way.

'Thanks, kid.' He wipes his upper lip. 'So. I spoke to Gerald and Ann this morning. Do you remember the story there?'

'Course. Ann's mobility scooter broke down outside Gerald's window and he lodged a formal complaint against her.'

'Bingo. Well, we had a Zoom call earlier. Gerald and Ann had to sit very close together because they were sharing a webcam. I was there as a mediator. Essentially I sat in silence while the two of them aired their grievances. It was rather simple stuff: Gerald was annoyed that Ann had failed to charge her scooter again, and Ann was annoyed that Gerald was annoyed with her. I piped up to suggest that they both stopped being annoyed. It worked! Gerald said he hadn't thought of that but that it was a very good idea and he would stop being annoyed right away. Ann was pleased that Gerald's annoyance was over, and she immediately dropped her own. They kissed and made up and decided to be annoyed with Sandra instead for cheating at Scrabble.'

'Fantastic. So the gang's back together. Except for poor Sandra.'

'Oh, they won't be annoyed with her for long. She's rubbish at cheating, so it doesn't really matter that she does it. And, like I said, they'll all forget about her crime by the time Christmas is over. Those old folks have awful memories.'

I narrow my eyes and tilt my head. 'Ummm . . .'

'Ellie Gibson! I hope you're not insinuating that *I* am an old folk? I'll have you know that I'm about to go ice skating along with all the young whippersnappers around here. And I'm not even that worried about my back giving out.'

I hold up my hands. 'Point taken. I'll never disrespect my elders again.'

We chuckle together and settle matters with another long drink. It goes down smoothly, the chocolate tasting even richer thanks to the deep woody flavour of the whisky.

'So what else is going on?' I ask. 'Other than your mates being mates again?'

'Ah, nothing much. I'm planning to go out for a spot of stargazing tomorrow morning. Dust off the old binoculars.'

I imagine the old binoculars will require a *lot* of dusting, given that Gramps hasn't so much as touched them for at least three years. He and Grandma used to go stargazing together all the time. He hasn't been able to face doing it since she died. Not properly anyway, with proper equipment.

'I thought it was about time I got out there again,' he continues. 'The weather is so lovely at the moment, especially for December, and I want to take advantage of the clear skies while we have them. I'm going to head out in the early hours tomorrow. Have a look at the constellations. See if I can finally track down a new star.'

My belly tightens. 'A new star?'

'Yes,' he says cheerfully. 'I haven't had a good look at the sky for a long time. There must be a few new stars since I last checked. Possibly some new planets too, although I know that's unlikely. If I find anything good, I'll show your grandma right away. She'll be so pleased.'

My tightened belly sinks. The boozy hot chocolate sits heavy in there. He's saying mad things again. Saying them as if they are perfectly normal and true.

Old folks and their memories indeed.

I am dimly aware of the table getting quieter around us. The little pockets of conversation all winding down as everyone takes notice of what Gramps is saying.

'I'm going to take the binoculars – did I mention that? I'll need to give them a good clean first. I'll do that tonight.

I'm going out very early tomorrow, so the binoculars need to be ready. I'm going in the early, early hours of the morning, when it will be nice and quiet outside. There won't be anybody else around. Unless the pony is out for a run. Yes, I might see the pony again! I haven't seen her for a couple of days now. Have you, Ellie? Have you seen the pony?'

Grandpa looks at me intently, waiting for an answer. I feel other eyes on me too. Mum's eyes and Dad's eyes, and Kate's and Ben's and Margot's. Chairs creak as people shift and fidget. Air stagnates as everyone holds their breath.

I don't stop to think about it: I look right at Margot. I need her support, and I find it right there waiting for me. Her entire face is etched with sympathy. Brown eyes holding mine. Mouth curved into the tiniest smile of encouragement. In this moment I feel seen. Not looked to for an answer or a way to deal with Grandpa. Just seen. Understood. It's comforting to know that even when Margot isn't here 'with' me, she is here with me.

'No, I'm afraid I haven't seen the pony.'

'Ah. That's all right, kid. We could ask Mitsi if she's seen her. Remember, Mitsi is friends with the pony.'

I nod. A few other people round the table nod. Stiff necks, tight smiles. How did it get to this: everyone nodding along indulgently to his random ramblings? No one knows what to say to him, how to react. We'll have to work this out one day soon. Decide to what extent we engage with his delusions or whether to ignore them and leave them be. We'll have to make a plan of action as a family. As of right now, there is no plan. All any of us can think to do is sit here in silence. Nodding. Thanks to our matching mismatched Christmas jumpers, we look like a festive range of bobbleheads.

Strangely enough I find yet more comfort in this bizarre scene. All of us bobbleheads bobbling our heads simultaneously . . . it's a very literal display of unity. Before we've even had the chance to plan how we'll respond to Grandpa, we've all responded in the same way. Me and my family, we've all found ourselves on the same page. Every single one of us. I can't remember the last time that happened.

It feels good. Like being part of a team.

'You're all being very strange right now,' Grandpa informs us. 'What are you all gaping at? Have I still got a chocolatey moustache on my upper lip? No? Enough staring then. Be more like my great-grandsons over here and get on with finishing your puddings. I want to get out on that ice!'

We all make our way on to the rink along with a new crowd of big families, chattering teens, and happy couples.

Dylan and Dominic shoot off right away, high on a heady mixture of sugar and pop-y Christmas tunes. Kate hurtles after them, demanding that they slow down and hold hands. Mum and Dad shuffle after Kate, offering their help in wrangling the twins. Not sure how they're gonna manage that or make good on their promises to skate as fast as cheetahs, because right now they both look like Bambi on ice. Still, gotta commend them for giving it a go. Ben is not being so brave. He has attached himself to the plastic wall around the rink and is tottering behind a gang of small children. Margot rolls her eyes good-naturedly at this and holds out an arm for him to grab on to instead. Just as my brother finally lets go of the edge and hitches himself to Margot, the twins whizz past them both. The little Duracell bunnies have only gone and completed their first lap already.

Grandpa gives the boys a big cheer as they overtake us next. He's skating along beside me, one hand on my arm and the other holding on to the plastic wall. He comes away from the edge every so often to get past the gangs of children that Ben had been queueing behind. I won't coax him into letting go of the side for good. Can't let him run the risk of slipping and injuring himself, especially since he's been on the whisky this afternoon. I highly doubt that a double hip replacement is at the top of his Christmas list.

'Those old farts at the home couldn't do this now, could they? I told you I was young and sprightly, Ellie. Maybe I'll do our next lap backwards. Or with my eyes closed. I'll be doing quadruple spins before we leave.'

'I'd pay good money to see that, Gramps.'

'Ah, unfortunately I can only do my tricks when nobody is watching me. Stage fright, you see. You'll just have to take my word for it that I can do ten backflips in a row.'

He's definitely back to his usual self again. He went back to normal almost as quickly as he went abnormal. The whole thing has left me with a spot of emotional whiplash, but my overriding feeling is relief that he's *him* again. Inhabiting the part of his mind that I recognize. It's like reuniting with a long-lost friend, even though he thankfully wasn't lost to me for long this time.

Margot and Ben skate past us, moving much faster than I think Ben would like to be moving. Their arms are still linked together, and they are chuckling away as usual. I allow myself a brief moment to fantasize about switching places with Ben and being the person that Margot is holding on to, and then I get back to simply being glad that she's happy. It's nice to see her getting along so well with my brother. With all my family. It's reassuring to think that once Ben's lie has been dropped, I could one day 'introduce' Margot to everyone and know for a fact that she'd go down well, since they've all already met her and started to adore her. Margot Murray has had the official stamp of approval. I was actually the last member of my family to give it.

Someone taps me on the shoulder. It's Mum. She and Dad have already given up on trying to catch up to Kate and the twins and they are now slowing down to a more natural pace next to me and Gramps. I notice Dad searching Grandpa's face to check that he's doing OK. I give him a small nod to let him know it's all good. He throws me a grateful smile in return. The four of us take to shuffling around the rink slowly, our skates chipping at the ice.

'There are so many familiar faces here today,' Mum says.

'Are there?' I cast a dubious look around. I haven't recognized anyone yet. Not properly. When we were waiting to get on to the ice I saw a few people I vaguely remember knowing once upon a time, but I couldn't recall any of their names. I just knew that I'd seen that guy with the upturned nose before, and those brothers with the matching unibrows, and that lady with the frizzy red hair. I nodded and smiled in their directions for the sake of being polite, but none of them noticed me as they trooped past to return their hired skates. Thank goodness. There's nothing worse than standing around trying to remember the name of some old acquaintance while they eagerly fill you in on the intimate details of their heart-wrenching divorce and their arduous but rewarding journey to finding themselves again afterwards.

Clearly Mum is better at matching a face to a name. She reels off the full names of everyone she's spotted on the ice so far, plus a short line of recent trivia about each of them. Eventually she mentions a name that I properly recognize: Ajay Gupta.

'Oh!' I say. 'I went to school with his brother Ashwin.'

'I know that, darling. That's how we know him.'

'Oh yeah. Of course. Well, I'm still friends with Ashwin. He's an amazing chef now, did you hear that? He was the one I mentioned the other day – the one who owns a catering company that specialises in modern Indian dishes.'

'That's very impressive,' Mum says.

'Does anyone else fancy a curry now?' Dad puts in.

I try to focus more on Mum's apparent interest than Dad's typical interruption. I think he's happy enough just getting to say his usual line. I'm sure it isn't even intended as an interruption. In fact, I haven't made it at all obvious that I'm trying to have another go at introducing one of my business ideas. I need to be clearer.

'I've been thinking, actually, that we could collaborate with Ashwin to offer up a new foodie option at the hotel,' I say. 'He wants to start branching out into doing supper clubs next year, and we could provide the perfect venue. Maybe one night a month? That means there would be curry served at the hotel, Dad.'

'Ooh!'

'What is a "dinner club"?' Mum asks.

I don't correct her. I just explain the concept of pop-up dining experiences in unique locations, and lay out my idea for our own supper club: an exclusive evening at the hotel, with a one-off tasting menu featuring delicious Indian dishes cooked fresh by Ashwin.

Grandpa beams at me. 'It sounds brilliant, kid.'

'It's a great idea,' Dad agrees. 'I do love a good curry.'

'It's an interesting concept,' Mum says slowly, shuffling along the ice just in front of us. 'But do we really have the facilities for it?'

'We have a huge commercial kitchen,' I say, trying not to sound impatient.

'But we don't have huge pots and pans. We're only equipped to cook a light breakfast for a small number of guests.'

'Ashwin would bring his own catering equipment for the day,' I explain. 'He has plenty of pots and pans. And a whole load of those silver balti dishes for serving.'

'And who would be doing this serving?'

'His waiters. He has trusted staff on his books that he'd bring with him.'

'OK. Will all this excitement disturb our overnight guests?'

'I don't think so. Ideally we'd have a good amount of overlap between room guests and dinner guests. We could offer discounted tickets for the meal when customers book a room for the same night, or vice versa.'

'You've thought this through,' Mum says, finally sounding impressed. 'OK. I think it could work . . . as long as you take the lead on the project. You clearly know what you're doing. Why don't you plan out a trial event, and we'll see how it goes?'

'Yes!' I say eagerly. 'I can do that.'

'Fantastic. Will you have some time to iron out the details after Christmas? Before you jet off again?'

'I haven't booked a flight yet actually. I'm planning on sticking around for a while.' I squeeze Grandpa's arm, and he squeezes back. 'I'll have plenty of time for project supper club.'

'I'm glad to hear it,' Mum says. 'I look forward to working with you, darling.'

'Me too,' Dad agrees.

I glow with pride and satisfaction. Maybe now would be a good time to ask for a more official job at the hotel, but I don't want to push my luck and risk knocking the shine off this lovely moment. I'm happy to wait a few more days.

For now I just keep skating, bobbing my head along to the cheesy Christmas music blaring from the speakers. When 'Frosty the Snowman' comes on, I automatically look to Margot. She's already looking back at me through the crowd. We both smirk at one another as her 'favourite Christmas song of all time' plays, and once again it's as if she's right here with me, even as we stand on opposite ends of a vast sheet of ice.

The twins zoom past me, catching my attention. I remember I mustn't stare at Margot, and she obviously comes to a similar conclusion because she looks away from me, a trace of that smirk still on her lips. I let myself take her in for a moment longer – her dark hair sticking out from under her black beanie, her long limbs moving gracefully over the ice – and then I look away too.

Kate finally gives up on keeping pace with her boys and joins my gang of slow shufflers near the edge of the rink. She links her arm through Dad's, who is holding Mum's hand, who slips a hand into mine, and I hold tight to Grandpa. We all move as one big chain. I let myself be present here: on the glistening ice, beneath strings of fairy lights, literally connected to my family in a way I haven't been in many, many years.

26

Margot

I arrange cheese on a wooden board. I had kept the goodies I bought at the market on Tuesday stashed in the mini-fridge in my room, and now I line them all up carefully: aged Cheddar, blue Stilton, classic Emmental, Stinking Bishop. Meanwhile, Ellie lights the twenty-odd candles that she collected from around the house to cut through the midnight darkness. Finally we both lounge back on a thick picnic blanket, our set-up complete. As well as cheese and candles, we have a bottle of vintage red Burgundy and two glasses, a hazy view of the moonlit lake in front of us, and Ellie's fairy lights draped over our bench behind us.

I love the romance of it all, and I am only slightly sur-prised about that. A new part of me seems to be coming out around Ellie – a part that doesn't find this kind of thing so overwhelming. Of course, the picture-perfect Hollywood-style stuff still seems a bit much. Even this new part of me would balk at the slightest whiff of a flashy grand romantic gesture. I would hate to receive one, because it wouldn't be rooted in love, intimacy, or any understanding of who I am as a person, and I would hate even more to give one, because I'd look silly. But this. This I can do. This midnight picnic for two under a canopy of glittering stars is some-thing that Ellie and I have put together, together. It is real and grounded and so very *us*. We are together in this beautiful moment, and we are also wearing seven layers each to ward off the cold, and planning to escape to the nearby greenhouse when it finally gets too much, and constantly relighting our candles as the wind keeps blowing them out. It is all slightly ridiculous, and truly and utterly perfect.

I uncork the wine and pour some into our wide-bowled glasses. We clink them together lightly, and I whisper, 'I missed you today.'

Ellie doesn't say anything. She looked down just before I spoke and is now focusing on her glass, swirling the deep red liquid inside. My whispered words must have been stolen by the wind.

'I missed you,' I say, louder this time.

'Oh, I heard.' She keeps swirling. 'I just wanted to hear you say it again.'

'Huh! Is my bleeding heart a joke to you?'

'Maybe,' she says coyly, still looking down. 'Why don't you try telling me again? Third time's the charm.'

I sigh. 'Fine. I missed you today. A lot. I've been itching to talk to you properly all day long and I've been counting down the hours until our date. How's that for charm?'

'It's perfect.' Ellie finally drops the act and knocks back some wine with a grin. 'I've been missing you all day too, even when you were right there next to me. I've been trying to sneak little looks your way without driving myself crazy. I've been *pining* for you, Margot Murray.'

'Sorry, I didn't quite hear that.' I cup my free hand around my ear. 'Repeat yourself?'

Now it's Ellie's turn to sigh. 'I *said*, I've been pining for you. I suppose that's a bit pathetic, considering that our first date was only last night, and I've spent most of my day around you in some capacity. But I don't care. I have missed you and I have been hopelessly pining for you all day. I have enjoyed every minute of it.'

'Wait, what? Really?'

'OK, maybe not every minute. It would've been nice if some of the minutes were spent with you and you alone. But yeah, I've enjoyed the feeling of wanting you. It's been a new one for me. I mean, I'm not really used to delayed gratification. Usually if I fancy someone, I tell them, and if they fancy me back then that's that. This thing with you is different. We've had more than a few stopping-off points on our way from A to B, haven't we? And we still have more detours to make. I'm still pretending to be your friend or your sister-in-law or whatever, when really I'm falling for you harder every day. There's still all this build-up and longing, even after we've kissed a zillion times. We still –'

I sweep towards Ellie and give her kiss number one zillion and one: a short but hungry kiss on the lips. I think it would have been physically impossible to stop myself. I feel weak at the knees, even though I'm sitting down on a blanket on the grass. I'm dizzy with the words my date has just said to me, about wanting me, longing for me.

Falling for me.

I find that every part of me is full of joy.

We graze on the cheese, along with some crackers, grapes and chutneys that Ellie picked up on her drive home from the ice rink. The platter we've put together is basically a charcuterie board. Minus the cured meats. And the finesse.

Sharing chunks of cheese with Ellie reminds me of the two of us sitting on a crumbling wall in Chester, smearing Brie on to chips and talking about my nana's homemade croquembouche. Looking back at that moment, it's tempting to view it as a first date of sorts. But really, that happened before Ellie and I had begun. It feels like half a lifetime ago, rather than a mere four days. It is wonderfully bizarre that we are now having candlelit dinner dates . . . of sorts. I top up both our wine glasses.

Suddenly there's a noise. A thump. It is quiet and distant but in the dead of night it feels far more immediate than it would if I could see where it was coming from.

'Did you hear that?'

'What?' Ellie smirks. 'Did you tell me something soppy again?'

'No, seriously. There was a sound, like a thud. I can't tell where it came from. Maybe from the other side of that field?' I point to my left. 'Or that one?' I gesture to my right.

'I didn't hear anything.' Ellie's voice is soft now. 'It was probably an animal running into a tree or something.'

'The "or something" is what worries me.'

'OK,' she says. 'I can see that. I promise you there's nothing to be scared of out here, but if you're not comfortable staying out in the dark, I totally get it. Do you want us to head back inside?'

'No.' I nudge her foot with one of mine. 'I don't want us to do that.'

She laughs gently. 'Fine. How about this then: If any fluffy night-time creature attempts to crash our picnic, I will scare it off right away. We have candles, right? I can use the flame as a deterrent. And here: we have a knife for the cheese. I can use that too.'

'*Ellie*. That isn't very vegetarian of you.'

'I don't care. If I have to choose between you and a wild animal, I choose you.'

'Aww.' I put a hand over my heart. 'That's the most romantic thing you've said all night. Your wooing techniques are improving all the time.'

She sinks her upper body into an exaggerated bow, folding all the way over her crossed legs. When she straightens up again, she pulls a few candles closer to her with a wink in my direction. The mysterious sound has not repeated itself. I pick up the rounded knife and slice off a generous chunk of Cheddar. We both return to the serious business of eating our midnight snacks. After a few minutes, Ellie sits back and fixes me with an earnest look.

'You know,' she says, 'I can take some more of your worries off your hands. If you want me to. If you get tired of carrying them alone. I meant what I said in my text this afternoon: I'm always here to talk to. And, FYI, I'm not gonna be put off by anything you say, in case you're worried about your worries worrying me.'

She's got me bang to rights there. I was already starting to worry about exactly that, because most of my concerns at the moment revolve around Taylor. It hardly feels appropriate to offload about my ex-girlfriend on a date with a new woman.

Then again, Ellie doesn't feel new to me. And she has never reacted badly to anything I've said to her. Not since she worked out that I'm not a gold-digger, at least. I believe her when she says she won't be put off easily.

'OK.' I put down my glass. 'Here's a worry I have at the moment. I think that Taylor emotionally abused me.'

I'm surprised that I led with that. I had expected myself to build up to it very slowly and with my guard way up. Instead, I've just said it. For the first time ever I've said it out loud.

The world hasn't stopped turning. Nobody has jumped out of a nearby bush to tell me that I'm a liar and that I'm over-exaggerating and that spousal abuse has to include physical violence or else you can't call it abuse, you massive liar and over-exaggerater and oversensitive drama queen. Nothing momentous has happened at all. There isn't even a discomfiting reaction from Ellie; she is clearly making an effort to appear neutral, keeping her eyes on me and her expression kind but largely unemotional. I'm grateful. It allows me to work through my thoughts without having to worry too much about what hers might be.

'I've never used the word "abuse" before,' I say. 'This is the first time I'm saying it, right now. Until recently I didn't even consider the possibility that I had been abused. I suspected that I might have been slightly mistreated, and I also suspected that it was as much my fault as it was Taylor's. But after I spoke to Ben about some of the stuff that happened with her, I started to see that our relationship wasn't normal. Ben read me this article, and I couldn't stop thinking about it. So much of it resonated with me. It had taken all these random behaviours that I'd never been able to recognize as being part of one larger context, and it grouped them together and gave them a name.

'Still, I pushed that name away. I dismissed the A-word any time it popped into my head. But I kept thinking about the article, and how all the worst things Taylor did when we were together might be connected. Then earlier today, after she tried to get to me through my mum, I googled some of those things. The ones she did most often. Like making me feel powerless and small compared to her, and giving me the silent treatment, and dismissing and belittling my feelings. Even more articles came up. All of them said the same thing, right there in the title: these were signs of emotional abuse.'

Ellie swallows, but she keeps her face as still as possible, her gaze steady. She doesn't wince with second-hand embarrassment upon hearing that I missed so many obvious signs of abuse. She is just silent and steady, giving me space to carry on without fear of judgement.

'I didn't feel ready to actually open the articles. Not yet. But those two words were everywhere. *Emotional abuse.* And I guess I have been thinking about that label over the last few days, even as I've tried to push away those specific words. It has kind of . . . sunk in. I've got used to the idea that the A-word is an appropriate way to describe what happened to me. The label fits, so I think it's OK to use it. Taylor emotionally abused me. I was emotionally abused.'

Ellie's hand twitches on her thigh, as if she wants to move it. I get the feeling that her instinct is to reach out and touch me, to provide some sort of comfort. But she stops herself. She is leaving me in charge, and so I lift up my own hand and take hers. I move across the blanket to be closer to her.

'You're allowed to speak,' I tell her. 'If there's something you want to say about all this, I want to hear it. Just as long as it's supportive.'

'I support you completely,' she says firmly. 'I am one hundred per cent on your side. And I am so, so proud of you right now. You are incredibly strong, and you deserve all the support in the world.'

I fidget slightly. 'I think I need all the support in the *universe.*'

'And you deserve that too. There's no shame in needing help with this, you know. You *should* get proper help with this.' She pauses. 'Can I say more?'

I fight the urge to fidget again, sitting in stiff stillness. And then I decide that I don't want to fight my urges and I let myself shift around on my bum, causing the blanket to bunch up under me. Ellie waits, keeping hold of my hand.

Finally, I nod.

'I think it would be good for you to see a therapist,' she says gently. 'And that isn't me calling you crazy or anything. I'm not judging you or trying to palm you off on someone else. I will help and support you in any way I can, and I'm sure Ben will as well, and your friends. But we can only do so much because we only know so much. A professional will know how to help you heal more deeply. And you truly deserve that. I won't nag you or push you to do anything you're not ready to do, but I think this is a good idea. I think you should do it out of kindness to yourself.'

I sit with this – not in stillness but in squirminess. Ellie remains just as steady as she has been throughout this whole thing. She doesn't seem bothered by my fidgeting in the slightest. She doesn't seem ready to run a mile in whichever direction will take her away from me. She is still here. And I am OK.

'I will consider a therapist. I will think about maybe

looking up some practices in London so that I can think about maybe seeing someone soon. Maybe. I kind of feel like it's way over the top, but I suppose it isn't a great sign that I see looking after my basic emotional needs as OTT. That's probably the kind of thing to discuss with . . . Yeah. I'll consider it, OK? I think it's a good idea. Thank you.'

'OK. That's OK.'

'Seriously, thank you. I really appreciate . . . everything. You. You've been so open and gentle and kind. You've really made me feel safe. And now I just want us to enjoy our date. I'm sure we'll talk more about this at some point, and maybe we'll even read some of those articles together when I'm ready? But right now I don't want to spend any more time thinking about Taylor. I want to focus on you, Ellie. I want to eat cheese and drink wine and look at the stars. I want my life to keep going on past all of this. So thank you for giving me space to talk, but for now could we leave this all behind us and say . . . fin?'

She studies my face in the half-light. Her green eyes travel across each of my features slowly and carefully. Finally she agrees. 'OK. Fin.'

The regret starts to creep in about twenty minutes later. Ellie and I have continued to pick at the cheese and we've kept chatting about things like music and comedy and the best places to find authentic tacos outside of Mexico, but things have changed. The whole vibe of the date has shifted. All thanks to me.

Ellie is now treating me like I'm delicate. She's holding my hand more gently, rubbing a thumb softly over mine. She's slicing off bits of cheese for me to eat, clearly wanting to do anything she can to help me. I can tell she wants to say more about the Taylor situation: words of comfort and support. The things that are left unsaid hang between us in the cool air, clouding up the atmosphere.

'I'm sorry,' I burst out midway through a very dry cracker. 'I didn't mean to bring the mood down earlier.'

'What?' Ellie looks genuinely confused. 'What do you mean? Because you spoke about your ex? I *asked* you to tell me about your worries.'

'Yeah, and I jumped at the chance and babbled on about all that dark stuff and tipped all my emotional baggage right into your lap. I have officially sucked every last trace of romance out of this date.'

'No.' Ellie holds tighter to my hand, finally giving it a proper squeeze. 'No. You opened up to me, Margot. You trusted me with this huge scary thing that you are only just starting to get to grips with yourself. That is genuine intimacy, and intimacy is a form of romance. Maybe it's not the most conventional way to get close to someone on the second date, but when have we done anything the conventional way? From the moment we met things have been bonkers, and they've only got weirder and wilder since. And I love it. We have taken a whole world of ridiculousness and turned it into our own sort of romance. That's kind of our thing if you ask me. So, I promise you, a bit of honest conversation is not suddenly going to make this whole affair too crazy for me to handle. I like the weird, messy, totally exceptional thing we have going on. That hasn't changed in the last half-hour. I still like things our way.'

For the second time tonight I leap on to Ellie to kiss

her. I overshoot it and unbalance her, so that we both find ourselves horizontal, half on the blanket and half on the damp, frosty grass. Ellie laughs and grabs hold of me where I'm splayed out on top of her, and she hauls us both back on to the blanket. She feels so strong and comforting and warm, and also she sends one of the wine glasses toppling over and lands my boot in the Stinking Bishop.

Once we are steady again, I remain on top of Ellie and she keeps her arms held tight around me. That frustrating delicateness is gone. The outrageous clumsiness is back. We leave the spilt wine to soak into the blanket, and we kiss each other with wild passion, and my boot reeks of stinky cheese, and everything is perfect.

Sunday, 24 December

27

Ellie

We stayed out late last night, finally leaving the steamed-up greenhouse at 3:30. We stumbled back to the house and kissed goodnight on the stairs about twenty times. In my room, I balled up all the picnic stuff inside the mucky blanket and chucked it under my bed to deal with tomorrow. Which is now today. I'm gonna tidy it all up this afternoon.

For now I'm sitting down to enjoy a big family brunch. It's a tradition of ours for Christmas Eve morning: we all eat a late breakfast together at the dining table, with silly Santa hats on and classic carols playing on the radio. As usual, Mum has put together an absolute feast. The spread she's laid out across the table is huge, even by Gibson family standards. We've got cinnamon rolls, gingerbread pancakes, fresh berries, toasted bagels, scrambled eggs. We are each given a plate and direct orders to load them all the way up.

Kate is sitting next to me. When she first took her seat, she apologized to everyone for her husband not being here with us today, but she seemed pretty laid-back about it. She showed us all a picture on her phone of Henry at his desk very early this morning, eating a cereal bar with a Santa hat on his head.

'He's still with us in spirit!' she said.

I'll admit I found that quite sweet. It's nice that Henry made the effort to engage with our soppy tradition, even when he's stuck at work miles away. Kate hasn't continued to apologize for him like she normally would. She is far too busy digging into a sesame bagel topped with scrambled eggs, smoked salmon, and fresh chives to keep saying sorry on her husband's behalf.

Dylan and Dominic also seem fine about their dad being AWOL. They are currently eating their way through two towering stacks of pancakes with syrup while singing along to the carols on the radio. They are getting all the lyrics wrong and delightedly revealing the mushed-up contents of their mouths with every note. Grandpa is sitting next to the boys, eating the exact same sugary breakfast that they're eating and occasionally joining in with the dodgy singing. Mum watches the three of them with a big contented smile on her face. Dad watches her watching them with pure adoration in his eyes.

Opposite me, Margot and Ben are sitting side by side. I give them both a bright, friendly smile. The same smile I've given everyone this morning. Margot beams back at me, and I feel a little fizz of heat deep in my belly. She is just so gorgeous, even with that bright red stocking cap placed skew-whiff on her head.

When brunch is finished, the two of us are going to pull Ben to one side and tell him about us. I'm looking forward to it. It will be amazing to be able to claim Margot openly and proudly as my date – even if it is only in front of one member of the family. She will obviously still be Ben's 'girl-friend' for the remainder of Christmas if that's what he wants. We'll follow his lead and go at his pace.

Whatever happens, Margot and I will be hanging out in the middle of the *day* today to have a second go at baking a pie for our Christmas dinner. It will be our last chance to get it right, but I'm not worried in the least. I know we'll nail it, because Margot and I make a great team and everything we do together is incredible and everything in my life is going perfectly right now. Also, we have a recipe this time.

I tear into a cinnamon roll and pop a handful of blueberries into my mouth along with the sweet pastry. '*Yum!*' I exclaim automatically.

Mum turns my way, surprised. 'Oh, thank you, my darling.'

'Thank *you*.' I take another big bite. 'This really is delicious. Everything is. You've officially outdone yourself this year.'

Everyone mumbles their agreement through mouthfuls of food, garbled *thank you*s echoing all around the table.

'You're welcome,' Mum says. 'I'm just delighted to have you all here to celebrate. Next year, I hope there's even more of us.' She offers Kate a sympathetic smile, then gives me a matching one. 'At least we have one happy couple at brunch this year!' She beams fully at Margot and Ben. 'And what a wonderful couple too.'

Margot smiles back, but her cheeks colour and her fingers twist around her napkin. Ben lights up completely, glowing with Mum's praise and happiness. I feel a little twist in my gut. Kate flares her nostrils.

Then Dad gasps. 'Are you suggesting we're not a happy couple, my love?'

'Am I, indeed!' Mum bats at his arm. 'You know I meant *young* couples.'

'And now I'm not young? This is a travesty. Kate, Ben,

Ellie – remove your mother from the table immediately. I want her out of my sight at once. *Seize her.*'

Kate cracks a smile and Ben laughs. I lunge across the table and pretend to reach for Mum. She leans back, out of my reach, and pushes Dad's arm again. He grabs hold of her face and covers it with kisses.

We all groan.

'Gross!'

'We're trying to eat here!'

'Now you both have to leave!'

Dylan and Dominic sense hijinks and start shouting along, spraying crumbs. Margot laughs and lets go of her napkin. Gramps keeps singing along to the radio.

After several minutes of chaos, Mum shushes us. 'Eat your food while it's hot.'

We keep tittering between mouthfuls. She frowns at all of us, but occasionally lets out a little laugh herself. I can't remember a time when we've all been so silly together. As calmness slowly descends again, I feel so full of love for everyone in this room that I think my heart might burst right out of my chest.

'Isn't the weather gorgeous?' Grandpa muses, swallowing some pancake. 'The sky is so clear. I could see every single star when I went out.'

'Oh?' Dad sounds weary. 'You did end up going star-gazing, then?'

'Of course. I said I was going, so I went. I'm sorry if I woke anybody up when I headed out in the early hours of the morning. The wind blew the door closed behind me, and it made quite a loud thud.'

Around the table people shake their heads. Nobody heard a sound.

Except, maybe, for Margot.

This thought shoots into my head as a random flight of fancy, and I dismiss it right away. Because it doesn't make any sense. The timeline doesn't work. Margot heard a thud last *night*. Not this morning. It can't have been the same sound.

Can it?

'So, Gramps –' I try to keep my voice light and casual – 'what time did you head outside, exactly?'

'I just said: in the early hours of the morning. About twelve thirty, twelve forty-five.'

My belly drops right down into my socks. Around me, conversation continues. Someone argues that midnight is *not* the early hours of the morning, it's the late hours of the night. I agree with whoever's speaking, but I can't focus on them enough to say so. My mind is racing a mile a minute. Grandpa was outside last night. He was out in the grounds at 12:30. At the exact same time that Margot and I were having our date. Margot clearly heard him slamming the door from where we were sitting. Does that mean he could have heard us too? *Seen* us?

I shoot a panicked look across the table. Margot's eyes bulge in response. She has clearly connected the same dots that I have. She looks stricken. Sick.

I force myself to tune back into the conversation. I need to be listening. Have to know what Grandpa is saying. Whether he saw anything. Whether he's gonna spill the beans.

'Well,' he says primly, 'whether you want to call it

night-time or morning, it was quiet and beautiful and clear. I had a full undisturbed view of the night sky.'

'See,' Kate cuts in. '*Night* sky.'

Grandpa considers this. 'Smart-arse,' is his conclusion. He pokes his tongue out at Kate. 'At one *a.m.* I got a good look at the stars. I'm afraid I didn't see any new ones, though. Isn't that a shame? I was out looking for quite some time. I could only see the old bog-standard constellations. And the pony was nowhere to be seen either. I suppose it was too early in the morning for her to be running about. Or too late at night, Kate. Either way.'

Everyone nods along as Grandpa speaks. Not the stiff nods of yesterday, when he was talking nonsense and we were all holding our breath. Today he is making more sense. Yes, he's still banging on about a new star and a runaway pony, but at least he hasn't had visions of those things. There is a palpable air of relief in the room.

I am still holding my breath.

Grandpa isn't done. 'I did see one strange thing out there. There was a young couple. I couldn't quite make out who they were, because they were facing away from me and they were all bundled up in coats and hats. But they did seem like a lovely pair, cuddled up so close together on a blanket. That was the strange part: they were dining al fresco. Having a candlelit picnic!'

The nods round the table become stiffer. I stop breathing entirely. It feels like I might actually die. Suffocate and die right here at the table. I have to instruct myself to take some air in through my nose. I am very aware of the coolness of it entering my nostrils. It feels wrong. Sharp. It doesn't matter – I take more in. And more. And more.

I need to get some oxygen to my brain. I need to think.

The stiff nods are a good thing. That's the first lucid thought I have as my little sips of air start going to my head. The tension that has suddenly filled the room is a sign that everyone thinks Grandpa is talking nonsense again.

Immediately I feel guilty for being relieved by this. My gut twists in on itself again. I can't throw Gramps under the bus – I can't let everyone think he's imagining things. But then again . . . he is. Sometimes. A lot of the time. Is it so awful if I let them believe this is another one of those times? Just for an hour or so? Until I've spoken to Ben?

I chance another look at Margot. Her face is almost green. And that decides it. I can't let her worry like this. I give her the tiniest nod I can manage, to say, *Yes, we're OK.* We have been saved by Grandpa's famously vivid imagination, and now we're safe.

I must not look as confident as I'd hoped, because Margot's face becomes etched with concern.

'Don't worry,' she mouths at me.

But *she* looks worried. That worries me.

I mouth back, 'It's all OK.'

There's a sudden screech.

A chair is being scraped across the wooden floor, the harsh sound echoing through the room, at odds with the soothing carols on the radio.

Ben stands up.

He looks from me to Margot and back again. He seems dazed. And dark. He has clearly seen it all. The mixture of worry and relief on our faces, the knowing looks and the mouthed words.

The truth.

With a pained recoil he turns and storms out of the room.

There is complete silence round the table. Confused glances. Furrowed brows. Some of them look at the door he slammed on his way out. Some of them look at their plates but ignore the food. I look at all of them. But not at Margot. And then not at anything. With my eyes closed, I don't have to think. I can't think. I let the silence swallow me, just for a moment, I allow the quiet to –

'Who'd like more juice?' Mum asks brightly.

I blink open my eyes. Mum is smiling wide, like she's pulled on a mask. She's holding a jug filled with orange juice. She's demanding that we move on.

Dad looks away from the door and passes Mum his glass at once. Kate frowns at the bagel she still has in her hand, left hovering near her mouth, and takes a tentative bite. Grandpa looks delighted as he tucks into his pancakes. I think he might have forgotten about the confusion already. I think everyone else is hoping to do the same.

They don't know what has happened. Of course they don't. There's no way they could have put all the pieces together to figure out why Ben walked out. They probably assume he was upset about Grandpa seeming all muddled again. Or maybe they think he needed the toilet. Urgently. Whatever their guesses, it won't be the truth. And it won't be discussed. Mum has signalled that we're getting back to our meal now. We're not to dwell on any negativity, and we're certainly not to allow Mum's perfect plans to be derailed by something as minor as an early exit from brunch.

So I've got a 'get out of jail free' card. Or at least a 'stay out of jail for now and eat a cinnamon roll, then sort out the messy bit later once Ben has cooled off and no one is around to witness the drama unfolding' . . . card.

But it's no good. I have to follow Ben. Staying put would mean fitting in with the family and avoiding a big spectacle, but it wouldn't be right. Ben deserves an apology right away, an explanation, anything he needs.

I leave my pastry behind. I avoid looking at Margot, hoping to avoid trouble, avoid us communicating without any need for words, avoid letting the cat any further out of the bag.

I chase after my brother.

He has been pacing. Hasn't got far from the dining room. As soon as he sees me he picks up the pace, walking away and tearing the jolly little hat off his head as he goes.

'Ben, stop.' I reach him and grab his arm. 'Talk to me.'

He spins around. 'About what?' he demands, his voice booming. 'Tell me what we need to talk about. What's going on?!'

I cringe at the question – at the anger and confusion and pain behind it. And at its volume. I cast a quick look over my shoulder at the door to the dining room. The rest of the family can only ignore this if we keep it down – if it doesn't spiral into another of my big screaming dramas.

'Oh, am I being too loud?' Ben asks, now in a sarcastic whisper. He doesn't sound like himself at all. 'Sorry. I wouldn't want to make you look bad. Imagine getting caught off guard in front of your whole family.'

'Ben.' My voice breaks. 'I'm sorry.'

'So it's true?' He suddenly sounds almost defeated. 'It was you and Margot having that picnic?'

I can only nod.

He sighs. His body slackens. His arm finally falls out of my grip.

'That's not very nice,' he says.

My heart breaks. He sounds just like himself again, all the anger now stripped away. I didn't expect this reaction at all. I never thought he'd be so upset about me dating his pretend girlfriend. His random employee. I never meant to hurt him like this.

But that isn't relevant. Whatever I intended, I *have* hurt him. I'm not gonna make excuses for myself or centre my own emotions in this. I don't want to escalate the situation like I normally do. I just want to make it right.

'I'm sorry,' I whisper. 'I'm so sorry. We both are –'

'We,' he echoes. 'You and Margot are a "we".' His low voice sounds hollow. 'You two only care about each other, hey? You went out on a date in our garden, not caring how pathetic it would make me look if someone saw you. But now you're whispering. You don't want this conversation to be heard, because now it's *your* image at stake. It's like you've followed me out here to do damage control, Ellie, not to apologize.' He shakes his head sadly. 'If you were really both sorry, Margot would be out here too.'

Right on cue, Margot comes out of the dining room.

'Ellie?' she calls.

Ben scoffs. 'See? You only care about each other.'

He stalks away, his shoulders rounded.

I want to chase after him and apologize properly. I want to run to Margot. I want to deal with this together. I want to be alone. I want to go back in and find Grandpa. I want to tell him he's not crazy, not confused. I want to believe that.

I want my head to stop spinning.

'It's OK,' Margot says, coming closer. Her voice seems shockingly loud after mine and Ben's whispering, the sound reverberating in the long hallway.

I can't deal with it. With her chasing after me instead of Ben. Proving him right. Making us look worse. Compounding my guilt.

Speaking so fucking loudly.

Does she *want* everyone to hear what's going on? Does she want to blow up Ben's secret once and for all? Make an even bigger drama for me to be the centre of?

No. I know she doesn't mean to do any of that. I shouldn't be feeling so angry with her – especially not when I want to take her in my arms at the same time. But I can't help it. My sudden fury is a strong, hot, familiar feeling in the middle of all this mess. It's something to hold on to. To keep me alone, like I so clearly need to be right now.

'Stop it,' I hiss at her. 'You're just making things worse.'

'But I –'

I turn away. 'Don't follow me.'

28

Margot

I stand alone, watching Ellie walk away from me. She doesn't look back. I am shocked by her hardness.

What can I do now? When I'm apparently making everything worse? I can't go back into the dining room to sit down at the table with someone else's family and pretend that I haven't just ruined their Christmas. I also can't follow Ellie. She's made that very clear. At the end of the hall she turns sharply and stalks off in the direction of the garden. Everything has come crashing down around us, and she has left me all alone in the wreckage.

Ben is alone too. My friend – hurt and angry and confused. I snap into action. I hurry down the corridor and towards the stairs. I have to find him and talk this all through. He is owed a proper explanation. An apology. I thought Ellie and I would be on the same page about giving him that. I thought we'd do it together. But that's not the point now.

I rush across the top-floor corridor to our bedroom. I knock twice on the door.

'Ben, it's Margot. I'm coming in.'

I'm not. The door doesn't open, no matter how much I jostle the handle. It must be locked from the inside. I knock on the wood again. I hammer at the door.

'Ben? Can you hear me?'

Silence.

I jostle the door again.

I rap my knuckles on the wood.

'Ben? Hello? Please let me in.'

'No.'

'*Please*, Ben. We need to talk.'

'No. We don't.' His voice is low and flat. 'I don't have to listen to a word you say.'

'But . . . I can explain everything. I swear. Just let me in. Just *listen to me.*'

'No. You listen to me.' His voice is still level – almost emotionless, aside from the slightest edge. I think I'd prefer if he just shouted at me. 'I am not interested in listening to what you have to say. I didn't "need" to talk to Ellie, and I don't need to talk to you. Just ask her what I said downstairs. Cut out the middle man.' He sniffs. 'Now I suggest you go.'

'But –'

'*GO!*' he roars. 'JUST BLOODY LEAVE!'

I stagger away from the door. I definitely don't prefer him shouting.

'You have humiliated me, Margot. Both of you. Do you not see that?! You have been running around with *my sister* behind my back, making an absolute mockery of me the whole time. Anyone could have seen you and Ellie together. Someone *did* see you. Do you know how stupid that makes me look? My confused old grandpa watching my girlfriend kissing someone else before *I* even knew I was being cheated on?'

'But –'

'BUT NOTHING. I know you weren't *really* cheating on me. That's irrelevant. None of them know that, do they? It doesn't make me look any less pathetic. Don't you think I already *felt* pathetic enough, having to bring a near stranger home for the holidays? God. I thought we were doing each other a favour here. I thought we were a team. But you couldn't even *act* like a decent loyal girlfriend for a few days, when that was the *only* thing you were here to do. It's no wonder nobody wanted you around for Christmas.'

He stops as soon as the words are spat out. There is a sharp intake of breath. I'm not sure whether it's his or mine.

'Sorry,' he says, his voice unnaturally level again. 'See. I can't talk. I'm too angry. I'll say things I don't mean. You just have to leave me alone. I don't want to see you. Go.'

I hear him retreating away from the door, further into the room. There's a loud sob of frustration, and I think a few muttered apologies. Another door slams shut, which I assume must be the one to the en suite. It makes sense. Ben wants as many barriers between us as possible. He can't stand to be anywhere near me, and I can't blame him for it. I wouldn't want me around either.

I realize I'm still holding on to the door. My arms are pressed against the wood, my hands curled into useless fists. I drop them, letting them hang heavy by my sides. It suddenly feels as if all my limbs are made of lead. With great effort I force my legs to move. I walk stiffly down the corridor. As soon as I reach the top of the staircase, I allow myself to stop. I sag against the nearest wall and let my heavy limbs drag me to the ground.

Ben's words play on a loop in my mind. He's right. He's right about everything. I have let him down completely.

I came into his beautiful family home and I took advantage of his generosity and I did whatever *I* felt like doing, thinking only of myself and my stupid self-indulgent *cloud of happiness*. That's what getting swept up in romantic fantasies will do for you. I am left all alone – the social pariah of the day. Ben doesn't want to know me. I can never face the Gibsons again. Even Ellie has turned her back on me at the very first sign of trouble.

Everyone has abandoned me.

I need connection. I need distraction. With shaking hands, I reach into my pocket for my phone. I scroll aimlessly, searching without knowing what I'm looking for. My eyes skim over my notifications. My fingers tap from one app to the next. I have a fleeting look at Twitter, then Instagram, then Facebook. I flick through my camera roll. I glance at my calendar. The weather. Even my online bloody banking.

Something finally catches my attention. A string of transactions from last night. Somebody has sent me a single penny. Then another. And another. In total, I have banked ten pence. Each transaction has a one-word reference.

Margot
Please
Talk
To
Me
I
Miss
You
So
Much.

I don't even have to check who the money is from, but her name is all over the screen. Ms T Webb.

Taylor.

I feel something inside of me shatter. I press my back against the wall. I draw my knees into my chest. I try to hold myself. I end up slumping, collapsing, caving in.

Some things, I think, are inevitable. Taylor is inevitable. She is here when nobody else wants to know. She sees the worst parts of me, and she takes me anyway. She always takes me. Pulls me in. Grabs hold. I should have known that this wasn't over. I wasn't making any 'progress' by sitting on my arse and searching up a few articles. I was kidding myself. This is where I belong. Taylor is the only person in the whole world who won't turn me away – who will work tirelessly to reach me, even when we are broken up and I am being bratty and ignoring her. She will never let me go. She was right about me being difficult to love. She is always right.

She is inevitable.

I unblock her number.

29

Ellie

I trudge across the field, boots crunching on frosty grass. Somehow it feels colder out at midday today than it did at midnight last night. A sharp wind snatches at my clothes and stings my cheeks. Dark clouds gather up above. No more clear skies now. Rain will start to fall soon in vast icy sheets.

I hear more footsteps behind me. Can't be arsed to turn around. I keep pushing on, driven forward against the wind by some inner force that I think must be anger. Or shame.

There's panting along with the footsteps, and then Mitsi is by my side. Tail wagging, tongue lolling out of her mouth. She must have broken out of the house shortly after I did. She skips along beside me, unburdened by her extra pregnancy weight and unaware that I am public enemy number one. She attempts to lead me off to the right, towards the furthest field of the estate. I ignore her. Press on in the direction I was going in: straight ahead. It's like I'm in some sort of trance, although it doesn't feel very relaxing. I must keep moving forward. Straight line. No detours.

Eventually we reach the lake.

The bench.

Immediately my single-minded determination to push onwards vanishes. My trance breaks. My legs buckle. I have to take a seat right here on the bench. Our bench. Margot's and mine.

The tears come as soon as I'm sitting down. Hot and salty and flowing so heavily that my vision blurs. Mitsi looks like a brown blob curled up at my feet. The lake is one big smudge of grey. I can't believe how badly I've messed everything up. Keeping a secret like that; hurting my brother; creating drama.

Worst of all: deserting Margot. Leaving her behind outside the dining room as I flounced away. *Why did I do that?* I can't make sense of my own thinking from only moments ago. I *wasn't* thinking, I don't think. Not properly. I was focused only on damage control, just like Ben said; on ensuring I didn't look any worse than I already did in the eyes of my family. I had a one-track mind, as per usual. I was fixating on a single irrelevant thing.

I was underthinking.

I was an idiot.

We should have stood together, me and Margot. It's so clear to me now. It's the only clear thing in this world blurred by tears. The damage was already done, after all: Ben was already furious, and brunch was already ruined, even if everyone was intent on pretending otherwise. I should have stayed with Margot as it all went down; allowed our eyes to meet as we both processed the shock of Ben storming out; left the dining room *with* her to face him and try to sort things out. The two of us should have been together in this. Instead, I've alienated her along with the rest. I've doomed myself to sitting on our bench alone, surrounded by tainted memories which are only making my tears fall faster.

I suddenly jump up, startling Mitsi. Startling myself. It's like waking up right in the middle of a dream. All I know is that I can't sit around here a moment longer, throwing myself the world's most pathetic pity party. I am not the victim here. I give my nose a rough wipe with the sleeve of my jumper and rub my eyes with the heels of my hands. I need to get back into that house and make everything right, right now. Margot needs to know that I haven't turned my back on her. Ben needs to know that I'm sorry.

It's time for me to stop crying and mop up this spilt milk.

I make my way upstairs the long way round, using the narrow staircase in the private wing so that I don't run into my family. I'm not ready to see them all yet. But I will be soon. I am going to fix everything – quietly, out of the spotlight, just like Mum would want – and then we can all resume festivities together.

The first thing I have to do is find Margot. I'm gonna apologize for pushing her away, for being so dismissive and rude. I was projecting when I told her she was making everything worse. I was ashamed of my own mess. Now I have to own my feelings and work through them instead of just reaching for the strongest, simplest emotion. I can do that *with* Margot. I just have to trust that she can find a way to forgive me. I know in my heart that we can get past this if I meet her with openness and honesty.

The next apology is for Ben. I will give him a full explanation about what's been going on, with no details hidden away. Margot and I will talk to him together – just like we planned. Grandpa's surprise revelation might have thrown our plan off course, but that doesn't mean we have to abandon it completely. We will weather this storm together. We will talk to Ben as a couple. He'll see that this isn't just another fling – a bit of silly fun I had at his expense. He'll see that it's real. He'll understand.

If it takes me all day and all night, I will patch things up with Margot and Ben. With everyone. We will all be together as a family for Christmas Day.

There's only one flight of stairs left between me and Margot. I know she's gone up to her room on the top floor. I can feel it. The same inner force that pulled me towards our bench outside is leading me to her now. I give my eyes and nose another quick wipe. I check that no one else is around to listen in. The coast is clear – even Mitsi has gone now, off looking for food. I have one last check for stubborn snot bubbles around my nose, and then I stride across the corridor towards the final staircase.

Before the steps are even in sight, I hear a voice coming from above. It's hers. I knew she'd be up there! I knew we were connected. My heart lifts, soaring up high in my chest. I hurry towards the sweet sound.

'It's not a joke,' she's saying. 'It's really me.'

There's a long pause.

'I missed you too, Taylor.'

All at once, every awful feeling comes flooding back. Anger, shame, embarrassment. The unmistakable feeling that I must be the biggest idiot to ever walk this earth.

But still I try to remain calm. To face up to these feelings without using them to jump to conclusions. With a great deal of effort, I dismiss any outlandish theories that come up in my mind – like Margot already getting back together with Taylor, or having never actually broken up with her in the first place. What Margot is saying right now doesn't line up with either of those options. She's asking what Taylor has been up to, and where she is at the moment. She doesn't sound overly familiar or comfortable.

The reality is that Margot was abused by Taylor. A twisted bond like that doesn't just go away overnight. Taylor must still have a hold over her, and I must try to be understanding about that. Of course it hurts to hear Margot talking to someone who treated her so horribly – telling her she misses her – calling her baby. It stings like a bitch. But I understand that Margot must be in distress.

And then she giggles.

She. Fucking. Giggles.

That isn't the sound of a woman in distress. This is not a situation I can be understanding about.

Margot is not someone I can trust.

Before I have to hear any more, I spin round so fast that I make myself dizzy. Hurry down the corridor the way I came. Race to the bottom of the stairs. I'm gone before Margot even knows I was there.

On the ground floor I keep running. I run down another hallway and past doorways and into the foyer. I don't care about anyone seeing me. No one could stop me long enough to ask questions. I swipe my coat on my way to the front door and then I run outside and I run across the driveway and I run to my car.

I don't give myself enough time to slow down, and I crash into the metal door. It reminds me of Margot on the night she arrived here, swinging her car door open and whacking Mitsi with it. I laugh bitterly at the memory, and the strangled sound is whipped up into the wind. Margot Murray has been bad news from the very start. I never should have gone anywhere near her. I should have trusted my gut.

I plunge a hand into my coat pocket. Grab my car keys. Unlock the door. I clamber into the driver's seat and shove the keys into the ignition. I'm in no fit state to drive – hell, I managed to crash before I was even in the car – but I don't care. I need to get away from here. That's what I always do when things go wrong: I run away. There's no new island for me to escape to this time, but I'm sure I can drive far enough away from this place that I start to feel free. I step on the accelerator and swerve round the gaudy stone water feature. Rain finally starts to fall, beating down on the metal roof and blurring the windscreen. I flick on my wipers and I turn the radio all the way up and I speed down the tree-lined driveway, leaving the manor behind me in the rear-view mirror.

30

Margot

'I've missed you so much,' Taylor says again. '*So* much, baby. I've been thinking about you and your sweet voice and your funny little jokes non-stop. You remember how we used to laugh until our abs hurt? I didn't realize how much I loved that until it was gone. It seemed like such a small thing, but it's been awful not having you around. I've been dreaming about you finally calling me back. Literally. I've had dreams about the phone ringing. That's how much I've missed you.'

I let her affection settle within me. I'm not sure how deep it gets. There is a pattern being followed here, a cycle that Taylor and I have been repeating for several minutes. I know what comes next.

'You should have at least replied to me,' she says. 'That wouldn't have been so hard to do, would it? I was so lonely. And you could've saved me so much worry with just one little text. I've been going out of my mind the last few days. Barely eating. Not sleeping.'

I bite the insides of my cheeks. I try not to feel guilty again.

It takes too much effort.

'I'm sorry,' I tell her. 'I missed you too. I should have answered.'

311

'Oh, never mind,' she says breezily. 'You're back now. I'm just glad to hear your voice. It's as adorable as ever – maybe even sweeter than I remembered. Can you believe I was starting to forget your voice? I missed it so much. I missed *you*.'

And so the cycle begins again. Taylor tells me about her sleepless nights and her dreams about the phone ringing; about missing me and being hurt by me. I apologize, and I tell her that I missed her too, and she brings us back to the start. It's easiest if I just relax into it. The repetition can be kind of soothing. Settling into a pattern with Taylor is almost like going back to the old times that she's been reminiscing about – the same old times that I was desperate to return to only a week ago. Back then, I thought Taylor didn't want me any more. It's an overwhelming but pleasant surprise that she still has such strong feelings for me.

Her voice keeps getting louder at random intervals, rising above all the background noise on her end of the call. She is clearly somewhere busy: there are loads of other voices around her, all of them chattering and laughing, and there is a heavy drum and bass beat thrumming away. The intense noise disorientated me when she first picked up my call – especially since it's only midday. I tried to ask where she was, but she could barely hear me. She moved further away from the crowd, and told me how alone she's been, and how I could have helped. The next time I asked where she was, she changed the subject back to how I left her high and dry. I probably shouldn't ask again. It's not really important, I suppose. It would just be nice to know.

Finally Taylor brings our cycle to an end. 'Enough,' she

says. 'Tell me how you've been, baby. Tell me what you've been up to.'

'Well, I –'

'Tell me where you are!' she continues brightly. 'I know you're not at the flat, because the downstairs neighbour said he hadn't seen you all week when I called to wish him a happy Hanukah. And I know you're not at your mum's, because she said she's been chatting to you on the phone every day. She couldn't hang up on *me* fast enough, though. There's always something more important for her to get to, isn't there? No time for anyone but herself.' Taylor sighs heavily. 'So where are you, then? Where in the world have you run off to?'

'Oh. Well!' I make my voice as upbeat as I can. 'Um, I'm just spending Christmas with a friend. Where are you? It sounds like there's a party going on?'

'Which friend?'

'A new friend. You don't know him.' I put a little extra emphasis on the male pronoun. Keep it light and happy. 'Are you with friends for Christmas as well?'

'What's this new friend's name?' Taylor asks. 'How can I not know him? How can you be sure that you're safe staying with him?' She pauses. 'Listen, you should give me his address. Someone you trust should know your location. Tell me where you are, baby. I'll make sure you're safe.'

I hold on to my phone, tight. 'There are people who know my location.'

'Good. That's good. But you should give me the address too. There's safety in numbers. You should tell as many people as possible where you are. Just let me know where he lives, so that I know you're OK.'

'Umm . . .'

I want to say no. Of course I want to say no. Something deep inside of me is screaming at me to say no.

But the word won't come out.

'Oh, Margot.' Suddenly Taylor's voice is full of pity. 'Do you even know where you are? Do you remember the address of the house you're in? I really hope you do. Please tell me you knew better than to run off with a strange man without knowing exactly where he was taking you?'

I bristle. Does she think I'm an idiot? My hand tightens even more around my phone. I press the screen hard against my ear.

'It will all be OK,' she coos. 'Just give me the address.'

I feel another surge of irritation. This repetition isn't soothing – not at all. Why can't she just drop the issue? It is very obvious that I don't want to give her my location.

And yet I'm not saying no, am I? She must have noticed that. She must be aware that I'm not able to fully deny her. She is using that to her advantage, repeating her question until it finally, inevitably wears me down.

Even though I know this and somehow recognize the tactic, I can't say no. The tiny, two-letter word won't leave my mouth.

'I'm in a manor house out in the countryside,' I say, my grip on the phone loosening. 'And where are you, Taylor?' I hug my knees even closer to my body, bracing myself. If I can't say no, my best hope is to keep deflecting. 'It sounds like you're at a club? Is it a daytime rave? Or are you abroad? Where are *you*?'

'Seriously?' she snaps. 'If you won't tell me where you are, why should I say where I am?'

'Well, I asked first . . .'

'Oh, don't act like a child, Margot. That's pathetic. If you really want to rank us based on who deserves an answer first, you should remember that *you* ditched me for the past week. Maybe it was some kind of revenge for me breaking up with you, so you've decided that it's justified – but it's actually just immature. I didn't deserve to be punished like that. And I don't owe you any answers. Now tell me the address of this manor house before I find some other way to find out. Where in *the countryside* are –'

That's it.

I can't take any more.

So I hang up the phone.

The quiet that follows surprises me. It is so complete. The only sound in the empty corridor is my hammering heart. Taylor's voice is gone, and so are the random voices around her and the booming music around them all. The silence feels clean. Freeing.

It's like my mind is my own again. In this new stillness, I start to run through some of the things Taylor just did. She belittled me, and she played the victim, made demands, and rapidly swung between moods. When it was all happening, I couldn't label any of it. I was too busy trying to find comfort in her familiar intensity. It was only when she pulled out the old classic of demanding to know my location while refusing to divulge her own that I finally came to my senses. That purposefully unequal dynamic was the first sign of abuse that really resonated with me in Ben's article.

Now part of me resists the A-word again – just like I have all along. I start to feel silly. After all, 'abuse' is a strong word for a slightly unpleasant phone call, and *I* was the one who initiated the conversation in the first place.

I try to silence those thoughts. It isn't silly or overdramatic of me to notice signs that *are* there. I must try not to trivialize my own experience. Ben's article mentioned that that can happen sometimes – often by the design of the abuser. That's one way you can become trapped. Another headline I stumbled across claimed that a high percentage of victims go back to their abuser, sometimes several times, before they manage to leave for good. So it's normal that I called Taylor. Doing so has made me feel stupid and pathetic and angry and weak and dirty and small, but it's normal. I don't have to hate myself for it. I can choose to let it go and move on.

I let my phone vibrate in my hand as Taylor calls me back, back to back, over and over. Very soon I will end this and block her number again. But first I look down at the incoming call on my screen and say one simple word.

'No.'

I feel myself becoming energized as soon as I press the block button a few moments later. I pull myself up from my seat on the ground. I'm in control again. I'm strong. I see now that I don't have to look backwards and settle for Taylor and her abuse, even if she does inundate me with messages and a whole ten pence worth of spending money. I deserve better than her. I *want* better than her.

I want Ellie.

That's a scary thing to be so certain about all of a sudden, especially since Ellie pulled away from me this morning. But I *am* certain – and that means that I have to work through this messy bit as best as I can. I have to be brave. Instead of panicking about feeling rejected and alone, and allowing that panic to push me back to familiar ground with Taylor, I have to step into uncharted territory. Maybe I have to run. That's what I want to do suddenly: as adrenaline courses through my body, I feel an overwhelming urge to run to Ellie. I have visions of myself racing through a tinsel-draped airport to stop her before she gets on a plane or dashing through the snow on a busy New York City street to kiss her at the exact moment the bells ring out for Christmas. Strangely I don't cringe at the romantic excess of these thoughts. This bit isn't scary. I want to be romantic. For her. For Ellie. I want to lay my heart on the line for her, because what we have is worth fighting for, even with all its complications.

Still, I stop myself from breaking into a run. Ellie asked me not to follow her, and I will respect that. There will be no mad dashes through the airport or sprints down Fifth Avenue today. I will simply give her a call. That doesn't count as following her, I don't think, and if she isn't ready to speak to me yet then she doesn't have to answer. I won't freak out about that. Or I won't freak out too much. Ellie is entitled to her own emotional response to this whole thing. I can give her more time if that's what she needs, and then we can work through it together when she's ready.

I tap on her contact name and press 'call'. I bounce slightly on the spot, with excitement rather than anxiety. I think she will be ready to talk to me now. I think we've both got our individual freak-outs out of the way. She'll pick up the phone and we'll be reunited and we'll fix this mess we have made with her family. We will deal with everything as a couple, just like we planned.

Seconds pass and there is no answer to my call.

Downstairs, music starts playing: an upbeat jingle. A *ringtone!* Maybe it's Ellie's phone ringing, which would mean she's right downstairs, which must mean she has come back to find me, which means –

No. It means nothing. Ellie isn't here. I have raced down the stairs two at a time, using some of my new intense energy, but Ellie is nowhere to be seen. There is nobody here at all. In the middle of the long corridor, a phone lies discarded on the floor. It is ringing loudly, and as I get close to it I see my name displayed in the middle of the screen. This is definitely Ellie's phone. She must have dropped it at some point this morning – though whether that happened before or after the disastrous brunch, I don't know. I hurry along to the very end of the corridor to look out of the nearest window. I see right away that Ellie's car is no longer parked in the driveway.

She's gone.

I hang up the phone.

Rain lashes against the windowpane. Dark clouds gather in the sky. Thunder claps far away. I keep bouncing on the spot as I watch the storm raging. The energy fizzing inside my body has not gone anywhere. I still have the vital urge to race towards my future.

I still feel strong.

Ellie will come back to me when she is ready – I have to believe that. Until then, it is up to me to deal with the mess. And that's OK. I can sort things out around here without needing someone to hold my hand through it.

I can do this alone.

31

Ellie

I don't want to be alone. I don't want to be stuck by myself in my crappy old car on the M56 in the pouring rain on Christmas Eve. The motorway is heaving with people driving home for Christmas, while I'm over here speeding away in the opposite direction. It's depressing. I don't want to be the one always running away.

I press my foot on the accelerator. I *am* running, so I'm gonna run fast. Fast enough to leave every ounce of pain behind me. I overtake cars full of happy families, swerving round them all to get into the fastest lane. Heavy rock music blasts out of my radio, shaking the car doors. I scream along to the lyrics. Some maniac behind me has started following me as I switch lanes, flashing headlights at me. I think of it as a challenge.

In the right-hand lane, I honk my horn at the sports car in front of me. The guy's driving *under* the speed limit. I zigzag to my left then cut back in front of him. Flash him my middle finger in the rear-view. I miss his response, because the rain is falling on to my rear window quicker than the shoddy wipers can get rid of it. My maniac challenger follows close behind me. The motorway comes in and out of focus for me. It doesn't matter. I step on it again and bolt down the road in a mostly straight line.

Lose myself in the wicked guitar solo playing right now. Speed up even more. Scream and sing and scream.

32

Margot

I step away from the window, turning my back on the rain outside. I feel another blast of energy as I think about sorting everything out. I am doing this for myself, because I can do things for myself by myself, and I am also doing it for Ellie. I want things at the manor to have settled down by the time she gets back home. Resolving all this for her will be a far better romantic gesture than running through an airport could ever be.

I'm going to start with Mo, AKA Gramps. He was right about seeing a couple having a midnight midwinter picnic last night, and it only seems fair that someone confirms that for him.

I find him downstairs, sitting on his own in the smaller family living room. He smiles at me as I knock on the open door, and beckons me in. I sit down gingerly on one end of the Chesterfield, and we exchange pleasantries for a few minutes. Mo tells me the rest of the family are off watching *The Grinch*, as Mrs Gibson ushered them all into the next festive activity almost as soon as half her brunch party walked out without warning. She apparently believes that 'everything will work itself out on its own', and that nobody needs to worry about anything they don't understand in the meantime. In her view there is no drama, no interruption to festivities. I am relieved. Mo doesn't seem hung up on the situation either, as he promptly moves on to complaining about that 'weird naked green thing'. I agree that the Grinch is off-putting.

When Mo asks after Ben, I tell the truth and say that he's taking some time to cool off upstairs. When he asks after Ellie, I am slightly surprised, but again tell him honestly that she has taken some time alone away from the house. Mo doesn't seem shocked to hear this. He says that they will both come round eventually, and then he offers me tea and biscuits.

'No, thank you,' I say. 'I'm still full after breakfast.'

He shrugs and drinks from the teacup he already has on the go.

I shift on the sofa. 'Listen, there was something I wanted to say to you, Mo. I hope it doesn't seem strange, but I wanted to let you know that you *did* see a couple having a picnic in the garden last night, with candles and everything.'

'I know. I'm the one who saw it, so I know I saw it. Whether other people believe me is a different matter . . .'

'I believe you.'

His cloudy eyes fix on mine for a long moment. 'I'm glad, Margot.' He takes another slow sip of tea. 'Everyone else thinks I'm off my rocker.'

I'm surprised by his frankness. I try not to let it show on my face.

'Thank you for not arguing,' he says, sounding relieved. 'It is simply a fact. Everyone thinks I've gone nuts because I notice things that most people miss. Also, I've gone a bit nuts.'

I must do a bad job of hiding my surprise this time.

'It's OK,' Mo assures me. 'I know that some of the things I notice are not really there to be noticed. I just never get to tell anyone that. It doesn't really come up in conversation. I . . . they . . . we don't talk about it.'

'We could.' I stop trying to hide my emotions and reach out to give his arm a gentle squeeze. 'You and I could talk about it.'

He looks down at where my hand meets his arm, and smiles. 'OK. Yes. Well, I do see things that aren't there. Usually people. Most often I see my late wife, or I hear her voice. She's normally telling me not to slouch or to lay off the sugar.' He sits up straighter and closes the biscuit tin in his lap. 'Since she died, I have become convinced that I will find a new star in the sky. Sometimes I think that the star will be *her*. Her spirit or her soul or something along those lines. Other times, I simply think it would be nice to discover something new and tell her all about it when we next talk. I do speak to her a lot, when we're – erm, when *I'm* alone in our bedroom. She harps on about my posture and my sugar intake, and I talk to her about everything else. In those moments, it honestly feels like she's here with me.'

'I think that's lovely,' I say gently.

'I think so too. It can be a little confusing, though. I get most confused when I see my mother. She died when I was a boy, so I haven't seen her for a very long time. When I speak to her, it's like I'm young again and my life hasn't happened yet.'

I keep my hand on Mo's arm. He gazes out of the window for some time. Then he snaps himself out of it, literally snapping his fingers.

'So,' he says in a lighter voice, 'when I imagine things that aren't really there, it's always based on something real. Like conversations with my wife or my mother. I am reimagining things that really happened in my life but which aren't happening now. On the other hand, I know that something is actually happening in the present moment if I have never seen it before in my life. If it seems utterly bizarre and as though I am making it up out of thin air, it's usually real. Like a couple having a picnic at midnight or a pony running around in my back garden.'

'I see.'

'My imagination doesn't seem to conjure up new things any more – it only focuses on bringing my old memories back to life. So that's how I sort the sane from the insane. The ordinary real-life things are a memory, and the impossible things are real. Of course, it isn't always easy to remember that rule when everything I see feels so very real in the moment, but I can usually sort things out for myself in time. It has been working well enough for me so far anyhow, and my memory is still sound according to the doctors, so I'm not too worried about myself for the time being.' He nods firmly, marking a conclusion of sorts.

Then in a smaller voice he adds: 'I haven't been able to explain any of this to my family yet. I'm concerned that the explanation itself sounds crazy and will only worry them more.'

'It doesn't sound crazy to me,' I say. 'I think it makes a lot of sense actually. And you talk about all this really well – if that isn't too strange a compliment to give you.' I bring my arm back into my lap. 'I think it's worth giving everyone your explanation.'

He sighs. 'I think you're right. Perhaps I will talk to them all after Christmas. I might test-drive my explanation on some of my old friends first. The likes of Gerald and Ann are rather used to hearing things that sound a bit loopy. You know, I have an interesting story about those two. Perhaps we could we talk about that too?'

'Of course we can.'

Mo cracks his biscuit tin back open, and over a round of custard creams he tells me about his two dearest friends and the fact that they are in love with one another. He doesn't think that Gerald and Ann know about this development themselves, but Mo is certain of it. He explains that he has been noticing the signs for several weeks now, even when his two friends were engaged in a bitter dispute, and he believes that the deal will finally be sealed today. In a game of Secret Santa at the retirement home Gerald pulled Ann's name and Ann pulled Gerald's. Over time, everyone else at the home dropped out of the game. Except for Gerald and Ann. Mo happens to know what they have bought one another: the exact same coffee pot from Whittard of Chelsea. He proclaims them soulmates and expects them to finally realize as much later today when the gifts are exchanged.

'I know I'm right about this,' he says. 'This is something I've never seen before. There's never been any hint of romance between those two, and they seem like a truly bizarre match on paper. So what I'm seeing now has to be real.'

'Like with the midnight picnic,' I say.

'Precisely. And with the pony.'

I want to ask about the pony, because if that is a real

thing then it is mighty hard to make sense of. I don't want to be rude, though, or sound like I'm doubting Mo when he has just opened up to me.

He somehow reads my mind. 'I know it seems impossible that there is a random pony frolicking around on the grounds, unseen by all except me. I haven't quite made sense of it myself yet. But if you believe me that the pony *could* be real, perhaps you could help me look for it? I last spotted it near the groundskeeper's bungalow on one of my early-morning walks. You could have a quick look around there if you're up for it?'

He has a cheeky glint in his eye as he speaks, which Ellie has described to me before as one of her favourite things about him. It makes me feel like leaping off the sofa and rushing straight out to the bungalow as Mo's lookout. The excursion would allow me some extra time before I have to work up the courage to talk to Ben again, and I think I could do with a bit of light fun. Energy rushes through me yet again.

Mo seems to notice my eagerness. 'Go on,' he says. 'Report back to me if you find anything good. And, Margot, thank you for stopping by to talk to me. You are a very kind and insightful young lady. I'm so glad that you're here with . . . us.'

My heart glows. His words are lovely, and I know they're deeply meant, and they aren't even built around the lie that I'm dating Ben because Mo sees me as being here with all the Gibsons. *With us.* That's the best thing he could have said – plus or minus the slightly panic-inducing pause towards the end. Now my adrenaline has spiked even higher, and I'm practically bouncing myself out of my seat, and I share a huge smile with Mo before hurrying off in the direction of the bungalow.

I arrive at the little home on the hill without much of a plan. Do I knock on the groundskeeper's door and ask him if he's seen any neighbourhood ponies lately? He'll think I'm mad. Even worse if I ask whether the rumoured pony is a) wild or b) an unlikely pet being stashed away in this very bungalow. The groundskeeper has never met me before, and that would be a truly bonkers introduction. You can't just accuse a man of having a pet horse. Especially not a man who has never even kept a goldfish or a hamster before.

I mustn't let on that I know that about him. Blurting out personal details like that will only make me look crazier. Plus, the poor man might think I'm accusing him of having a contraband animal. Didn't Ben say that pets aren't allowed in the bungalow? He theorized as much, at least. I don't want the groundskeeper to think I've come to bust him on behalf of the Gibsons.

It's irrelevant anyway, because he obviously doesn't have a pet pony to get busted with. When did I even decide that was the most likely scenario? Why have I got so carried away with this? It's all nonsense. That seems so obvious all of a sudden. What was I thinking?

Just as I'm coming to my senses and turning around to leave, there's a loud crashing sound from the bungalow. A huge animal comes bounding towards me through the rain. The beast jumps up at me, standing on its hind legs. It rubs its muddy feet all over my clothes, tearing at the material of my jumper. I try to move backwards, but it keeps rearing up at me, panting heavily and . . . wagging its tail?

It's only a dog.

As soon as I realize this, I start to calm down. So does the dog. It returns to all fours, taking its dirty paws off me. It gives my leg a curious sniff. It cocks its head.

It humps me vigorously.

'STALLION!' someone shouts. 'SIT!'

The dog does as it's told. A chubby man with a shock of red wiry hair on his head is stomping out of the bungalow. He wears navy overalls with an oversized flannel shirt thrown over the top.

'I'm so sorry about him,' he says, glaring at the dog. 'I'm Stan, the groundskeeper. And he's Stallion, the idiot.'

'Um. I'm Margot, I'm here with –'

'I'm really so sorry,' Stan repeats. He doesn't seem to have heard me speak, and he doesn't seem able to take his narrowed eyes off Stallion. There isn't really anger there – more discomfort and embarrassment. 'I know he shouldn't be here. I know. He definitely shouldn't be running out like that. I'm so sorry. I opened the door too wide . . . that's my fault . . .' Stan tugs at his shirt sleeves. 'I saw you standing out here in the rain and was just coming to ask if everything was all right, when Stallion kicked the door all the way open and charged at you before I could stop him. The great oaf. I feel awful.'

'It's oaf-kay.'

I cringe as soon as I've said it. Stan is clearly worried, and I've gone and brushed him off with a stupid pun. I must not be thinking straight thanks to all the questions racing through my head. Like, is Mo's 'pony' really just this dog? And what are the odds of the not-a-horse being called Stallion? How long has Stallion even been here? Has he broken out of the bungalow before now? And was he caught quickly that time? Or did he have time to cause some trouble? Did he have a co-conspirator? A kindred spirit on the estate?

Did he make mischief with Mitsi?

Before my head can explode with thoughts, Stan snorts out a laugh. I look at him with surprise. I guess my joke wasn't so awful, after all. It seems to have helped Stan relax a little. He even makes eye contact with me at last.

'I s'pose it's a relief to finally be caught,' he says. 'I haven't felt right about having a dog here when my contract clearly says no pets, and I've been meaning to come clean to the Gibsons for a while. I just kept putting it off and somehow days turned into months. The truth needed to come out.'

'How . . . how have you managed to keep him hidden for so long?'

'Well.' Stan shifts from one foot to the other. 'We've got into a decent enough routine over the past few months. I drive him to a park miles away every day so he can have a proper run around, and I only walk him on the estate very early in the morning or late at night, always keeping him well away from the main house. The rest of the time, he's happy enough to be curled up in the living room, napping or eating.'

It does sound like a decent routine.

'He got away from me once or twice in the early days,' Stan continues, 'and it took bloody ages to find him again in the dark, but I've got a firmer hold of him now. Just as long as I keep the door closed.' He glances back at the bungalow. 'I really shouldn't have opened the door so wide.

He'll take any chance to run free, even if he's just come back from a two-hour stint at the park. He still has that puppy-ish energy, even at a year and a half. And he . . . well, he hasn't been neutered yet, so he tends to get overexcited. As you've seen.'

Stallion continues panting at me, ogling the leg he just humped.

Stan tuts. 'All of this should have been sorted out a long time ago, I know. It would have been if he was my dog. Then again, I never would have snuck a pet in here in the first place. Especially not a great big Great Dane. Not if I hadn't been begged by someone I can't say no to.' He shakes his head. 'I'm sorry again, love. Are you OK?'

In truth, I'm a little confused. Stallion isn't Stan's dog? I was just thinking I had everything worked out, and now there are new question marks. Still, it seems that my budding Stallion-Mitsi Pregnancy theory is correct. I just don't want to worry Stan with it until I'm absolutely certain. So I simply nod.

'I'm completely fine. There's no harm done.' I resist the urge to brush the mud off my clothes. 'And don't worry, it's none of my business if you have a pet. I think he's . . . cute.'

Stan laughs. 'No you don't. And no he's not. He's a hooligan and he's bloody humungous. D'you know he might get even bigger than this? He'll outgrow my house if he stays here another month.'

'That's why I named him Stallion,' calls a female voice. 'He's as big as a horse!'

The new voice belongs to a tall woman I've not seen before, wearing a light purple raincoat with the hood pulled up over her head. Another question mark. The moment she steps outside, Stallion rears up again on his back legs. She rolls her eyes at him.

'I wish he'd calm down for five minutes,' she says. 'But at least now he can burn off the excess energy – since he's revealed himself once and for all, we can finally stop with this hiding malarkey and he can run free.'

As if he understands her words, Stallion suddenly bolts. We all turn to watch as he races down the hill and halfway across the stretching field. Before long, he crashes into another beast. Mitsi. As soon as they collide, Stallion rolls over on to his back, completely submitting. The smaller (but very obviously rounder) dog clambers on top of him and licks his face all over. Both their tails wag wildly.

I feel absolutely zero surprise, but the tall lady's mouth hangs open as she watches them. She brings a hand to her head, which pushes her hood back slightly. This reveals a few curls of ginger hair – a vibrant shade that is a perfect match for Stan's.

And finally I have the full picture. This bewildered woman must be Bobbi, Stan's daughter and Ben's childhood sweetheart. Stallion is *her* pony-sized dog who is unneutered, overeager, and clearly not shy around Mitsi. The puppies are definitely his.

'What's going on?' Bobbi asks no one in particular. 'I thought bringing Stallion here would keep him *out* of trouble. I swear, I never would've snuck him in if I knew that he'd . . . Goodness. I suppose this is a fairly good reason for dogs to be banned from the bungalow, isn't it? I just assumed the no-pets-allowed thing was a short line thrown into a boilerplate contract that was written and signed decades ago and that nobody would care about any more.

Especially not if we checked in with Mr and Mrs G first – which I *did* want to do. But, no, even then, this is too much. I clearly shouldn't have bought Stallion here. I just . . . this seemed like a much calmer environment for him than a cramped house in Liverpool full of seven strangers and their various hook-ups. Not that *I* ever had anyone over to stay,' Bobbi adds quickly, shooting a look at her dad. 'I've been flying very, very solo since getting back to the UK sans boyfriend. That's why I needed Stallion here to keep me company. But . . . it wasn't fair to have him with me until I could get back on my feet and find us somewhere more spacious to live. It was much better for him to have room to run around, somewhere that he couldn't cause anyone any bother.' She looks back to her dog, who is licking the very plump Mitsi all over. 'That was the idea anyway.'

I still don't know exactly who she's aiming her words at, and I can't fully process her entire stream-of-consciousness in one go. But I feel excited. Because this endless chatter lines up so perfectly with Ben's description of his old flame.

'You're Bobbi,' I say simply.

She finally turns fully away from the canine love-fest. 'I'm Roberta these days actually. I'm sorry, do I . . . know you? Oh my goodness, you're not Kate, are you? Or Ellie? I hardly recognize you! How awful is that?'

'No, no. I'm not a Gibson. We've never met. I'm Margot. I'm here with Ben for Christmas.'

'Oh. I'm here for Christmas too. I arrived a few days ago to join Dad and Stallion.' She smiles my way, but it feels to me like there's a tiny flicker of disappointment somewhere on her face. Is it because I mentioned being with Ben? Is that a crazy conclusion to jump to?

'Ben and I are just friends, though,' I blurt out. Just like that. Maybe I should have put a bit more thought into sharing this secret that I've been guarding all week and which I was intent on keeping safe even after the spectacular fallout at brunch. But it feels right to have shared it now. I truly believe this could be for Ben's good, and it's not like Roberta and Stan are about to run off and report back to the Gibsons that Ben has a pal. Most importantly of all Roberta looks relieved at what I've said. I'm sure she does – her shoulders have relaxed and her smile has brightened. So I decide to go a little further. 'He's told me a lot about you.'

'He has?' She blushes. 'That's cool. Um, yeah, Ben and I used to be really close as kids. I've been meaning to come up to the house and say hello to him. To everyone, of course. But I haven't quite found the time yet. Dad and I have a lot of catching up to do here. This is the first Christmas we've ever spent together!'

Stan takes a break from staring slack-jawed at the dogs to beam at his daughter, apparently unable to help but light up at her words.

'Plus, I worried that if I visited the house, I'd let slip about Stallion,' Roberta continues. 'I'm not very good at . . . not talking. And Dad wasn't ready *to* talk. So I had to steer clear. I really didn't want to get Dad in trouble for doing me the huge favour of letting Stallion crash at his.' She winces guiltily. 'Oh, this is such a mess. That rottweiler *is* pregnant, isn't she? Is there any chance that some other guy is responsible?'

I open my mouth to rep–

'Wait. Don't answer that. I don't want to know.' She shakes her head. 'What a fiasco. I guess this is why Stallion has been scratching to go out constantly and tugging at the leash to get closer to the main house. He must have done this one of those times he managed to run off. Goodness. I'll have to go and apologize to the Gibsons as soon as possible. For what Stallion has done – and for my smuggling him in here in the first place.' Roberta scratches her neck. 'Are all the Gibsons here for Christmas?'

'Yep,' I say. 'Everyone's here.'

'Good, good. I definitely need to talk to Mr and Mrs G about the dogs. But I should probably talk to Ben too. He's really good with animals. Or he always was. We used to play with the birds and the squirrels around here, all summer long, and one time he even mended a sparrow's wing, and . . . Anyway. I bet Ben is great with that dog. So he'd be good to talk to about this. And to say hello to. I really have been meaning to come by and say hi. I just wasn't sure about . . . Well, I didn't know whether he'd remember me after all these years . . .'

Oh, these two *have* to see each other. To say that Ben still remembers Roberta would be the understatement of the century, and I don't think I'm completely off-base in thinking that she might still hold a flame for him too. At the very least, she clearly wants to chat to him – and she stated earlier that she's 'flying solo'. If I play this right, it could be an incredible reunion. I could go just a little way to putting things right with Ben by playing matchmaker. I'd so love to do this for him – to play a part in helping him find the happiness and romance he's been hoping for all these years.

But Ben isn't feeling happy or romantic right now. I can't risk springing Roberta on him on the one day of his life when he might not be open to finding a connection. I have to make sure he's ready for this. I have to talk to him again – even if it is only to say that I'll shut up and get out of his way.

I will bring him back to his usual self.

I will bring these two together.

'Stay here,' I say. 'Please. Ben will want to say hello to you too. I know he will. I just need to check that he's . . . free. Please don't go anywhere. I'll be back as soon as I can.'

Before anyone can question my sanity, I break into a run, racing across the drenched fields and through the pouring rain towards Ben.

33

Ellie

I can't shake off this prick in the car behind me. He makes every turn I make, flashing me with those stupid LEDs in his stupid massive SUV. I check my own lights are turned on. I know my tyres aren't flat. I keep screaming along to my music even though my throat is starting to hurt, as if the sheer force of my vocal cords will somehow scare the persistent bastard off.

I'm getting really bored of having him on my tail. Getting really bored of this whole bloody thing. I don't want to keep running. I want to be home. With my grandpa, and my dog, and my family. With Margot. I want to be still.

I keep speeding down the motorway.

34

Margot

I am halfway across the grounds, my calves burning, when I decide that I can't wait any longer. I pull out my phone, trying to shield it from the rain with my arm, and call Ben.

He picks up on the fourth ring.

'Hi! You answered. Hi.' I stop running, trying to catch my breath. 'Listen. I need to tell you something. But first, I have to say I'm sorry. I'm not asking you for forgiveness, and I'm not asking to talk it all through if you're not ready for that. I just want to apologize. I can explain everything if and when you want to hear it, but none of my explanations are excuses. I never should have gone behind your back. I never, ever intended to make you look stupid. You've become a real friend to me, Ben, and I care about you a lot. I hope beyond hope that I haven't ruined that completely. But whatever you think and feel about me, I really want to tell you this one thing. I promise you it's good news. Do you . . . do you want to hear it?'

Ben is quiet. Even his breath barely makes a sound, unlike mine. I force myself not to fill the silence. I've said my piece, and now I have to respect his response — whatever it may be. I distract myself by stretching my calves.

Then finally: 'That was one hell of a hello,' he says. 'Were you trying to get it all out before I could hang up?'

'Yes.'

'I wasn't going to hang up. I . . . I actually wanted to apologize as well. I was so rude to you earlier.'

'No, no. You had every right to be.'

'I didn't. I had every right to be *upset*, but there was no need for me to scream at you and hurl insults your way. I'm sorry. I was just shocked to find out about you and Ellie, and I felt so stupid for feeling shocked.' He pauses. 'I was jealous mostly. It didn't seem fair that you started dating someone for real, when I was stuck faking a relationship to get myself through Christmas. It encapsulated how pathetic my love life really is. I'm in my thirties, I've never had a long-term girlfriend, and I'm still into the girl I dated as a teenager. How sad is that?'

'No, it's not –'

'Bobbi is a thing of the past. I have to accept that. She's gone.'

'*Ben*, she hasn't –'

But he isn't listening.

'So why can't I let go?' he ponders. 'Every time I catch a glimpse of ginger hair anywhere near here, I think it might be her and my heart soars. It's ridiculous. I'm bloody delusional.'

'YOU'RE NOT!' I shout into the phone. 'Listen to me – you're not delusional. That's what I wanted to tell you. She's here. On the estate.'

'She . . . ?'

'Bobbi is here.'

He is quiet again – so quiet that I think the line might

338

have gone dead. Just as I pull the phone away from my ear to check whether he's hung up, I hear him laughing. A giddy, joyful, disbelieving laugh.

'Oh my gosh, I have to say hi.'

'No, no. I can't say hi,' Ben says a minute later, having called me back almost immediately after hanging up. 'It's all too sudden. It might be weird. I mean, it's been years and years. What if we have nothing to say to each other?'

'I don't think that could ever be a problem for you two,' I say.

'Ha. Fair point. But what if I come on too strong?'

'By saying hi?'

'By being me,' he says. 'I don't want to seem all intense. How . . . how do you even know she wants to see me?'

'Because she said so.' I avoid rolling my eyes, just in case Ben can see me through a window or something. 'Listen. You wait up there in the house, OK? I'll bring her to you. That way, you can be absolutely certain that she wants to see you and we'll know that she doesn't feel ambushed. OK? It's only saying hello.'

There's a long pause.

Then he laughs that giddy laugh again. 'OK!'

As soon as I knock on the bungalow door, it opens. Roberta is standing right there in the doorway, waiting.

'Ben would love to say hello,' I tell her quickly. 'He's free right now. So . . . will you come back to the house with me?'

She doesn't move. Nobody does. Stallion is still lying on his back on the grass. Mitsi is still lounging on top of him. Roberta is still standing motionless.

Finally Stan appears behind her in the doorway. 'For God's sake, go. There's a reason you've been standing right here this whole time. Go and see the Gibson boy. You can start apologizing for Stallion's little adventure with the Rottweiler.'

She laughs. It is a bright and jubilant and slightly crazed laugh that sounds incredibly similar to Ben's. Before I know it, she's pulling the hood of her raincoat back over her head and setting her sights on the main house.

We run together. I wasn't really sure whether I should still be involved, but Roberta was talking to me over her shoulder as soon as she'd set off.

'And is his hair still curly? I've always pictured him with curly hair, obviously, because that's how it was when we were young. But some people grow out of that kind of thing. Hormones, you know. I didn't, though. My hair has probably gotten curlier with age. I have all the right products now, which helps tame the frizz, but it does get expensive. I used to make do with one-pound shampoo. So bad for the hair. It's got too many sulphates in. Or not enough sulphates? I forget . . .'

The still and silent Roberta from moments ago is long gone.

As soon as we reach the house, the front door swings open. Ben was waiting eagerly on the other side of the door – just like Roberta was at the bungalow.

Now the two of them are standing just shy of touching distance. Finally face to face. Staring at each other.

'Bobbi,' he breathes, just as she says, 'Ben.'

They both break into self-conscious smiles.

'It's Roberta now,' she says. 'I assume you're still Ben. You still look like Ben. You have curly hair! I . . . I wasn't sure whether you'd remember me.'

'Of course I remember you. You still look like Bobbi. Like a tall, grown-up, Roberta version of Bobbi. You look great. Of *course* I remember you. I still remember every single thing about the last summer you were here. Everything.'

Roberta colours. 'I do too. We . . . erm, we went swimming, didn't we? And I broke my arm.'

'What? I don't remember that!?'

'Really? It was a huge deal. I fell off my bike on the last day of August. My dad had to take me to the hospital, and when my mum met us there she was *hysterical*. She was raving about how the manor wasn't safe for me, going on and on as if I was a child and my dad was a neglectful parent. We had to sweet-talk her into letting me even pick up my stuff from the bungalow. Your parents helped us pack everything up quickly. Then Mum took me back to her house that night, with my arm in the pink cast she chose for me.'

'I never knew about this,' Ben says slowly. 'I didn't hear a word about a bike accident or broken bones or the hospital. Not even about speedy packing. I guess my parents didn't want to upset me with the gory details of your accident? Or my mum just wanted to sweep anything remotely dramatic under the rug as usual.' He sighs. 'I . . . I thought you just left without saying goodbye.'

Roberta looks stricken. 'I thought *you* didn't want to say goodbye. I thought you didn't care about me getting hurt, because you didn't come to see how I was doing when I picked my stuff up from Dad's.'

'Because I didn't know you were picking your stuff up! I didn't know anything.'

'Huh.' Roberta shakes her head. 'We both seem to be pretty big on the "not knowing" thing, don't we?'

Ben nods his head.

Roberta switches to nodding with him.

They shake their heads at themselves and laugh.

'We have to get to the bottom of this,' Roberta says.

'We have *a lot* to talk about,' Ben agrees.

I tiptoe round them and slip through the wide-open doorway, leaving them to it.

It's getting dark by the time Ben comes back up to our room several hours later. I have been trying hard not to worry about things I can't control – like Ellie, like Taylor, like the Gibsons. Like what Christmas Day will possibly look like tomorrow. I have just been curled up on my bed with a book, listening to the rain tip-tapping on the leaded window.

'I like her,' Ben says now as he sits down on his own bed. 'I like her, I like her, I like her.'

I turn to face him, hoping for more chatter, like normal. I really hope things can be like normal.

'She had to go and start prepping her turkey for tomorrow,' he says. 'She's making it with a Bourbon glaze. How clever is that? She picked up the recipe when she was living in Nashville. You know how they love to eat in the States. She said she'd cook me some classic Southern dishes sometime soon. How nice is that? It's almost like a date, I think. Kind of. I wish it could be tonight or tomorrow, but, you know, Christmas. Hopefully we'll get together mid-week.

I'll miss her until then, though. I already miss her. How silly is that?'

'So silly,' I say. 'And so clever and so nice.' And so much like normal.

'It was amazing to talk to her again,' he says. 'We had so much to catch up on. *So* much. Did I mention that she lived in Nashville? She moved there when she was nineteen with an American guy she met at a club. Nineteen! She did it to get away from her mum. But then she had to get away from the guy too. And that was tricky because she had married him for a green card, and also for his abs. She listed those things in the opposite order, though. She said she was crazy for his . . .' Ben stops. 'This is too much information, isn't it? I'm going to go ahead and skip to the end. Which is that she finally moved back to England this year, and adopted a dog, and reconnected with her dad. They had drifted apart because of Roberta's mum, well, keeping them apart – and then because of Roberta going off to the US. She loved it out there, did I mention? She had this really cool job as a radio host – the Yanks *love* an English accent – and she had this new boyfriend for a while, once things were properly over with her husband. She liked the *boyfriend* for his . . .' Ben stops again. 'Sorry. I can't seem to shut up. She told me everything. Basically: she's finally ready to get back home, to her roots.'

'Right. Well, that all sounds great.' I pause. 'So she's divorced?'

'Yep,' he says brightly. 'She was divorced by the age of twenty-two. And *I've* never been in an official relationship. Aren't we a good match?' He chuckles to himself, the laugh ending with a happy little sigh. 'Seriously, though, Margot, thank you for getting us to talk. It was incredible. She's so chatty. And so funny. And so . . . wow. She's just wow.' He sighs again, then pauses, thinking something through. 'Is this how it is for you? Do you feel this way about her?'

'Umm. Well, I only met her a few hours ago. So I don't really . . .'

'I mean Ellie.'

Oh. My stomach starts flipping at the mention of her name. Like normal. But also like anxiety. I have no idea how I'm supposed to answer this.

'Well, I only met *her* a few days ago. So, um, I don't know whether I can really compare those feelings to the ones you have about a love story that's a lifetime in the making. I wouldn't want to be dramatic or anything . . .'

Ben holds up a hand. 'Margot.'

'Yes?' I look right at him. I give in. 'Yes. I feel like that about Ellie. I like her. I like her, I like her, I like her.'

He looks right back at me. He smiles. 'Good. I'm happy for you. I really am. You'd make a cracking sister-in-law, so I have no complaints.'

I want to hug him. So I get up off my bed and do just that.

'Thank you,' I say. 'I'm sorry, and thank you, and I promise we can keep up our fake relationship if you want to. But, oh – I assume you realize that Roberta knows you and I aren't dating? I'm sorry for letting that slip. It seemed necessary. But obviously we can still keep up the act for everyone else . . . ?'

He squeezes me. 'I think it's time to give it up now. It's all right. Why don't you tell me about something real instead? I'm ready to hear about you and Ellie.'

So I tell him the entire story – from clumsy beginning to moonlit dates to wherever we are now. I explain why we chose to keep things secret for that first night, and how we ended up keeping the secret for several more days. I apologize again for going behind his back. I swear that I never meant to get involved with his sister, but that I do really like her. I admit that I have no idea where she is right now, and that just like Ben with Roberta, I miss her so much already.

'See,' he says at the end of my spiel. 'I told you we were both losers.'

I laugh, but only by exhaling through my nose.

Ben frowns. 'Are you worried about her?' he asks softly. 'Because this is not the first time Ellie has run off. She always comes back. Trust me. I'd be feeling far more guilty right now for having a go at her if I thought she was gone for long. She just needs to blow off some steam and then she'll come right back home when she's ready. I promise you she'll be all right. She can take care of herself.'

I let his words soothe me, resisting the urge to overthink. I don't need to know exactly where Ellie is or exactly what she's doing. I just need her to be safe. And Ben is right: she can handle herself. She doesn't need me fretting over her and she certainly doesn't want me following her. The most supportive thing I can do right now is leave her to it. So for once in my life, I will not strap myself into someone else's emotional rollercoaster. I'll just be here for when she gets back.

'The only thing I'm worried about,' I say, 'is you calling me a loser. Cos I'm not. Even with all these big feelings, and even when I'm sitting around waiting for Ellie, I don't feel like a loser at all.'

'Oh, you lose by the way.'

Ben looks up at me from across the room. He makes a noise that almost sounds like 'huh', his mouth too full of pasta to respond properly. We both have huge bowls full of pesto rigatoni in our laps, smuggled upstairs by Ben for us to scoff in bed.

He swallows his mouthful. 'Huh?' he says more clearly. 'I thought we agreed earlier that neither of us are losers.'

'Nope. I agreed that I'm not a loser. And I'm not. I'm a winner. Because *I* have solved the mystery of who got Mitsi pregnant before you.'

He sits up like a meerkat and pushes his bowl to the side.

'Ah,' I say. 'So Roberta didn't mention it then.' I luxuriate in having a piece of top-notch gossip to share with my friend over a huge portion of carbs. 'Shall I spill?'

'*Yes*,' Ben demands. 'Give me all the goss! Right. Now.'

35

Ellie

Headlights are flashing at me again and my petrol light has started blinking and I cannot be arsed with any of this any more. I am tired. I am hungry. I am the slightest bit nervous about this nutter behind me. I take another quick look at his looming SUV in my rear-view mirror, then flick on my indicator and dart into the middle lane. I'm done with this now. I'm going to lose this guy once and for all, then stop off for petrol and snacks, and then finally think about heading home.

Obviously I won't actually *go* home. I am so not ready to face that shitshow yet. But I might go in the direction of home. A pub in the general vicinity. Give myself at least the option of being nearby for when it officially becomes Christmas Day.

I spot a sign for services and take note of the junction leading off to them. I stay put in the middle lane. Keep an eye out for gaps in the left-lane traffic. Don't touch my indicator. Stay put.

Stay put.

Stay put.

GO. I spin my steering wheel all the way to the left, cutting in front of a Mini and making it to the junction just in time. I shoot down the slip road with nobody following me. Relief blooms, relaxing all my muscles.

And then tyres screech behind me. Lights flash.

The SUV skids on to the slip road.

My heart hammers in my chest and even my throat as I pull into the petrol station. I have no other choice – I can't risk running out of fuel on the dark roads. I pull up as close to the building as possible, desperate for the safety of bright lights and other people. I look in my mirrors and then over my shoulder at this relentless, terrifying, reckless –

Woman?

I see her better now that we are not surrounded by other headlights, now that we are shielded from the rain by the forecourt canopy, now that my windscreen is finally clear.

I see that I know her.

I see Kate.

She stops the car in the middle of the forecourt, not making even a slight attempt at parking it properly. She throws open the door and flings herself out. Is pulled back by her seat belt. Unclips the belt. Flings herself out.

I get up and stumble towards her, feeling dazed.

She stops just in front of me.

We face each other.

It is silent.

And then, 'Why did you drive like that?' we ask in near unison.

'ME?!' Kate explodes. 'I was following *you*. You're a menace behind that wheel. If you drive like that normally, it's a miracle you're not dead by now. It's a miracle *I'm* not dead. I followed you for miles at breakneck speed. I kept flashing but you wouldn't pull over, and I kept calling and calling but you never answered your phone. You are an absolute nightmare of monumental proportions.' She finally pauses for breath. 'Are you OK?'

I blink at her. I'm still in shock that my chaser was Kate all along. I'm even more shocked that she broke so many rules behind the wheel of her pristine yummy-mummy Range Rover. I probably should have recognized her car from the start, but the pouring rain and the smeared windscreen and the intense emotion all conspired to confuse me.

'Why did you drive like that?' I ask again.

She looks at me as if I'm stupid. 'I just said, I was following you. I had to keep up somehow, didn't I?' She rubs her temples. 'I saw you leaving the house earlier. I watched through the window as you went running out and bumped into your car as if you hadn't even seen it parked there. I didn't think you were in any fit state to drive, so I came out to talk some sense into you. You had already driven off, so I followed. It took almost twenty minutes to catch up to you on the motorway, what with all your speeding and swerving. If only you'd pulled over at one of my very obvious and very frequent signals, instead of carrying on like an imbecile. I just wanted you off the roads and back home safe and sound where you belong. Obviously you will pay all my tickets when they arrive, and you'd better take any points on my licence, and –'

I hurtle forward and throw my arms round her.

'You drove like that for me,' I say, sniffling.

She stands stiffly. 'Yes. I suppose I did. For you, and for all the innocent people out on the roads tonight.'

I hold her closer. She relaxes slightly, and even puts an arm round me. That makes me sniffle even more, feeling like a little kid. Feeling safe.

'You're coming home now,' she says after a while, letting me go. 'It's about time, don't you think? You're going to suck it up and come back to the house to fix whatever it is that's gone wrong. And you're going to follow *me* in *my* car.'

'OK.'

'Don't even bother arguing with me,' she continues briskly. 'I have an awful lot to do tonight, and I've already wasted more than enough time on this wild goose chase. You're coming back home, and that's –' she frowns, apparently having just processed my agreement – 'that. OK, good. We'll get going right away. I'm already several hours behind schedule.'

'What do you need to do?' I ask.

'Oh, everything.' Kate rubs her bare arms. 'Henry had to stay late at work tonight and won't get back here until tomorrow morning. *Christmas* morning. So I have to sort out all the festive bits for the boys on my own. I have to make hot chocolate and cookies for Santa, and then wrap up the presents from Santa, and then become Santa to drop off the presents and eat all the hot chocolate and cookies. Tomorrow, I have to be up at the crack of dawn to act surprised that Santa has visited. I'll clear up all the wrapping paper, and set up all the new toys with new batteries, and get the boys washed and dressed and looking smart enough to impress Mum and Dad.' Her shoulders sag. 'I just wish Henry was here for it all. To make special memories with us, and to help me with the mundane bits in between. Maybe that's selfish. I know his work is important, but sometimes . . . well, sometimes, I feel almost like a single mother.'

I reach forward and hug her again. This time *she* feels

like a little kid in my arms. I realize suddenly that I've never really seen her in that way – not even when we were children. She has always been the big sister, steady and sensible. I couldn't relate. But this vulnerability . . . I get it. I finally recognize some of myself in her, and some of her in me. We hold on to one another in the middle of the forecourt, letting the cars in search of petrol inch round us. Rain keeps tumbling down from the sky, bouncing off the canopy roof that covers us. Sharp wind stings our exposed skin, so we hold each other closer.

'I'm sorry for giving you the run around,' I murmur. 'I didn't know it was you behind me and I'm pretty sure I left my phone at home somewhere, so I never got your calls. I really didn't mean to pull you away from everything you have to do tonight. I really, really appreciate you following me.' I swallow and realize that a lump has formed in my throat. Yet more tears are tracking down my cheeks. 'I'm sorry I always create so much drama. I promise that I'm not turning on the waterworks to make it all about me.'

'No. No, it's OK.' She brings her open palm to the back of my neck, just like Grandpa does. 'It's good to let it all out. It's healthy. If you don't, you end up like me, having a breakdown over Santa Claus because you never let yourself release your negative emotions. Trust me, Ellie, I'd rather be like you.'

'Like me?'

'Yeah. You're always so in tune with your feelings. If you need to cry, you cry. If you need to shout, you shout. If you need to drive like a lunatic auditioning for *Fast and Furious 103* in order to release some tension, that's exactly what you do. I've always admired that. You have so much *passion*, and you're never afraid to act on it. You wear your heart on your sleeve every day of your life and you follow through on all your emotional impulses. I think that's so brave. And stupid. But mostly brave.'

I am more shocked by this sentiment than by everything else that has happened today combined. I always thought everyone in my family saw me as tempestuous and difficult – Kate most of all. It never crossed my mind that she might admire my openness.

Not that I actually am as open as she thinks. I don't wear my heart on my sleeve – not really. I rush into new situations with unbridled passion, but I always rush away again just as quickly. I run away before I can get attached or hurt, tucking my heart back under my sleeve as I go.

But no more. I want to be the woman that Kate thinks I am. I want to be truly passionate and open-hearted, bravely honouring my deepest and most vulnerable emotions. I hold on to my sister, and I know that I genuinely want to follow her back, to clean up my mess so that I can be with everybody for Christmas and beyond. I give her one more squeeze and then pull away.

'Let's go home.'

Kate comes back downstairs from her shower at 11:00 p.m., just as I'm pulling the chocolate-chip cookies out of the oven. She passes a beady eye over the tray to check that I've got them right, then thanks me again for taking over for her.

'No problem,' I say. 'Thank *you* for bringing me home, and for sorting out the admin-y stuff, like calling Mum in the car to let her know we were OK and asking her to please not wait up. I really needed the space.'

'We both did,' Kate replies.

I arrange the cookies on a plate and pour hot chocolate into a mug while my sister looks around for carrots for the reindeer. We carry the treats up to the twins' room along with the presents that Mum had already wrapped up beautifully by the time we got home.

Together Kate and I complete the full Santa experience. We fill stockings up with gifts, sip on the hot chocolate, nibble at the cookies, and take huge bites out of the carrots. The snacks might not have been laid out before the boys went to bed as per tradition, but at least now they'll wake up to see that Santa has enjoyed them. Kate even sifts some flour on to the carpet so that it looks like snow has been trodden in through the window.

'Thank you,' she whispers as we tiptoe out of the bedroom.

'No problem. Now go and get yourself some sleep. You deserve it.'

'Aren't you going to bed too?' she asks.

I shake my head. Kate looks at me quizzically in the dim light of the hallway. I don't know where to begin with explaining to her that I have to stay awake for the rest of the night down in the kitchen. It's all part of my new resolution to open myself up and really put my heart into something. The plan started coming to me when I was mixing Santa's cookie dough for Kate. It felt good to really *do* something for a loved one, and now that the sweet treats are delivered, I want to do more. I want to do something for Margot. Obviously there are some things that the two of us need to talk about. But I actually want to have that conversation for a change – far more than I want to cut my losses and give up on this thing with her. I want to fight for Margot. I like her, and I am going to honour that feeling. I am going all-in on Margot Murray, and I'm staying up all night to put together the perfect Christmas gift for her.

'I don't have time to sleep,' I say. 'I've got a lot of baking to do.'

Monday 25 December

Monday 23 December

36

Ellie

At 5:00 a.m. I am so delirious with exhaustion that the rain starts to look almost white.

At 6:00 a.m. the white stuff is still tumbling down, fluffy and flurrying.

At 7:00 a.m. I finally accept that we are actually, miraculously having a white Christmas. Snow has settled over the fields and trees outside like a glimmering blanket, and yet more snowflakes are drifting down past the window to the great hall.

In here I've got all the lights turned on. Lamps cast out a warm glow. Fairy lights twinkle on the tree. A fire roars and crackles in the grate. There's even a selection of candles lit, releasing a cinnamon-spiced scent into the air. I've gathered up all the Santa hats that got discarded at brunch yesterday and I've placed them all around the room, along with as many Christmas jumpers as I could get my hands on. I've laid it all out neatly, with proper folding and everything. Each stack of clothes has a striped candy cane on top of it, plus an individually wrapped peppermint cream from my personal stash. I'm hoping that all of this will create a sense of wonder for everyone when they come downstairs later this morning. I want my family to step into the perfect Christmas from the moment it begins. They deserve it.

My pièce de résistance is the *grande* French dessert I'm currently carrying into the room. I've been holding my breath since I left the kitchen with it, terrified that I might trip over and drop the lot. My hands grip the plate as tight as they can. There are now just three small steps left between me and the side table. I take them slowly and carefully, as if I learned how to walk only last week. I lower the plate on to the table. Remove my hands.

The dessert wobbles.

Teeters slightly.

Steadies.

I finally release my breath. Everything is still in one piece. The dessert stands tall and proud at the centre of the table. It looks just like a golden Christmas tree, exactly as Margot described it to me last week. Loads of little round pastry balls stack up in a triangular shape, all dipped in dark caramel sauce and filled with vanilla cream. Hidden away inside the structure is a column of salted caramel sponge cake. The whole thing is decorated with spun sugar. It leans ever so slightly to the left and some of the pastry is browner than it should be, but I think it looks pretty damn good. It will remind Margot of her beloved nana and it will show her how much I care about her, and that's all that really matters to me.

Screw that. I also want it to look perfect. I lean over and fuss about with the croquembouche, fiddling with the pastry in an attempt to straighten everything up. When I step back to admire my handiwork, the structure is now leaning to the right.

I force myself to walk away from the table. There's nothing more I can do now. I've been up all night making cake and cream and choux and caramel and gossamer-thin strands of decorative sugar. The pantry has been ransacked and every shelf of the oven has been used. Culinary skills I did not know I possessed have been pushed to their limits, and now I'm spent. I sink down on to the sofa and let myself relax. The cake is perfectly imperfect, and that's OK.

No it's not. I leap up again and make a beeline for the table. I use the very tips of my fingers to rearrange strands of spun sugar. I want the decorations to be evenly distributed over the pastry balls. I want this thing to stand up straight.

While I'm working away, I become aware of music playing somewhere nearby. I take my hands off my balls and turn towards the sound. It's coming from the hallway. A Pixies song. One I've loved since I heard it played live in 2004. Heavy drums clash with loud guitars and even a theremin, but the vocals are soft and tender as the lyrics proclaim adoration for *my Velouria*.

Margot appears. She stands under the archway, with a Christmas wreath round her neck and fairy lights wrapped round her torso. She holds a tiny Bluetooth speaker above her head like it's an old-fashioned boom box, and she doesn't say anything. In her other hand, she has a huge sheet of paper with blocky letters printed across it: TO ME, YOU ARE PERFECT. Behind her I finally notice Ben, who has just wrestled the projector screen down and is now playing a video of various snowy cityscapes, making it look like Margot is standing in front of the Empire State Building, then the Eiffel Tower, then the multicoloured houses of Notting Hill.

'It's every romantic gesture I could think of,' she says proudly. 'I don't care how ridiculous it makes me look. I had to welcome you home properly. So if you want to laugh at me, Ellie, I'll just be glad to see you smiling. You are the most wonderful person I have ever met, and I want to do ridiculous things to make you happy. Before I found you, I didn't believe in romance. I thought it was fake and showy and I couldn't understand the excess of it all. Now look at me. I like you so much that it's bursting out of me. That's what all this flashy romance stuff is about, I think: I can't contain my feelings for you, so I'm getting them out in the form of music and notes and . . . buildings.' She grins. 'That's it, Ellie Gibson. I like you more than I know what to do with, and I wish you a very merry Christmas. Fin.'

I stare at the beautiful, bizarre woman standing in the doorway. She has got me literally lost for words, so I simply step aside to reveal the table hidden behind me. I point at my leaning tower of caramel-coated pastry balls. Margot gasps. She drops her speaker and her paper and rushes forward, but before she can get to me I race over to join her under the archway. I take her in my arms. She grabs my face. Music swirls. We tangle together. Intense feeling surges through every inch of my body.

We both glance up at the mistletoe hanging above our heads,
    and we kiss,
    and kiss,
    and
    kiss.

37

Margot

It is the perfect moment. We finally pull apart and beam at each another, and that becomes another perfect moment. I suddenly remember what I wrote on the other side of my giant piece of paper, and I pick it up to show Ellie the three little words – ARE YOU WOOED? – and she hoots with laughter and nods vigorously, and every moment of it is perfect.

A few seconds later, I remember that Ben is standing behind me. I turn towards him and Ellie follows suit. He looks almost as happy as I feel.

'You two are perfect together,' he says. 'I should have set you up from the start.'

'No way,' I protest. 'I wouldn't trade you in for anything, Just Ben Gibson. You've been the best boyfriend I've ever had.'

He narrows his eyes at me. 'Have you ever had a boyfriend before?'

'Nope!'

We all laugh.

And then we're not quite sure what to do.

Because we are all just standing around here: me and my ex-fake-boyfriend and his sister who might just be my new real girlfriend.

Ben throws open his arms. He pulls us both into a hug,

and the moment of awkwardness evaporates as if it never even existed. He speaks over the top of our heads. 'I'm really sorry for kicking off yesterday.'

'No,' Ellie says into his shoulder. '*I'm* sorry for giving you something to kick off about. I swear, I never wanted to hurt you. Neither of us did.'

'It's true,' I put in, pressing as close into the hug as my wreath-turned-necklace will allow. 'I'm sorry again, Ben. And, Ellie, I have something to apologize to you for as well.' I take a breath. 'I called Taylor yesterday, after everything went wrong. It was a mistake. I'm not proud of it, but I don't want to hide it from you. I'm really sorry.'

Ellie nods, her head still pressed against Ben's shoulder. 'It's OK. We can talk about that later if you'd like to. If it would help *you*. I'm here for you one hundred per cent.'

'I am too,' Ben says gently. 'I'm here for you both.'

'Thank you,' I murmur. 'I know. I'm here for both of you as well.'

'OK, OK.' Ellie disentangles herself from the group hug. 'Everyone here is here for everyone else. It's lovely and it's beautiful and it's too sweet to stomach much more of this early in the morning.' Her eyes twinkle. 'So who wants cake?'

I immediately run across the room to have my first proper look at the croquembouche. It's beautiful – almost exactly like the one Nana used to make, if a little lopsided. I can't believe Ellie made it for me. It must have taken her half the night and a whole lot of baking know-how that she didn't possess this time yesterday. I never imagined that I would eat this cake again. I could only picture myself having it if someone baked it for me out of love, like Nana used to. I can't wait to take my first bite. This dessert is exactly what Christmas tastes like for me, and it looks like Ellie has been delightfully generous with the caramel sauce. Nana would be impressed. More importantly she would be overjoyed to see that I've found myself such a kind and thoughtful woman.

I spin round to face Ellie. She kisses me before I get the chance to thank her. I melt into it and my stomach swarms with butterflies. It is the most perfect moment yet.

The moment comes to an abrupt end when I hear a high-pitched squeak of surprise. I look around to see Mrs Gibson standing in the doorway, her mouth hanging open. She brings her hands up to the gaping hole, as if that will push her involuntary squeak back in. She looks from me to Ellie to Ben, then to her husband who is standing beside her, and back to me again, and to Ellie.

Before anyone can think of anything to say, the twins come racing into the room. They head straight for the Christmas tree, grabbing at the presents underneath. Kate follows them in, yawning, and Mo isn't far behind her. Mitsi rounds out the crowd, strolling over to the fireplace and curling up for a nap. Mrs Gibson keeps darting her eyes between me and Ellie and Ben. It's like her brain is buffering. I know she's used to a neat and tidy version of life, and this scene certainly doesn't fit into that.

It's Ben who breaks the silence. 'Merry Christmas, everyone,' he says in a cheery voice. 'Just to let you all know, Margot isn't really my girlfriend.'

Everyone stares at us. Mrs Gibson's mouth falls even further open, and Kate looks like she's trying to solve a very long equation. Mitsi wakes back up from her slumber to cock her head, matching Mr Gibson's reaction exactly, and even the twins stop assessing their presents to glance our way. Mo stands apart from the crowd, giving a sage and knowing nod. On the whole, it seems that a bit more of an explanation is required.

'Every year,' Ben says, 'I come home for Christmas single and alone. I wanted that to change this year, so I drafted Margot in. I thought we looked pretty good together and I knew you'd all love her, so it seemed like the perfect way to fit in with all the . . . perfection.' He looks at his feet, the cheeriness gone from his voice. 'I just wanted to impress you all, to not be the odd one out for once. I wanted to finally be good enough to meet the Gibson family standards.'

Mrs Gibson squeaks again. She flies across the room and throws her arms round her son. Mr Gibson follows close behind and crashes in on the cuddle. Together the older couple almost unbalance Ben and he staggers backwards to steady himself, knocking into the Christmas tree as he does so. A couple of baubles fall off the perfectly decorated tree, and the star on top comes tumbling down.

Mr and Mrs Gibson ignore the mess and keep holding Ben close.

'You are more than good enough,' Mrs Gibson says. 'You are the best son we could have asked for. You're perfect, darling. You never, ever need to have somebody else with you to impress us or fit in. We love *you*. Just as you are. Just as Ben.'

Mr Gibson agrees, nodding his head enthusiastically.

'I'm so sorry if we put too much pressure on you, my darling.'

Mr Gibson disagrees, shaking his head rigidly. 'We're sorry that we *did* put too much pressure on you, son.'

There is a stunned quiet moment. Then Mrs Gibson nods. Just once. 'Absolutely. We are sorry that we made you feel like you're not enough. All of you.' She lets Ben go and looks to Kate and Ellie. 'You are all perfect. You always have been, and you should never have been made to doubt that.'

Kate looks like she might cry. Ben is already tearing up.

Ellie grins. 'I always knew I was perfect.'

Mrs Gibson looks closer at her. At me.

'We're together,' Ellie confirms. 'For real. I stayed up all night making her this cake.'

There's a long pause.

Then: 'How marvellous!' Mrs Gibson comes over to take hold of our hands. 'This is wonderful news – this is perfect. You are lovely, Margot, and I'm delighted that you are *someone's* real girlfriend. And, Ellie, my darling. What a catch! And what a *cake*. How have you managed to keep it upright when it so clearly wants to collapse? It won't hold for long, I can't imagine. It's like the Leaning Tower of Pisa.'

Behind us, Mr Gibson coughs.

His wife catches herself. 'By which I mean it is a feat of architecture and creativity.' She squeezes our hands. 'Really, Ellie, this is incredible work. It must have required so much focus. And an awful lot of passion. That's an excellent combination, you know.'

'I know,' Ellie says, 'I could use those skills to help run the hotel.'

'Yes! You want to work at the hotel? Do you mean it, darling? Yes. Yes, yes, yes!'

A short while later, we all settle down on the sofas. We pull on Christmas jumpers and Santa hats and we divvy up the croquembouche. Ellie insists that I have the first taste.

It is phenomenal. Sweet and rich and toasty. The flavours coat my tongue from the first bite and the choux pastry practically melts in my mouth. I can't stop eating it for long enough to speak, so I give everyone a thumbs up to let them know to go ahead and dig in. Forks clatter eagerly on china plates as everyone gets stuck into their light breakfast of decadent French patisserie dipped in sugar and coated in sugar and decorated with a bit more sugar.

And so Christmas Day has officially begun. Snow falls outside the window and lights twinkle around the room. Everything is out in the open and all those niggling complications have been resolved. We are all ready for the perfect –

Chaos.

Total unfettered mayhem.

It all starts happening at once . . .

Mitsi starts pacing, shivering, and whining. Ben calls out, 'Her labour is starting! The puppies will be here by the end of the day.' He runs out of the room to fetch her a 'whelping box', whatever that is.

The twins, standing by the door, cheer as Ben leaves, which confuses me until I see Henry striding into the room like a long-retired boxer returning to the ring. He has armfuls of chocolate for the boys, all of which goes flying when he slips on one of the baubles that fell from the tree. He jumps back up, his machismo gone, and proclaims, 'I have finally set a hard boundary at work. From now on I will only be doing overtime *one* day a week.'

Dylan and Dominic cheer even louder, celebrating this news that they don't understand by jumping right up on to the sofas. Kate watches them both with a straight face, then she slips her shoes off, ties her hair back into a sensible ponytail, and starts jumping on the sofas with them. Henry makes four, bouncing wildly.

Mrs Gibson's entire face turns red as she restrains herself from saying anything about the messy, dangerous, uncontrolled bouncing. A moment later, she leaves the room. Ellie snuggles up under my arm, playing lazily with the fairy lights I still have round my waist. Then she spots one of her presents under the tree and gets very excited. 'A BANJO! Wow. I didn't see that under there before. Amazing. I've always wanted to try a quirky instrument. A banjo is the perfect thing.'

Mr Gibson hears this and shakes his head. 'It's a frying pan, Ellie. Your mother's idea, not mine. But a banjo? Really? How do you reach these conclusions?'

Ellie shrugs, blows a raspberry, and settles back down in my arms.

Mo hears the fart noise and shouts, 'That was Mitsi!'

'*What was Mitsi?*' Ben cries, running back in with a big box full of old blankets. Just as Mo starts to explain, the doorbell rings and Ben immediately rushes out again to answer it. He comes back in, looking dazed, with Roberta behind him, who herself is followed by her pony-sized dog and her father. Stallion runs straight over to Mitsi, tail wagging wildly.

Stan looks mortified. 'We are so sorry about the dog.

We are so, so sorry.' The other half of 'we' is ignoring her dad's apologies, staring right at Ben with cheeks flushed an impressive shade of red. Stan is blushing too, glaring at the Great Dane lying next to Mitsi. He continues, 'He hasn't stopped begging to go out since he saw your dog yesterday, and just now he shot out of the door and ran all the way here before we could catch him. I am so, so sorry. I didn't mean for us all to drop in uninvited. We'll be on our way very soon, I promise – we've left a turkey in the oven.'

At that, I remember with a jolt that Ellie and I never got the chance to make our pie for Christmas dinner. Mrs Gibson comes back into the room then, looking aghast. 'The kitchen is an absolute tip, and the oven is broken. I think a fuse must have blown.' Nobody says anything for a while, most likely afraid of the way her nostrils are flaring.

Then Mo steps forward and attempts to calm her down. 'We can use the kitchen in the family wing. It will be a squeeze, but it will work.' She doesn't seem to hear him.

Stan raises a hand to speak. 'You can use my oven in the bungalow too – just as long as you're happy to transport your food across a few acres of land each way and squeeze your stuff in with our turkey.'

Mrs Gibson comes back to life when she notices that we have company. She immediately dives down to the ground to tidy up the baubles and redecorate her perfect tree. Mr Gibson mucks in without hesitation, scrabbling around on his hands and knees. Kate and Henry and Dylan and Dominic keep bouncing on the sofa, apparently lost in a world of their own. Ben and Roberta slink off into a corner, looking only at one another. Mitsi climbs into the whelping box, and Stallion attempts to follow her in. One of the twins launches himself from one sofa to the other. Mo catches him in mid-air and cries out, 'Ow – my back!' Mitsi kicks her boyfriend out of bed, stretches out and releases an almighty howl.

Everything stops at the sound.

And then starts again.

I keep my arms wrapped round Ellie as all the craziness plays out around the room. Somehow my girl has managed to fall asleep amid the chaos. I pull her closer to me and watch as mayhem rages all around us.

I smile. I suppose there's always next year for a nice normal Christmas.

One Year Later

Margot

I sit in my room alone, working away on my laptop. It's getting late and my eyes are starting to hurt from staring at the screen for so long, but I have too much to do to stop now.

The door opens a crack, and Ellie pokes her head in. I close the lid of my laptop right away. She comes into the room, kicking a crumpled pile of her clothes out of the way to get to my desk. She drapes her arms round my shoulders and drops a kiss on to the top of my head. I lean back against her and breathe in her lovely lemony scent.

'Dinner soon?' she asks gently.

'Yep. Yes. I just have one last project to finish up here, and then all my work is done for the year. I'll be free to take a whole fortnight off for Christmas. Or, at least, I'll be free to be very, very busy with you.' I turn to give her a quick kiss. 'Another half an hour and I'll be done. Do you want to get a takeaway? Your choice. Take my credit card and order whatever you want.'

'You are such a crap gold-digger.'

I give her a playful slap on the arm. She gives me one back. We push and shove and end up having a not-so-quick kiss. When we come up for air, my eyes track instinctively towards our bed.

'Careful,' Ellie says. 'You've got work to be focusing on.'

I sigh and get back to it. Almost an hour later, at a few minutes to midnight, I head through to our airy living room for a late dinner. We eat takeaway burritos on the sofa and comment that the vegan cheese in them is really good. We're both lying. Giving up dairy has been the hardest part of our transition into veganism over the last few months. Trying to get a decent Christmas dinner at the Gibsons' is going to be another thing entirely. Last year, we ended up eating stuffing and Brussels sprouts because we couldn't find time to make our pie and Mrs Gibson cooked everything else in duck fat. Miraculously that was the only major disaster on Christmas Day. After the chaos of the early morning, everything went ahead smoothly. Mitsi giving birth to nine healthy puppies was the cherry on top.

I scrunch up my empty burrito wrapper and put it to one side. Through our big bay window, I can see the first snow of December starting to fall, and beyond that a busy Manchester high street. Ellie and I moved into this flat perched atop a bakery seven months ago. She can drive to Cheshire for work in under an hour, and I have the space in our bedroom for a pretty swanky desk set-up. The only issue is that we don't have a garden, but we make sure we get to the park a couple of times every day so that the dog can have a proper run around. As a Rottweiler and Great Dane mix, she requires a lot of exercise, which fortunately keeps me from spending all day glued to my computer screen. Now Pixie emerges from under the sofa – one of her favourite tiny spaces to squish herself into for hours at a time – and starts sniffing at my discarded burrito packaging.

Once Ellie has also finished her food and handed the empty wrapper over to Pix, I lean forward with my game face on. Tonight, we are running through our Christmas plans to check that they are airtight. We have an awful lot to fit in.

Firstly Ellie has a few more shifts to get through at the hotel before her parents close up shop for Christmas break. She then has a meeting with Ashwin about next year's curry nights; a lunch date with a new prospective chef; and a festive-themed supper club to run, which is going to be a *two*-night-only event because there was so much demand for it.

While Ellie is still working, I'm going down to Reading to spend a few days with Nikita. It will be my third time meeting her adorable baby girl, and I can't wait. After that, Ellie and I are jetting off for a quick weekend away in Cyprus. We're flying back via London, so that we can visit Ben and Roberta at their new house in the suburbs and drop in on my mum for dinner. She's going to be coming to the Gibsons' manor for Christmas Day a week later, along with her new beau, but it will be nice to enjoy a more private celebration with her first.

Once we're back in Manchester, I have my weekly session with my therapist to attend. I had kind of expected to be done with therapy after a few months, but it turns out that complex trauma takes a little while to heal. I have no plans to discharge myself any time soon, and that's OK.

As soon as that standing appointment is out of the way, Ellie and I are off to the manor. Kate, Henry, and the twins should be there when we arrive, and then everyone else will be joining us a day later. If we're lucky Mitsi will deign to come over from the groundskeeper's bungalow, where she has practically moved in with Stallion, who himself has moved in with the groundskeeper. None of the Gibsons mind Stan having pets after all, just as long as he lets them all visit often. Ben and Roberta ended up taking two of the puppies for themselves as a sort of trade and they are now constantly telling everyone very long and involved stories about what their 'fluffy children' have been up to lately. Mo adopted the runt of the litter and gives the skinny thing a new name every few weeks. It is unclear whether he has forgotten the original name or has simply evolved beyond it. Ellie and I will be taking him to an appointment with his neurologist a few days before Christmas, and we have sweetened the deal by agreeing to drop him off to see his friends at the care home on the way back. Right after that we will all be going ice skating in our best ugly Christmas jumpers, as the twins have decreed it a family tradition. And then Ellie and I will set ourselves up in the kitchen to bake Nana's Christmas cake together.

I tap around in my phone's calendar to sort through all the details and make sure that nothing clashes. Ellie shouts out imaginary snags in our plans, like a zombie apocalypse breaking out, or aliens crash-landing on Earth hoping to discover the true meaning of Christmas. I roll my eyes and pummel her with my feet, and we end up play-fighting again. I abandon my phone on the sofa as we make our way into the bedroom. I've done enough planning for one night. Whatever happens this Christmas, it is sure to be wonderfully complicated.

Fin 😉

Acknowledgements

I have dreamed about publishing a book since I was a very tiny child, and I have hoped that it could be a joyfully queer book since I was a teen. My heartfelt thanks are owed to all LGBTQIA+ authors who came before me and paved the way for books like this one to exist, and to all the pioneering activists who fought and continue to fight for the rights of our community.

Thank you to Emily Glenister, my brilliant agent, for your endless support and kindness. I would feel truly lost in the publishing world without having you in my corner, along with the rest of the fabulous D H H literary agency family.

Huge thanks to my editor Rebecca Hilsdon, for always providing incredibly encouraging and insightful notes, and for running the PMJ Christmas Love Story competition along with Madeleine Woodfield and any others behind the scenes. Thank you also to Jorgie Bain, Beatrix McIntyre, Courtney Barclay, Steph Biddle, Jen Harlow, and everyone else at Penguin Michael Joseph, as well as Nina Elstad for the gorgeous cover design. In the US, thanks to Melissa Rechter and the entire Alcove Press team for bringing *The Christmas Swap* to American readers.

The world's biggest thanks to my incredible Mum, Lara Samuels. You are gentle and strong at the same time, and I hope I grow to become even half the woman you are.

Thanks to Joshua Samuels, my amazing brother, and again to Frances and Derek Braham. I lovingly remember my dad, Paul Samuels, along with Papa Jack. I am so thankful for the Samuels family I still have with me: Grandma Pam, Auntie Sue, Auntie Den, and my brilliant cousins. Thank you also to Nick, Linda, and Jessye – you are not yet my in-laws, but you are certainly my family. Thanks to any other family members I haven't mentioned – I had included you (yes, you) by name but something must have gone wrong with the printers.

Thanks to one of my oldest friends, Jonah Solomons, for being the very first person to read the opening of this book and provide feedback, and thank you to Alycia Miller and Sarah Duffy for supporting me so generously in good times and bad. I dare not single anyone else out for fear of leaving anybody off, but I am endlessly grateful for all my wonderful friends – from new writing pals to old friends who I simply couldn't imagine my life without.

To any and all readers of this book, I am so honoured that you let me tell you a story.

Thanks to my beloved dog, Lola. I have my best ideas when I'm walking you.

Finally, to Asher Berkowitz, thank you for being my partner, my best friend, and my home. My heart is always yours.